I0729738

Betting
on
Clay

John Cranberry

Author's Note

Too many years have passed since I first began writing this book, making it difficult to recall the exact moment of inception. I read very few books as a child; dyslexia was my mortal enemy. "When I stepped out into the bright sunlight from the darkness of the movie house, I had only two things on my mind: Paul Newman and a ride home." That was the opening dialogue from S.E. Hinton's novel, The Outsiders. A book I read many times as a struggling teen, finding it all too relatable. I still have my original copy, with tarnished pages and a faded cover. It was only in adulthood that I began to write my first book. I had no plan, story, or idea about what I would write. All I remember is creating a character in my own image, and everything that followed would ultimately begin to fall into its rightful place. Creative writing can sometimes feel like purgatory; you become immersed in a fictional world, trapped inside, reliving it in your mind over and over again. You're never satisfied, constantly changing the storyline and dialogue. You want everything to be perfect. But the reality is, just like life, it's never perfect. All we have are moments of perfection that go by so fast. "Nothing gold can stay, Ponyboy." So, the story you're about to read is my own, imagined by my younger self. There is some truth to what you're about to read, truth in parallels. Looking back at my life, I often wonder how things might have turned out differently if I had taken chances, spoken up, or pushed back. It's a dangerous thing to look back; it can make you feel like you've made nothing but mistakes your whole life. But now, this story is complete, and that chapter in my life is closed. Will I write again? Maybe, who knows what my future holds?

For those who suffer in silence.

Betting on Clay

John Cranberry

Copyright © John Cranberry 2025

The right of John Cranberry to be identified as author of this work has been asserted by the author in accordance with sections 77 and 78 of the Copyright, Designs and Patents Act 1988.

All rights reserved. No part of this publication may be reproduced, stored in a retrieval system, or transmitted in any form or by any means, electronic, mechanical, photocopying, recording, or otherwise, without the prior permission of the publishers.

Any person who commits any unauthorised act in relation to this publication may be liable to criminal prosecution and civil claims for damages.

This is a work of fiction. Names, characters, businesses, places, events, locales, and incidents are either the products of the author's imagination or used in a fictitious manner. Any resemblance to actual persons, living or dead, or actual events is purely coincidental.

Table of Contents

Chapter 1

September, New York City, Detective Frank Languetti leans over the still, bloodied body of a young woman.

"Is she alive?"

An inquisitive voice travels over the detective's shoulder. Languetti gently pulls back her sodden hair, exposing the side of her bruised face, her left eye swollen shut.

"Hey Frank, is she breathing, man?"

Frank sighed as he witnessed a faint breath exit the woman's lips. He turns to look at his partner. "Yeah, she's still alive." Languetti rises to his feet, his eyes shifting about the room as he navigates the victim's residence.

Across the room, an inebriated man lay on his stomach with both hands interlocked behind his head. Detective Shaun Miles has one knee pressed on the assailant's back and the nozzle of his Beretta firmly at the base of the man's head. The detective twists as he reaches to the rear of his belt, taking hold of a pair of handcuffs as he leans forward, shifting his weight onto the perpetrator. "Don't fucking move, arsehole." Miles returns his gun to its holster and then proceeds to cuff the man's arms behind his back. "Oh man, this guy stinks." The stench of alcohol revolts Miles. "You hear me, arsehole? You stink!"

Languetti returns to the living area, now grasping a woollen blanket in his right hand; he kneels by the woman, gently covering her naked torso. "Miss, I'm Detective Frank Languetti." The woman lay still, staring into nothingness, a collapsed lung hindering her ability to breathe freely. "You're safe now," Languetti speaks softly, doing what he can to reassure the woman. "An ambulance is on its way; everything is going to be alright now."

Frank Languetti (pronounced: Lan-getti), an Italian American, has been a detective for the past sixteen years. He joined the police academy when he was twenty-three, and after several years as a beat cop, he worked his way up to detective. At age thirty-eight, he was promoted to Sergeant Detective and has served in that role since. Frank has a medium build with dark hair combed back, exposing his hardened, defining features. He is always meticulously dressed, usually in a dark brown or navy suit, a sensible tie, and his black leather coat, but only in the year's colder months. Over time, Frank has developed a reputation as a fair and kind-hearted man, but the many years exposed to the brutal crimes of the city have left Frank with little sympathy for criminals, especially for men who beat defenceless women and children.

"Hey Frank, you okay, man?"

Frank remains crouched by the woman, looking miserable as he turns to face his partner. "Yeah, I'm good," Languetti affirms.

Miles surveys the room, the trademark settings of a typical crime scene. An empty whisky bottle on the ground, overturned furniture, scattered food on the floor and bloodstains on the walls and clothing of the victim. "Don't worry, Frank. She's gonna make it."

Miles, always the one to exercise caution, has partnered with Languetti for almost four years. The thirty-four-year-old clean-shaven detective is of African American descent and grew up in the tougher parts of New York City. Well-educated, he earned a scholarship at eighteen and attained his Master's in Criminal Psychology at the University of New York. Detective Miles is methodical in his approach to crimes and has made a rule of distancing himself emotionally from his work. Using his healthy sense of humour, Miles considers himself the leveller out of the two detectives, managing his and his partner's emotions to ensure they don't cloud their better judgment during an investigation.

A black and white pulls up to the residence's curb, accompanied by a blaring ambulance. The officers and the two medics jump out of their respective vehicles and tear up the stairs of the apartment building. They enter the room; the medics move towards Languetti, who remains crouched over the victim.

Languetti rises to his feet and looks across at the two police officers. "Get him out of my sight." Languetti gestures to the restrained assailant on the floor.

"Yes, Sir." The two officers veer towards the assailant, taking a firm hold of his arms and pulling him up off the ground. He groans incoherently.

"Shut the fuck up." Miles glares as they escort the man outside the room. "Make sure I get my cuffs back." Miles turns to face Languetti as he approaches. "We're all done here, Frank. Come on, let's get out of here."

One of the attending medics looks up at Languetti. "We'll take good care of her, Detective. Don't worry about it, we've got it from here."

Languetti looks at the woman one last time, the image of her as she lay there all too familiar, ingrained into his mind. He turns to Miles, an indignant look on his face.

"Come on. I'll buy you a cup of coffee, Frank." Miles pats Languetti on the back as he strides out of the room. He casually follows, adjusting his belt as he takes one last look around the crime scene. He looks at the woman as one medic applies a brace to support her neck, inhaling a long, deep breath, exhaling the bitter grief as he exits the room.

Chapter 2

Streetlights begin to flicker as the electrical current flows through the cables; one by one, the bulbs illuminate the quiet street known to residents as Parkway Avenue. A hum surrounds the neighbourhood with sounds of distant traffic, and a single voice of a mother summons her child for dinner. The sky has turned purple as the sun drifts behind the horizon, and the iridescent moon brings yet another night filled with adventure for those who seek it.

On Parkway Avenue is a grand old building riddled with the heritage of our ancestors, built in 1932 with large blocks of sandstone and the sweat and blood of men who slaved an honest day's work to bring home bread for their families. Passers-by will often stop and observe the structure that stands four levels high and has many windows for peering into the souls of those who live there. Detailed carvings on its exterior acknowledge the craftsmanship of the men who built it, and two large wooden doors made of oak act as the entrance into the heart of this old abode to many.

The foyer is laid in decorative marble, surrounded by green foliage to breathe oxygen into the lungs of those who pass through. A grand staircase spirals up to all levels and is used by many who live there as their daily exercise routine. Many residents have lived there most of their lives, some recalling the original wallpaper that has since been replaced; a much-needed renovation was completed in the early nineties. Too few paintings are hung by artists who are long forgotten, who were never able to make a name for themselves, but whose work still hangs in memory of their once-inspired talent. Carefully positioned lighting throughout the foyer and hallways creates a sense of warmth and comfort for the residents who come in from the cold to rest their weary legs from a long day's work. The hallways run deep at the top of the stairs, with timber floors made from stained oak, covered by runners woven from wool and designed to dampen the sound of a heavy stiletto.

On the upper level, down the soft-lit hallway, a single door makes for the entrance to Apartment 34, the home of Audrey Mills, for almost four years now. Beyond the door, the oak floor seeps into a narrow hallway that leads into the largest room of the apartment. The living area extends to a dining area and beyond to a practical kitchen fit for any chef. Two more doors feed off the living room to both bedrooms; one that Audrey has made her sleeping quarters and another to accommodate a tired guest if needed. The walls are painted in soft sand, with flat white decorative ceilings and skirting boards. Two Noir paintings hang on adjacent walls, lending a small taste of character to the room, which also houses three comfy sofas made of a claret velour fabric. The coffee table is stained Hackberry, with a matching dining table near the far wall. Black marble surrounds a working fireplace, and adjacent are two large windows that face Parkway Avenue, draped with thick velvet curtains to keep out the frosty winters when drawn. An antique upright Steinway, handed down to Audrey when she was still a child by her grandmother, was positioned at one end of the room.

The kitchen cupboards are plentiful and constructed of practical timber, which Audrey painted a soft chalky green to complement a black granite bench top. A classic black and white tile pattern covers the kitchen floor, and an aptly sized window positioned directly above the porcelain kitchen sink houses an assortment of fresh herbs. A third door makes for the entrance to the only bathroom in the apartment, still in its original heritage tile. The bathroom houses a large cast iron tub, a modern ceramic toilet, and a pedestal basin with chrome fittings.

In the main bedroom where Audrey sleeps, the walls are dressed in striped wallpaper, with velvet drapes covering the windows. An immense heritage bed and two matching wardrobes occupy the far wall. A chest of drawers sprawled with old pictures of friends and family at one end, and next to the window is a small dresser with a matching chair, a parting gift by her mother the day Audrey left home and moved to The Parkway.

It is a September Saturday, six forty-five in the evening and on the edge of her bed sits a nervous Audrey, fidgeting with her hair and wrestling with the one thing on her mind. Earlier that week, her closest friend Veronica had convinced Audrey, known as somewhat of a recluse, to attend a party with her at a colleague's house on the Upper West Side.

Audrey is twenty-seven years of age and has milky white skin and long dark hair, which falls from her thin frame. She is five feet six inches tall, has brown eyes and a beautiful smile. Audrey works at a small florist a few blocks from Parkway Avenue and spends most of her spare time reading and playing her grandmother's piano. Audrey has never felt comfortable in large gatherings filled with unfamiliar faces, and accepting Veronica's proposal has ignited her anxiety.

To make matters worse, the host is a very wealthy patron of Veronica's, and the people attending this lavish party are a different class of people that Audrey would typically associate with.

"I can't believe I'm doing this," Audrey says as she rises. "I'll never understand why I let Veronica talk me into going." Audrey looks straight into the mirror and lets out a grumbled sigh. She begins to berate herself out loud, pacing up and down the room. "What are you doing, Audrey? You know, as soon as you get there, you will find a dark corner to hide in, and the first chance you get, you will exit unnoticed like a vampire." Audrey tries to control her anxiety; she closes her eyes, taking long, deep breaths. A solemn moment passes; she opens her eyes, folding her arms in dispute. "I can't do this, seriously...no."

She eyes her cell from across the room. "I'm going to call V and cancel. I'll tell her I'm not feeling well, and that will be that." Audrey says emphatically. She snatches her phone off the dresser but is startled as it unexpectedly rings in her hand. Audrey knee-jerks the phone to her ear, neglecting to check who the caller is.

"Hello?"

"I bet anything that you are pacing up and down right now, thinking of excuses to cancel on me tonight. Am I right?" It's Veronica.

Audrey looks out the window as if expecting to see Veronica with a pair of binoculars. "No!" Audrey is not at all surprised at how well Veronica knows her.

Veronica Park was born and raised in New York. Her family descends from Korean heritage. She has naturally dark brown hair but chooses to dye it fiery red; she claims it goes better with her personality. She is the same age as Audrey, and they met at college when they shared several classes together. Veronica studied business and now works for a large financial firm in the city. They have managed to remain friends since college, but when it comes to their social lives, they are polar opposites. Veronica is an extrovert and often encourages her timid friend to venture out more often and meet new people. Needless to say, this never sits well with Audrey.

"Great, pick you up in fifteen, babe. Mwah." Veronica hangs up.

Audrey tosses the phone onto the bed in a huff, placing her palm onto her forehead as she exhales with grief. "I hate... arr." Audrey concedes defeat; she begrudgingly snatches her coat and purse and heads for the door.

Now outside her apartment, Audrey places her right hand firmly on the smooth rail of the spiralling staircase; still unsure of her footing in the black stilettos she seldom wears. She is draped in a long black satin dress falling off her shoulders, garnished with a silver pendant shaped like a dove, aptly placed over her cleavage. As she clears the final steps, Audrey enters the foyer, looking across to see Charlie standing outside his office, cleaning rag in hand. Charlie ceases his movement; the sound of Audrey's stilettoes, as they meet the floor, distracts his concentration.

"Audrey!" Charlie smiles delightfully. "You look gorgeous."

Audrey is still feeling bitter. "Thanks, Charlie."

Charlie is the caretaker of The Parkway and has been so for the past twelve years. He is sixty-two years of age and of African American descent. Charlie's wife passed away seven years ago from heart failure, and his only daughter lives in Chicago with her husband and Charlie's two grandchildren. Charlie spends most of his time at The Parkway and keeps himself busy with the upkeep of the grand old building. He has a big heart and, over the years, has become like family to many of the residents at The Parkway, including Audrey herself. Charlie looks forward to Christmas every autumn, as he loves decorating the building with tinsel and erecting the customary eight-foot Christmas tree. He enjoys listening to the residents compliment him on his efforts and has consistently advocated for spreading the Christmas cheer.

"So, where are you off to this fine evening, all dressed up like you are?" Charlie places his hands on his hips, eyeing Audrey like a proud parent.

"I'm going to a blooming party with Veronica; Charlie."

Charlie smiles laughingly, knowing how Audrey likes to spend her time alone. "Well, good for you. It will do you some good to get out and meet new people. That's how people make new friends, Audrey." Charlie can't help being condescending.

Audrey rolls her eyes. "Sure…whatever, Charlie."

"Well, you look stunning, Audrey. Very much like Audrey Hepburn!"

Audrey forces a smile. "Yeah? Thanks, Charlie."

Charlie and Audrey have developed a close relationship over the past four years. On many occasions, Audrey would come down to the foyer on a Saturday evening, and she and Charlie would eat popcorn and watch old movies in Charlie's office, which is furnished with a comfy lounge and flat-screen television.

"And what will you be doing this fine evening?" Audrey inquires.

"Oh, I don't know, don't have anything special planned tonight." Charlie says.

"Would you like to come along? You can be my date, Charlie." Audrey winks, a cheeky tone evident as her spirits begin to rise.

"I think you can do better than me, Audrey." Charlie chuckles at the thought.

Audrey tilts her head to the side and smiles. "He'll be a hard man to find, dear old Charlie."

Suddenly, there are several loud knocks on the frosted glass of the entrance doors. Charlie and Audrey both turn to see Veronica standing there in a red dress, waving her arms, and gesturing to Audrey.

Charlie turns to Audrey. "Veronica looks very...eager tonight."

Audrey gives Charlie a nervous smile. "Yeah, she's a real firecracker."

"Best not to keep her waiting," Charlie says. "You go and have a lovely night, Audrey."

"Thanks, Charlie, see ya."

Audrey gathers her courage one last time and heads for the door to greet Veronica. As Charlie watches Audrey tap towards the exit, he softly utters. "God be with you, Audrey."

Chapter 3

A polished yellow cab pulls up onto the grand driveway of the Harrington Estate. Enthusiastically, Veronica leaps out of the rear door, followed by an anxious Audrey. Veronica leans forward and hands a twenty to the driver through the passenger window.

"Keep the change, mister. And thank you."

As the cab departs, Veronica adjusts her cleavage; she turns to see a pale-faced Audrey standing there, motionless.

"Hey," Veronica places both hands on Audrey's shoulders. "Breathe before you keel over, silly."

Audrey manages a little smile.

Veronica takes hold of Audrey by the hand. "Come on, let's go have some fun."

Veronica pulls Audrey along a winding path that leads directly to the entrance of the estate. The two-acre Harrington Estate rises three levels above ground and includes an enormous wine cellar below. It comes complete with three fountains, several small gardens separated by cobblestone pathways, a small lake, a swimming pool, and a tennis court. The house itself is white and resembles the actual presidential White House.

"Does the President live here?" Audrey remarks.

As the girls approach the front of the house, they make their way up a small flight of stairs, confronted by two vast doors with oval patterned glass. Audrey begins to feel overwhelmed with the view and again regrets her decision to attend. Veronica reaches over to sound the doorbell. A heavy chime sounds: Audrey leans slightly towards Veronica.

"I think I'm going to puke." Audrey presses down on her stomach. Veronica rolling her eyes at Audrey.

"Fine, do it in the bushes."

Audrey takes a calming breath. "You know I don't socialise with these types of people, V. We have absolutely nothing in common whatsoever."

"You'll be fine; there's free food. If you get bored, just eat something." Veronica says.

"What?" Audrey gives Veronica a confused look. "You better not leave me, V. This was your idea."

"Don't be silly; I won't leave you." Veronica rattles her head as she straightens her dress one last time. "Just try to relax. They're not royalty, they're just...extremely wealthy."

The door swings open, releasing sounds of laughter and soft music. Trish Harrington, the lady of the estate, dons a long shimmering gold dress garnished with a pearl necklace. Trish immediately gazes at Veronica, her face beaming.

(In a ludicrously posh tone)

"Veronica, how wonderful that you could attend my little soiree! You look stunning in that dress."

Veronica presents Trish with her biggest smile. "Thanks, sunshine."

Trish shifts her attention to Audrey's not-so-familiar face. "And who might this be?" Trish curiously wondered.

"Oh, this is my bestie, Audrey...and she's delighted to be here too."

Audrey presents her pearly whites, secretly hoping not to chuck up over Trish's four-thousand-dollar dress.

"Splendid." Trish gives Audrey a wink of approval. "Well, please come in and make yourselves right at home." Trish guides the girls inside. "We have plenty of food and refreshments for everyone."

Veronica moves ahead of Audrey. Audrey follows, muttering softly under her breath. "Splendid."

Veronica and Audrey are led into a large room filled with guests, laughing and sipping their beverages. The room is everything Audrey would have expected when first approaching the house. It has a high ceiling with two large chandeliers that reflect the navy-blue metallic paint on the walls. The room has several paintings and an assortment of leather furniture rearranged for the occasion. The floor is Italian tile with a Mediterranean design that borders the rectangular room. The large windows surrounding the house are dressed in heavy drapes hanging from thick brass railings.

As she enters the room, Audrey's eyes shift to the women who appear elegantly dressed, donning their best jewellery out on display for all to admire. The men look confident as they strut about in their fine leather shoes, their drink cradled in hand, all seemingly sporting identical designer silk suits.

"Why do I suddenly feel like I'm in an *F. Scott Fitzgerald* book?" Audrey says under her breath.

Trish grabs the attention of a servant holding a drinks tray. They approach and offer Veronica and Audrey a beverage, both girls reaching simultaneously and opting for the white wine. Excitedly, Trish addresses Veronica.

"You have to see what Donald bought me today!" Trish takes hold of Veronica by the hand, carelessly pulling her away from Audrey and whisking her out of the room. Standing by her lonesome now, Audrey's mouth is wide open, notably astonished at the sudden turn of events. She shakes her head, taking a generous mouthful of her wine. She eyes the crowd of people unimpressively.

"Well, I'll just wait here then."

At the opposite end of the room, three young men triangulate together, bantering about stocks, equities, and investments.

"That mining stock was up three and a quarter points today." Jarrod announces optimistically. "That sixteen-footer is definitely in the bag, fellas and I can't wait to take her to sea and catch me a big fat, Marlon."

Percy is giddy as he listens to Jarrod.

"In six weeks, my dear and loyal friends, we'll be cruising the deep blue seas with nothing but the wind in our hair."

Jarrod and Percy join in the laughter.

"I'll drink to that." Percy raises his glass to Jarrod.

Jarrod looks over at William. "What do you say, Will? Up for some big game fishing when I get my yacht?"

William looks distracted; he refocuses, grinning but only slightly as he responds to Jarrod's invitation. "It should be an intriguing outing at sea," he says as he raises his glass, "considering neither of you knows how to sail a yacht." William takes a sip of his drink, looking into the crowd, dissecting the other patrons in the room as they converse.

"It has a motor too, William." Jarrod shakes his head, miffed by William's retort.

Audrey has since ambled her way over to a nearby table catered with plentiful hors d'oeuvres. She stands there staring at the food, contemplating the risks, not keen to ingest food she cannot recognise. After a wise selection, Audrey raises her head from the table and scans through the crowd. Her eyes focus on dresses with open backs, gold watches, perfect hairstyles, and red stilettos with what appear to be diamonds on the heels. *Has to be fake.* She thinks to herself.

As Percy and Jarrod talk in detail about fishing techniques, William becomes disinterested, focusing on individuals in the room. Catching his attention is Audrey, who is still surveying the crowd. Inevitably, Audrey looks in William's direction and notices him looking directly at her. Audrey suddenly freezes and then quickly looks away. She looks back again out of the corner of her eye, only to see William remain fixated on her. This time, William gives her a little smile. Audrey attempts to smile back but finds herself behind a moving crowd of people.

"So, Will," Percy distracts William, "what do you think is the best bait to catch Marlon?"

William polishes off his whisky, raising his empty glass to Percy as he responds. "Plenty of alcohol." William walks off, heading directly for the bar in the adjacent room.

Audrey sees that the handsome young man who smiled at her is no longer there. She exhales her disappointment but then notices two young women conversing nearby. "They look normal from here," remarking sarcastically. Audrey summons a little courage and decides to introduce herself. They notice Audrey approaching.

"Hi." Audrey greets both women with a wave and a smile. One of the women gives Audrey a curious look, unable to place her from previous outings.

"Hello." Both women are in unison.

"My name is Audrey." Audrey sips her wine.

"Hello Audrey, I am Sandy, and this is Mindy."

Audrey raises her left hand, presenting another playful wave. "Hey."

"I haven't seen you at one of these before. Are you a new friend of Trish's?" Sandy inquires.

"Or of Donald's?" Mindy snickers, nudging Sandy with her elbow.

"Yes…I mean, no, well, I don't know them. I'm friends with Veronica." Audrey takes a nervous sip of her wine.

"Oh, Veronica…yes, we know Veronica." Sandy raises her eyebrows at Mindy, both sharing another chuckle.

Audrey presents a confused look; she quickly dismisses her thoughts, deciding to skip over whatever that was. "So, what were you two chatting about before I rudely interrupted?" Audrey inquires.

"Well, Sandy and I were just discussing the effects of global warming on our planet." Mindy covers her mouth, muffling her laugh; her immaturity becomes unbearable.

Audrey realises she's joking and forces herself to laugh. *When in Rome.* Audrey thinks to herself, concealing her sigh.

"Of course, she's just teasing, girl." Sandy places her hand on Audrey's arm, offering a truce. "So, do you work with Veronica?"

"Oh no, I work at a florist on 29th." Audrey flings her arm in an easterly direction, so she believes, taking another sip of her wine, which is depleting at a rapid pace.

"That's on the other side of town." Sandy is quick to point out.

Audrey looks at Sandy and affirms with a definitive nod. "Yep, it is…way over the other side," Audrey emphasises, her eyes agape.

At the bar, William stares down at his double shot of whisky, the mysterious dark-haired girl he smiled at still occupying his thoughts. Wearing a dark grey designer suit with a crisp eggshell, textured shirt and elegant tie, William stands six feet, two inches tall. He is thirty-two years of age with a solid athletic build and light brown hair. He has a defined jawline, likened to the men from those shaving commercials, and sports a Longines watch on his right wrist, which he often admires, a gift from his grandfather when he passed the Bar.

Audrey finds herself alone again after her brief but memorable conversation with Sandy and Mindy ends with an impromptu bathroom visit. Audrey wanders to examine one of the paintings on the far wall with her second wine in hand. The idle sounds of chatter fade into the distance as she gazes in thought, recalling a spring day, Charlie and she went to the Art Gallery together. As Audrey stands there, mesmerised by the intricacy of the artwork, she is entirely unaware that a stealthy William has walked up behind her. With his eyes fixated on her flawless profile, William allows several moments to pass before deciding to announce his presence.

"It's a Monet."

A startled Audrey turns and looks at William. "Excuse me?"

"The painting you're looking at," William motions with his glass of whisky, "The View at Rouelles, Le Havre. It's a Monet." William takes a sip of his whisky.

Audrey views the signature on the bottom right of the painting. "Oh, wow!" she raises her eyebrows. "Must be expensive then."

William smiles, exposing his gleaming white teeth. "The real one is. That one is a replica. The original is in London. It is worth around two million."

Audrey nods and looks back at the painting, awkwardly realising that a brilliant piece such as a Monet would never be hanging in such an exposed area. She bravely turns around to face William.

"Have you been to London?"

"Several times," William explains. "I often go there on business. The law firm I work for has an office in London." William extends his right hand to Audrey. "My name is William."

Audrey reaches out and places her hand gently in William's palm. "I'm Audrey."

"It's a pleasure, Audrey."

Audrey begins to feel at ease with the sound of William's soothing voice. "So, you're a lawyer?"

William takes another sip of his whisky. "Yes, I am with Bloodworth and Crane."

"Cool name. Sounds...established." Audrey fidgets with her glass. "Criminal law?"

William smiles. "No, Bloodworth and Crane specialise in business law for companies dealing with acquisitions. It was established in 1962 in London by Charles Bloodworth..." William notices a hint of disinterest in Audrey's eyes and cuts himself off. "Well, I won't bore you with the whole history."

Audrey chuckles, taking a generous mouthful of wine to calm her jitters.

"So, Audrey, what do you do for a living?"

"I work at Gloria's Flowers. It's a florist on 29th."

William smiles, mesmerised by Audrey's beauty; he quietly gazes into her eyes.

Audrey begins to feel awkward with the momentary silence and anxiously adds. "We sell flowers to people." Audrey turns her head to the side, rolling her eyes inconspicuously.

William's admiration for Audrey begins to flourish. "I've heard that florists do that."

Audrey shows her sheepish face to William, both sharing a chuckle.

"Are you here with someone?" William asks.

"No...I mean, yes. I mean, I came here with Veronica."

William has met Veronica previously at several gatherings such as this one and is familiar with her outgoing personality. "Ah, yes...Veronica. She's quite a handful."

Audrey acknowledges William's statement with a firm nod. "Yes, she certainly is." Audrey takes a mouthful of wine, the alcohol working its magic on Audrey's nerves. William notices that Audrey's glass is almost empty.

"Would you like another wine?"

Audrey looks at her glass. She extends her neck, pushing her shoulders back. "Yes, I think I will have another; thank you, William."

Bent at the elbow, he extends his right arm to Audrey. Visibly delighted by the gesture, Audrey places her hand around William's forearm. William leads a gleeful Audrey towards the bar.

"These parties bore me," William confesses.

"Oh, they do, do they?" Audrey has a playful tone, and the two glasses of wine help her fall into character. "And why is that?"

"I think it's the people. I know them all too well, and their stories no longer interest me."

"So why do you come then?" Audrey frowns.

"I'm not sure; I guess I'm an optimist. I believe that one day I will meet someone different. Someone with stories to tell me that I haven't heard before."

"Someone from another world, perhaps?" Audrey begins to enjoy herself.

"Yes, an alien with six fingers on each hand and detachable ears."

Audrey holds up her hand; her fingers spread as she presents them to William. "I only have five fingers, William, and my ears don't detach. But I can dislocate my left shoulder on command!"

"Ouch, that sounds painful, Audrey." William cringes.

Audrey giggles. "Yes, it is fricken painful, William."

Chapter 4

After leaving the crime scene, Languetti and Miles have taken their regular seats at Carmen's Coffee House on Broadway. Florence, a long-time waitress at Carmen's, brings over two cups of black coffee and places them on the table. Miles leans back and looks up at the waitress.

"Hey Flo, can I please have a slice of your delicious pecan pie?"

Flo winks at Miles. "Sure can, handsome." Flo looks over at Languetti. The grim look on his face is visible. "Would you like some pie to cheer you up, Frank?"

"No thanks, Flo. I'm not hungry; thanks anyway."

"Alrighty then, be back in a jiffy, hun."

As Flo heads off, both detectives are mute as they prepare their beverages. Frank has a sweet tooth and adds three sugar packets to his black coffee. Meanwhile, Miles slowly stirs his coffee while adding a generous amount of fresh cream. Flo promptly returns with a slice of pecan pie and places it in front of Miles.

"Here you go, sweetness." Flo pats Miles on the shoulder as she leaves.

"Thank-you-Flo." Miles rubs his palms together, inhaling the aroma of the roasted pecans. He wastes no time, taking possession of his fork, his mouth salivating at the thought. As he's about to slice into the pie, Miles notices his partner eyeing his dessert, a recurring habit on Frank's part. Miles glares directly at Frank. "Can I help you, Frank?"

"What?" Frank acts innocent.

Miles shakes his head. "Why do you always do this, Frank? Whenever I order a piece of pie, you stare at it like a sad, hungry puppy." Frank leans back, taking a sip of his coffee. Miles continues to rant. "I heard Flo ask you if you wanted a piece of pie, and I also heard you say you weren't hungry."

Frank shrugs his shoulders. "I'm not hungry."

"Oh! You're not hungry. Then quit staring at my pie, Frank."

"I'm not. Stop whining and eat your pie." Languetti props himself upright; he looks across the Diner. It's quiet, with only a few customers occupying tables.

"I will. And I will enjoy every bite." Miles exclaims.

After a few moments of silence, Languetti discreetly shifts his eyes onto the dessert.

"Can I have a little taste? A small piece, nothing too big."

Miles lets out a sigh, dropping his fork onto the table. "Here." Miles slides the plate to Languetti. "Take as much as you want, Frank. Have it all. Go on."

Languetti manages a slight grin. "I just want a little taste. I don't understand why you're so possessive. Sharing is healthy and good for the soul."

Miles raises his coffee off the table. "A little taste," he remarks, shaking his head.

Without much hesitation, Languetti consumes a mouthful of pecan pie. Miles sits there sipping his coffee peacefully, his thoughts to himself as he watches his partner unapologetically devour the whole dessert in minutes. Frank leans back into his chair and lets out a satisfied groan. "I'll pay for the check tonight," Languetti says with a grin, Miles delivers a blank stare. "That was a nice piece of pie, you should get Flo to bring you a piece."

Miles looks away. "Screw you, Frank. I'm not hungry." Miles takes a mouthful of coffee, the hot liquid a welcome relief as it consumes his chest.

Minutes pass by as both detectives enjoy their beverages in complete silence. Languetti looks past Miles' shoulder at a young woman sitting at a table not too far from theirs. Her golden hair resembled the night's assault victim. Languetti's facial expression quickly changes—the image of the bloodied young woman invading his calm.

"That fucker broke her ribs."

Miles turns his attention to Languetti. "What was that?"

Languetti takes a sip of his coffee. "The woman, her ribs were broken."

"Yeah, I could hear the wheezing." Miles pulls his arms over his head, letting out a tired groan. "Don't worry about it, Frank, we got the son of a bitch now. He'll get what's coming to him."

"If she testifies." Languetti is quick to scrap his partner's statement. "A guy who would do that to a woman could just as easily walk." Languetti taps his index finger on the table. "If she doesn't press charges and testify, he walks. It's that simple." Languetti takes his final mouthful of coffee, placing his cup on the table. "That never seems to bother you, though. Why is that, Miles?"

Mile's voice is tepid. "No, Frank, it doesn't because I don't let it bother me." Miles leans forward. "That's how you get ulcers and high blood pressure, Frank. I don't get emotionally involved with the victim."

Languetti looks right at Miles. "Is that what your master's in criminal psychology from NYU has taught you?"

Miles' reply is confident. "Yes, Frank, it has. We have to worry about what we can control. We're cops, not lawyers. We arrest these pricks, and the rest plays itself out." Languetti shows Miles the side of his face.

"Maybe next time, Frank, we can shoot the perp in the head, plant a gun and then call the black and whites to clean up." Miles leans back into his chair. "Will that make you happy, Detective?"

Languetti waves dismissively.

"Listen, Frank, I am sorry for what happened to that lady tonight, and I hope she decides to press charges." Miles slowly rises to his feet. "We have to evolve, Frank. If we don't, we become just like those assholes. I'm better than that, and so are you, Frank. So, stop your bitching."

Miles walks off, passing Flo on his way to the bathroom.

"How was the pie, handsome?"

Miles displays his resentment as he looks directly at Flo. "Next time I ask for pie, bring me two pieces, Flo."

Chapter 5

After a short visit to the bar, William takes Audrey to the second-level balcony located off a guest lounge at the rear of the house. Audrey has managed to amuse William in great detail on the right floral arrangement for the right occasion for almost an hour. The moon has since dipped below the horizon, exposing the night sky, a blanket of stars shining ever so bright as Audrey and William stand there, looking up in silence.

"Wow, the sky looks so beautiful tonight," Audrey says. "I can't remember the last time I've taken the time to just look at the stars."

William continues to gaze. "I always look up at the stars; I remind myself to do so every chance I get."

Audrey turns to William; his expression appears calming. "You do. Why is that?"

William holds his gaze, mesmerised by the galactic view. "It reminds me how insignificant we all are."

Audrey tilts her head. "Insignificant?"

William turns to face Audrey. "Maybe that's not quite the right word," William chuckles. "So many of us go through life believing everything we do matters. We continuously strive to achieve our goals because we believe that we must accomplish so much in life." William pauses momentarily. He returns his attention to the night sky. "But everything we do can seem insignificant when you look at the stars."

"I'm not sure I understand," Audrey questions. "I mean, what you're saying doesn't sound very optimistic; actually, it sounds rather depressing, William."

"It's just the way I feel sometimes, Audrey." William pauses. "Do you ever stop and think about why we do what we do? Is it what we want to do or what society expects us to do? We go to work to earn our daily bread to buy our nice clothes, pay for our shelter, and join others who go through life doing the same. And when we encounter each other, we exchange pleasantries for a while, and the next day we go off on our daily routine."

"But what choice do we have?" Audrey interrupts. "If we don't do what we require to survive, then I guess we end up homeless, without a place to sleep or food to eat. It's what we or any self-respecting human being must do to survive."

William looks into Audrey's eyes. "You think all those homeless people decided one day to be different, and ended up that way?"

Audrey shrugs. "I don't know, maybe. Maybe they tried and failed. If they did, they are braver than most, I guess."

"An unfair punishment for wanting to try something different."

"Are you unhappy with what you are doing with your life, William?"

"I have wanted to be a lawyer since I was young. But sometimes, I feel like I will wake up one morning, be sixty-five, and look back at everything I've done and realise it was meaningless. What if I've been so busy doing what everyone expects me to do, that I missed the opportunity that is life, to be something else, something unique, or simply, something that truly matters."

Audrey reaches over and takes William's hand, sensing his moment of insecurity. "I think we all feel like that sometimes. I often wished I had practised more to play the piano for a living instead of cutting stems off flowers for the rest of my life." Audrey smiles.

William looks down at Audrey's hand. "My grandfather and I used to go fishing before he passed away two years ago. I remember one day he told me that; a man's significance is measured by the people who love him."

"Sounds like you loved your grandfather very much."

"I did. My father died when I was little, and my grandfather would spend time with me while I was growing up."

"I'm sorry, William." Audrey squeezes William's hand.

William manages a sincere smile. "I realised soon after my grandfather passed that what he meant was that you need to find someone to love, someone you can care for and who can love you as much as you love them." William looks directly into Audrey's eyes. "I guess when you find that person, everything you do begins to matter again."

Audrey's eyes glaze over as she gazes up at William. She feels her heart rate increase as William slides his thumb across her fingers. Audrey holds her breath, the tender moment catching her off guard.

"Kiss her!" A whispering voice distracts them both. They both turn and see Veronica standing with a glass of wine, clutching the doorway. She begins to bellow out a laugh.

"Oh no, I think she's hammered." Audrey cringes.

"It appears so."

Veronica staggers over to greet them both. "So, what is going on here? Holding hands under the stars. So romantic, guys." Veronica gives William a wink.

Audrey laughs. "We are just talking, V."

"Oh, really, seemed to me like a little more than that. Lucky, I found you when I did."

Audrey takes the wine glass from Veronica's hand. "How much have you had to drink?"

"Hey, it's a party." Veronica staggers.

Audrey sighs. "I think we'd better call a cab and get you home."

"No way!" Veronica frowns. "I'm having fun."

"I have my car here, and I can take her home if you like."

"Are you sure it's no trouble?" Audrey asks.

Veronica throws both arms around William. "Yes, William, take me home, you big stud."

Audrey laughs. "Come on, let's go." Audrey peels Veronica away from William.

Veronica throws her arm around Audrey and whispers. "He's very handsome."

"Come on, you." An embarrassed Audrey drags Veronica away from the balcony and towards the stairs. William casually follows them, amused by Veronica's antics, his eyes on Audrey's physique. As they reach the bottom of the stairs, Sandy hears the commotion and spots the trio as they struggle towards the door. Mindy returns from another visit to the bar.

"What are we looking at?" Mindy follows Sandy's line of sight, stirring her drink with her straw.

"William, he's leaving with that weird girl we were talking to earlier."

Mindy peers across the room. "You mean the flower girl?" Mindy focuses on Audrey, quickly identifying William and an animated Veronica by his side. "Oh man, Veronica looks plastered."

"She's always plastered." Sandy notices Audrey rubbing up against William's shoulder. "I guess our little friend fell for William's charm."

Mindy glares intently at William, taking a long sip of her Vodka mixer. "He probably used that – 'I like to look at the stars because they make me feel insignificant.' routine crap on her, I bet." Mindy purses her lips. Sandy snickers.

"Is that why you fucked him?"

Mindy screws her face at Sandy. "Shut up." Mindy sips her drink and stares at William intently. "He's a real sleaze when you get to know him, anyway."

Sandy takes a sip of her drink; she too intently eyes William as he places his hand on Audrey's back. "Not only; I've heard other disturbing shit about him too."

A gleaming silver C-Class Mercedes pulls up onto the driveway. Veronica clumsily tries to get in with Audrey's help. A cautious William watches from the driver's seat.

"Watch your head."

Veronica plops herself in the back seat, with Audrey squeezing past and securing herself by Veronica's side.

William gestures to Audrey. "Maybe you should hold on to her 'til we get her home."

Audrey affirms as she pulls the door closed. "Oh yeah, I'll hang on to her, don't you worry."

William places the car in gear and slowly drives off, heading directly towards Veronica's place. Audrey sits quietly, admiring the lush interior of the Mercedes and secretly praying that Veronica doesn't throw up all over the leather seats. William, too, remains silent, focusing on the moment he and Audrey were having before Veronica interrupted.

After a short while, they arrive at Veronica's apartment block. William quickly gets out as he, too, is aware of the fortune of making it this far without Veronica throwing up all over the interior of his car.

"Here, let me help." William takes Veronica by the arm and encourages her to rise to her feet.

"I'm fine. What's all the fuss about?" Veronica's grumpy as she wakes from her short nap in the back seat. "Let go!" She pushes William's arm away and springs onto her feet, momentarily dizzied by a head rush. "See, I'm fine...woah!" She staggers onto the footpath and towards the front door of her building, waving her arms about and yelling aloud. "Goodnight, sweet dreams, don't let the *beg buds bite*."

William and Audrey look at each other and laugh in amazement at Veronica's sudden antics.

William places his hand on Audrey's shoulder. "Come, I'll take you home."

Audrey opens the front passenger door of the luxury car and gets inside. Once inside, William puts on a character voice.

"Where to, Madam?"

A charmed Audrey smiles and falls into character once again. "The Parkway, please, sir."

William tilts his head slightly forward, tipping his imaginary hat. "Yes, ma'am, The Parkway it is."

Chapter 6

In a small office inside The Parkway's lobby, Charlie lies comfortably on a compact two-seater sofa, holding a half-eaten bag of buttered popcorn. The residents of The Parkway all lobbied to have cable installed several years back, and typically, Charlie has opted to watch an old movie on his Saturday night, as he so often does.

"Thought I'd find you here."

Charlie turns to see Audrey standing in the doorway. "Well, hello there, Audrey," Charlie says with a surprised smile.

Audrey makes her way over to the sofa and then reaches down, snatching the bag of popcorn off Charlie's lap. With a big grin, she sinks back into the couch, flicking her shoes across the room. "So, how was your evening, Charlie?" Audrey asks, her cheeky grin clearly evident.

Charlie feels delighted by Audrey's cheerfulness. "I think the question we should ask is, how was your evening, Audrey?"

Audrey fills her mouth with a handful of popcorn. "Preffy goob."

An amused Charlie reaches down to a small bar fridge beside the sofa and takes hold of a soda bottle. "Here you go, Audrey. Drink something before you choke on the popcorn."

Audrey twists the cap, taking several gulps. "Ahh...that hit the spot." She wipes her mouth with her forearm. "So what movie are they playing tonight?"

Charlie looks over at the television. "Scaramouche, but it ended about an hour ago, Audrey."

Audrey's face turns to disappointment. "Oh, I love that movie. I can't believe I missed it."

Charlie remains curious and is quite eager to find out what events transpired at the party Audrey attended. "Oh, I wouldn't worry, Audrey. They will show it again in a month or two. They constantly repeat the good ones." Charlie reaches for the remote and reduces the volume on the television to a whisper. He then turns to face Audrey, his eagerness on full display. "So?"

Audrey becomes coy, teasing Charlie a little, as she occasionally likes to do. "So...?"

Charlie sighs. "Audrey, I'm very old and tired, so spill it."

Audrey lets out a laugh. "O... *kayee*. Keep your knickers on, Charlie." Audrey leans forward and places her drink on the floor. She adjusts herself on the sofa, ensuring she is most comfortable. Charlie watches her fuss, quickly losing his patience. "So, I met a very handsome man named William at the party."

Charlie's eyes widen. "Really, 'very handsome', you say."

"Yes," Audrey nods, "he was very charming, and he is also a highly successful lawyer."

"Oh, I could use a good lawyer." Charlie acts impressed. "Will you be seeing this very handsome, charming, and successful lawyer again?"

Audrey slaps Charlie on the knee. "As a matter of fact, yes, I think I will, Charlie. He has asked me to dinner next Saturday night and will come here to pick me up at seven p.m. sharp."

Audrey leans forward, placing her hand on Charlie's shoulder. "In his Mercedes-Benz," she whispers with a definitive wink.

"Did you say Mercedes-Benz?" Charlie milked his reaction.

"Certainly did, good sir. A Benz-C-Class-Sedan-Iridium-Silver-Metallic 'merc', as we highbrow say."

Charlie's thoughts immediately go to Audrey's detailed knowledge of the make and model of William's car, figuring that at some point, William would have talked about it in great detail, as men tend to do. "Well! Good for you, Audrey." Charlie grins. "See, I told you it would be good for you to socialise. And look what happened."

Audrey rolls her eyes. "Yeah, yeah, whatever, Charlie. You're very intuitive." Audrey lets out a love-struck sigh as she leans back, placing her head on the arm of the sofa. "Oh, Charlie, the night was so wonderful, he was so wonderful."

Charlie sits quietly and listens to Audrey as she reminisces about her encounter with William. A short while later, Charlie had fallen fast asleep from the soothing sound of Audrey's voice. Audrey leans forward, waking her weary legs as she rises from the sofa to retrieve a woollen blanket that Charlie keeps on top of a bookshelf. Careful not to wake him, Audrey covers Charlie from neck to toe.

"Sweet dreams, Charlie."

Charlie is all curled up on the sofa in a peaceful sleep. Audrey leans forward, giving Charlie a gentle kiss on the forehead. Collecting her shoes, Audrey makes her way over to the door. She takes one final look before easing the door closed.

Chapter 7

The following morning, Audrey rose early, feeling refreshed from a good night's sleep. With a noticeable spring in her step, she makes a short visit to the corner shops to buy groceries for her lunch. Audrey returns with an assortment of lettuce leaves, a punnet of cherry tomatoes, a packet of ready-made croutons, two pieces of raw chicken breast and some Parmesan cheese. After placing the items in her refrigerator, she brews herself a cup of Brazilian coffee, taking several mouthfuls to warm her chest, commencing her morning cleaning ritual. She begins by playing her favourite CD, Linda Ronstadt—Greatest Hits. First, Audrey tackles the bathroom, picking up her damp towels from the floor and wiping down the sink and bathtub. Her next stop is the bedroom, where she manages her soiled clothes, tidies the bed linen, and puts the items on her dressing table back in their exact places. Audrey then moves on to the lounge area, where she straightens the cushions on the sofa, hides old magazines in the end table drawers, and dusts the furniture with a polishing cloth. Finally, she fills a bucket from the kitchen sink with hot water and adds a special floor-cleaning solution for the oak floors that Charlie gave her. She then begins to mop the entire apartment strategically, ensuring she finishes back inside the kitchen.

An exhausted Audrey now stands in the kitchen, keeping her tired body upright by clutching the mop handle and admiring her meticulously clean apartment. Her method for trapping herself in the kitchen is that she can now prepare her lunch, giving ample time for the floors to dry, so she can later return to the living area and relax. As Audrey stands there, allowing herself to catch her breath, her admiration soon turns to anguish as she notices a mistake she has made often. Looking across the living room, Audrey realises she neglected to open the windows. This means the floor will take longer to dry, as no air is circulating in the apartment.

"Oh, rats." Audrey submits to what she now must do. She puts the mop aside and tears a handful of paper towels from the spool on the kitchen wall. Rising to her toes like a Prima Ballerina, arms extended, she carefully inches her way over to the windows, cautious not to slip. After opening both windows, she then proceeds to make her way back to the kitchen. Placing the paper towels beneath her feet, she glides back like a clumsy figure-skater, careful to wipe off each imprint as she slides back along the floor. Once inside the kitchen, Audrey turns and flings the dampened towels into the trash. "Nothing but net," she joyfully celebrates.

Wiping her brow, she retrieves the groceries from the refrigerator to begin preparations for lunch. She removes a large ceramic bowl, a stainless-steel colander, and her trusty non-stick pan from the cupboards below her knees. After thoroughly washing the lettuce and tomatoes, she tears the leaves into even pieces and places them into the colander along with the cherry tomatoes. She takes the chicken breasts out of the airtight package, lays them whole on a plastic chopping board, scores them diagonally, and gently coats them with olive oil. Below the windowsill, Audrey has a collection of dry spices. After a careful selection, she sprinkles the chicken pieces with some salt and paprika, using her small fingers to massage the spices into the scored openings. Holding the pan in her left hand, Audrey leans forward to ignite the stovetop. After several failed attempts, she realises something is wrong. She lets the pan drop on the stove, letting out a frustrated sigh. "Fricken 'ell, stupid stove."

Suddenly, there's a loud, heavy knock at the door; Audrey is startled and swiftly turns her head. She clutches her chest, patting her heart to settle herself as she approaches the door. Audrey cautiously treads on the dry patches of the floor, which isn't completely dry. She takes a moment to straighten her bandana before pulling the door open to greet her visitor. Audrey catches her breath as she gazes at the figure standing before her. Towering over six and a half feet tall, a large black man wearing freshly pressed dark green overalls and polished military-style boots, carries a battered red toolbox and peers down at Audrey. His colossal torso and biceps strain the stitching on his shirt, with his bulging muscles visible through the delicate fabric. His head is clean-shaven, featuring a prominent scar on the left side of his temple. Audrey stands there momentarily, a glint of fear in her eyes as she marvels at the man's sheer size.

"Can I help you?"

Audrey's first words are a reflex as she looks directly at the young man's face. She notices a hint of vulnerability in his brown eyes.

The reticent man replies in a soft yet deep voice. "Miss Mills, I'm here to repair your stove."

Audrey gives the large man a wondrous look, utterly unaware of who this man is, and confused as to how he knew about her stove. Just then, Charlie appears out from behind the large man's frame.

"Audrey, I see you've met Clay."

Audrey lets out a faint sigh of relief at the sight of Charlie. "Hey, Charlie."

Charlie smiles and places his hand on Clay's shoulder. "Audrey, this is Clay. He started working for me today."

Audrey extends her arm to Clay. "Nice to meet you, Clay."

Clay nods his head forward. "Miss Audrey."

"Is it all right if we come in, Audrey?" Charlie requests.

Audrey moves to the side to make way for Clay and Charlie. "Yes, of course, it is. Please, come on in."

Audrey waves her arm around. Charlie pats Clay as a gesture of consent. Clay slowly moves down the hallway, passing Audrey, who has pinned herself against the wall, making room for Clay's broad shoulders. As Clay walks past, Audrey is in awe of his size. *His bicep is larger than my thigh*, Audrey thinks to herself. She then turns and gives Charlie a curious look, not recalling Charlie mentioning anything about a new employee in recent conversations.

Charlie places his arm around Audrey. "How are you this fine morning, Audrey?"

"I'm well, Charlie. How did you sleep last night?"

Charlie smiles at Audrey. "Like a baby."

Charlie and Audrey make their way over to the kitchen. They pass Clay, who stands in the middle of the room awaiting further instructions from Charlie.

"How did you know that my stove isn't working?" Audrey inquires.

"My dear Audrey, after twelve long years, I know almost everything that goes on in this building."

Audrey looks over at Clay, who remains mute on the topic. "Come on, Charlie, tell me."

Charlie continues to act coy. "Old men have many secrets, Audrey."

Audrey gets impatient and tries a serious face. "Charlie, I want to know if you're spying on me."

"Nope; sorry, Audrey. You need to be a member."

Audrey places her hands on her hips. "A member of what?"

"A member of the Caretakers' Secret Society," Charlie says with a grin.

Audrey tilts her head to the side. "Charlie, you're being very annoying."

Seeing that Charlie is in the mood for games, Audrey walks over to Clay. "Clay, please tell me how you knew my stove wasn't working?"

Clay looks across at Charlie. Charlie gives a nod of approval to Clay. "The light, Miss Audrey."

Audrey squints. "The light; what light?"

"The light downstairs," Clay says.

Audrey turns to Charlie. "Charlie, what light is Clay talking about?"

Charlie motions to Clay. "Clay, would you please bring me my toolbox?"

Clay politely excuses himself from Audrey and walks over to Charlie.

"Thank you, Clay." Charlie places the toolbox on the kitchen counter and retrieves a small packet containing an assortment of fuses.

"Hello, Earth to Charlie."

Charlie looks over his shoulder to see Audrey. "Audrey, I'm trying to repair your stove."

Audrey peers down at Charlie momentarily before turning her attention to Clay. "Clay, would you like a glass of lemonade?"

Charlie looks up from the toolbox. "Oh, I'd love a glass of lemonade."

Audrey acts miffed. "I was addressing Clay; Charlie."

Charlie is amused. Audrey looks at Clay and smiles. "Clay?"

Clay politely accepts Audrey's offer. "Yes, Miss, I would."

Audrey opens the fridge and takes out a jug filled with homemade lemonade. She removes two glasses from the cupboard above her head and pours some lemonade for Clay and Charlie. "Here you go, Clay." Audrey presents Clay with a glass of lemonade.

"Thank you, Miss."

"You're very welcome, Clay."

Audrey takes the other glass to Charlie and places it on the counter next to him. As Charlie reaches for the glass of lemonade, Audrey pulls it away from him. "Spill it, Charlie."

Charlie again smiles, recalling using the exact words to Audrey last night when trying to get her to give him information about the party she attended. "Clay was referring to the light on the large panel of lights below the front counter."

"You mean downstairs in the foyer."

"Yes. About a year ago, I had a technician come out and restore the panel of lights to working order."

"And...what does the panel of lights do?" Audrey glares with eyes wide open.

"The panel of lights is wired to every fuse box in the building. When you blow a fuse, a light appears on the panel, which indicates whose apartment it is."

Audrey crosses her arms. "Well, how come I never knew about this, panel?"

Charlie gives Audrey a cheeky grin. "Again, Audrey, I pose this question to you. Are you part of the Caretakers' Secret Society?"

Audrey frowns at Charlie. "Just drink your lemonade, Charlie."

Audrey walks over and takes Clay by the hand. "Come on, Clay, let us sit in the living room."

As Audrey attempts to pull Clay, she soon realises that her efforts are no match for his size and strength. Audrey looks up at Clay with a smile. "Come on, Clay, help me out here."

Clay hesitates, unsure if he should go with Audrey and looks at Charlie. Charlie, again, gives his nod of approval. Clay shifts his weight forward, allowing Audrey to take him into the living room. Audrey sits on her sofa and then looks up at Clay, patting the cushion beside her.

"Have a seat, young man."

Clay eases himself down onto the sofa cushion next to Audrey. Audrey notices that Clay has a quiet way about him and imagines him as a large, sweet teddy bear. She pats her hand on his knee to put him at ease.

"Do you like the lemonade?"

"Oh, yes, Miss, it's very nice." Clay takes another mouthful.

"I made it myself, with real lemons." Audrey proudly admits.

Clay murmurs as he swallows the mouthful of lemonade, concealing his anguish from the beverage's excessive bitterness.

"Would you like some more?"

Clay's eyes widen slightly. He raises his arm and shows Audrey his palm, simultaneously shaking his head. "Oh...no, thank you, I've had enough." Clay looks over at the piano. "You play, Miss Audrey?"

Audrey admires her grandmother's Steinway. "Yes, my grandmother taught me when I was a child." Audrey sees a rare opportunity to impress her guest. "Would you like me to play for you?"

Clay shifts his weight forward. "Yes. I would love to hear you play."

A thrilled Audrey jumps up from the sofa and skips over to the piano. She positions herself rightly on the stool and raises the cover, the ivory keys tarnished with a hint of yellow. Clay joins Audrey by the piano, leaving his beverage behind on the coffee table. Audrey extends her elbows; with her fingers interlocked, she pushes her palms towards her chest. Audrey then releases her hands and violently shakes her fingers about. Carefully placing her fingers on the desired notes, she closes her eyes momentarily; she begins to play, softly pressing down on the ivory.

The room quickly fills with the distinctive notes of *Beethoven's Moonlight Sonata.* Clay becomes mesmerised, watching Audrey's hands effortlessly scroll over the keys. Goosebumps begin to appear on his forearm, the bass notes of the piece penetrating his skin. Charlie stops momentarily and looks across the room in admiration; the familiar score pillows the air; long-forgotten memories of his wedding occupy his thoughts as Audrey gently sways back and forth, immersing herself into the piece's rhythm. Clay's eyes begin to well; the nostalgic music ignites a feeling of sadness in his heart; painful memories from his childhood still haunt his fragile mind.

Clay grew up on the outskirts of Philadelphia as an only child. His mother, Claire, almost died giving birth to Clay. Claire was a kind and loving mother; quite often, she would protect Clay from the other children in the neighbourhood.

Clay's size became apparent from his early teen years, and many of the children, some much older than Clay, would gang up on him and tease him, calling him cruel names and throwing empty bottles at him. Clay would often come home from school with bruises on his body and face, and this one time, he came home with blood streaming down the side of his face: a glass bottle catching Clay unaware. He needed twenty-seven stitches that day to mend the wound. A scar remains to this day as a reminder of his torment.

Clay's father, Samuel, was a solid man who worked at the local steel factory. He had a hardened nature and would repeatedly arrive home drunk and hurl abuse. He often cursed at Claire and lashed Clay with his worn leather belt.

'Why don't you stand up for yourself, coward?' He would bark, taunting Clay for his refusal to fight back.

Claire was the only comfort Clay had growing up. She would hold her son tight in her arms and protect him as best she could from her husband's tyranny. 'You will grow up and be a gentleman.' She would whisper in his ear as she kissed him goodnight. On his eighteenth birthday, Claire gave Clay some money she had put away over the years and instructed him to go live with her sister in New York. 'Catch the next morning's bus to the city.' She instructed. 'It arrives at 7:44, and Clay, you will be on that bus. Your father will have already left for work, and when he returns tomorrow evening, you will already be gone. He won't be able to hurt you anymore. You will finally be free.'

Claire's sister lived in New York and arranged for Clay to stay there and look for work. Clay didn't want to leave, but Claire got firm with him. 'It's time to grow up, Clay. It's time to be a man and learn to stand on two feet.' Claire places her palm on the side of Clay's face. 'I love you, Clay, and I will always be your mother, but now, it's time for you to find a better life, a life of your own, full of love and happiness.'

That same night, Clay's father arrived home late from work, fumbling his way inside, the stench of alcohol on his person. He looks around, noticing Claire and Clay sitting on the sofa together. He staggers towards them.

"What the hell is this?" He remarked, pointing at a half-eaten chocolate cake on the coffee table.

"It's Clay's birthday today, Samuel."

Samuel gives Clay an enraged stare. "Why didn't you wait for me?"

A frightened Claire stands up and walks towards her husband. "We waited, Samuel, for two hours."

Samuel glares at Claire.

Claire attempts to reconcile the situation before it escalates. "Would you like some chocolate cake, Samuel?" Silence fills the room as Samuel shifts his sights on Clay. Claire puts her hand on her husband's shoulder. "Come on, let us sit and have some cake together." She forces a smile.

Seething with hatred, Samuel grabs Claire by the arm and throws her to the ground. Whipping his leather belt free, he begins to beat her violently. "Why didn't you wait for me, you selfish bitch?" He thrusts the leather onto Claire's back, Claire wailing from the immense pain.

Clay's eyes fill with rage as he watches his father hurl the leather. Clay lunges forward, taking hold of his father by the neck, squeezing with all his might. Samuel takes hold of Clay's wrists, grimacing as he tries to pry them apart. Clay's arms shake from adrenalin as he clutches tight, Samuel kicking Clay in vain as both men fall to the ground from the struggle. Clay pins his father to the floor. "You are not gonna hurt, mama..." Clay's voice trembles with fear as he squeezes hard; Samuel's efforts to free himself from Clays choke hold are futile, the lack of oxygen taking its toll. Inevitably, Samuel ceases to resist; his arms falling limp by his side. Claire struggles as she lifts her head off the floor. She looks across to see Clay easing his grip on his father's neck. Claire begins to cry as she realises what has happened. Clay falls back on his haunches; he looks across at Claire; his father lies motionless on the floor. Tears begin to stream from his face as he comes to realize what he has done.

"I'm sorry, Mama." A frightened Clay cries out, remorseful as he slowly rises to his feet. He takes one last look at his mother as he runs from the house.

"Clay!" Claire yells out as she begins to weep uncontrollably.

Two days later, the police found Clay hiding in an old, abandoned shed by the river. He was charged with manslaughter and sentenced to twelve years in prison. Clay's mother passed away from cancer while he was serving his sentence, and he was never able to attend her funeral. He visited her grave on the first day he was released. He still regrets not being able to spend time with his mother and comfort her during her illness.

Audrey pushes down on the closing notes, holding them momentarily, completing her inspiring performance. Clay quickly puts his palms together, giving her a resounding applause. Audrey notices a small tear running down Clay's face. "I see that my playing has moved you, Clay."

"Oh yes, Miss Audrey, you play nice," Clay responds softly.

"Thank you, Clay." Audrey turns her head and sees Charlie looking at them both. "Charlie, I'm getting hungry and am not paying you just to stand there. Hurry up and fix my stove."

Charlie points the screwdriver in his hand towards Audrey. "You're a very cheeky girl, Audrey, talented, but cheeky."

Audrey pokes her tongue out at Charlie.

"Are you hungry, Clay? Can I make you something to eat?"

Clay politely declines. "No, thank you, Miss Audrey. I have my lunch with me today."

"Let me teach you chopsticks!"

Charlie crouches down into the cupboard beneath the stovetop, groaning from his efforts to replace the burnt fuse. "That should do it." Admiring his excellent work, Charlie picks up his toolbox and walks over to the living area. "Time to go, Clay."

Audrey interrupts her lesson, looking up at Charlie. "Are you finished?"

"Yes, Audrey, you may now cook your chicken."

"Finally, Charlie," Audrey smirks.

Charlie glares at Audrey. "You're welcome, Audrey."

Audrey stands up and extends her arm to Clay. "It was a pleasure meeting you, Clay. We shall continue our lesson another time, I'm sure."

"Yes, Miss Audrey, it was nice to meet you, too," Clay says humbly.

Charlie turns and heads for the front door. Audrey places her hand on Clay's back as they walk behind Charlie. "Look after Charlie for me, Clay. Make sure he stays out of trouble."

Clay nods his head forward, chuckling at the thought. "Yes, I will."

Charlie turns to peer at Audrey, her playful humour relentless.

"See you later, boys." Audrey waves her hand, exaggerating her gesture as she closes the door.

Chapter 8

Charlie groans as he and Clay make their way down the spiralling stairs. "My back is playing up again. I need to do more stretching exercises; bending down and crawling into cupboards is not as easy as it used to be."

Charlie looks over at Clay, who's smiling with admiration. "What are you grinning about, big fella?"

"Audrey is a very nice girl," Clay says.

Charlie smiles at the thought, delighted that Clay and Audrey had a moment to bond. "Yes, she certainly is, Clay."

As Clay continues down the stairs, Charlie falls behind, stopping midway, fixated on his thoughts. Clay is quick to notice and concerns himself.

"Are you all right, boss?"

Charlie looks at Clay before taking a seat on the steps. "Have a seat, Clay. I want to talk to you about something."

Clay hauls his heavy frame back up the stairs and sits beside Charlie. Charlie ponders for a moment before addressing Clay in a sincere tone.

"Clay, I want you to take good care of Audrey for me."

Clay looks at Charlie, feeling confused at his request.

"I won't always be here, Clay. I'm getting older by the day, and now that you're here helping me, well, one day soon, you'll be running this place." Charlie looks down momentarily before continuing. "Audrey is special to me, Clay. She's like a daughter. A sweet, annoying, and often stubborn one, but nevertheless, she's like family to me. Do you understand what I'm telling you?"

"Yes, sir, I understand. I'll take good care of her."

Charlie smiles at Clay, patting him once on the shoulder. "I know you will." Charlie rises to his feet, letting out another small groan. "Come on, big guy, let's have some lunch."

Clay smiles at the thought of food. "Yes, boss."

Chapter 9

It is a sunny Wednesday morning, and Audrey is busy preparing arrangements for the day's orders. Gloria's Flowers is a small florist established in 1987. Many locals purchase their flowers there, despite the area's heavy competition. A family-owned florist, Gloria Lipstein, bought what was then an empty space with the money given to her when her husband, Lenny, tragically passed away at a young age. Gloria and Lenny managed to have only one child before Lenny died: a daughter they named Rose. For the past seven years, Gloria has entrusted the responsibility of running the florist to Rose. Now in her late sixties, Gloria comes into the store only twice a week, on Wednesdays and Fridays. She often sits behind the counter, greeting customers as they enter the store.

Rose, who never married, has always relied on her mother for assistance in running the store. One day, however, Gloria fell ill and was bedridden for two weeks, so Rose decided to hire a full-time employee. Rose now runs the florist with Audrey, who was hired when she moved to Manhattan. On her first day in the big city, Audrey stopped at Gloria's Florist for directions to The Parkway. Rose immediately liked her and asked if she wanted to work at the florist. Audrey had already arranged to start work as a receptionist at a local accounting firm the following week. Still, after speaking with Rose for almost an hour, Audrey was humbled by the offer and accepted immediately. She has worked there ever since.

It's 10:25 am, and Gloria is sitting in her usual place behind the counter, knitting a red sweater, which she boasts is for Audrey. Gloria looks across the counter to see Audrey smiling.

"What are you smiling about, dear?"

Audrey turns to look at Gloria. "Nothing, I'm just happy."

Gloria adjusts the half-knit sweater on her lap. "I know that look, dear. You have something on your mind, or should I say someone?"

Audrey tries to act coy while she carefully prunes the stem of an orchid. "Don't be silly. I'm just happy."

"You can't fool an old lady, dear. Something in your eyes tells me a tall, handsome gentleman has recently walked into your life; last Saturday night, to be exact."

Audrey gives Gloria a suspicious look. "What did Rose tell you?"

Gloria looks down at her lap momentarily and lets out a little laugh. "Oh, she told me everything, dear."

Audrey raises her eyebrows. "Really now. Well, you don't need to hear it from me then."

Gloria gives Audrey a pleading look. Audrey ignores the plea and continues with her work, wrapping the half dozen Orchids she has trimmed and tying them off with a pink ribbon. Placing the Orchids aside, she turns to face Gloria, who continues to knit her sweater in silence.

"He was very nice."

Gloria looks up. "What, dear? I didn't hear what you said."

"The gentleman I met last Saturday night, I said he was very nice."

Gloria ceases knitting. "So, I heard, dear."

Audrey walks over and leans on the counter. With one hand placed on her cheek, she lets out a sigh. She picks up a pen and doodles on a scrap piece of wrapping paper. "We spent most of the night just talking and looking at the stars, and afterwards, he took me home, as a proper gentleman would."

Gloria's full attention is now on Audrey. Audrey is doodling love hearts on the wrapping paper.

Gloria asks hopefully. "Not before asking you out again?"

Audrey looks across at Gloria, who is smiling eagerly. Nodding her head once, she acknowledges Gloria.

Gloria leans back into her chair. "That's wonderful, dear. I'm so pleased for you."

Audrey's eyes glaze over—her thoughts with William, reminiscing about the evening they spent together. Gloria stands, deciding to leave Audrey with her thoughts. She heads to the back of the store to make a cup of tea.

"Would you like some tea, love?" Audrey doesn't respond. Gloria smiles and continues on her way—the familiar jingle of the door chimes, distracting Audrey from her thoughts. A young man walks into the store wearing a NY baseball cap, torn blue jeans, sneakers, and a grey T-shirt. The young man slides towards Audrey.

"Hey, Audrey."

Audrey smiles. "Hey, John!"

John works for Rose and Gloria delivering flowers and helping around the store two or three days a week, and occasionally on weekends. Rose hired John eight months ago when she found herself run-off her feet delivering orders. John is in his first year at NYU, studying biochemistry and biology.

"Got anything for me?" John removes his cap, running his fingers through his silky, dark hair. Audrey points to the bench.

"Pink Orchids, for a Kate Pritchard, AMEX building downtown. I've put the slip with the flowers."

John makes his way over to the bench. "What time is she expecting them?"

Audrey looks curiously at John. "I'm sure she's not, John."

John concedes with a grin.

"The gentlemen who called said, 'before noon if possible'."

John looks at his watch. "Cool, I'll head off now, then."

Audrey raises her finger, alerting John as she hurries behind the counter. "Oh, hold on a minute." She opens the till, removing a twenty from the tray. She extends her arm, gesturing to John to take the money. "Here you go."

John grabs the note from Audrey. "What's this for?"

Audrey becomes distracted as the door chime sounds. She looks over John's shoulder to see who it is. John waves the note in front of Audrey's eyes to regain her attention, but it is to no avail as William strides into the store, looking directly at Audrey as he enters. John continues to wave the note in front of Audrey's eyes.

"Hello, earth to Audrey."

Audrey looks at John. "What?"

John frowns at Audrey. "What's the money for?"

"Oh, umm, can you buy some food on your way back?"

John pushes the note into the rear pocket of his jeans.

"Sure; food, no problem."

Cradling the bunch of Orchids under his arm, John scoots from the store. Audrey turns and looks at William, who is standing there, smiling. Audrey is surprised. William takes a step closer; he removes his black leather gloves as he greets Audrey.

"Hello, Audrey."

Audrey opens her mouth to speak, but her words have deserted her. She is still stricken by the sight of William standing there in a dark grey suit, with what appears to be a cashmere scarf hanging unevenly from his neck.

"Hi." Audrey manages a whisper.

William looks around the room, admiring all the floral arrangements. "So, this is where you work."

Gloria hears the chatter of an unfamiliar male voice and takes a sneaky peek from the back room, catching only a glimpse of William's steely profile as he meanders around the store.

"Yep, this is it," Audrey responds.

Audrey admired that William remembered where she worked, thinking to herself that she had forgotten the name of the law firm where William worked. Audrey spontaneously decides to be a little cheeky with William.

"So, are you here to buy flowers for someone…special?"

William smiles, sensing Audrey's tone. He brushes his hair back, unsure of his response.

"Perhaps your…mother?"

William nods his head. "Yes, my mother."

Gloria continues to watch with intrigue; peering from the slit in the curtain that hangs in the doorway.

"Anything particular in mind, sir?" Audrey inquires.

William raises his eyebrows in uncertainty. "Maybe you can suggest something, miss?"

"Certainly."

Audrey walks from behind the counter, leading William to the displays around the store. Gloria continues to watch, noticing Audrey place her hand on the man's shoulder, now suspecting that the man Audrey is talking to may also be the same man she met at the party the other night.

Audrey points to an arrangement of daffodils. "Does your mother like daffodils?"

William raises his eyebrows. "I'm sure she does. I've seen them in her home many times."

"Very well then, daffodils it is."

Audrey takes a dozen daffodils from the bucket and walks to the bench. As William looks on, he notices the soft glow on Audrey's face as it catches the sunlight from the store window. He looks on as Audrey arranges the flowers, aligning the head of each flower before taking the clippers in her hand and pruning the stems at the exact length.

Gloria looks more straightforwardly at William as he turns in her direction. She smiles as she appreciates the defining features of William's face, but only for a moment, her emotions stolen by a long-forgotten memory that quickly surfaces. Gloria clutches onto her sweater with frail hands as she looks in disbelief.

"You love your work?"

Audrey looks at William and smiles before gathering the flowers in a bunch and placing them on a piece of yellow wrapping paper. "Yes, I do," Audrey says as she gently wraps the flowers. "It's peaceful here, and it smells great!"

William laughs. "Yes, it does smell nice in here, much better than my stuffy office."

Audrey cuts herself a piece of ribbon off the selection of spools and ties off the bouquet. "I'd imagine that your office is anything but stuffy." Audrey picks up the daffodils in both hands and presents them to William. "I think your mother is going to love these."

William takes the flowers from Audrey. "Yes, and she will most likely think that I may want to borrow money for bringing them to her so unexpectedly."

Audrey looks into William's eyes, her voice softening above a whisper. "Well then, she will be surprised, won't she?"

William continues to gaze into Audrey's eyes. Audrey looks away as she begins to blush.

"I had a wonderful time the other night," William admits.

Audrey fusses with the items on the counter. She eventually looks up at William. "So did I, William."

A moment passes; William clutches the bouquet. "Well, I better get back to work then," William says as he reaches into his coat pocket. "How much do I owe you for these?"

Audrey collects her thoughts. "Um, forty-five."

William retrieves the exact number of denominations from his leather wallet. He extends his hand to Audrey, placing the money in Audrey's palm. Audrey falls into character once again.

"Thank you, kind sir."

William nods his head, pretending to tilt his imaginary top hat. "Good day to you, Ma'am."

Audrey beams as William turns to exit the store. "See you Saturday night," Audrey yells out regretfully.

William places one foot outside the door, turning to look at Audrey one last time. "See you Saturday night, Audrey."

Audrey takes a deep breath as the door closes, exhaling the butterflies in her stomach. She becomes curious about Gloria's whereabouts, making her way to the rear of the store to find Gloria seated on the sofa against the wall.

"Hey, what are you doing back here?"

Gloria remains silent, holding off her response to Audrey. Audrey sits beside Gloria, placing her hand on her shoulder.

"Are you feeling alright?"

Gloria continues to look down, taking Audrey's hand into her palms. She looks up at Audrey. "Audrey dear, I need to tell you something."

Audrey is perplexed at Gloria's tone, unsure of her thoughts. "What is it?"

Gloria takes a deep breath, choosing her words with care. "The man you were just talking to, was this the man Rose told me about?" Gloria holds her breath, waiting for Audrey's response.

Audrey grins slightly at the thought of William. "Yes...that was William."

Gloria closes her eyes momentarily, and with sorrow filling her heart, she reopens them. Audrey looks on, sensing Gloria's uneasiness. She removes her hand from Gloria's shoulder and places it on her head.

"I completely forgot my manners. I should have introduced him to you."

Gloria removes Audrey's hand from her head; she clutches Audrey's hands tightly in her palms. With a solemn look, she stares directly into Audrey's eyes, lowering her voice above a whisper. "I need you to listen to me very carefully, dear."

Audrey loses her smile; she takes note of the seriousness in Gloria's demeanour. Her attention heightened as Gloria began to recount her thoughts to Audrey. After several minutes, Audrey's emotions become conflicted, as she shakes her head in disbelief. Almost sure that Gloria's assumptions are inaccurate. Gloria's eyes well up as she concludes, deeply saddened by the information she has imparted to Audrey, praying that her memory has let her down. Uncertain of her emotions, Audrey gently removes her hands from Gloria's palms, leaning against the sofa. She sits quietly, reflecting on her thoughts, unwilling to comprehend what she has learned.

Chapter 10

The following Saturday, a morning chill hovers over the city as Audrey walks to the grocery store to purchase some goods. Rugged up in a navy-blue coat that hangs past her knees, leather gloves, a scarf and a beanie, Audrey walks with her arms firmly folded, her thoughts occupied with Gloria's revelations earlier that week. Eyeing the cracks in the sidewalk, Audrey feared that if Gloria's conclusions were accurate, she would inevitably have to confront William later tonight on their date.

As Audrey nears the store, she decides she will not spend any more time dwelling on the topic, as it will only make her more anxious by nightfall. Outside the store is an older man smoking a pipe that Audrey has encountered almost every Saturday morning for four years. Audrey smiles as she waves to the man, who smiles back, exposing his remaining four front teeth. Audrey continues to grin, entering the store, remembering that he had seven front teeth when first encountering the older man. She calculates that he will only have one front tooth remaining in another four years.

Audrey collects a carry basket from the stack to her right, loosening her scarf as the warmth of the air conditioning engulfs her face. Audrey casually walks around the store with the basket hanging from her forearm, unsure what she may be hungry for, come noon. After several minutes wandering the aisles, Audrey decides to have a fruit salad for lunch, fearing she may spoil her dinner with William if she eats anything too heavy. She collects her thoughts and heads for the fruit and vegetable section of the store. As she nears the fruit arrangements, Audrey notices two teenage girls giggling with each other and pointing to a man who is kneeling, fumbling with several oranges that have fallen at his feet. Audrey looks across and immediately smiles, recognising her new acquaintance Clay as he struggles with the troublesome fruit.

Audrey sneaks up behind Clay, careful not to be noticed. She watches Clay for a moment, suppressing a chuckle, deepening the tone of her voice as she alerts Clay to her presence. "You'll have to pay for those, sir."

Clay quickly looks up at Audrey with a frightful look on his face.

Audrey laughs and places her hand on Clay's shoulder. "I got you good, Clay?"

Clay smiles, feeling relieved to see Audrey standing there. "I'm having some trouble with the oranges, Miss Audrey." Clay stands, cradling several oranges against his chest.

"Here, let me help you with those, silly boy." Audrey reaches over, taking the oranges from Clay. She places them carefully on the pile. "There we go," Audrey says as she looks up at Clay. "How are you doing, Clay?"

Clay smiles. "I'm well. And how are you this fine morning?"

Audrey removes her beanie. "I'm pretty good, thanks, Clay."

Clay looks down at Audrey's basket. "What are you shopping for today, Miss Audrey?"

Audrey lets out an exhausted sigh. "Fruit, I've decided."

Clay chuckles. "Healthy decision, me thinks."

Audrey wraps her arm around Clay's forearm. "Can you keep me company, Clay?"

Clay feels Audrey clutching his arm tightly. "Yes, Miss Audrey, I guess I can."

"Are the oranges for Charlie?" Audrey inquires.

"Yes, Charlie asked me to get some oranges for him before I came to work today."

Audrey smiles at the thought of Charlie as she selects a couple of oranges for herself. "Charlie loves his orange juice." Audrey continues to enlighten Clay about Charlie's love for orange juice. "He has this big electric orange juice machine that he received two Christmases ago, just like the ones you find at those juice places, you know, where they make all those mixed power juices."

"Yes, I 've seen them in the city."

Audrey takes hold of an apple. "Charlie has one of those machines now and keeps it in his office."

Clay recalls noticing the juicer. "Yes, I've seen it. It's a big silver thing on top of the filing cabinet."

Audrey widens her eyes. "Yes, and he keeps it so clean," Audrey says as she smells a pear before continuing. "One time, I went down to see him early in the morning, and he had all the parts laid out. He sat at his desk, polishing every part with a tea towel."

Clay lets out a laugh, admiring Audrey's energy. Audrey reaches for half a cantaloupe.

"And he won't let anyone touch it, not even me."

"We should hide it from him one day as a joke," Clay whispers.

Audrey shakes her head. "No way, he would kill us if we did that. Seriously! I reckon that if we did, he would call the police." Audrey holds her weighty basket in front of her. "Can you please hold this for me, Clay?"

Clay takes the basket in his hand. Audrey moves towards the collection of stone fruit and berries. She raises her finger, tapping her bottom lip.

"Now, what should I get?" She reaches over and takes a peach, placing it gently into the basket.

Clay points to the papaya. "That one is sweet."

Audrey agrees, placing one in her basket as she makes yummy noises. She then takes a couple of passion fruits and presents them to Clay.

Clay cringes. "I don't like those, Miss Audrey; they don't taste very nice."

Audrey laughs. "Yes, they do."

"They are kind of bitter," Clay says, presenting his tongue to Audrey.

Audrey places the passion fruit in her basket. "It's an acquired taste," Audrey argues, "like wine!"

Audrey suddenly remembers she is out of tomatoes and meanders between the stalls towards them. "Do you drink wine, Clay?" She enquires over her shoulder as she walks away.

Clay follows Audrey, holding the basket out in front of him. His facial expression changed as the notion of alcohol induced memories of his drunken father, remembering the empty wine bottles scattered around the house when he was a child.

"Clay?" Audrey notices the change in Clay's mood. "Are you alright, Clay?"

Clay gives Audrey a reassuring look. "Yes."

Audrey is not convinced. "Did I say something wrong, Clay?"

"No." Clay feels shame for concealing his past. "It's just that I never drink alcohol, Miss Audrey."

Audrey chooses not to pry. Instead, she quickly diverts Clay from his thoughts. "I bought some new earrings, Clay."

"Earrings, Miss Audrey?"

"Yes, would you like to see them?"

"Sure," Clay says, a wondrous look presenting itself.

Audrey picks up a cherry tomato in each hand. Holding them by the vine, she raises them to her ears as she faces Clay. "What do you think?"

Clay gives Audrey a colossal smile. "They look great," Clay says laughingly.

"They are practical as well. If I get hungry, I can eat one of them." Audrey exudes her delight. Clay is amused as Audrey stands in the middle of the produce section, holding the tomatoes up to her ears. "They are only good for about a week, though," Audrey chuckles.

Clay watches as she walks further along and picks up two pieces of celery sticks, concealing them behind her back.

"Clay, I have a big secret to tell you," Audrey says sombrely.

"Secret, Miss Audrey?"

Audrey nods twice. "Yes, Clay, a big secret. Not even Charlie knows this secret."

Clay takes a step forward, feeling a little anxious. "What is it, Miss Audrey?"

Audrey takes the celery sticks and places them on her head like antennas. "Clay, I'm an alien from Venus," Audrey announces worriedly.

Clay laughs at Audrey's antics. "Miss Audrey, you are a crazy girl."

"Don't call me crazy, Clay, or I will use my alien antenna powers to zap you into stardust," Audrey says in character, taking a few steps towards Clay.

Still holding the celery sticks, Audrey bends over and pokes Clay in the stomach with the vegetables. An old lady standing nearby looks on as Audrey makes zapping noises, poking a hysterical Clay in the stomach—a ticklish Clay retreats with laughter. Audrey watches Clay for a moment as he continues to giggle hysterically. Clay catches his breath before he looks Audrey in the eyes.

"You are a fun girl to be around, Miss Audrey; a little crazy but fun."

Audrey laughs as she places the celery sticks in the basket. "Charlie would agree with you on that." Audrey takes hold of Clay's arm. "Come on, Clay, let's get some fromage."

Clay gives Audrey a confused look. "From...what?"

"That's French for cheese," Audrey explains with a giggle.

Clay nods his head. "Oh! I didn't know that, Miss Audrey. My French isn't too good."

Audrey and Clay make their way over to the supermarket's dairy section. Audrey notices several shoppers staring at Clay as they pass by. She wonders for a moment what it may be like for someone like Clay to have people constantly staring at you because of your sheer size. Audrey turns to Clay, who is looking curiously ahead for the dairy section.

"Does it bother you, Clay?"

Clay looks down at Audrey. "Sorry, Miss Audrey?"

"Does it bother you that people stare all the time?"

Clay ponders, thinking at first how much his size affected him growing up, and how the other children treated him. On the first day of prison, the guards and inmates gawked at him as he walked down the prison corridor in handcuffs. But during his time in prison, Clay befriended an older man named Caesar, who was serving a life sentence for the murder of his brother. Caesar worked in the prison library where Clay spent most of his time, keeping his distance from the gangs in the prison yard. One day, Caesar told Clay, 'Think of yourself as a god amongst men. And that when people stare, you should pretend they are staring at you because you are special, benevolent, like a god.'

Clay found Caesar's advice amusing at the time, but later understood it was a clever way to rid himself of the feeling of self-consciousness, a sense Clay had known all too well since he was a child. Clay remembered those words the day Caesar passed away, just six months before Clay was released. The first day Clay was released, he found himself in Central Park. He walked around, admiring his surroundings and freedom from the dark prison walls. Removing his shoes to feel the softness of the green grass beneath his feet, Clay spent several hours there after visiting his mother's grave earlier that morning. He noticed the passers-by frequently staring at him that day and remembered what Caesar had told him in prison and how he should feel about himself. Since that day, Clay has always smiled when he notices someone staring at him, recalling Caesar's sound advice.

"No, Miss Audrey, I kinda like it. It makes me feel special."

Audrey smiles at Clay. "You are special, Clay."

Audrey looks across the selections as they reach the dairy section, hunting for a specific cheese. Clay leans in, whispering to Audrey.

"What cheese are you looking for, Miss Audrey? I can help you look for it."

"Bocconcini," Audrey whispers. Her eyes scan the various kinds of cheese. Clay, too, examines the assortment of cheeses, sounding out the name.

"Buck-a-cheesy."

Audrey is amused at Clay's pronunciation. "What did you say?"

Clay giggles, aware that his pronunciation is a little off. He makes another attempt. "Bock-a-chooni?"

Audrey cackles, mimicking the pronunciation. "Bock-a-chooni." Audrey repeats the correct pronunciation, breaking the word into syllables. "Bo-ccon-cini."

"Bo-ccon-cini," Clay repeats, making another attempt.

"Yeah, you got it, Clay!"

"What does it look like, Miss Audrey?" Clay inquires.

Audrey forms a circle with her thumb and forefinger. "It looks like little round balls of white cheese. They're sometimes called Cherry Bocconcini."

"It has cherries in it?" Clay asks.

"No, silly, they call it cherry because of its shape. They usually pack them in a small container."

"Little white balls of cheese," Clay repeats as he examines the produce. After a moment, he points to a small container filled with little white cheese balls. "I think I found it, Miss Audrey?" Clay takes a container from the shelf and presents it to Audrey.

"That's it. Good work, Clay."

"It looks like delicious cheese. Do they taste nice?"

"Let's find out, Clay."

To Clay's horror, Audrey tears off the safety seal and pries the lid open. Clay quickly wraps his hands over the container before Audrey can remove the cover.

"Miss Audrey, you will get in trouble. You must pay for it first."

"It's alright, Clay; I promise to pay for it," Audrey smirks. Audrey frees the container from Clay's grasp, offering a cherry Bocconcini to Clay. "Here, try one."

Nearby, a young store clerk looks on. Clay reaches into the container and takes a cheese ball with his fingers. The store clerk curiously watches as the enormous black man holds the itty-bitty cheese ball before his lips.

"Put it in your mouth, Clay," Audrey encourages.

Clay looks around and notices the store clerk watching him. He whispers to Audrey. "We are being watched, Miss Audrey."

Audrey turns to see the young, pimple-faced clerk staring at Clay. "What are you gawking at, kid?" Audrey asks in a curt tone.

The pale young clerk looks directly at Audrey, an expressionless look on his face. He draws his attention back to Clay, deciding it may be in his best interest not to concern himself with the young lady and her giant. He scampers down the aisle.

"I think you frightened him, Miss Audrey."

"I think I did," Audrey says laughingly. "Quick, taste the cheese, Clay, before the manager comes."

Clay quickly pops the cheese in his mouth.

"Well? Tastes nice, right?"

Clay nods in agreement as he swallows the cheese. "Yum. It's so soft."

Audrey pops the lid back on and places it into her basket. "Come on, let's get out of here."

"Where to now?" Clay inquires, still licking his lips.

"Well, I need to get some bread."

"The bakery down the street bakes nice bread," Clay informs.

"Do you want to go to the bakery?" Audrey asks.

Clay nods with excited anticipation. "Yes, Miss Audrey. We can get some of those hot jam rolls they make for breakfast."

The bakery is renowned for the jam and cinnamon rolls they produce in the mornings. Most New Yorkers line up for them in the chilly winter months, and Audrey herself has been guilty of having more than one on many occasions. Audrey smiles as she pats Clay on the belly.

"I can see you like those jam rolls, Clay."

Clay lets out a giggle. "Yes, I do. They are delicious. I had three this past week."

After paying for their goods at the checkout, they head to the bakery. Audrey feels comforted as she leans against Clay's shoulder. It is warm inside the bakery, and a young Indian girl offers her service from behind the counter.

"What would you like?"

"Hi. Can I have one of those loaves and four cinnamon and jam rolls?" A smiling Audrey greets the young girl as she removes her beanie again.

Clay smiles as he watches Audrey order, clutching the bags of groceries with anticipation. Audrey places the beanie under her arm as the young girl returns with her order.

"Is there anything else?"

"No, that's it for today. Keep the change," Audrey says as she hands over a twenty. She collects the goods from the counter. Clay watches her closely as she turns to face him, keen to get his hands on those jam rolls.

"You're like a kid in a candy store, Clay," Audrey says as they head back towards The Parkway.

"Did you buy four jam rolls?"

Audrey sighs. "Yes, I got four of them, one for you and Charlie and two for me," Audrey teases.

Clay's facial expression changes, stopping at the thought of only having one jam roll for himself.

"Maybe we should buy two more, Miss Audrey."

Audrey laughs aloud. "I'm messing with ya, Clay; you can have two." Audrey pulls Clay by the hand. "Come on, Clay, I'm getting cold."

Clay continues to walk with Audrey as she leans in close to keep warm.

"I must watch what I eat, anyway. Otherwise, I'll get fat, and no man will want to marry me, Clay."

Clay wraps his arm around Audrey. "I'll marry you if you get big, Miss Audrey," Clay chuckles.

Audrey smiles as she leans her head on Clay's shoulder. "You're a sweetheart, Clay, you know that. A big sweetheart."

Chapter 11

The sun has set in the evening, and a crescent moon appears in the night sky. Audrey sits nervously on her sofa, waiting for William to arrive; the same thoughts occupy her mind as her date with William draws near. Could what Gloria had said be true? Is William the man she spoke about? She must be mistaken. It was over four years ago, and people can often look different in photos. She has to be mistaken. After all, William didn't seem the sort of man who would do something so horrific, as Gloria had described. Audrey briefly looks at her watch and sees it is 6:43 pm. She stands up and walks over to the window. Inching the curtain to one side, she peers down the street, looking for Williams' Mercedes. Her eyes sweep the street. No sign of William's car, she thinks to herself. Audrey turns and slowly walks over to the sofa. Standing there with her arms folded, she suddenly feels ridiculous and smiles.

"Oh, Gloria, what are you doing to me?" Audrey lets out a frustrating groan and heads for the dresser to collect her coat and purse. She decides to go downstairs and wait for William in the lobby.

Downstairs, a preoccupied Charlie is crouched by the television in his office, attempting to correct the poor reception. Charlie addresses the television in frustration. "What is the matter with you tonight?"

As Charlie continues to prod away with his screwdriver, outside, Ms Fellstone is making her way up the front steps of The Parkway, cradling a cumbersome grocery bag.

Ms Fellstone, a long-time resident of The Parkway, lives on the second floor. As she clears the last step, she places the groceries on the landing and reaches into her purse, removing her key to the front entrance. As she extends her arm to insert the key, she is startled by a soft, deep voice.

"Would you like a hand with your groceries, Ma'am?"

Ms Fellstone turns to see a tall man standing beside her, dressed in a sharp dark blue suit, holding tiger lilies in his left hand. With a smile, he reaches down and picks up the grocery bag. Unable to recognise the man, Ms Fellstone begins to feel nervous, clutching her keys tightly against her chest.

"I apologise if I frightened you. I'm William. I'm here to pick up Audrey." William pauses momentarily. "Do you know Audrey?"

Ms Fellstone begins feeling at ease, as she is familiar with Audrey. "I do know Audrey. A lovely girl. Thank you, you're so kind to help." Ms Fellstone laughs nervously, patting her chest with her keys. "I have to admit you startled me, young man."

"I apologise. That was not my intention."

Ms Fellstone feels embarrassed. "I'm sorry too, dear; it's just that you can't be too careful in this neighbourhood."

"Yes, I understand how you feel," William says, cradling the groceries under his arm.

"I'm Ms Fellstone. Audrey and I know each other quite well. She sometimes comes over for tea."

William raises his brow. "I have only known Audrey for a short while. Tonight will be our first dinner together."

"Oh! Well, you mustn't keep her waiting then. Never keep a lady waiting."

William smiles. "Yes, you're right."

Ms Fellstone opens the entrance, allowing William to enter the lobby. As she closes the door behind her, she turns and whispers. "You should go up and surprise her with those flowers. Women like that sort of thing."

"That's thoughtful advice; I'll do just that."

As William escorts Ms Fellstone up the spiralling stairs, Charlie is entirely unaware, still hustling with the television's antenna cable. As they reach the second level, Ms Fellstone takes possession of her groceries.

"Audrey's apartment is one more flight up, William. It's apartment 34, at the end of the corridor."

"Thank you. You're truly kind."

"You're welcome, dear. You have a lovely evening with Audrey. I am sure she will enjoy your company."

William wraps his middle finger over his index finger, presenting it to Ms Fellstone. "Fingers are crossed."

Upstairs, Audrey stands in front of her bedroom mirror one final time. Wearing a white dress with lace trim, she looks herself up and down and takes a deep breath. "Okay, everything looks good." With her purse in hand and winter coat draped over her arm, Audrey exits her bedroom and heads directly for the front door. "You'll be fine; you'll be fine."

Taking hold of the handle, Audrey unconsciously swings the front door open, her thoughts in disarray. She looks up to see William standing with one arm raised, his hand formed into a fist, poised to knock. Audrey quickly mutes her scream. She uncovers her mouth.

"What are you doing here?" She yells in fright.

William leans back, lowering his clenched fist. "Audrey, I'm so sorry. I didn't mean to frighten you." William is somewhat amused. "I came up to surprise you."

Audrey's heart is still racing, chaotic thoughts running through her mind as she looks up at William. William takes a step forward, placing his arm on Audrey's shoulder.

"Are you okay, Audrey?"

Audrey remains silent, urging herself to say something. She nods ever so slightly.

"You look a little pale. Let's go inside for a minute so that you can catch your breath."

William leads Audrey down the hallway and into the open living area. "Let me get you a glass of water, ok?" William walks over to the kitchen. A startled Audrey finds the nearest sofa and eases herself down. She covers her face with both hands, realising that her reaction is abnormal because of everything Gloria had told her. Audrey now dreads what William may have been thinking of her.

After getting his bearings in the kitchen, William returns with a glass of water. He sits beside Audrey and hands her the drink. "Here you go." William can't help but smile. "I'm truly sorry, Audrey. I didn't think that I would scare you as I did. Am I that frightening to look at?"

She manages a smile. "No," Audrey shakes her head as she sighs. "It's just that I didn't expect you'd be standing there." Audrey feels mortified as she looks at William. "You must think I'm a real nut job."

"Well, you may be a little nutty. But that's what I like about you."

As Audrey looks directly into William's eyes, fond memories of the first night they met come rushing back. His sweet smile and handsome looks begin to overshadow any unfavourable thoughts. Audrey turns her attention to the glass of water; she ponders momentarily; she knows her feelings for William are uncharacteristically strong for someone she has only seen twice before. *Maybe what Gloria had told me was inaccurate.* She thinks to herself. *Maybe William has a right to know what I am thinking.* Audrey takes a sip of her water, deciding to confront William. She repositions herself on the sofa, doing her best to appear relaxed.

"Do you mind if we sit here for a minute?"

"Sure, there's no hurry."

Audrey looks down at her glass, searching her mind for the right words, wondering about his reaction when she finally reveals what she has learnt, even if it is a total fallacy.

William focuses on Audrey's long, dark hair flowing down her milky back. Her thin, frail arms and elongated fingers as they clasp the glass of water. He feels aroused as Audrey nervously moves her elbows closer together, emphasising her bosom. His lust for her emerges as he watches her breathe.

"William, I need to tell you something."

William's eyes have glazed over; she's the perfect woman to him, and he adores her completely as she sits there. "What is it, Audrey?" He whispers.

Audrey places the glass of water on the coffee table before turning to face William. "The other day, when you visited me in the florist, Gloria, the owner, saw your face. She was watching us from the back of the store."

William raises a brow. "Sounds like she was spying on us?"

"Yes." Audrey clenches her hands together, letting out a nervous chuckle.

"After you left, she told me something upsetting. Something that I haven't been able to stop thinking about."

William becomes curious. "What did she tell you?"

"She said that you looked familiar to her."

William's curiosity deepens. "Familiar?"

"Yes. Gloria told me about her friend and her daughter." Audrey pauses. "Her daughter, Amy."

Audrey looks directly at William. William was no longer smiling. Audrey continues, deciding to rip the band-aid off. William listens intently as Audrey narrates the information imparted to her. Audrey's mouth begins to dry; her hand trembles as she again reaches for the water. She takes a quick sip and returns the glass to the table. Audrey collects her thoughts. She closes her tear-filled eyes as she senses William's mood shift. With tears now running down her face, Audrey looks up at William.

"Is it true?" She asks, her voice trembles. William's sullen expression all but confirms to Audrey that it is. She bows her head in anguish.

William casts a steely look at Audrey before rising slowly to his feet. Audrey's heart races as she senses a terrifying change in William's aura. He strides towards the kitchen, resting his hands on the countertop. The bouquet he bought catches his eye as he lunges forward with his head bowed. Audrey wipes the tears from her face, crossing her arms to prevent herself from trembling. William remains motionless, the silence of the room palpable.

"William?" Audrey speaks; her throat is coarse.

William remains motionless.

"William, please say something," Audrey pleads. "You're scaring me."

William pushes himself off the countertop and turns, taking a few steps towards Audrey. He looks aimlessly around the room; his frustration is evident. William faces Audrey, standing there with purpose, arms by his side, looking directly at her; his charm is absent, and his face is cold. Audrey cannot look away; her emotions are a mess, and she feels nauseous recalling the details Gloria had described. Audrey wills herself to speak.

"William, I think you'd better go."

William redirects his focus to the piano by the far wall.

Audrey nervously rises to her feet. "Please, William, just leave. We can discuss this another time."

William turns and looks at Audrey. "Sure, you'll call me, right?" A condescending tone.

Audrey continues to wipe the tears from her face. "William, I didn't mean to..."

"To what?" William interrupts. "Look at you; standing there, terrified and looking at me like I'm some monster."

Audrey bows her head momentarily, mustering all her courage, a firmer tone she feels is needed. "William, I'm sorry. But I didn't want our relationship to end like this."

William looks away, concealing his immediate hatred for Audrey's retort. He repeats Audrey's words in his mind *...our relationship to end.* William clenches his jaw, contemplating the situation as he takes a deep breath. He casually walks towards Audrey; her heart begins to race as William approaches her. William extends his arm.

"Give me your hand Audrey."

Audrey reluctantly extends her hand to William. William wraps both his palms around Audrey's trembling fingers.

"Can I ask you for one last favour before I leave?"

Audrey hears sincerity in William's voice; she feels regretful. She knows their relationship will never be what she hoped for after tonight. William leads Audrey over to the piano.

"Will you play something for me?"

Audrey develops sympathy for William as she looks into his pleading eyes.

"Please, Audrey, just this one time, for me."

William looks helplessly at Audrey. Her thoughts confusing her as she looks up at William. Audrey nods her head.

"All right, William."

Audrey wipes the drying tears one last time before seating herself at the piano. Closing her eyes, Audrey files through many pieces of familiar music. She makes her selection, resting her delicate hands on the keys for the opening notes. William stands beside her, anxiously eyeing Audrey's neckline. Audrey gently presses down on the keys. The room's mood quickly changes, the familiar sounds of *Clair de Lune* invigorating the stale air. William follows Audrey's hands as they selectively meander the ivory; the gentle sounds of Debussy's music sweeten William's bitterness. He places his hand on Audrey's shoulder, closing his eyes to reflect on the night he first met Audrey. He remembers how she smiled at him, with her cheeky grin and that unrealised moment on the balcony as their eyes met, anticipating a first kiss. Audrey begins to sway, disrupting Williams' thoughts; he opens his eyes, the harsh reality tainting his blissful memories. Audrey's revelation, a knife piercing his chest, that first kiss that never was, is now destined to become only a fantasy. William now struggles to maintain his composure. He envisions the look Audrey gave him moments earlier, a look of disappointment and despair as she revealed what she had learnt of his past—no benefit of the doubt in her summation. William clenches as he glares down at Audrey, who has now fallen into tranquillity, as she strikes each note.

William resigns at the thought of not seeing Audrey again after tonight. He concedes that any effort to reconcile their relationship will forever be tainted. He focuses on her cleavage, aroused by the smooth white skin of her breasts as it falls away from the lace of her dress with every exhaled breath. William's eyes fill with rage, taunted by his past, taunted by the realisation that their relationship will cease soon after Audrey stops playing. William gently lifts his hand off Audrey's shoulder. One final resentful thought, erasing all his compassion for Audrey.

In a sudden movement, William takes hold of the piano cover, thrusting it down on Audrey's hands; simultaneously wrapping his hand over Audrey's mouth, muffling her scream. The notes stifled as Audrey anguished in pain. He presses firmly down on the cover, crushing her hands onto the keys, her frail bones snapping like twigs from the force of William's shoulder. William maintains a firm grip as Audrey struggles to free herself from his clutches. The shooting pain from her pierced skin flows into her arms as tears run down her face. Her weak frame cannot free itself from William's grasp; his torso is taut with anger, vilifying Audrey with his rage. Audrey tires from her struggle, only a tiny amount of oxygen now able to fill her weary lungs. Barely conscious, William pulls her away from the piano; her arms and bloodied hands dangle to her sides as he throws her to the ground, her shoulder and head striking the dense wooden floor with force. William eases himself down on one knee, fixated on Audrey's rosy cheek, taking one last look as she lies there, conscious for the moment. The blunted weight of William's clenched hand plunged her into darkness.

Chapter 12

Charlie takes a few steps back from the television, admiring his handy work, celebrating with a foot shuffle.

"Clean as a whistle," he says, his enthusiasm evident as he prepares for a night of visual entertainment. Charlie walks over to his desk and retrieves a packet of microwave popcorn from the bottom drawer. Tearing the cellophane wrapping with his teeth, he opens the microwave oven door and places the bag inside, setting the timer for two minutes exactly. While waiting for the corn to explode into mouth-watering puffs of white gold, Charlie fetches a Budweiser from the bar fridge, promptly removing the cap and taking a well-earned mouthful of cold beer. "Ahh, that's just what I needed."

Charlie stands in the middle of the room, patiently waiting for the timer to run down, his attention diverted by a faint but familiar sound, the building's front door as it hits against the recess. Charlie places his beer on the table, walks out of the office and enters the lobby. He looks at the entrance before surveying the area. Charlie sees no one. His thoughts quickly go to Audrey as he looks at his watch. He begins to wonder why she never came to his office. Earlier in the day, Audrey promised Charlie she would introduce William before they left for dinner.

Charlie walks towards the front entrance for a closer look. *That's not like her,* he thinks to himself. He deliberates, looking across and up the stairs. Then, unexpectedly, he begins to feel uneasy. *Maybe he never showed,* Charlie wonders. Feeling dissatisfied, he decides to make his way up to Audrey's apartment.

After reaching the top of the stairs, he gradually walks down the corridor. As he approaches, Charlie notices the front door to Audrey's apartment is slightly ajar. Charlie feels concerned as he gently places his fingertips on the front door, pushing it open. "Audrey?" Charlie looks cautiously down the dimly lit hallway; he slowly edges his way towards the open living area. Charlie turns his head to the left; the kitchen is empty. He begins to examine the living area for signs of Audrey. The glass of water placed on the coffee table catches his attention. He takes another step, his concerned expression disappearing into horror as he notices a figure on the floor by the piano.

"Oh, dear god." Charlie's heart races as he inevitably realises the figure on the floor is Audrey. Charlie kneels beside Audrey. "Oh, dear god, no." Charlie carefully moves in closer to examine Audrey; his eyes fill with tears as he sees the bruises on her face, her eye swollen. "Oh no, my dear Audrey." Tears emerge as he looks upon Audrey's injured hands in disbelief. Her mangled fingers turn Charlie's stomach; he looks away in horror. Feeling helpless, Charlie staggers to his feet. He hurries to the phone for help; Audrey lies there, lifeless.

Chapter 13

Detectives Languetti and Miles arrive at The Parkway at 7:46 p.m. They survey the exterior of the building before entering; a uniformed police officer mans the entrance. As they enter the lobby, they spot two more police officers at the base of the stairwell.

"What have we got, fellas?" Miles inquires.

Officer Ross gestures up the staircase. "Top of the stairs, Detective, Apartment 34."

Officer Yuen glances at his notepad. "Mitch and I were first on the scene, sir. Assaulted female; late twenties." Officer Yuen takes another peek at his notes before continuing. "The caretaker, Mr Charlie Brown, found her around twenty minutes ago and called it in."

"Where's the caretaker now?"

"He's still upstairs in the girl's apartment; he won't leave. EMS is up there, too."

"We got a suspect?" Languetti asks.

The police officer shakes his head. "Nothing yet, Sir. The caretaker hasn't said much. He's pretty shaken up."

The two officers move aside as Languetti and Miles go up the stairs to Audrey's apartment. Officer Ross yells out to Languetti and Miles. "Up the very top, Detectives. End of the hall."

Languetti and Miles make their way to the top of the stairs, noting another police officer outside the apartment, standing guard. As they near the apartment, Languetti reaches into his coat pocket and pulls out a pair of latex gloves. The officer moves aside and casually nods as Languetti walks through the door of Audrey's apartment.

"How are you doing this fine evening?" Miles acknowledges the officer at the door.

As Languetti enters the main living area, he sees Charlie standing by the sofa, observing the two Medics as they attend to Audrey. Languetti takes a few steps towards Charlie before he looks down at the Medics, hunched over the body. Detective Miles glances around the room before turning his attention to Charlie. He walks over, and in a soft voice, he addresses Charlie. "Excuse me, sir."

Charlie remains unresponsive. His thoughts are on Audrey. Detective Miles places his hand on his shoulder.

"Charlie?"

Charlie turns to look at Detective Miles, his face distressed. Charlie remains silent; Miles notices the redness in Charlie's eyes. One of the Medics sits up and addresses Languetti.

"She's alive, Detective."

As he hears those three words, a small sense of relief washes over Charlie.

Miles gently pats him on the back. "Charlie, I'd like to ask you some questions. Is that ok with you?"

Charlie responds to the detective with a slight nod. Miles walks Charlie over to the kitchen area. Languetti moves closer to the body; he takes a photo with his phone before crouching down and focusing on Audrey's wounds.

"What's her condition?" Languetti inquires.

One of the medics proceeds to inform Languetti. "Not good. She has multiple bruises and fractures, her collarbone and maybe her left arm might be broken, and she received a heavy blow to the side of her face. Jaw appears broken from the swelling." Languetti's eyes circle the floor.

"You find a weapon?"

The medic shakes his head. "Didn't see anything near the body, Detective."

Languetti takes a photo of Audrey's hands. "What about her hands?"

The medic looks to his right. "The piano has blood all over it, Detective."

Languetti rises to his feet and steps towards the piano—the keys covered in Audrey's blood. Languetti looks down at the overturned stool as he pieces together the events.

Miles removes his writing pad from his jacket and begins questioning Charlie. "Mr. Charlie Brown, is it?"

Charlie nods. "Yes, that's correct."

"You're the caretaker here, Charlie?"

"Yes, I am." Charlie's thoughts are still with Audrey.

"And you found the girl?"

Charlie nods, looking in Audrey's direction.

"How well do you know the victim?"

Charlie wills his focus on the detective. "We were close, Detective. We spoke almost every day."

"Do you know who might have done this to her?" Miles is direct.

Charlie looks up at Miles, nodding slightly. "Audrey had dinner plans."

"Audrey? Is that her name?"

"Yes, Audrey Mills."

Detective Miles becomes attentive. "You said she had dinner plans? With whom?"

"Yes, his name was William."

Detective Miles continues to take notes. "So, she had a date tonight with this William? Do you know his last name?"

"No, I never met him. Audrey mentioned him to me last week."

Detective Miles notices Charlie becoming distant in thought.

"How did he get upstairs?" Charlie whispers.

"What's that?" Miles prods Charlie to include him in his thoughts.

Charlie shakes his head, trying to figure out how William got into the building. Charlie collects his thoughts for a moment and then addresses the detective. "I was downstairs in the office. I was expecting Audrey to come down. She told me she would come and see me before she went to dinner."

"With her date? William?" Miles confirms.

"Yes. I heard the door to the entrance of the building close and went out to look to see who it was."

Detective Miles interrupts Charlie. "What time was this?"

"Oh, about thirty minutes ago."

Miles looks at his watch. "Did you see who it was?"

"No, I didn't see anyone," Charlie says regretfully.

"And then what happened?"

"I came up the stairs to see if Audrey was still home, and found the door was open. When I came inside, she was..." Charlie pauses as images resurface of Audrey spread out on the floor, covered in her blood. Miles motions with his pen.

"So, you found her on the floor like that?"

Charlie nods. "Yes."

"And you think it may have been this William who did this to her?"

Charlie shakes his head. "I'm not sure. I never saw him. I didn't see anyone come in or leave."

Detective Miles gives Charlie a curious look. "She may have buzzed him in?"

Charlie shakes his head. "No buzzer in this building, Detective. You have to come down to let your visitors in yourself."

"Maybe that is what she did?" Miles speculates.

"I don't know; I don't think so."

Detective Miles decides to give Charlie a moment to collect his thoughts. "Charlie, I want you to wait here and try to think of anything that may help us with this investigation. I'll be back in a minute."

"Yes, Detective."

Miles walks towards Languetti. He briefly looks at Audrey's body, the medics shielding his view. "You figured anything out?" Miles asks.

Languetti looks at his partner, directing his attention to the piano. "It looks like someone crushed her hands using the piano cover."

Miles looks at the bloodied keys. "Jesus, that's messed up."

Languetti's temper is tested as he looks around the room. "Someone was here, and they worked her over pretty good, leaving her here to die."

"Caretaker says the victim had a date."

Languetti looks directly at Miles. "You get a name?"

"Just a first name, William. Old man says he never saw anyone enter or leave the building."

Languetti looks down at Audrey. "Maybe she can tell us." Languetti glances at Charlie across the room. "Take him downstairs and find out where the fuck forensics is. I want this whole place swept from top to bottom."

"Yes...sir."

Detective Miles escorts Charlie down to the lobby while Languetti continues to survey the apartment. His eyes focused on the lone glass of water on the coffee table. *A possibility of obtaining fingerprints of the assailant,* he thinks to himself. Languetti looks down at Audrey once more as the two Medics secure her frail body onto the gurney, now wrapped in bandages and braces to stabilise the damage, carefully removing Audrey from the crime scene.

Miles seats Charlie on a cushioned sofa in the lobby; Charlie is now seemingly calmer than before. The detective continues his deposition.

"Charlie, you said that Audrey mentioned William last week?"

Charlie nods, now feeling a little eager to help the detective. "Yes, she told me she met him at a party last weekend."

Miles continues to take notes. "Do you know where this party was?"

Charlie shakes his head. "No...upper west side of town, I think."

"Did she go to this party with anyone else?"

Charlie's eyes fire up with conviction. "Yes, her best friend, Veronica."

Miles is distracted by the footsteps of two men from forensics who enter the lobby. "About fucken time." He mutters under his breath.

Charlie continues. "She left with Audrey last Saturday night from here, around 7:00 pm, Detective." Charlie begins to consider the possibility that Veronica may know William. "I have Veronica's address and number somewhere in my office. I can get it for you."

Detective Miles takes hold of his cell phone. "You have Veronica's address and number? Please get it for me, Charlie."

Charlie jumps up and heads for his office.

Miles calls his partner. "Hey, Frank. I've got a possible lead on this guy, William. We should check it out."

"I'll be down in a minute."

Frank's voice pierces the phone's speaker. Miles takes another look around the lobby. He admires the décor as Charlie returns promptly, holding a piece of paper in his hand.

"That's Veronica's home address and cell number, Detective. Audrey gave me this a while ago to book taxis, as such."

Miles looks at the paper for a moment before addressing Charlie. "You did good, Charlie. You should go home and get some rest; you look tired."

Charlie nods. "I will. Good luck, Detective."

Languetti scurries down the last few steps; his heels clacking as they meet the marble floor. He peers at Miles as he crosses the lobby.

"Gotta go, Charlie. Get some rest, okay."

Miles joins his partner as they both head for the exit. For a moment, Charlie feels a sense of accomplishment before images of a wounded Audrey invade his thoughts, now wondering if he was partly to blame for what happened.

Chapter 14

A midnight blue Chevrolet Impala pulls up in front of an apartment building on the east side of town. Languetti and Miles exit the cruiser. Languetti takes a moment to look at the fourteen-level opulent high-rise apartment block before following Miles to the front entrance. Miles retrieves the small piece of paper from his shirt pocket, taking another look at the unit number before reaching for a keypad adjacent to the entrance. 8…7…#.

"Be home," Miles mutters as he files the note in his coat pocket. He quickly glances at his watch as he removes his badge from his waist belt. Languetti instinctively looks over his right shoulder as they wait for a response from the intercom.

"Who are you guys?" A curious voice crackles. Miles raises his badge to the intercom's camera.

"Miss Park?" An extended silence. "I'm Detective Miles."

Veronica takes a closer look at the two men. "Yes?"

Miles reattaches his badge. "My partner and I need to come up and ask you a few questions. Can you let us in, please?"

"Yes, I guess so. I'll buzz you in." Veronica feels baffled.

The sound of the magnetic clack releases the locking mechanism. Languetti moves forward, pushing the front door open. Languetti and Miles make their way towards the building's elevator. Upstairs, Veronica scurries around the room, nervously tidying up, feeling uncomfortable at the impromptu visit, and wondering if she has done anything to bring the detectives to her apartment. She glances at the clock on the wall, wiping the sweat from her palms onto her jeans. Exiting the elevator, Languetti and Miles peer down the hall, taking note of the numbers as they pass each door.

"This is it," Miles announces, raising his arm and knocking twice. The door swings open, revealing a nervous-looking Veronica, arms folded, as she looks curiously at the detectives.

"Veronica Park?" Detective Miles asks.

Veronica nods at the detectives. "Yeah, that's me."

"May we please come in for a moment?"

Veronica eyes the detective's badge. "Sure."

Veronica steps aside, inviting the detectives inside. Detectives Languetti and Miles proceed into the apartment, making their way to the open area of the living room. Miles peers around the room, noticing the large impressionist painting hanging on a purple-coloured feature wall. The remaining walls are painted in Arctic white, a simplistic décor which houses two brown leather sofas, a smoked glass top coffee table and a 74-inch flat-screen television. Closing the door behind her, Veronica follows the men barefoot, the floor covered in a wool blend carpet extending throughout the living area. Veronica warily approaches the detectives.

"So, what's this about?"

Miles places his hands on his hips. "We are here to talk to you about Audrey Mills. You are friends with her, is that correct?"

Veronica is surprised to hear Audrey's name mentioned by the detective. "Yes, we are like best friends. What did she do, steal a pack of gum?" Veronica snickers.

Miles hesitates, searching for the right words to break the news to Veronica. An extended silence from Miles sends a chill down Veronica's spine. Suddenly, she realises that this isn't about something Audrey has done wrong, but rather something that has happened to Audrey.

"What the hell's going on?" Veronica becomes slightly agitated. Languetti moves towards Veronica.

"Maybe you should sit down for a moment." Languetti places his hand on Veronica's shoulder, guiding her to the sofa. He takes a seat beside her, taking a moment before speaking. "The police were called to Audrey's residence about an hour ago. She was found in her apartment, severely beaten." The blood drains from Veronica's face as she listens to the detective deliver the horrific news. "She is alive, but she has sustained several serious injuries."

Veronica places her hand on her head in disbelief. "What the fuck happened?" She yells out unexpectedly. Languetti is unresponsive; Veronica looks up at Miles. "Who did this to her?"

"We don't know yet." Miles stands firm. "Do you know of a guy Audrey met named William?"

A distressed Veronica tries to collect her thoughts. "Yeah. Audrey met William last week. It was at a party we were at." Veronica covers her mouth as she begins to feel nauseous.

"Do you know William?" Frank asks.

Veronica refocuses, acutely aware that the detectives suspect William. "Did William do this to her?"

Languetti is reluctant to implicate William without evidence.

"We're not sure at this time. We want to speak to him."

Veronica looks at Frank. "Yeah, I know him."

"Do you know his last name or where he currently resides?" Miles retrieves his notebook in anticipation.

Veronica rubs her temple. "Oh fuck." Veronica collects her thoughts. "Yeah, I do...fuck. His name is William Burrows. I don't know where he lives, but I do know where he works." Veronica thinks for a moment. "Bloodworth and Crane. It's a law firm."

Miles scribbles the information down. "Caucasian?"

"Yeah, he's white," Veronica says, her hatred visible.

Veronica turns to Languetti, eager to know more about Audrey's condition. "Where is Audrey now?" The conviction is evident in her eyes.

"She was taken to the Bellevue hospital for emergency treatment."

Veronica springs up from the sofa and quickly wipes her tears. "I'm going to see her."

Languetti reaches into his jacket, pulling out a small business card. "Miss Park, if you need to speak to us or remember anything you think we should know, you can reach us on this number."

"Okay, sure." Veronica says, her adrenaline evident as she takes the card from Languetti.

Languetti wastes no time, turning to exit the apartment.

Miles eyes Veronica one last time. "I'm sorry about your friend," he says as he leaves to join his partner. Veronica appreciates the sentiment.

Languetti and Miles exit the apartment and head towards the elevator. Veronica closes the door and takes a moment to itemise her thoughts; she presses her forehead against the door, closing her eyes momentarily. "Oh god, Audrey," she begins to cry.

As they exit the elevator, Miles takes his cell from his coat pocket and speeds dials a number for a co-worker in his precinct. A chirpy female voice answers the call.

"Hi, Shaun."

"Hey Stephanie, are you at your desk? I need a small favour." Miles loosens his tie.

"Sure am. What's up, handsome?"

"I need a home address for one William Burrows, aged between twenty-five and thirty-five, who works at Bloodworth and Crane; it's a law firm."

"Burrows..." Stephanie voices as she dictates.

Miles pushes the outer door, exiting the building. "Put a rush on that order, Steph." Miles adjusts his attire, tucking his shirt into the rear of his trousers as he walks towards the car.

"Okay, I'll call you back when I have something."

"Check for priors too, Steph."

"Sure, hun."

Miles hangs up the phone. He lets out a frustrated sigh as he swings open the vehicle's door.

"You wanna go for coffee?"

Languetti slips into the driver's seat. "Yeah sure," he says as he fires up the engine of the squad car.

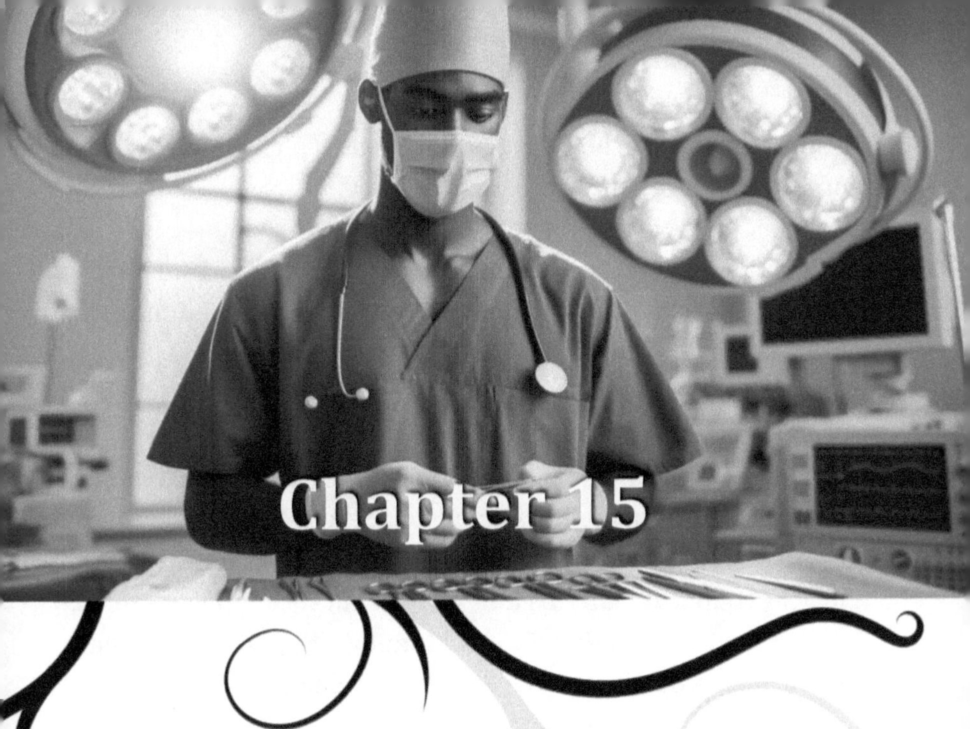

Chapter 15

Dr Wakefield stands over a stainless-steel trough, vigorously and meticulously scrubbing his hands in preparation for surgery. He leans forward, placing his hands one at a time underneath the running water, using his left elbow to bring the water flow to an end. He shakes off the excess water before facing Nurse Hoang, a first-year resident at the ready with a sterilised towel. Nurse Hoang hands the towel to Dr Wakefield and waits patiently as he thoroughly dries both hands. The nurse holds out a pair of latex gloves. Dr Wakefield carefully slides his hands into each glove one at a time. The doctor repositions his surgical mask as he walks towards the door to the operating theatre. The doors mechanically slide apart, permitting Dr Wakefield to enter the room. Dr Wakefield walks towards the patient; he looks directly down at the young girl, who lies still, her arms by her side, prepped for surgery. A rubber tube was inserted into the patient's gullet, assisting her in breathing, while a nurse carefully monitors the patient's heartbeat on the ECG nearby. A third-year resident,

Dr Sims, stands by the bed, waiting to assist Dr Wakefield in the surgery. Dr Wakefield addresses his crew.

"What have we got, Doctor?"

Dr Sims refers to the patient's chart. "Patient has a fracture to the right-side cheekbone, several fractures to both hands and ribs on the left side of her torso."

Dr Wakefield examines the patient; Dr Sims continues in greater detail.

"The patient has sustained trauma to the right side of her face, leaving fractures of the Ramus, Zygomatic and Mandible. She also has sustained trauma on the left side of her upper torso with the Clavicle, Humerus, and ribs four and five, all sustaining fractures." Dr Sims takes a breath before continuing. "Both her hands have several fractures. Many of the Proximal Phalanges and Metacarpal bones have suffered breaks."

Dr Wakefield focuses on the patient's battered hands before responding. "How did she sustain these injuries?"

Dr Sims looks at Dr Wakefield. "Attending said she was assaulted."

Despite the twelve years of experience as a surgeon, Dr Wakefield feels deeply disturbed as he looks down upon Audrey. He stares intently at Audrey's face momentarily before refocusing on the task. He addresses the room. "Let's get to work."

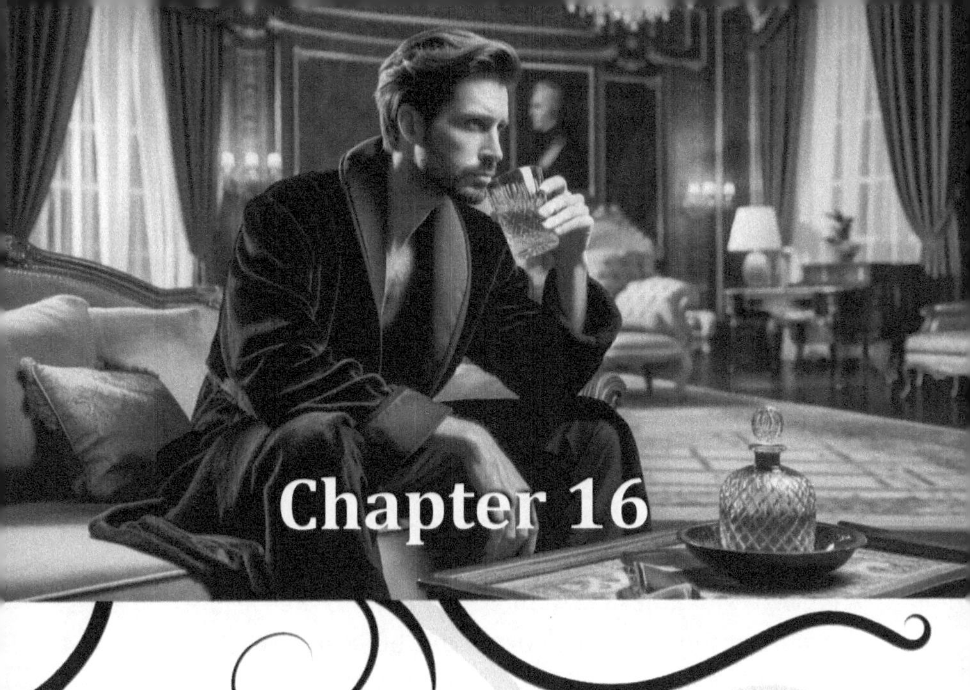

Chapter 16

In his lavish apartment, William sits peacefully, his feet comfortably placed on a stool cushion, and images of his encounter with Audrey occupy his thoughts. When he arrived home earlier that evening, he immediately removed his clothing, taking a long, hot shower. William meticulously scrubbed his body clean of any sign of Audrey's blood before drying off his muscular physique. Wearing only a black pair of Jockey underwear, William sits on his sofa, taking small sips of the Chivas Regal scotch whisky that he poured earlier. Still, he feels the bitterness of the encounter as he takes another sip to dull his emotions. His muscles begin to relax as the golden liquid begins to take effect. William gazes across the room through the glass doors of his balcony; he notices that a naked woman is visible in the adjacent complex. He remains emotionless. Raising his glass to his lips, William takes another mouthful of whisky, his thoughts unexpectedly interrupted as the intercom chimes, announcing he has a visitor. William rises to his feet and makes his way over to the intercom.

"Who's there?"

The voice on the other end is direct and to the point. "William Burrows, this is Detective Frank Languetti. I need to ask you a few questions."

William takes a moment before responding. Downstairs, Languetti looks at Miles, who patiently waits for the response. William tilts his head to one side, cracking his neck before casually responding to Languetti's request. "Come on up, Detective."

William presses the button, which releases the door lock. Without any sign of anxiousness, William walks into the bedroom; Languetti and Miles make their way over to the elevator, pushing the button for the top floor of the building. Reaching into his wardrobe, William retrieves a long black robe from the hanger, the letters W.B. embroidered in gold on the right lapel. He wraps himself tightly with the luscious fabric and proceeds to the living area. With whisky in hand, he patiently waits for Languetti to arrive at his door.

Arriving at the penthouse level of the apartment building, Languetti quickly locates a door numbered 1101. Holding his badge ready, Languetti reaches forward and knocks on the door. Miles stares down the long hall, his hands by his side; a clicking sound from the door lock gathers his attention. The door opens, revealing William, who stands taut, cradling his whisky, his other hand brushing his hair back.

"How can I help you, Detective?"

Languetti presents his badge to William. "We would like a word with you regarding your whereabouts earlier this evening."

William takes another sip of his whisky, refusing to verbally invite the detectives inside; instead, he walks towards the living area. Languetti looks over at Miles before proceeding to follow William, Miles closing the door behind them. William turns and faces the detectives before casually planting himself on the sofa, taking one more sip of his whisky before speaking.

"So, what's this about, Detective?"

Miles takes out his notebook.

"Where were you earlier this evening?"

William looks up at Languetti. "I was out, Detective."

Languetti prompts William to elaborate. "I'm going to need you to be more specific."

William takes another sip of his whisky, prolonging his response, Languetti unmoved by William's demeanour. "I went for a drive."

Languetti tenses; William's attitude digging into his skin. "Did you visit anyone?"

William is calm, avoiding the detectives' questions. "I might have, why?" William tests their patience.

"Do you know an Audrey Mills?" Miles interacts.

William refuses to look at Miles, eying the reflective pattern of the crystal glass.

Languetti, slightly agitated, repeats Miles' question. "Do you know a young woman by the name Audrey Mills?"

William looks up at Languetti. "Yes, I do, Detective."

Languetti nods with impatience. "Did you visit Audrey at her place earlier this evening?"

William takes another sip of his whisky before responding, keeping Languetti on edge. "As a matter of fact, I did."

Miles intercepts. "So, you were in her apartment earlier this evening?"

"Yes, I was," he says, confirming the fact. William holds the glass of whisky to the level of his eye, remembering the glass of water left on the coffee table; his prints would likely be found.

"What time were you at her apartment?" Languetti eyes William.

William shakes his head slightly, as if unsure of the time. "Maybe seven. I don't remember the exact time, Detective. I had a brief chat with her and then took off." William pauses, looking through the glass doors; the naked woman is now dressed in lingerie. She sits on her bed, reading. Languetti follows William's line of sight; he notices the woman. "Why do you ask, Detective?"

Languetti returns his attention to William.

Miles keeps his composure as he responds to William. "Audrey was found in her apartment unconscious. Someone assaulted her," Miles reveals.

William acts concerned as he looks at Miles. "That's terrible." William mocks.

"How well did you know Audrey?" Languetti asks.

"I didn't know her that well at all, Detective," William says, taking another sip of whisky, "we only met last week. Wouldn't even call her a friend to be honest."

Languetti looks at his partner.

"Do you know who assaulted her, Detective?"

Miles takes a small step towards William. "We got a pretty good idea," Miles says as he peers down at William.

"Is that so?" William sounded resentful. "Well, speaking as a Harvard lawyer, I hope you gather enough evidence to arrest and prosecute the guilty party." A spiteful grin is evident on William's face; it triggers Languetti.

"You think you can hide behind the law. I've buried bigger men than you, you fucken cock sucker."

Miles places his hand on Languetti's shoulder. "Take it easy, Frank."

William's displeasure is apparent, resentful of the aggressive accusation. He addresses Miles, locking eyes with Languetti. "You better take control of your partner, Detective."

Miles decides to end the interview. An arrest at this time is a futile exercise. He tugs Languetti by the arm, motioning for him to let it go. "Don't leave town. We may need you to come to the station tomorrow and answer a few more questions," Miles announces.

William rises to his feet; a steely glare blankets his face. "You better have concrete evidence before you go and accuse me of anything, Detective."

Miles stares back at William before he guides a reluctant Languetti towards the front door. William takes a few steps, making one parting remark to Detective Languetti.

"Give my best to Audrey, Frank."

Miles takes a firm hold of Languetti's arm.

Languetti turns and glares at William. "We'll be seeing you again, you prick." A grim grin on Frank's face as he points his finger at William.

Miles opens the door before placing his other hand on Languetti. "Come on, Frank, let's get out of here."

William stands firm, watching the detectives leave his apartment, with Miles casting one last glance at William before shutting the door behind him.

"Look forward to it, Detective," William utters, throwing back the remaining whisky, clenching his jaw as he swallows his vexation.

Out in the hall, a visibly agitated Languetti waits for the lift to arrive. "I'm gonna nail that fucker."

Miles adjusts his jacket and lets out a sigh. "Take it easy, Frank, we'll get him."

"Don't tell me to take it easy. That prick one hundred *per cent* did it, and he sat there mocking us, hiding behind his law degree. He didn't give two shits for what he did to that girl." Languetti loosens his tie as he lets off some steam. "We should go back and haul his ass downtown right now."

Miles looks ahead as the lift chimes. "And then what, Frank? He'll be out in an hour if we arrest the prick now. He'll call one of his lawyer friends, and the asshole will be back home by midnight tonight."

The lift doors open; Miles follows Frank as he steps into the lift. He presses the button for the lobby before turning to Languetti. "Look, Frank, we'll go to Bellevue first thing tomorrow and talk to the girl. If she, I. D's him; we'll pay the prick another visit."

Languetti remains silent, his thoughts now with Audrey.

"We have to play by the rules, Frank, otherwise he'll walk."

The doors open to the lobby, and Miles pats Languetti on the back as they exit. Miles unexpectedly wonders if Audrey is going to make it through the night. Inside, his mood is sombre, and the detectives call it a night.

It's early the following morning, and the air is crisp. Languetti and Miles arrive at the Bellevue hospital, both rugged up in heavy coats and scarves, eager to interview Audrey. They enter the building and head straight towards the main counter. Languetti eyes out a young nurse standing behind the registration desk, clasping several papers in her hand. She looks up, the heavy stride announcing Languetti as he approaches her. He flashes his badge at the young nurse.

"Hello, Miss, I'm Detective Frank Languetti. I'm here to check on the status of a young woman who was admitted last night, around eight."

Miles removes his scarf. The nurse lays the paperwork on the desk and moves to a computer situated to her right.

She taps several keys before she looks up at the detectives. "Do you have her last name?"

"Mills, Audrey," Languetti says as he takes another step towards the nurse.

Miles looks at an enormous man sitting in the waiting area, consuming a bear claw. The man wipes his hand on his shirt. "Jesus," Miles murmurs under his breath.

The young nurse types the name into the computer. "Mills, Audrey, you said?"

Languetti nods at the nurse. "Yeh, that's her."

The nurse turns to face Languetti. "She's on the fourth level, room 412. That's the post-surgery wing. I'll have to page the on-call doctor to meet you there."

Having received no call from the hospital last night, Languetti concluded that Audrey had survived the surgery. Just the same, a small wave of relief fell over him as the nurse delivered the news.

"So, she's alive?" Languetti asks, managing a smile.

The nurse returns the gesture in kind. "Yes, she is. She's in recovery, sir."

"Thank you."

Miles clenches his fist in celebration, knowing too well that too many assault victims end up at the morgue, even after surgery. Languetti eagerly takes off towards the lifts with a welcome calmness in his chest.

Miles looks at the young nurse. "You have a lovely day, miss."

The young nurse can't help but smile as Miles walks off to catch up to his partner.

Ping. The doors slide open as the elevator stops on level four. Languetti smartly spots the sign on the wall opposite the lift. Rooms 400–420 ☞.

"It's this way," Languetti says as he paces down the corridor, looking both ways at the numbered rooms. Up ahead, at the opposite end of the long hall, a man in a white coat walks towards the detectives. As he approaches the men, he addresses Languetti.

"Detective Languetti?"

Languetti stops. "That's right."

The man extends his hand to Frank. "Dr Wakefield. I performed the surgery last night on the young woman brought in."

"And you're still here?" Miles is looking impressed.

Dr Wakefield chuckles. "Well, I got home late but managed a few hours of sleep. I was back here at seven in the morning. No rest for the weary."

Languetti concurs with a nod. "How is the girl doing?"

"She's well, she's stable. Her room is this way."

Dr Wakefield turns and proceeds back down the corridor; Languetti and Miles follow. Miles peers into the open doors of the passing rooms; Dr Wakefield stops at one of the doors to his left. Languetti looks at the door, numbered 412. Dr Wakefield gently pushes the door open and proceeds to go inside. He momentarily holds it open, allowing Languetti and Miles to enter the room. The room is dimly lit, with only one bed by the far wall. Languetti looks across to see Audrey lying silently, appearing to be asleep. Miles looks around the room, feeling uneasy at the surroundings.

In his youth, Miles remembers the many times he had to visit his father in the hospital in his final weeks. His father died from respiratory failure caused by a lung disease; asbestos was the likely culprit. The hospital became his second home for many weeks, and after his father passed, he was never keen on ever returning. The sights and smells still bother him to this day.

Dr Wakefield takes a few steps towards Audrey and stops in the middle of the room. He then informs the men of Audrey's condition, lowering his voice to a whisper. "We operated for three hours last night. She suffered minor haemorrhaging in the left side of her brain, and her left lung is bruised but luckily not punctured. Her jaw is broken, and we had to insert a pin in the mandible. That is the bone in her lower jaw. Several bones in her hands and fingers are also broken. They should heal, and she should regain full use of both hands. Two ribs and her arm are fractured and will also heal in time. She is sedated for the moment and needs plenty of rest before she can fully recover."

Languetti takes a step towards Audrey, finding it difficult to speak. "Has she suffered any...brain...issues?" Languetti fumbles his words. "How's her memory?"

Miles rolls his eyes. Languetti looks to Dr Wakefield for a positive response.

Dr Wakefield smiles. "The blow to the head caused some internal bleeding, but it won't have any long-term effect on her memory. She should remember what happened if that's what you're implying."

Miles, feeling anxious, decides to include himself. "When can we speak to her, Doc?"

Dr Wakefield looks at Miles. "She won't be able to speak for at least a week or two, but she should be able to acknowledge your questions, maybe in a couple of days. However, I'm afraid you won't be able to question her successfully at this point."

Languetti reaches into his coat, retrieves his wallet, and extends his arm, offering his card to Dr. Wakefield. "Doctor, I would appreciate it if you would please call me when she is able to have visitors?"

Dr Wakefield politely nods as he takes Languetti's card. "I understand it's none of my business, but do you know who did this to her, Detective?"

Languetti looks down at Audrey, the metal clamps over her jaw, the plaster on her arm and hands. His eyes glisten, his resentment visible. "We have a pretty good idea."

Dr Wakefield acknowledges the distress on Languetti's face. "I'll call you as soon as she is awake and well enough to answer your questions."

Languetti turns and looks at Dr Wakefield. "Thank you for your time, Doctor."

"Thanks, Doc," Miles says as he turns for the door, eager to leave his surroundings. Languetti follows.

Dr. Wakefield takes one last look at Audrey. "Looks like you got yourself a pair of guardian angels, miss."

As Languetti and Miles enter the lift, Miles presses the button for the ground floor. "So, what do you want to do now?"

Languetti thinks for a moment, stoic in his demeanour. "We're gonna wait."

Chapter 18

That same morning, Charlie had risen early, unable to sleep, his mind consumed with the image of Audrey lying on her apartment floor, battered, covered in her blood. Charlie couldn't shake the thought that he might have prevented Audrey from being assaulted if he had been more alert that night. He kept wondering if he would have witnessed William entering the building that evening, if he had greeted him, William might have been reluctant to hurt Audrey.

Standing in front of his bedroom mirror, Charlie buttons his woollen vest, his face bleak, his eyes sunken from the lack of sleep. As he prepares to visit Audrey in the hospital, he concedes that there is little he could have done; yet, he is still puzzled about how William managed to get into the building without a key. Unlike most apartment buildings, residents at The Parkway cannot buzz the door open for visitors. *I'm almost certain Audrey didn't come down and let William inside; I would have heard something; Audrey would have...* Charlie's thoughts on a loop, tormenting him still. Someone else let him inside last night, he concludes.

Charlie covers himself with his winter coat; he closes his eyes in anguish, again picturing Audrey lying on the floor of her apartment, the image that kept him awake during the long wintry night. Charlie reaches for his house keys and wallet from the nightstand before heading towards the door to exit his home, a comfortable abode in Chelsea. Checking his pockets, Charlie finally opens the door and proceeds into the cold autumn air. He takes a deep breath before proceeding down to the footpath, taking another moment before heading east to the nearest bus stop. Charlie wonders what he would say to Audrey when he sees her; his throat swells at the thought of Audrey not surviving the night. As Charlie reaches the bus stop, he looks upon two young women standing nearby, rugged up in autumn clothes and conversing with laughter. Charlie looks at his watch for a moment before retrieving a bus schedule from his coat pocket, taking another look at the arrival time of the next bus headed towards Bellevue Hospital.

Except for any emergencies that may arise, Sunday was Charlie's day off from his caretaking duties at The Parkway. Since employing Clay, Charlie looked forward to his first Sunday without concerning himself with unexpected emergencies at The Parkway. He remembers boasting to Audrey during the week how he looked forward to spending this Sunday lazing around the house, with nothing to do but eat his favourite meals and relax on his lounge by a warm heater. Even though Sunday is generally a quiet day at The Parkway, part of Clay's employment agreement was that he had to work as a caretaker every Sunday. Clay also worked on Saturday, but only till 4 pm. Charlie often hung around till late on Saturdays, watching old movies on the cable channel and was occasionally joined by Audrey. Clay was given Tuesday and Thursday as his days off in lieu of the weekend, but Charlie told him he could switch between days off during the week if he needed to. Charlie was nice like that.

Charlie looks ahead as the rumbling sound of the bus engine draws closer. He checks the bus's number, ensuring it denotes the correct destination. Charlie retrieves several quarters from his coat pocket as he boards the bus to Bellevue Hospital, handing over the fare before taking his seat just behind the driver. As the bus proceeds down West 23rd Street to the east side of Manhattan, Charlie sits quietly with his thoughts, gazing at the bustling traffic as it passes by and keeping his thoughts to himself. There is no such thing as a quiet Sunday morning in Manhattan. There is always something to do in this city full of locals, tourists, wannabe actors and approximately 12,500 yellow cabs. As the bus nears Madison Square Garden, Charlie tries to distract his mind from Audrey, turning his head to read the venue's billboard. Nicks vs. Celtics. It proved pointless as he recalls a night not too long ago when he invited Audrey to a basketball game at The Garden. Audrey seldom watched basketball with Charlie; she had never been to a live game. That day, Charlie presented Audrey with two tickets, adamant that she would enjoy the game surrounded by the live atmosphere. That night, Charlie had great seats just behind the players. He remembers Audrey remarking to Charlie about the unbelievable size of the players.

'I can't believe how big they are,' she would say aloud, her eyes agape. Charlie remembers laughing when Audrey pointed out that they looked so tiny on the television back in Charlie's office. Charlie had bought Audrey a giant foam hand to wave at the players that night and remembered how she took it to the streets after the game and kept waving at the people passing by in the street. As the bus makes a right turn on 5th Avenue, Charlie continues to eye out people on the street, noticing the differences between the tourists and the locals. There is always something similar about how tourists dress, and you can always identify them by their clothing and accessories—typically, donning New York baseball caps and jerseys, an attempt to fit in with the locals.

Digital cameras hang off their wrists, and some have hotel maps of the island in front of them. There is a look of confused concentration as they try to find specific landmarks, like treasure hunters searching for gold hidden in the city.

As the bus makes a left at Madison Square Park, Charlie prepares to disembark, watching ever so closely as the bus nears 1st Avenue. Charlie steadies his hand, ready to signal; the bus turns into 1st Avenue, drawing closer to his destination. Charlie finally presses the button, signalling the driver to stop at East 28th Street, adjacent to the Bellevue Hospital. As the bus steadies to a stop, Charlie promptly stands and turns to the driver.

"Thank you, driver," he politely says before stepping onto the sidewalk. As the bus continues its journey, Charlie stands in awe of the massive structure; he takes a deep breath before proceeding towards the building's entrance, silently praying for Audrey's well-being. Attentively, Charlie walks through the foyer, inconspicuously wiping his sweaty palms on the sides of his coat. He looks ahead, noticing two nurses standing behind the front desk. The same young nurse, Languetti and Miles, encountered earlier that morning, along with a senior nurse, were conversing as they hovered over a document. The young nurse looks up. She notices Charlie walking towards her and addresses him as he approaches the counter.

"Hi, how may I help you, sir?"

Charlie responds with a whisper in his voice. "I'm here to see Audrey Mills." The young nurse remembers the name from earlier this morning. "I was informed that she was admitted to this hospital yesterday evening," Charlie adds.

"Are you family, Mr.?"

"Brown, Charlie." Charlie nervously clutches his hands. The young nurse smiles, slightly amused by Charlie's name. Charlie quickly realises that the hospital may only let family in to see Audrey, so he pleads his case to the young nurse. "I'm the closest person Audrey has to family in Manhattan, miss. I work as the caretaker in the building where Audrey lives. We have been close friends since she moved here."

The young nurse hesitates to respond, not wanting to break the hospital's strict rules. The senior nurse notices the desperation in Charlie's eyes.

"I know which room she's recovering in. I will take you to see her."

Charlie looks appreciatively at the senior nurse; he takes note of her nametag. "Thank you very much...Nurse Carter."

Nurse Carter places the folder on the desk and smiles at Charlie, signalling him with a head tilt to follow her. They both proceed towards the elevator, and Charlie again praises Nurse Carter as they reach the lift.

"It is very nice of you to allow me to see Audrey."

Nurse Carter turns to Charlie. "Some rules are meant to be broken occasionally, Mr Brown."

"Please, call me Charlie."

The doors open, and Nurse Carter steps inside.

"Only if you call me Nell, Charlie." Nurse Carter requests as she winks at Charlie. Charlie finds it difficult to smile, his thoughts again with Audrey, feeling anxious about seeing her. He enters the lift, reluctantly deciding to inquire about Audrey's health.

"How is Audrey doing?"

Nurse Carter presses the button to level four before responding to Charlie. "She's going to be just fine, Charlie," she informs, placing her hand on Charlie's shoulder. "It will take some time, but she will be her old self soon enough."

Charlie feels a sense of relief as he listens to Nurse Carter, conflicted by feelings of distress and misery, wishing he could go back and prevent all this. The lift doors open, and Charlie is led down the long corridor towards Audrey's room. Nurse Carter approaches the room and opens the door, allowing Charlie to enter. She turns to look at Charlie, who remains in the corridor, taking a moment before entering the room.

"It's okay, Charlie, you can go inside."

Charlie nods slightly before entering the room, immediately fixating his eyes on Audrey.

"Take as much time as you need, Charlie."

Charlie barely responds, the sight of Audrey overpowering his senses to acknowledge Nurse Carter; she gently eases the door closed. Charlie takes a few steps closer to Audrey, his eyes welling up as he notices a steel brace covering the lower part of Audrey's face. His eyes move across her torso, taking note of her arms covered in white bandages and plaster, placed neatly by her side. Charlie takes a few more steps, his eyes focusing on the heart monitor by Audrey's side, a little green heart blinking on the top left corner of the screen. Charlie can only gaze at Audrey, unsure of what he will say to her once she wakes from her deep sleep. A few moments pass before Charlie decides to speak to Audrey.

"I don't know if you can hear me, Audrey," Charlie sighs, his voice trembling, "I don't know what to say to you." Charlie clutches his clothes. "I always imagined it would be you, standing here, watching over me one day." Charlie wipes a tear from his face. "When you get better, I will make you your favourite meal. Roast chicken with pumpkin pie. You can eat as much as you like." Charlie emits a nervous laugh as he wipes his face again, taking a moment to regulate his breathing. He looks intently at Audrey, no longer able to suppress his emotions.

"I am so sorry I wasn't there for you, Audrey." Charlie covers his face with his hand as he breaks down in tears, willingly blaming himself for Audrey's suffering. Audrey is lying in a tranquil state, unaware of Charlie's pain.

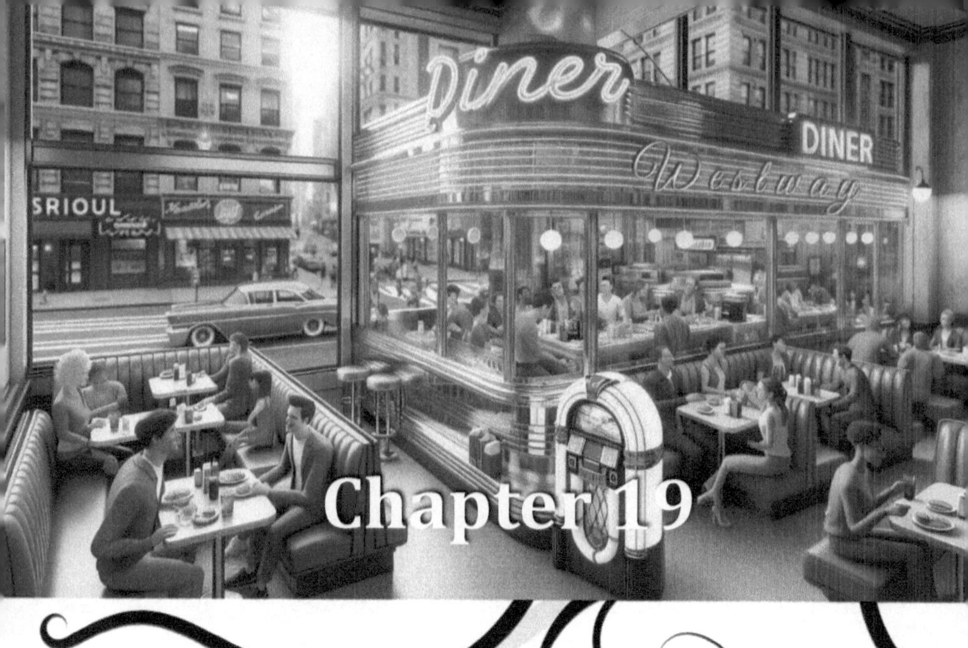

Chapter 19

It's almost midday, and Languetti and Miles are preparing to have lunch at one of their most frequent diners. Established in 1988 in Midtown Manhattan, the Westway Diner is considered a dining institution in New York amongst the locals. Languetti ordered his usual steak and egg open sandwich with fries and a large Diet Coke. Miles ordered a tuna sandwich with tomato and mayo on whole grain bread, a side order of salad, and orange juice. Beryl, the long-time hefty waitress, walks up to their table, placing their food in front of the hungry detectives.

"Here you go, boys. Is that everything?"

Miles looks up at Beryl, who has beads of sweat on both her chins. "Yes, that's all we need for today. Take a load off, Beryl."

Beryl is no stranger to Miles' wittiness. "Sure, I'll go in the back and lie in the hot tub, naked," Beryl says, letting out a stunted laugh, gleaming as she leaves.

Miles cringes at the imagery. Languetti begins his ritual, as he often does, before eating his meal. He turns his plate so that the steak faces his stomach. Then he adjusts his plate of fries to the right and the glass of soft drink to the left. He refers to it as the 10 and 2 positions. He takes the salt in his left hand and shakes it several times over his fries and then over the steak and eggs before placing it back on the table. He then takes two paper napkins from the dispenser, tucking one into his collar and putting the other neatly on his lap. With the fork in his left hand and knife in his right, he leans forward, inhaling the aroma of the steak, smacking his lips in anticipation. Miles watches his partner with reservation as he prepares to eat.

"I can't believe you're still eating like that for lunch, Frank."

Languetti gives Miles a curious look. "Why, what's wrong with my food?"

Miles shakes his head. "Heard of the ongoing cholesterol problem in America, Frank?"

Languetti slices off a piece of steak and places it in his mouth. "Nope, I can't say that I have," Languetti says as he forks the fries. "We have a cholesterol thing here. Are you sure?"

Miles rolls his eyes. "It's called an epidemic, Frank. And yes, we do. Every second guy we meet is like twenty pounds overweight."

Languetti widens his eyes as a single thought arises. "I forgot the ketchup!" Languetti announces as he looks around the table in a panic; there's no ketchup. He turns to the booth behind him, interrupting two young women eating lunch. "Excuse me, ladies, sorry to disturb your pleasant lunch, but can I please use the ketchup on your table?" Languetti's eagerness to have the ketchup bottle sparks laughter in the two girls.

"Sure." The girl sitting directly behind Languetti takes the bottle in her hand and passes it over. "Here you go, enjoy your lunch," she says, giggling. Languetti smiles as he snatches the bottle.

"Thank you, Miss." Languetti squirts several dollops of ketchup onto his steak and fries. He looks up at Miles, who is watching in amazement as Languetti drowns his food with the red condiment.

Languetti offers the ketchup bottle to Miles, just as he prepares to bite into his sandwich. "You want some ketchup?"

Miles pulls the sandwich from his mouth and looks directly at his partner. "I'm having tuna, Frank."

Languetti places the bottle of ketchup on the table and continues eating. Miles takes a bite of his sandwich; he peers at Frank, deciding to inquire about Languetti's sudden change in mood.

"Why so happy, Frank?"

Languetti takes a big gulp of his beverage before responding to Miles. "She's alive."

Miles raises his glass to his mouth. "Who, the girl?"

Languetti nods as he stabs the plate of fries with his fork. "Yep."

Miles takes a sip of his juice. "I know; I was there, remember?"

Miles watches Languetti fill his mouth with fries dipped in egg yolk before raising his glass and taking another mouthful of soda.

"She's alive, and that son of a bitch lawyer thinks he got away with it."

Miles continues to take bites from his tuna sandwich, washing it down with his beverage; he listens intently to Languetti. Languetti continues to devour his meal, sharing his thoughts with a mouth full of steak.

"He expects us to pay him a visit today, but we won't." Languetti exclaims with his finger in the air; he takes another sip of his drink. "For the next few days, he'll think that we don't have a case against him because we didn't show up to arrest him."

Miles nods in agreement, picking up on his partners' train of thought. Languetti cuts another piece of steak and holds it on the end of his fork.

"But the girl is alive. And in a few days, she's going to ID him. And then, we pay the prick a visit," Languetti says with conviction as he places the steak into his mouth, nodding firmly at Miles, anticipating a response from his partner. Miles takes a sip of his juice, drawing out his rebuttal.

"You know what we should do, Frank?"

Languetti looks eagerly at Miles. Miles leans back, wiping his mouth with a serviette.

"We should arrest him at his work." Languetti looks impressed, his face alit, clearly enjoying how his partner thinks. Miles continues. "We can barge in there, kick in the door to his office, flash our badges, and cuff his arrogant *ass* in front of all his co-workers."

Languetti wipes his hands in thought. "I hope he's with some important client at the time or, maybe, in a meeting with a bunch of his lawyer friends."

Miles delivers a smile, delighted at the thought. They both sit quietly for a moment, peacefully enjoying the scenario. Languetti's high spirit is brief as he looks across at an adjacent booth. A young girl with dark hair like Audrey's, sits alone, drinking coffee, reading her book. Languetti reflects on Audrey and how she suffered, the image of her lying on the floor covered in her blood still visible in his mind. Miles notices the young girl also, his partners' expression noticeable.

"We'll get him, Frank, I promise you. We'll get this guy. One way or another he'll pay for what he did."

Languetti looks at Miles, acknowledging his statement. Frank continues with his meal. Miles takes another bite of his sandwich as he reflects on the case, patient but eager for the day to come when they can again confront William.

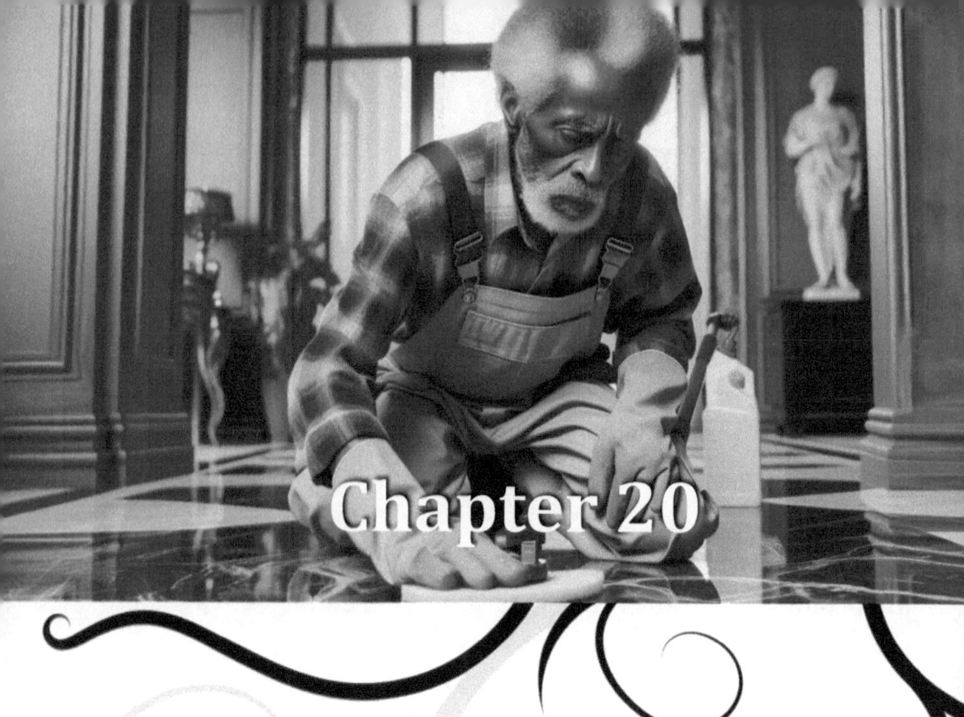

Chapter 20

The following morning, Charlie arrives at The Parkway a little earlier than usual, hoping to occupy his mind with his daily chores and help take his mind off Audrey for a while. After leaving Bellevue Hospital yesterday, Charlie stopped by Gloria's florist as he intended, informing Rose of the events that took place on Saturday evening. Rose was distraught. She regretfully remembered what her mother had told her the previous Wednesday evening during dinner. Rose confessed this to Charlie and was immediately consumed with guilt, admitting to Charlie that she believed her mother was mistaken. She dismissed her caution, thinking her mother was being overprotective of Audrey. Charlie was visibly upset at Rose's admission, but comforted Rose, knowing she was not to blame for what had happened. Charlie stayed with Rose for a while, informing her of Audrey's condition and how he planned to revisit her later in the week when she was better rested.

In the lobby of The Parkway, Charlie is kneeling on the floor, a container of floor wax by his side and polishing cloths, one in each hand. Haggard, from the lack of sleep he has had the two previous nights, Charlie begins to wax the lobby floor by hand, covering each tile with gentle circles of wax, wiping it clean, leaving a dull gleam on the surface. Charlie usually waxes the lobby floor once a week, using a cumbersome rotor he keeps in the storeroom. But today, he opted to do it by hand, avoiding the reverberating noise the machine makes as it circulates, fearing it may only lead to a headache. Charlie remembers admitting to Audrey that he hates getting headaches. So now, peacefully, he kneels on the floor with nothing but empty thoughts, making continuous circles with each hand, ensuring the wax is completely removed from each tile before he moves on to the next.

As Charlie reaches to apply more polish to the cloth, his harmony is distracted by a rattling knock on the entrance doors. He looks up and sees Clay through the patterned glass, standing there, motioning to him to open the door. Charlie groans as he rises to his feet, feeling the aches of his withered body. Walking towards the entrance, he wonders why Clay doesn't use the key he was given to let himself inside. Charlie pushes down on the lever, pulling the large door open. Clay is quick to explain.

"I'm sorry, Boss. I accidentally left the keys to the building here last night," he said sincerely, ashamed for forgetting to take the keys with him. Charlie smiled, stepping aside to make way for Clay to enter the lobby.

"That's alright, Clay; I, too, forget sometimes. That is why I keep a spare set at my home."

Clay feels some relief. "I won't forget again, boss, promise."

Charlie continues to smile as he looks up at Clay. "Yes, you will, Clay, but that's all right. We all forget sometimes."

Charlie walks back to continue with his work; Clay hesitates for a moment before going over to Charlie, who has now taken his position on the floor. Clay watches Charlie as he applies the wax to the tile. He takes a deep breath through his nostrils, preparing to reveal his thoughts to Charlie.

When Charlie was visiting Audrey in the hospital yesterday, two forensic detectives came to Parkway, flashing their badges to Clay and inviting themselves to Audrey's apartment. Clay became curious but was asked to return downstairs and remain in the lobby as the detectives entered Audrey's vacant apartment. Clay called Charlie's home, but there was no answer at the time; Charlie had already departed from his home in Chelsea. That evening, Clay went home around six and, in haste, forgot to take his keys, his mind riddled with questions he had no answers for.

Clay stands over Charlie; he wipes his palms on the side of his trousers, removing a hint of sweat that has formed from his anxiousness. Clay finally addresses Charlie.

"Boss."

Charlie turns to look up at Clay, who stands there with a bleak expression on his face. Charlie briefly examines Clay, noticing his demeanour and concluding that he must have heard something about Audrey yesterday while on duty at The Parkway.

"What is it, Clay?"

Clay stands there motionless, visibly cautious. "Police were here yesterday."

Charlie looks down for a moment; he tosses the cloth in his hand onto the floor. "Take a seat next to me, Clay."

Clay positions himself on the floor beside Charlie. Charlie takes a moment to think, unsure of what the police may have told Clay yesterday.

"Did the police tell you why they were here, Clay?"

Clay starts to feel a bit nauseous, remembering that the apartment was empty, a yellow police sticker stuck to the door reading, Crime Scene, Do Not Cross. "They went up to Miss Audrey's apartment. They asked me to unlock the door and told me to go back downstairs." Clay bows his head, feeling oddly shameful. "I was afraid to ask them any questions."

During his time in prison, the guards constantly reminded Clay not to make eye contact with them, as it was a sign of disrespect and often a way prisoners displayed intimidation. A man of Clay's size was not someone the guards wanted to be intimidated by, and it was the guard's way of keeping their dominance over the prisoners. They constantly reminded him of this in prison, 'look ahead when spoken to,' they barked; 'don't you dare eyeball me,' they would add. It was a common trend in prison, and Clay never looked into the eyes of any guard during his time there. When the detectives flashed their badges at him yesterday, Clay immediately looked ahead, avoiding eye contact with them, a quirk from his time in prison. When they asked Clay to let them in Audrey's apartment, he did not question the detectives and promptly led them upstairs. He remembers the detectives murmuring amongst themselves, chuckling at Clay's oddity, before following him up the stairs to Audrey's apartment. Charlie is a learned individual and understands where Clay's uneasiness comes from.

"That's alright, Clay. You didn't do anything wrong."

Clay waits patiently, Charlie takes a moment, preparing himself to deliver the sad news.

"Clay, I have some upsetting news."

Clay remains still, struggling to keep his thoughts free of conclusions; he listens intently to Charlie, Charlie cautious about being delicate in his delivery, remembering how quickly Audrey and Clay bonded this past week.

"A couple of nights ago, after you had left for the day, I remained here for a while. I was in my office fiddling with the television." A hint of a nervous smile on Charlie's face. "The damned reception was on the fritz again." Charlie wipes his smile as he continues. "I was waiting for Audrey to come down to see me. She was going to introduce me to her date. This man she met at a party the week before."

Clay remembers Audrey sharing her dinner plans while they walked home from the supermarket the other morning.

"She never came down to see me, so I became a little concerned and decided to go up and see her. I mean to see if she was still home." Charlie pauses for a moment; he looks directly into Clay's eyes, taking a breath and sighing as he exhales. "The door was open, so I went inside and found Audrey lying on the floor by the piano."

Clay held his breath. Preparing himself for the worst.

"She was… Someone had hurt her badly."

Clay feels tense, horrified at what Charlie may say next.

"Her dress was covered in her blood," Charlie reveals. "She wasn't moving, she just lay there." Charlie is visibly distressed as he relives the moment. "She was breathing, thankfully. So, I called the ambulance, and they came and took her away. The police, too, were here."

Clay swallows, his throat swollen. "But she is still alive?"

Charlie nods, his voice is coarse. "Yes, Clay, she's alive, thank God."

Clay places his hand on Charlie's shoulder. He ponders for a moment. "Who did this to her?"

Charlie looks up at Clay. "Police aren't sure yet, Clay."

Clay makes his conclusions. "That man Audrey met?"

Charlie takes a moment to regain his composure. "They suspect it might be him. Yes."

"Did you see him?" Clay inquires.

Charlie shakes his head. "I never saw anybody come inside or leave Clay. I remember hearing the door; maybe someone had left the building, but I can't be sure. I was in the office the whole time."

Clay sits in silence for a brief moment.

"You went to see Audrey yesterday? I tried calling you but had no answer."

"Yes, Clay, I went to the hospital yesterday. She is doing well for now."

Clay feels relieved. "So, she's going to be all right then?"

"I think so, Clay. I mean, I hope so. She needs her rest right now."

Clay and Charlie both sit, reflecting on their thoughts. Clay feels unsettled, bewildered as to why anyone would do something like this to Audrey. Remembering the types of inmates he encountered while in prison, he recalls that some would be triggered even if you looked directly at them. They would turn violent to assert their dominance and show no remorse for causing pain to human life. Clay couldn't understand why they were like this; memories of his father's hatred surface, still tormenting him. Charlie interrupts Clay's thoughts.

"Clay, did the police say they were coming back here? Did they tell you if they needed to see the apartment again?"

Clay shakes his head. "No, I don't think they are coming back. They took the crime scene sticker from the door. I went up to ensure the door was locked, and the sticker was not there. They said they were done before they left. They didn't say they were gonna come back, boss."

Charlie looks towards the stairs and thinks for a moment. "I'd better call them, just to be sure," Charlie considers. "Clay, I'd like you to do something for me."

Clay sits up at attention. "What is it, boss?"

"I'd like you to clean Audrey's apartment for me."

Clay's thoughts go straight to Audrey's blood on the apartment floor, something he has yet to witness.

"You think you can do that, Clay? For me and Audrey?"

Clay affirms Charlie's request. "Yes, sir, I can clean it. I will clean it really well."

Charlie smiles at Clay. "Thank you, Clay," Charlie says, rising to his feet. "I'd better call the police detective first to ensure they are through with their work before you clean away any evidence they may need."

"Sure thing, boss."

Charlie walks towards the office; he turns his head to the side, catching Clay with the corner of his eye. "I'll bring your keys when I return, so you don't forget them here again before you leave to go home today."

Clay's voice is barely audible as he acknowledges Charlie. "Thanks, boss." Clay stands in the lobby, facing the stairs, dreading the moment he must enter Audrey's apartment for the first time since the crime. His thoughts turn to Audrey and then to a faceless man who did this to her, unaware that he has clenched his large hand into a fist, his heavy heart sinking.

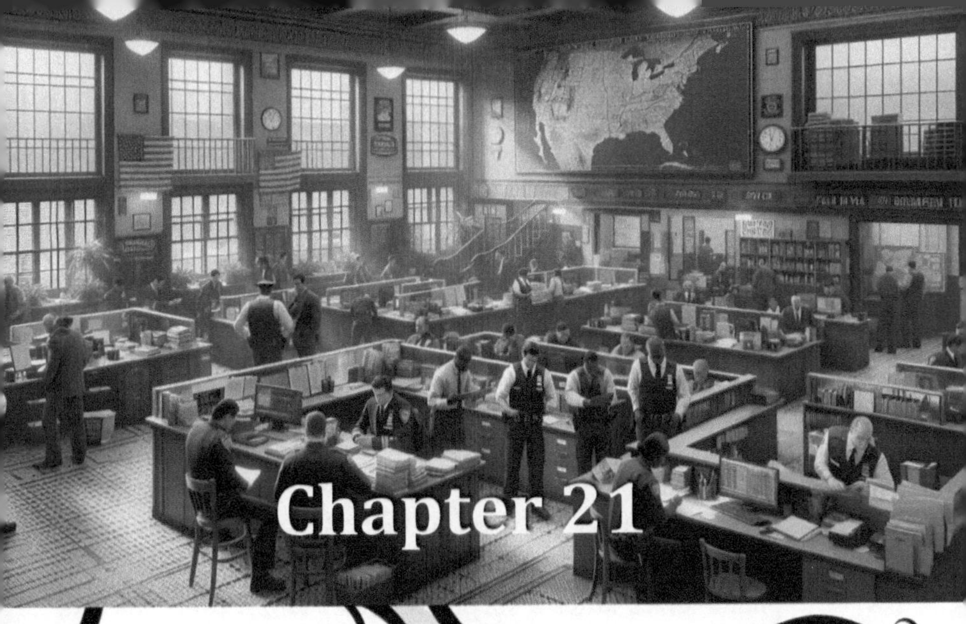

Chapter 21

It's Thursday, 10:17 in the morning. Languetti and Miles are down at the Precinct, filling out paperwork for a DUI they encountered the night before. The drunk driver had swerved into Languetti's lane, clipping the front fender of his undercover squad car. When Languetti pulled the vehicle over, the disoriented man exited his Ford Taurus. He verbally abused Languetti, unaware that the car he hit belonged to two police detectives. An agitated Languetti opted to arrest the man himself instead of calling in a black and white to do the honours.

Languetti sits at his desk, pen in hand, fumbling through several pages of a questionnaire he must now complete for the arrest he made the previous night. "I can't believe I have to fill out all this crap for one DUI."

Miles is by the fax machine, trying to remember whether to place the paper facing upwards or downwards into the machine. "I don't know why I must help you do this, Frank. You're the one who arrested this drunken asshole. I was just an innocent bystander."

Languetti, looking annoyed at Miles, reaches into his trouser pocket and removes his ringing cell. "Languetti." A voice at the other end responds. Languetti's attentiveness heightens. Miles becomes curious, his attention now on his partner. Languetti rises from his chair. "Thank you, we'll be right over." Languetti whips the phone from his ear and turns to face Miles. "She's awake; let's go." Languetti wastes no time, throwing on his coat as he heads out of the building.

Miles is prompt, stopping at Stephanie's desk on his way out. "Hey Stephanie, you sweet thing, fax these documents for me, will ya?"

Stephanie gives Miles a surprised look. "What! Do I look like your secretary?"

Miles is quick-witted in his response. "No, you're too ugly, but fax them anyway."

Miles darts off as Stephanie rises from her chair, a peeved look on her face as she clutches the documents. "Mother Fu...," she mutters under her breath.

Now at Bellevue Hospital, Languetti's exterior is calm as he rides the elevator, eyeing the floor numbers as they illuminate on the digital screen. Miles loosens his tie as he again feels uncomfortable with the hospital's surroundings. The elevator doors open, and Languetti exits. His walk has a purpose as he heads for Audrey's room, a reluctant Miles following, trying to keep up with Languetti's long strides. Room 412, Languetti places his palm on the door, easing it open. As he enters the room, he notices a familiar face; Charlie is sitting by Audrey's side. Charlie rises from his chair to greet Languetti, Miles hangs back, careful not to overcrowd himself with bodies.

"Detectives," Charlie says.

Miles stands firm, placing his hands into his trouser pockets as he acknowledges Charlie from a distance. Charlie greets the detectives with a smile. Languetti nods at Charlie before turning his attention to Audrey. Audrey is awake; she shifts her eyes to Languetti, a face she doesn't recognise.

"Hello, Audrey. I'm Detective Frank Languetti."

Audrey is unable to speak because of the brace fixed to her jaw. She lifts her bandaged fingers from the blanket and waves a little at the detective.

Charlie addresses Languetti. "Dr Wakefield told me you would be coming. Audrey can't talk yet, but she can understand and acknowledge you." Languetti directs his attention to Charlie. "You can ask her yes or no questions, Detective, and she will blink once for yes and twice for no. I've been speaking with her since I arrived this morning." Charlie smiles. "She is getting quite good at it." Charlie takes a step back, making room for the detective. Languetti moves a little closer to Audrey.

"Hello, Audrey. I would like to ask you some questions. Is that alright?"

Charlie smiles as Audrey blinks once at Languetti. "That's a yes," Charlie says.

Languetti gives Charlie a brief smirk before turning to face Audrey again. Languetti's voice is sincere as he continues to question Audrey.

"I understand this is difficult for you, but I need you to clarify some details from the night you were assaulted."

Audrey's eyes remain open for several moments, shifting her eyes over to Charlie and then back again, acknowledging the detective with a single blink. Languetti takes a brief look at the heart monitor by Audrey's side before continuing.

"On the night you were assaulted, you had plans to go out for dinner. Someone was coming to pick you up from your residence. Is that correct?"

Audrey stares momentarily at Languetti before again responding with a single blink.

"Charlie informed us this was a man you met at a party the previous week. A party you attended with your friend, Veronica?"

Audrey responds with a single blink. Languetti nods with affirmation.

"Was this man you met at the party and arranged to have dinner with, William Burrows?"

Audrey looks across the room at Miles; she hesitates for a moment, returning her attention to Languetti, her eyes well up as she blinks again. A single tear runs down Audrey's cheek, and Languetti notices a slight increase on the heart monitor. Languetti looks over at Miles, aware of the distress he is inflicting, mentally preparing to deliver his final question and end Audrey's agony.

"Audrey, I need to ask you one final question."

Audrey looks away, focusing again on Miles, unmoved by the circumstances. Languetti politely requests Audrey's attention.

"Audrey?"

Audrey looks back at Languetti, the change in mood is evident in her eyes, the heart monitor reflecting her distress.

"Is William the person who did this to you?"

Audrey is unresponsive; she stares back into Frank's eyes. The detective rephrases the question.

"Audrey, was William Burrows the man responsible for assaulting you that night?"

Audrey's eyes linger open for several moments; she looks over at Charlie, closing her eyes firmly, pushing more tears down her face. Charlie becomes uncomfortable at Audrey's distress; he decides to intervene.

"Detective, maybe we should let Audrey rest now."

Unsatisfied with Audrey's response, Languetti directs his attention to Charlie, placing his hand on his shoulder. "Can I have a word with you outside?"

Charlie nods, acknowledging Languetti before turning to Audrey. "It's all right, Audrey. Just rest now." His voice is soft. Charlie follows Languetti outside into the corridor. Miles joins them, closing the door behind him as he leaves the room. Languetti ponders for a moment before he approaches Charlie.

"Charlie, can I call you Charlie?"

"Yes, you may, Detective."

"You said earlier that you spoke with Audrey before we arrived. What did you talk about?"

Charlie looks over at Miles, who is watching from several feet away, leaning casually against the wall. "Well, nothing significant, Detective; I was just telling Audrey about my week, trying to cheer her up."

Languetti pushes for more information. "Specifically, what did you tell Audrey?"

Charlie thinks for a moment before responding. "I told her I spoke with Veronica and that she would revisit her later this week. I mentioned that I had been by her work and that they knew her situation." Charlie shrugs his shoulders. "Just information I thought may put Audrey at ease. Nothing else, really."

"Did you and Audrey talk about William or the night she was assaulted?"

Charlie props himself upright, feeling somewhat offended at the question posed by the detective. "No, Detective, I thought it best not to bring that up."

Languetti looks sympathetic as he again places his hand on Charlie's shoulder. "Charlie, I know this is difficult for Audrey, but the man who did this to her has to pay. If Audrey doesn't identify him, we can't arrest and charge him for attempted murder."

Charlie briefly looks at Miles, his emotions torn. "I understand how this works, Detective, but Audrey doesn't want to talk about it right now, and I won't allow you to push her. She's been through hell, Detective, and she's afraid." Languetti shifts his torso. Charlie continues. "In time, I'm sure you will get your desired response," Charlie adds.

Languetti looks at Miles, who seems bewildered as he shrugs his shoulders at his partner. Languetti reaches into his coat to retrieve his wallet. He hands his card to Charlie. "We'll give her some time. But I'd like you to call me when she is ready to talk to us."

Charlie takes the card in his hand. "Audrey is like a daughter to me, Detective, and I, too, want this man to pay for what he did to her. But it's Audrey's decision; she must make it alone."

Languetti acknowledges Charlie with a nod. "Take care, Charlie."

Languetti takes off towards the elevator, Miles peeling himself off the wall as both men return down the corridor. As they approach the lift, Languetti frustratedly stabs the button with his index finger. Miles lets out an anxious sigh.

'The D.A. won't touch this unless the girl talks, Frank. William has connections."

Languetti places his hands into his pockets; he takes a long, slow breath to calm his nerves. "She'll talk. We'll give her some space for now."

Miles looked surprised by his partner's uncharacteristic response. "You're not upset, Frank?"

Languetti shrugs his shoulders at Miles. "No, I'm fine. Why?"

Miles raises his eyebrows. "It's just that you behaved calmly back there; given that good ole Charlie pretty much told you to take a hike."

Languetti steps inside the elevator; he casually reaches across to press the button for the lobby. "You overthink, Miles. You're always over-analysing stuff like this. It would help if you learned to go with the flow. Do not swim against the current."

Miles squints. "What the fuck book have you been reading?"

Languetti adjusts his coat. "I'm just trying to be more accepting of our current situation."

Miles shakes his. "I think Bellevue has a psychiatric ward, Frank. We should stop by, and have you checked out before we leave." A smirk appears on Frank as the doors open to the lobby. "I'm serious; I think you're having a mental breakdown, Frank."

Languetti steps from the elevator. "I'm hungry. Let's get some doughnuts and coffee."

Miles spots the hospital's directory located adjacent to the lifts. It denotes each floor level with a brief description. "Here you go, Frank, Psychiatric ward. It's on level nine, the very top floor."

Languetti continues his walk to the exit, choosing to ignore Miles. Miles catches up to him, placing his hand on his partner's shoulder.

"You know why it's on the top floor, Frank? If the therapy doesn't work, you don't have far to go if you decide to jump off the roof."

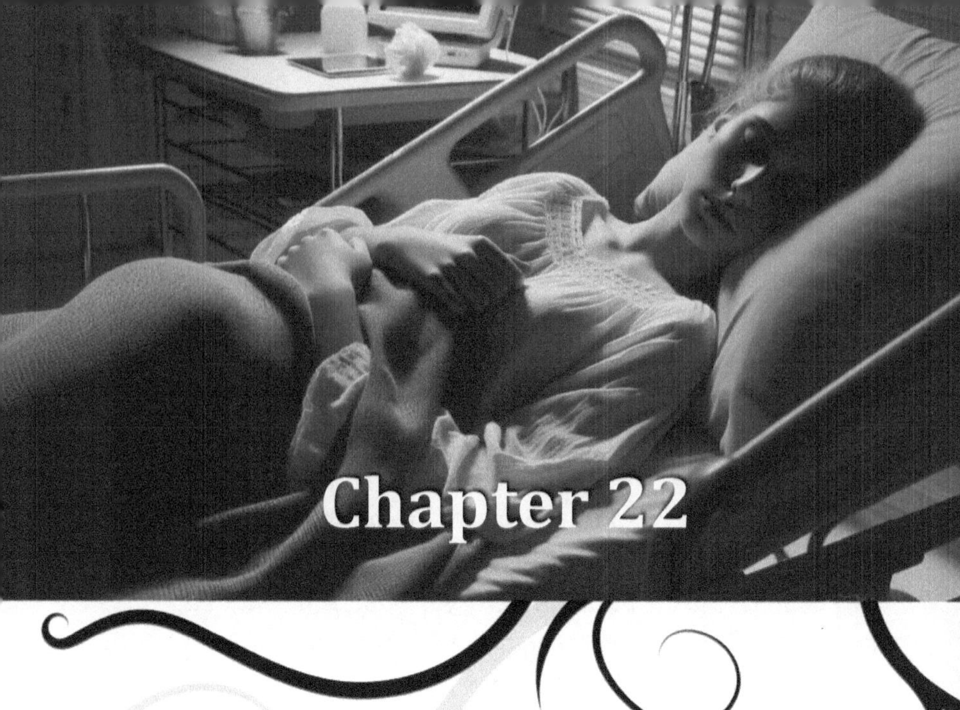

Chapter 22

After spending most of the day with Audrey, Charlie decided to head home for dinner that evening. He was exhausted and eager to climb into his comfortable bed for a well-earned good night's sleep. Audrey had fallen asleep, and Charlie was careful not to disturb her much-needed rest as he exited the room. The sun is just about to set in New York, and Audrey sleeps peacefully, alone in her room.

Audrey's eyes snap open, inhaling a deep breath, something waking her from her slumber.

Am I awake? She questions herself, struggling to focus her tired eyes. Audrey scans the room, unable to form a clear image of the objects that surround her. Nonsensical thoughts race through her mind, frustrated as she is unable to speak, wanting desperately to voice her thoughts. Audrey's blood runs cold as she feels a presence in the room, shifting her eyes frantically. Her vision remains blurred as she becomes aware of what seems to be a human figure standing in the shadows by the window. Her heart rate elevates as the figure begins to move towards her. Completely frozen from fear, Audrey blinks repeatedly, desperate for her vision to return as the human figure draws closer. To her horror, the figure now stands beside her, a deep whisper as the figure leans forward from the shadows.

"Hello, Audrey."

Audrey is horrified, her eyes entirely focused; she struggles to breathe, identifying the man beside her. It's William. Audrey feels her heart thumping against her chest, unable to move; she remains fixated on William. William's eyes begin to snake across Audrey's body, focusing on her heaving breasts and then her bandaged hands. William is calm as he remarks on Audrey's condition with a condescending tone.

"You really should be more careful, Audrey."

Audrey notices an unfamiliar tone in William's voice, which was non-existent when they first met. The man she met no longer exists, or did he ever? she wonders. William observes Audrey as she glances over at her side, her hand prodding the covers, desperately looking for the remote button that summons the nurse on duty. William takes note of what Audrey is doing, smirking at her efforts.

"Looking for something?"

Audrey's eyes shift back to William. Her heart raced, feeling his breath on her face as he leaned closer.

"I thought we should be alone," he whispers in her ear.

Feeling completely helpless, Audrey closes her welled-up eyes, praying for this nightmare to end. William tracks a single tear as it rolls down Audrey's cheek, collecting the sap with his index finger. Audrey opens her eyes, sensing William's touch on her face; she watches him intently as he slides his tongue across his finger. William's face turns rigid; he places his hand on Audrey's forehead, swiping his thumb across her brow. His voice is deep as he locks eyes with Audrey.

"If you talk...I will kill you."

A stone-faced William continues to glare deep into Audrey's eyes, affirming his warning. Another tear runs down Audrey's cheek as she closes her eyes momentarily. Her breathing heaves as William leans forward; he presses his lips onto her forehead.

"Such a sweet girl," he whispers, disappearing into the shadows like Nosferatu. Silence fills the room; Audrey cautiously lifts her head and examines the void, a sense of reprieve as she certifies the room is empty. Tears emerge again as she rests her head on her pillow, closing her eyes in anguish.

Outside Audrey's room, down the other end of the corridor, Nurse Carter is making her evening rounds. With a clipboard in hand, she enters the rooms, checking the status of each patient. As she makes her way down the corridor, she notices a tall man up ahead, standing in front of the elevator. Looking briefly at her watch, she notes the time before looking up and calling out to the man.

"Excuse me, sir?"

The man is unmoved and steps into the elevator. Nurse Carter takes several quick steps towards the elevator, calling out to the man once more.

"Sir?"

The doors close as Nurse Carter approaches, and she only catches a glimpse of the man's face. She looks down at the empty corridor; she feels uneasy. Her thoughts go to Audrey as she now heads directly to Room 412. As she enters the room, she immediately notices the distress on Audrey's face.

"Audrey? Are you all right, my dear?"

Audrey puts on a brave face, nodding her head ever so slightly.

"Try not to move your head, dear." Nurse Carter removes a clean handkerchief from her uniform, wiping Audrey's tears. "Why are you crying? Are you in pain?" The nurse places her hand on Audrey's forehead. "You are so brave." Nurse Carter is tender in her admiration. "I'll tell you what. I have to finish my rounds for now. Afterwards, though, I'll come by, and we can spend some time together, okay?"

Audrey blinks once at Nurse Carter, wishing she could throw her arms around her. Nurse Carter gives Audrey a warm smile as she leaves, her toe brushing against an object at her feet. She leans down and retrieves the remote.

"What is this doing on the floor?" She places the remote by Audrey's side. "Here you go, dear. Just buzz if you need anything, I'll be by a little later."

As Nurse Carter exits the room, Audrey slides her hand over the remote, clutching it tightly as she waits. Her thoughts remain on William taunting her only moments earlier. They continue to lacerate.

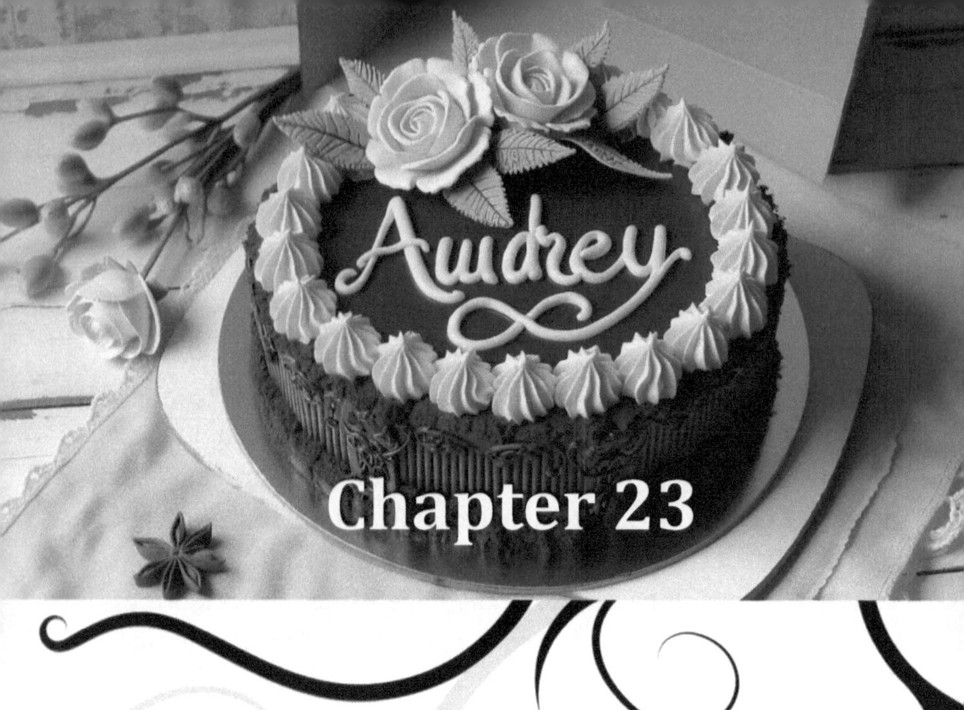

Chapter 23

Five weeks have passed since the night Audrey was assaulted, and Dr Wakefield has now removed the metal brace from Audrey's jaw. Over the past week, Audrey has begun to speak again, but with both hands still in plaster, she is finding it challenging to hold utensils. Audrey has been in great spirits with all the attention she has received, and Dr Wakefield authorised her to be released from the hospital. Charlie and Veronica arrived at the hospital early this morning to greet Audrey and assist with her departure. Charlie and Veronica visited Audrey often over the past month, as did Gloria and Rose, bringing her several bouquets to garnish her hospital room.

It's a typical cold Sunday morning in October, and with Clay's help, Charlie has prepared Audrey's apartment for her arrival. Charlie purchased some paper and a box of crayons during the week, which Clay used to make a banner. The banner reads: Welcome Home Audrey and hangs on the wall above the fireplace in Audrey's apartment. Charlie picked up a Chocolate mud cake from the local bakery, which he preordered especially for Audrey, and has Audrey's name scripted in pink icing.

As Audrey collected her things, Dr Wakefield dropped by her room, wishing Audrey all the best and reminding her to return in two weeks so the nurse could remove the plaster bandages from her hands and arm.

"Take care, dear." Nurse Carter wraps her arms around Audrey, giving her a comfortable hug before helping her inside the cab. Charlie and Veronica join Audrey on the trip home. As the cab makes its way across town, Audrey sits quietly, gazing out the window and admiring the abounding views of the city, a sight that has been languishing these past weeks. Faint honking is heard in the distance as the cab pulls up to the curb, Charlie propping forward to view Audrey, who leans against the glass, seemingly unaware they have reached their destination.

"We're home, Audrey," Charlie announces.

Audrey lifts her head from the glass, turning to look at Charlie. She presents Charlie with a little smile as Veronica reaches over and gently rubs Audrey's shoulder before stepping from the cab.

"That comes to $22.50," says the cab driver.

Charlie hands the fare to the driver. "Don't forget; we have luggage in the trunk." Charlie reminds him before he exits the cab.

The cab driver removes a small suitcase from the rear and places it at Charlie's feet. Veronica walks over to the passenger side to assist Audrey onto the sidewalk. Audrey looks up at The Parkway, feeling somewhat uncomfortable as she prepares for the long walk up to her apartment, fully aware that she will be revisiting the place where she was assaulted only six weeks ago.

"Are you okay, sweetie?" Veronica cuddles Audrey's shoulder.

Audrey thoughtfully looks ahead, hesitating to take another step towards the entrance, nodding ever-so-slightly. Charlie picks up the suitcase and walks over to Audrey, who is in a trance.

"Audrey? There is someone inside keen to see you." Charlie engages Audrey's attention. "You don't want to keep him waiting?"

Audrey smiles as she looks ahead, joyously receptive to Charlie's reference to Clay.

During her stay in the hospital, Clay would take the bus to visit Audrey at least twice a week. On his first visit, Clay brought his copy of John Steinbeck's *Of Mice and Men* to read to Audrey. Every time Clay visited Audrey, she would listen to Clay read, often falling asleep from the deep, soothing tone of Clay's baritone voice. Clay confessed to Audrey that this book was his favourite because he related to the character, Lenny. Clay's mother purchased a copy of the book for his twelfth birthday, and Clay would often read a little each night before he went to sleep. When Clay was released from prison, he went to live with his aunt in New York, as Clay's mother had planned. On his first night there, Clay's aunt gave him a box with some of his parents' belongings left behind after Claire passed away. When Clay sifted through the box, he found the copy of the book that his mother had given him. Clay keeps the book on his nightstand and still reads a little each night before he falls asleep.

Audrey takes a deep breath, exhaling the crisp air as she first steps towards The Parkway. "It still looks the same?" Audrey remarks.

Charlie's eyes scan the front of the building for a moment before responding to Audrey. "You've only been gone for six weeks, Audrey, not six years."

Audrey pulls a squinted face at Charlie. "Just open the door, Charlie; I'm freezing my butt off out here."

Charlie tilts his head to Audrey. "Yes, Your Majesty, at your service."

Charlie pushes the door open; Veronica helps Audrey inside the welcoming warmth of the lobby. Audrey takes a moment to look around, focusing on the counter, hoping to see Clay.

"Where's Clay, Charlie?"

Charlie shrugs his shoulders. "I don't know, Audrey; I just got here myself. He's probably around here somewhere."

"He'll turn up, Audrey." Veronica is becoming impatient. "Let's get your slow ass upstairs so I can have some wine."

Audrey screws her face at Veronica. "It's like ten in the morning, V."

Charlie makes his way towards the elevator, assuming Audrey would prefer not to climb the three flights of stairs.

"Where are you going, Charlie?"

Charlie stops and turns to Audrey. "Don't you want to take the elevator?"

"Charlie, I've been lying on my butt for six weeks, and it has gotten so big that I can feel the seams in my knickers wanting to burst open."

Charlie sighs, realising he now must lug Audrey's luggage up the stairs. "What is your obsession with your butt Audrey? That's all you've talked about since we arrived."

Audrey raises her arm, pointing to the stairs, gleefully grinning at Charlie. "After you, Charlie Brown."

Veronica laughs as Charlie moans at Audrey. "Good to see you're back to your old self, Audrey."

Charlie starts muttering as he proceeds up the stairs. Audrey follows Charlie, clutching Veronica's arm as she makes her way up the plentiful steps.

"Move it, Charlie." Audrey giggles as she commands.

"You two are like an old married couple," Veronica says, shaking her head as she helps Audrey.

Audrey stops to catch her breath as they all finally reach the top of the stairs. "Boy, am I out of shape."

Charlie turns to look at Audrey, resting the suitcase on the floor. "I told you to take the elevator, Audrey."

An impatient Veronica walks over and picks up the suitcase.

"Here, Charlie, I'll take this the rest of the way for ya."

Charlie glares at Veronica. "Where was this grand gesture at the bottom of the flipping stairs, Veronica?"

"What? I was busy helping Audrey drag her fat *ass* up the stairs," Veronica smirks.

Audrey walks over to Charlie, extending her arm out to him. "Come on, Charlie. You can help me the rest of the way."

Veronica leads Charlie and Audrey down the corridor towards Audrey's apartment. As Veronica reaches the door, she stops and drops the suitcase on the floor. "Shit, that's heavy," she laughs to Charlie, who is clearly unamused. "You got the keys, Charlie?" Veronica extends her hand, her palm facing up.

Charlie begrudgingly reaches into his trouser pocket, retrieving the keys to Audrey's apartment. He hands them to Veronica. "Are you okay to do the honours, or are you too exhausted from the twenty feet you had to carry Audrey's suitcase?"

Veronica snatches the keys from Charlie. "I can manage, Charlie."

As Veronica fumbles through the keys, Audrey wonders what feelings may be triggered when she is again in her apartment. Charlie notices that Audrey has gone quiet. He places his arm around her. "You'll be fine, Audrey. It may take a few days, but soon things will return to normal."

"Thanks, Charlie," Audrey says as she leans against Charlie.

Veronica finally manages to open the door. "I've got it. Far out, so many bloomin' keys."

Audrey watches as Veronica paces down the narrow passageway of her apartment. She feels reluctant to follow, delaying the inevitable of stepping inside. Charlie rubs his palm back and forth on Audrey's coat.

"Off you go, Audrey."

Audrey takes incremental steps down the hallway. Finally, she looks up as she reaches the end of the passageway, her view becoming clear as Veronica steps aside. Audrey is exalted as she looks ahead, seeing Clay standing proud by the fireplace, a massive banner with her name on it, and Clay holding a chocolate cake. He presents the cake to Audrey with a colossal smile.

"Welcome home, Miss Audrey."

Audrey takes several quick steps towards Clay, reaching out to him eagerly and wrapping her plaster-covered arms around his belly. Audrey closes her eyes as she rests her cheek on Clay's chest.

Veronica rolls her eyes. "Get a room, will ya?"

Charlie collects the cake from Clay before turning to address Veronica. "You make the coffee, and I'll cut the cake."

"Do I look like a barista?" Veronica mutters as she heads towards the kitchen.

Audrey leans back, managing to clutch onto Clay's sweater with her bandaged hands. She looks up at Clay. "Good to see you, Clay baby."

"Good to see you too, Miss Audrey." Clay giggles for a moment, his admiration on display. "It's so nice to see you back home, where you belong."

Audrey leans her head back, groaning as she extends her neck. "It's good to be home, Clay." Audrey releases her hands from Clay's sweater and looks at Veronica and Charlie, wondering if they need assistance.

"We've got this, Audrey." Charlie presents the cutlery to Audrey. "Sit on the sofa; we'll bring everything out to you."

Audrey salutes Charlie. She looks over the furniture, noticing how sterile the room is. Taking a deep breath, she slowly walks over to the sofas, looking down at her spotless coffee table, all the magazines fanned neatly in one corner. Audrey glances across the room, catching the sun's rays visible through the cracks. She turns her attention to her grandmother's Steinway, taking a moment to collect her thoughts. Audrey takes watchful steps towards the piano, running her eyes across the hardwood floor where she lay the night she was assaulted. Clay looks on as Audrey stands by the piano, looking down at the buffed surface of the fallboard that covers the keys. She ponders momentarily, using her plaster cast to ease it open, exposing the keys. Clay respectfully looks on as Audrey runs her eyes across the keys, noticing how the once tarnished keys now have a noticeable sparkle that was once non-existent.

"Did I clean everything well, Miss Audrey?" Clay asks, curious as he watches Audrey examine the piano.

Audrey turns to face Clay, her eyes now glistening. Her emotions unexpectedly get the better of her, and several tears escape, finding their way down her cheeks. "Yes, Clay, you cleaned everything real good."

Audrey drops her shoulders and lets out a stuttered cry, Clay rushing forward and cradling her in his arms. Charlie and Veronica cease their actions when Audrey unexpectedly expresses her grief. Charlie drops his head, unable to comprehend what it must be like for Audrey, finally returning home, once her safe place, now a reminder of her brutal assault. Clay continues to embrace Audrey, frustrated, knowing that he can do nothing but comfort her, silently praying for Audrey's suffering to cease.

Chapter 24

Miles applies the brakes, causing the squad car to stop abruptly at a set of traffic lights. Languetti grasps his morning coffee as he lunges forward, grimacing at Miles.

"What the hell are you doing? You're going to get coffee all over me."

"The light turned yellow," Miles pleads.

"Yellow? Just drive through it. I'm not going to arrest you, Miles."

"I can't be sure of that, Frank." Miles releases a strenuous sigh, stretching his arms over his head as he looks out the window. His eyes land on a homeless man rummaging through the trash for breakfast. *New York City in all its glory*, he thinks.

It's Monday, 10.23 in the morning, the day after Audrey arrived home from Bellevue Hospital. Languetti and Miles are on their way to see her after receiving a call from Dr Wakefield yesterday, informing them that Audrey has been released. Many weeks have passed since the last time Languetti spoke to Audrey, and he is keen to interview her after deciding to step back and give her some time to recover. Languetti takes a sip of his coffee.

"Do you think she'll talk?"

The lights turn green; Miles gently eases down on the accelerator. "It's hard to tell, Frank. Giving her time was a good idea, though. The longer she spends in the hospital, the more resentment she builds for her attacker."

Even though Languetti has spent more time on the job as a detective, he has come to value Miles' opinion when assessing the victim's psychological profile. Miles has always been able to distance himself emotionally from the victims and, therefore, has proven to Languetti, on several occasions, to be entirely accurate in his psychological evaluations.

"You should be careful what you say to her today, Frank. Don't come in too hard, or she'll clam up."

Languetti takes another sip of his coffee. "I'm not going to come in hard. I'm going to, ever so gently, ask her to name the prick that did this to her."

Miles pulls up at another set of lights, careful not to jolt the car. "That is exactly what I'm talking about, Frank. We'll lose her if you get emotional and push her on this. Even if she names William, we still need her to testify in court. Take it easy on her or she'll clam up."

Languetti waves his arm through the air, a trait he picked up as a child, growing up with his Italian uncles, who were quite animated when they debated topics. "What the hell are you on about? Who's getting emotional? I want the prick to pay for what her did to her. It's my job, my passion in life."

Miles scoffs, shaking his head at Languetti. "Yeah, right, Frank."

"I'm not emotional, Miles; I'm Italian. There's a difference."

Miles makes a right turn. "Yeah, those Italians never let their emotions get in the way, do they, Frank?"

Languetti gawks at Miles. "What the hell are you going on about? You've seen The Godfather. I'm just like Don Vito Corleone. Cool and in control."

Miles eases off the accelerator, turning to avoid a careless pedestrian. "Get the fuck off the road, idiot." Miles pulls up at another set of lights. "The Don put a horse's head in some guy's bed, Frank."

Frank raises his finger at Miles. "But he remained calm when doing so."

Miles sweeps his hand through the air, brushing Languetti off. "I'm done with this conversation, Frank."

Languetti smirks, sipping his coffee as he files through his thoughts on Audrey, rehearsing his opening questions in his head. "She'll talk." Languetti quietly proclaims.

Miles looks over at Languetti. "And if she doesn't, Frank?"

Languetti reflects on the possibility of knowing all too well how female victims can behave in these situations. After some time, most victims want to put the whole ordeal behind them. Pretend it never happened. If Audrey talks now, she'll open up those wounds that have been healing these past six weeks. Audrey is home and feeling safe right now. Languetti knows the best time to interview the victims is in the first 48 hours of the crime. This was not possible with Audrey, and Languetti knows he has a challenging task ahead of him if he has any chance of arresting and convicting William. A smirk appears on Languetti's face.

"If she doesn't talk, I'll cut the head off a horse and stick it in her bed."

Miles grins slightly, shaking his head as he approaches The Parkway. "I'm working with a psychopath."

Miles pulls up to the curb, right in front of The Parkway, Languetti taking one last gulp of his coffee.

"You ready, Frank?"

Languetti places the empty cup on the dashboard of the cruiser. "Yeah, let's go."

The detectives step out of the car and head towards the entrance of The Parkway. Inside, Charlie is standing at the counter, scheduling in his notebook; he looks up, hearing three loud knocks on the door, Languetti pressing his face against the glass to peer inside the lobby. Charlie places his pen on the counter and heads to the door. He opens the door, greeting both men with a nod as they enter.

"Detective."

Languetti extends his hand to Charlie. "How are you doing, Charlie?"

"I'm well, Detective," Charlie replies.

Miles eases the door closed before greeting Charlie with a hand gesture in the form of a pistol. "Charlie."

Charlie acknowledges Miles and turns to Languetti to inquire about their visit, even though he knows they have come to see Audrey. "How can I be of service, Detective?"

Languetti places his hands on his hips. "We have come to see Audrey, Charlie. We're hoping to have a word with her now that she has had time to recover somewhat."

"I see."

"How's she doing, Charlie?" Miles inquires.

"She's doing well, Detective. She arrived home yesterday morning and was a little emotional at first. But she seemed to be her normal self by the time the sun went down."

Languetti is curious. "Emotional, how?"

"Well, we thoroughly cleaned her apartment while she was recovering in the hospital, making sure there were no traces of blood left behind. But Audrey was shaken up a little when she stepped into the living area, seeing her grandmother's piano. That room is a reminder...well, you know, Detective.

"That's understandable," Miles remarks. "It's difficult for victims to go back and visit the crime scene."

Charlie looks right at Miles. "Yes, I understand it would be difficult, Detective, especially if the crime scene is your home." Charlie takes a deep breath and continues. "She broke down and cried for a while, which was expected, I guess, and then she went to her bedroom and rested. We ate dinner with her last night. She seemed fine."

Languetti removes his hands from his hips, becoming slightly impatient. "We'd like to go up and talk to her now. She's home?"

Charlie acknowledges the importance of the visit while also being aware that Audrey may feel somewhat resentful towards him for allowing the detectives to question her. "She's home; I was only up there a few moments ago. You can go up."

Languetti pats Charlie on the shoulder before heading towards the stairs.

"See ya, Charlie." Miles follows Frank. Charlie remains behind, his thoughts with Audrey, wondering how she may react when she sees the detectives at her door.

As they make their way up the stairs, Languetti reaches into his pocket and removes his notepad. Miles examines Languetti, who suddenly stops on the first level and begins to rifle through the pages.

"What are you doing, Frank?"

Languetti continues to inspect his notes. "I can't remember the apartment number."

Miles looks up at the tunnel of the spiralling staircase. "It's the top floor, at the end of the hall."

Languetti looks up from his notes. "You certain?"

"Yeah, you don't remember?" Miles replies.

Languetti looks at his notes. "If I'd remembered, I wouldn't be looking it up, Miles." Languetti finally locates his notes on the investigation. "Found it, Apartment 34," he announces. Frank replaces the notebook in his coat pocket and continues climbing the stairs to Audrey's apartment. Miles stretches his eyes.

"And there goes his memory."

At the top of the stairs, Languetti walks down the corridor leading to Audrey's apartment. Slightly out of breath, he navigates his way towards the door. Miles follows, adjusting his jacket and always being self-aware of his appearance. The lighting is dim; Languetti approaches the door numbered 34.

"This is it."

He knocks twice. A few moments pass, and both men patiently wait; the atmosphere in the hall is subdued. The sound of heavy footsteps can be heard. The door swings open; both detectives immediately look upwards, a large man filling the void, a curious look on his face. A deep voice greets them both.

"Can I help you?"

Languetti is momentarily bewildered, reaching into his coat and wondering if he wrote the apartment number down incorrectly. He retrieves his badge and presents it to Clay, who is peering down at the two men.

"Sir, I'm Detective Frank Languetti, and this is my partner, Detective Miles," Languetti announces, looking over at Miles before raising his question to Clay. "Is this where Audrey Mills lives?"

Clay's expression changes as he takes note of the badge, now feeling slightly awkward at the presence of the two detectives.

"Yes, sir." Clay nervously whispers, "this is Audrey's place."

Languetti replaces his badge in his coat pocket. "We would like to speak to Miss Mills and ask her a few questions."

Clay hesitates, unsure whether to call Audrey or invite the detectives inside.

"Can we please come in and see her?" Languetti inquires.

Clay looks over at Miles, who is in awe of Clay's enormous physique. "Charlie said it was okay to come up to see her," Miles explains.

Clay feels flustered. "I will go and get her." Clay spontaneously runs off to inform Audrey of her visitors, leaving the front door wide open.

"Should we go inside?" Languetti asks Miles, who shrugs his shoulders.

"I guess so."

Languetti leads Miles inside the apartment, down the narrow corridor and into the open area of the living room. "Where did he go?" Languetti wonders, browsing the room with his eyes.

Miles shakes his head. "No idea," he says, taking a few steps further into the room. "Who is that guy, Frank?"

Languetti shakes his head. "I don't know."

Miles continues to look around the room, focusing on the Steinway. "Maybe she hired a bodyguard," Miles remarks.

A shadow appears from one of the bedrooms, catching Languetti and Miles' attention; both men look across the room to see Audrey moving towards them; she holds her ground at the edge of the room. Clay moves up behind her, avoiding direct eye contact with the detectives.

"Miss Mills, I'm Detective Languetti. We met briefly several weeks ago while you were in the hospital."

Audrey stands there mutely, inspecting Languetti and Miles as she contemplates a response. Languetti looks at his partner before addressing Audrey once again.

"Do you remember us, Miss Mills?"

Audrey nods her head. "I do, Detective."

Languetti takes a step towards Audrey. "I'd like to talk to you, Audrey. Please, if that's okay with you?"

Audrey takes a breath and gives Languetti her consent, nodding before walking to the sofa. She turns to Clay before seating herself.

"Clay, would you please get some water for me and the detectives?"

"Sure, Miss Audrey." Clay heads for the kitchen.

As Languetti makes his way to join Audrey, he motions towards Clay as he addresses Audrey.

"You hired a bodyguard, Miss Mills?" he says jokingly.

Audrey smirks at Clay. "Yes, I did, Detective."

Clay giggles when hearing Audrey's response. Miles meanders by the window, conscious that two detectives may overwhelm Audrey. Languetti sits next to Audrey; he looks at her plastered hands, removing his notebook and pen from his coat. He purposely clears his throat.

"So, how are you doing, Audrey?"

Audrey tilts her head; a wry smile appears. "I'm just dandy, Detective. And how are you doing?" Audrey makes light of the detective's opening question.

"I'm fine, thanks for asking."

A shadow is cast over Audrey as Clay appears, holding a tray with three glasses of ice water. He leans down and places the tray on the coffee table.

Audrey reaches up and rubs her cast on Clay's shoulder. "Thanks, Clay."

Clay smiles at Audrey, noticing the other detective by the window; he takes one of the glasses into his hand and walks over to Miles. Languetti looks down at the two remaining glasses, noting that one has a straw. He immediately concludes that the glass is meant for Audrey and offers it to her. Audrey grasps the glass of water in both hands, placing it on her lap.

"You *are* a detective!"

Languetti smiles, taking a small sip of the water to wet his palate.

"So, Detective, you have a few questions you would like to ask me. Yes?" Audrey syphons a mouthful of water through the straw.

Clay and Miles stand a few feet apart by the window.

Languetti places his beverage on the tray before responding to Audrey. "I understand this is difficult for you, Audrey, but the person who did this to you will go unpunished if you don't come forth and implicate him."

Audrey looks down at her glass, the water glistening from the refractive light. "No one on this earth goes unpunished, Detective. We all pay for our sins, one way or another."

Hearing Audrey's theological response, Languetti becomes cautious about insulting her religious beliefs or intelligence. "You're right, Audrey; we all pay for our sins. But I have a responsibility as a police detective to ensure that the people who commit these sins are tried and punished here, on earth. In their lifetime." Languetti looks at Audrey hopefully. Audrey remains silent, again looking down at her beverage. Languetti takes a risk, playing on Audrey's conscience. "And so do you, Audrey."

Audrey immediately looks up at Languetti. "Is that so, Detective?" She refrains from raising her voice.

Languetti senses Audrey's resentment but pursues the argument. "I don't mean to insult you in any way, Audrey, and I can understand if you're afraid. But if you choose not to implicate the person who did this to you, then you, yourself, may somehow feel, in part at least, responsible for any women this man may hurt in the future."

Miles cringes, fearing Frank went too far, too soon.

Languetti gazes sympathetically, adding one more remark. "In the same way, William, hurt you."

Audrey remains calm, choosing to respond with a question of her own. "Tell me, Detective, what's the guilt like that *you* feel for a woman who dies, trying to uphold your theory?"

Languetti refrains to argue the point.

"Can you guarantee my safety, Detective?" Audrey asks with a blunt tone.

Languetti sees his reflection deep in Audrey's eyes and upon hearing those exact words, a memory deep in Languetti's subconscious surfaces. A case from many years ago: a woman who was beaten by her fiancé, not unlike how Audrey was. Languetti was determined to convict this man and endeavoured to persuade the young woman to come forward and implicate her assailant, even though she was reluctant to do so. After several days of persistence, the woman posed this same question to Languetti.

'Can you guarantee my safety, Detective?' The frightened woman pleaded. Languetti knew that he couldn't protect her, but his response did not reflect his thoughts that day. Two weeks after she pressed charges, Languetti received a call to the woman's home, where police found her severely beaten. She later died in the hospital. The man was convicted and incarcerated, but Languetti never forgave himself. His promise to the young woman was a lie, and to this day, he visits her grave on the anniversary of her death. Languetti knew there was no guarantee that the circumstances would have been any different if he hadn't pushed her. Still, nevertheless, he vowed that his determination for justice would never cloud his judgment, present false hope to any victim and compromise their safety. Languetti continues to gaze into Audrey's eyes, choosing his following words carefully.

"No, Audrey, I can't."

Audrey's lips part, her eyes widen, and her surprise at Languetti's response is quite evident. "Well. This part of the job must be most frustrating for you, Detective?"

Languetti glances in thought, seemingly conceding defeat. Audrey gently brushes her hair back, wanting to share her thoughts with Frank.

"I can understand your determination to make this man pay for what he did to me, and it is appreciated, Detective. It is. But it's over now, and I want to put it behind me and move on with my life. I hope you can understand and respect that decision."

Languetti hides his frustration, familiar with Audrey's response, a song many victims often play.

"I understand, Miss Mills."

"So, what now, Detective?" Audrey inquires.

Languetti reaches into his coat pocket, presenting his card to Audrey. "Audrey, you've made your decision. But I would like for you to make me a promise."

"What's that, Detective?" Audrey glances at the small white card in Languetti's hand.

"I was informed that you don't have any kind of relationship with William, and statistically, the chances of him returning to your apartment are unlikely. But if he does try to contact you and threaten you in any way, you will let me know immediately." Languetti extends his hand, offering Audrey his card.

Audrey reaches forward, taking the card in her fingertips before looking up at Languetti. "I promise I will, Detective."

Feeling his mouth dry up, Frank reaches for the beverage to quench his thirst. Audrey tilts her head, looking past Languetti's shoulder at Clay, standing by the window, with a hint of awkwardness in his posture.

"You okay, Clay?"

Clay takes a step towards Audrey.

"Yes, Miss Audrey, I'm fine. How are you doing?" Clay asks.

"I'm okay, Clay," Audrey replies, smiling as she shifts her vision to Miles.

"Would you like some more water, Detective?"

Miles looks at the glass in his hand. "No, I'm good, Miss Mills." *It's scotch that I could use right now,* he thinks to himself, offering Clay the empty glass.

Clay heads for the kitchen sink.

Languetti places his beverage onto the tray, glancing up at Clay as he walks by. "Most women in your situation usually buy a German Shepherd."

Audrey snickers. "I'm not a huge K-9 lover personally, Detective, being such a clean freak and all." Audrey winks at Clay. "Besides, Clay makes for better conversation."

Languetti eyes Clay, instinctively curious as to how Audrey and Clay met. "Well, at least you can be assured that as long as he's around, no man will be brave enough to come within a hundred feet," Languetti says, replacing his notebook in his coat pocket, lifting himself off the sofa. "We should go. I've taken up too much of your time as it is."

Audrey leans forward; she struggles to reach the serving tray. Languetti quickly leans down, taking the glass from Audrey, helping her to her feet.

"Thank you, Detective." Audrey exhales as she rises. She escorts Languetti towards the exit, Miles joining them; Audrey suddenly turns to face Miles, who attracts her attention.

"Miss Mills, do you mind if I ask you a question?"

"Sure," Audrey replies, shrugging her shoulders, surprisingly.

"Since that night you were attacked, have you at any time encountered the man who assaulted you?"

Audrey feels blindsided. The suppressed memory of William visiting her that night in the hospital rushes back, sending a chill down her spine. She keeps her composure, smuggling her true thoughts. "No." Audrey wondered if the detective somehow knew about William's premeditated visit.

Miles locks eyes with Audrey. "Does William know where you work, Audrey?"

Audrey hesitates for a moment, her discomfort evident. He remains persistent, demanding validation.

"Yes, he does, Detective."

Audrey's eyes begin to glisten. Clay becomes concerned as Miles makes his point, staring deep into Audrey's eyes. Frank intercedes.

"Thank you again, Miss Mills. We'll get out of your hair now."

Audrey's thoughts are distracted by Languetti's departing remark.

"Yes, thank you for coming, Detective." Audrey struggles to smile.

Languetti leads Miles to exit the apartment. Clay follows them, Audrey returning to the sofa, contemplating whether there was anything the detectives hadn't told her. Languetti steps out into the corridor; Miles holds his ground just outside the door, performing an about-face. Clay is alert as Miles looks him squarely in the eyes.

"The guy who did this to her...is bad news, brother."

Clay stands there feeling conflicted about what Miles said to Audrey moments ago.

"You understand what I'm telling you, big guy?"

Clay nods at Miles. "Yes, sir, I think I do."

Miles briefly holds his poignant look before exiting the corridor, Languetti joining him by his side. Clay watches the men momentarily before easing the door closed. He wanders back to the living area, Audrey sitting alone, lost in her thoughts.

"Hey Audrey?"

Audrey turns to look at Clay. "Hey." She forces a smile.

Clay moves towards her, reluctant to ask Audrey the one question on his mind. Audrey senses Clay's hesitance and invites him over to sit with her.

"What's on your mind, Clay?"

Clay takes a moment. "The man who hurt you…do you think he'll try to hurt you again?"

Audrey looks appreciatively into Clay's eyes, making light of his concern for her safety. "Not with you around to protect me, he won't," Audrey says with a smile. She takes a moment before sharing her thoughts with Clay. "Do you think I'm a coward, Clay, for not saying anything? You know…pressing charges and all that."

"No, Miss Audrey, I think you're brave."

"How am I brave, Clay?" Audrey huffs. "I didn't do anything."

Audrey laughs at herself. She rests her head on Clay's chest, unable to shake her thoughts from William, closing her eyes and picturing his face as he leaned over her in the hospital. Audrey is frustrated; her sense of comfort, once again, is absent. Clay is unaware of her secret.

Chapter 25

Frank looks annoyingly at his partner. "What the hell was that about?" Languetti says unimpressed.

"Just giving her something to think about, Frank," Miles says.

"You've probably got her all paranoid now."

Miles adjusts his jacket in a display of prowess. "Good, paranoia keeps people like her alive in this city, Frank."

Frank shakes his head. "A little too harsh, in my opinion."

Miles pulls up at the top of the stairs. "You went soft on her, Frank."

Frank peers at Miles, recalling Miles's lecture about taking it easy on Audrey. Miles raises his hands.

"We can't touch him now. Case closed." Miles dusts off his palms as he continues down the stairs.

"We did what we could. Besides, he's not going to go near her again, anyway. There's no motive." Languetti points out.

"Can't be certain of that. Can't be certain of anything anymore, Frank." Miles suppressed frustration emerging—his analytical prediction is based on a pattern of psychological profiles encompassing similar circumstances.

"What the hell are you on about?"

Miles stops and faces Languetti. "Girl gets the crap beaten out of her, almost dies, and she just wants to forget it ever happened. Right?"

"Yeah, so what. Happens all the time," Frank states.

"She may forget Frank, but he won't. You know how these sick fuckers think; we both do. They get obsessed with the pretty ones. William had a thing for this girl. He lusted for her, but she rejected him. Once is never enough. After enough time passes, they almost always go back. Especially if they feel they can get away with it."

Frank glances in thought. "She's never going to forget about this, Miles. You know this will follow her around for the rest of her life, and maybe that's enough to keep her on her toes until enough time passes for him to lose interest."

Miles shakes his head at Frank. "I don't get you, Frank. For the last month, all I've heard is you want to put this guy away, and now, you make out as if it doesn't matter."

"It does matter, but not to her. So, until that changes, there is no point worrying about it or making her feel like shit for not talking to us." Languetti is poignant.

"That smells like bullshit, Frank. You needed to push her more, for her own sake." Miles feels frustrated. "Let's just get the fuck out of here." Miles continues down the stairs. "You better hope that big guy never leaves her side."

Languetti catches up to an agitated Miles as he hurries down the stairs. "You hungry?" Languetti pats Miles on the back. "You get grumpy when you haven't eaten for a while. I could go for a bite myself."

Miles shrugs. "Yeah, sure, whatever, Frank."

Chapter 26

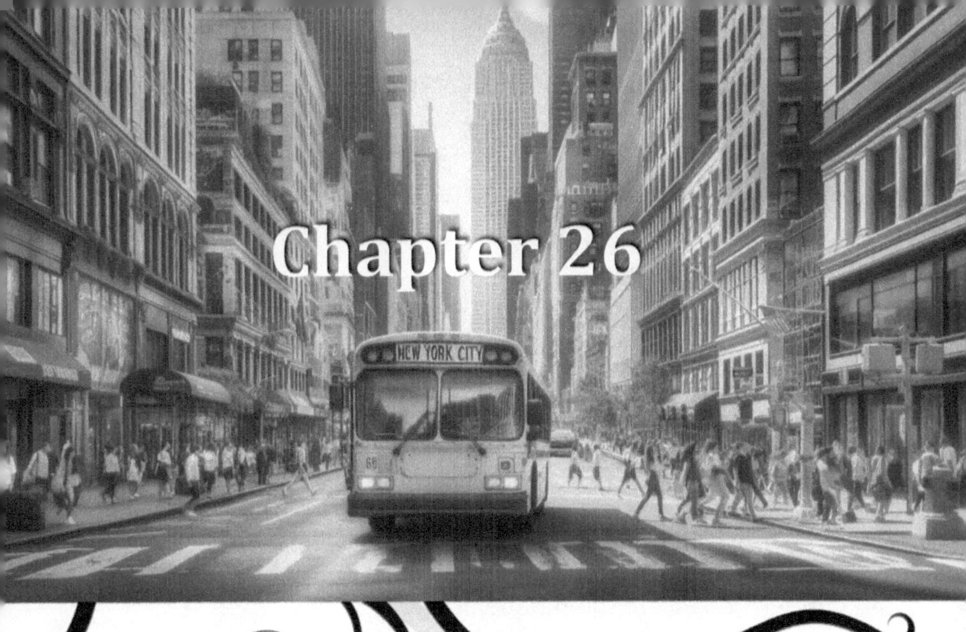

It's a warm Sunday morning, two weeks since Audrey was released from Bellevue. Charlie escorted Audrey back to the hospital last Wednesday to have the nurse remove the cast and bandages from her arms and hands. Dr Wakefield visited her then and gave her a foam rubber stress ball as a gift. He asked Audrey to continually squeeze it several times a day to help regain the strength in her hands. With all the time off work she accrued over the past two months, Audrey has eaten up a substantial chunk of her savings and is keen to return to work at the florist on Monday. She asked Charlie if he would cover for Clay this Sunday so that she could take Clay to Central Park for a picnic, a gesture of appreciation for Clay's time over the past two weeks helping her with various chores. Charlie happily agreed.

Charlie is situated at the bottom of the stairwell, dust cloth in hand, polishing the banister. He looks up, hearing footsteps from above.

"There they are," he says with a grin, catching sight of Clay and Audrey carefully descending the stairs. Clay offers his arm to Audrey, guiding her down each step and finally into the foyer.

"You made it!" Charlie remarks.

"Hey Charlie!" Audrey is full of glee.

Charlie sees Clay holding a picnic hamper in his left hand and a bright red backpack thrown over his right shoulder.

"So, you're all set, I see." Charlie observes the sunny beams of light through the windowpanes, sketched across the marble floor. "Bright, warm, sunny day today," Charlie says as he turns to Audrey. "Great day for a picnic, Audrey." Charlie motions at the hamper. "What's in the hamper, Clay?"

Clay gives Charlie a befuddled look, unsure of what Audrey has packed into the hamper.

"Well, Charlie, we have some roast chicken, coleslaw, fresh bread rolls that Clay was kind enough to bring on his way here this morning and three large helpings of chocolate cake." Audrey's eyes widen.

"Three helpings of chocolate cake, you say?" Charlie raises his eyebrows. "Chocolate cake is my favourite." Charlie expresses his interest to Clay. "But there are only two of you, the third piece must be for me?" Charlie teases, undoubtedly knowing that the third piece of cake is meant to satisfy Clay's enormous appetite. Charlie looks at Audrey, amused, as Clay clutches the hamper tightly to his chest.

"We better get going, Clay, before Charlie steals your dessert," Audrey says with laughter.

"Yes, Miss Audrey."

Clay hurries along; Charlie watches as Clay clutches the hamper close to his chest. As they reach the doors, Audrey turns to address Charlie.

"Hey, Charlie."

"What is it, Audrey?"

"Thanks again for today."

"Not a problem, you kids have fun today."

Clay holds the door open for Audrey. They both exit, Clay careful with Audrey as they step onto the sidewalk.

"The bus stop is just down on that corner. I think the next bus goes directly by Central Park, Clay." Audrey straightens her coat. "Shall we?"

Clay nods. Audrey hangs onto Clay's arm as they journey towards the bus stop. Audrey looks to the bright blue sky, closing one eye as she catches a glimpse of the morning sun poking its yellow face through a cirrus cloud. "Ooh! I'm blinded." Audrey squeals, fluttering her eyelids to get rid of the sunspots.

Clay looks down at Audrey. "Are you ok?"

Audrey stretches her eyes. "Oh, wow, that was not a wise decision," Audrey says as she reaches into her coat pocket to retrieve a pair of dark tortoise sunglasses. "I'm okay, Clay, just seeing poker dots everywhere."

Clay foolishly looks to the sky, unable to elude the sun's rays. "Oh…that is…very bright," Clay exclaims, pressing his thumb and forefinger onto his squinted eyes.

Audrey chuckles. "Idiot, I just did that."

Clay continues to knead his eyes with his fingers.

"How do I look, Clay?" Audrey poses. "Do I look like anyone familiar?" Audrey waits in bated breath for Clay to look at her. Clay regains his vision and eventually looks down to see Audrey, smiling, donning her stylish sunglasses.

"Sorry, Miss Audrey?" Clay is bemused by the question.

Audrey again asks as they approach the curb. "Whom…do I remind you of?" Audrey quickly reaches out, pressing the pedestrian push-button before resuming her pose. Clay gawks at Audrey, searching his mind for an answer to satisfy her. Audrey raises her hand next to her face, palm facing outwards, as she tilts her head back.

"Who am I, Clay?" She says once more, this time altering the pitch of her voice.

Clay looks dumbfounded, spotting his blank expression reflected in Audrey's lenses. "I can see myself in your glasses, Miss Audrey," Clay says smilingly.

Audrey lets out a frustrated sigh, dropping her arm by her side. The street signal prompts them to walk. "Come on, time to walk again, Clay." Acting slightly miffed, Audrey takes Clay by the arm, pulling him onto the road.

Clay is amused, knowing how Audrey often acts this way intentionally. "Are you someone famous?" Clay laughingly inquires as he is pulled across the street.

"Yes, someone very famous, as a matter of fact," Audrey replies in a definitive tone. "Even Charlie has mentioned it to me."

Clay smiles. "Who are you, Miss Audrey?"

Audrey draws out her responses. "Audrey Hepburn."

Clay lets out a little giggle. Audrey snaps her head, peering up at Clay over the rim of her glasses. He quickly loses his smile.

"Oh, yes, I see it now, Miss Audrey." Clay nods. "You look just like her."

Audrey looks condescendingly at Clay. "Some people have said there is an uncanny likeness with these particular glasses."

"People?" Clay thinks for a moment. "You mean Charlie?"

"Not just Charlie; there are others you know."

"Who?" Clay asks.

"People, Clay, many people you don't know." Audrey asserts as she steps up onto the curb. "You know, I bought these glasses on Amazon. They are replicas of the ones Audrey Hepburn wore in Breakfast at Tiffany's. Clay amuses himself.

"So, they're magic glasses?"

"That's not funny, Clay." Audrey again peers at Clay above the rim of her shades, her elbow poking Clay, doing her best to remain serious, a hint of a smirk revealing her true disposition.

Just ahead, Clay notices a woman standing at the bus stop shuffling through her purse. He suspects she is preparing her coinage for the bus driver and looks over his shoulder to see if a bus is approaching.

"I think that might be our bus coming?"

Audrey turns her head and looks at the oncoming traffic. She immediately notices a white bus with its distinct blue stripe and the words New York City Bus written on the front and sides. Audrey looks above the driver's head at the destination signage. It reads 109: Central Park W.

"Yep, that's our bus, Clay!" She says excitedly.

Clay and Audrey hurry towards the bus stop. Clay looks over his shoulder again, noticing the bus is now stationary.

"It stopped at the traffic light."

Audrey looks over her shoulder. "That's a relief. I'm so out of shape still," Audrey says, draping her tongue over her bottom lip.

"I have not seen her on television, but I have seen her in a book once. It was a book with all the famous people."

"You mean Audrey Hepburn?"

Clay nods at Audrey.

"You haven't seen her in one of her movies?"

"No, Miss Audrey."

"Well, we'll just have to rectify that fact."

Audrey pats Clay on the arm. As the bus approaches the stop, Audrey takes a ten-dollar note from her purse to use as bus fare for herself and Clay.

"I have some money on me, Miss Audrey," Clay says, reaching for his wallet.

"Don't worry, Clay, this ride's on Miss Hepburn," Audrey says as she flicks her head back in a pose.

Clay lets out another giggle.

"Still not convinced?" Audrey lowers her glasses to peer at Clay. "Watch; I'll prove it to you."

A look of concern appears on Clay's face as he senses an embarrassing moment approaching. The bus pulls up; a hydraulic hiss as the driver opens the doors. Audrey waits for the woman to board before stepping nonchalantly onto the bus. She looks directly at the bus driver, who appears as a hardened New York local.

"Do you get many movie stars on your bus?"

The driver looks directly at Audrey, unsure of what to say. Audrey prompts the driver for a response.

"Well, you do know who I am, don't you?"

The edgy driver looks Audrey up and down.

"I don't know, lady; I just drive the bus. You getting on or what?"

Audrey drops her shoulders with exasperation; she extends her arm, presenting the money to the driver. "Two, please," she requests with a hint of contempt.

Clay covers his mouth, snuffing out any oral reaction. The driver gives Audrey a disturbed look as he takes the money. He punches out two tickets, collects the exact change, and presents it to Audrey. Audrey seizes the tickets in her hand. "Thank you, Mr bus driver." She purses her lips and removes her glasses, feeling dissatisfied as she heads off to the bus's rear.

Clay awkwardly steps onto the bus with the hamper in hand, looking directly at the driver. "Nice day today, isn't it?" Clay asks with a grin.

The bus driver gives Clay a strange look. "You must take your seat now so that I can leave." The driver peevishly instructs.

Clay apologetically nods his head. "Yes, okay, sir, thank you."

Clay heads down the aisle, looking ahead to see Audrey taking comfort on the bus's rear seat. Some passengers peer up at Clay, his size distracting their focus. The driver observes Clay through his rearview mirror, shaking his head as he puts the bus in gear.

"Every day, there's something weird in this city," the driver mumbles, releasing the brake and putting the bus in forward motion once again.

Audrey lets out a tired sigh, spreading herself out onto the elongated seat as she looks up at Clay. Cautiously, Clay navigates his bulky frame between the seats, suddenly losing his footing as the driver shifts gears.

Audrey lets out a snicker. "You alright there, Clay?"

Clay grins, placing the hamper on the empty seat beside him. The driver shifts another gear, causing Clay to unexpectedly fall back onto the rear seat, positioning himself beside Audrey. Clay looks fearful at Audrey, who reacts by curling up into a semi-foetal position.

"Oh! Sorry, Miss Audrey." Clay almost crushes Audrey.

"That's ok, Clay." Audrey absolves, with an anxious look quite visible.

Clay places his hands on his thighs. A huge grin covers his face as he looks around excitedly, like a young child on his way to a school excursion.

"I like the back seat," he says smilingly. "I mostly have to stand up when I ride the buses because the back seat is usually occupied, and I'm a little too big for the other seats."

Audrey sniffs.

"I almost sat on a little girl last week because I didn't see her. Her mother yelled out, and everyone on the bus turned and stared. It was so embarrassing."

Audrey laughingly places her hand on Clay's shoulder. "You're precious, Clay, you know that."

Audrey rests her head back, looking out the window at the New York visage. Clay mimics Audrey's quiet admiration as the bus heads west of the city. Destination: Central Park.

Chapter 27

Outstanding in every way, the Bethesda Terrace is the architectural achievement that defines the heart of Central Park as it seamlessly joins the Mall with a Terrace overlooking the lake and the wooded Ramble beyond. It is built of New Brunswick sandstone in a mixture of Romanesque, Gothic and Classical styles, with decorative elements designed by Jacob Wrey Mould. The amazingly intricate sandstone carvings reflect nature's significance, featuring birds and seasonal plants along the stairways and on the terrace's main posts. This magnificent split-level terrace creates a heavenly atmosphere with its upper terrace and grand stairways on either side. Many visitors stand on the Upper Terrace and gaze towards the famous Angel of the Waters fountain (or Bethesda Fountain, commonly called). The fountain features a neoclassical winged female figure that symbolises and celebrates the purifying of the city's water supply when the Croton Aqueduct opened in 1842, bringing fresh water to all New Yorkers. The stimulus for the 'Angel of the Waters' comes from the

Gospel of Saint John, Chapter 5, the story of an angel bestowing healing powers on the pool of Bethesda in Jerusalem.

Audrey holds on tight to Clay's arm as they walk down the sandstone steps that lead to the terrace below. As they reach the bottom of the stairs, Clay immediately looks up at the Bethesda Fountain, becoming fixated on the eye-catching figures.

"It's beautiful, isn't it, Clay?" Audrey remarks.

Clay shields his eyes from the sunny glare as he walks towards the fountain. "Yes, it is Miss Audrey." Clay becomes absorbed with the statue's dazzling beauty and intricate features surrounding the fountain.

"It was designed by a woman, Clay." Audrey points out as she walks over to the fountain, resting momentarily on the sandstone rim.

"Do you know her name, Miss Audrey?"

Audrey leans her head back, looking towards the sky. "I think her name was Emma something. There's a plaque over there with her name on it."

Clay looks at the terrace floor. "I think I see it." He rushes over to read it. "It says her name was Emma Stebbins." Clay looks across to see Audrey absorbing the sun's rays.

"Yep, that sounds right." Audrey clutches onto the rim, leaning way back over the water.

Clay walks over towards Audrey. "Careful, Miss Audrey, you might fall in and drown."

"What?" Audrey says laughingly as she raises her feet off the terrace floor, leaning further back.

Clay hurries towards her. Audrey laughs as Clay approaches. She pulls herself upright.

"Drown in a fountain? Can you swim, Clay?"

"I don't think so. I have never tried, Miss Audrey." Clay places the hamper on the pavement.

"Why not?" Audrey inquires.

"Don't know, never been anywhere with a pool."

Audrey looks up into the heavens. "I like spending time at the beach in summer. You haven't been to the beach either, Clay?"

"No." Clay takes a seat next to Audrey.

"New York has beaches, you know, Clay."

"Florida has nice beaches," Clay exclaims. I have an uncle who lives in Florida, and I remember visiting him when I was young.

"I'd like to go to Australia one day and swim at the beaches in Sydney."

"That is a faraway place."

"I'm going to go one day. I was saving up for a holiday...but." Audrey looks out into the wooded area beyond the terrace, imagining herself on the beach.

"Maybe Charlie and I can come with you?"

"That would be a fun trip." Audrey's voice is soft.

"And we can all swim together at the beach," Clay says excitedly.

Audrey raises her sunglasses, placing them aptly above her brow. "Swimming, you say, ay, Clay?" Audrey casually leans back, cupping her hand and scooping her palm in the fountain's water. "You have to learn how to swim first, Clay." She pitches her hand towards Clay. Clay leaps up as multiple droplets of water are propelled towards his face. Audrey begins to laugh uncontrollably as Clay wipes the water from his eyes. "Got you good, Clay," Audrey says with laughter.

Looking to even the score, Clay intentionally walks towards the fountain, extending his arm towards the pool of water. Audrey jumps up as Clay begins to reach down into the water.

"Don't you dare, Clay?" She screams, running off across the terrace. Clay stops his hand just shy of the water's surface, his intent enough to alarm Audrey. A giggling Clay picks up the hamper and hurries across the terrace to catch up with Audrey. "I will get you back later," he assures himself.

The cool air begins to warm as the dissipating clouds give way to the sun's rays. Audrey heads down to the lake's edge, just beyond the terrace. She looks over her shoulder to see Clay not far behind.

"Over here, Clay, this looks like a great spot."

Clay looks around at the park's foliage. "This is a great spot," he agrees, placing the hamper on the plush green grass.

"Let's put the blanket right here, Clay."

Audrey walks over to assist Clay with the backpack. Clay and Audrey begin to set up the picnic area. They remove each item from the hamper, placing it onto the blanket. Minutes later, the picnic area is meticulously set with all the food neatly spread out, ready for the feast. Both admire their handiwork.

"It looks great. Doesn't it, Clay?"

"Yes, ma'am." Clay grins at Audrey.

Audrey directs her attention towards the lake. "Come, Clay, let's check out the lake." Audrey takes Clay by the hand, pulling him towards the lake. "I love this place." Audrey sighs, gazing out across the lake's glistening water. She closes her eyes momentarily, absorbing the serenity of her surroundings.

"Look, Miss Audrey." Clay extends his arm, pointing towards the middle of the lake. Audrey follows Clay's finger to view a Northern Pintail swimming along the water's surface.

"He's beautiful."

"And there's another one over there too." Clay points out.

"I think that might be a Red-Breasted Merganser." Audrey pronounces, taking a few steps closer to the water's edge.

"You mean the duck?"

"Yeah."

"How do you know that, Miss Audrey?"

Audrey turns to look at Clay, closing one eye as she catches a glimpse of the sun. "I came here with Charlie once, and he was showing off how much he knew about the animals in the park."

Clay snickers. "I've noticed he sometimes does that when we fix stuff back at The Parkway."

"Look, Clay." Audrey points further along the lake's edge.

"They are swans; I recognise them," Clay announces proudly.

Audrey brushes her hair back. "They look like Mute Swans."

"Did you say mute Swans? You mean they don't talk?"

"Not unless you're Dr Doolittle." Audrey kids. "They don't really make much noise, unlike other swans. They make hissing noises and sometimes barking sounds if you go near them."

"You seem to know a lot about birds. You're super smart."

"*Gee*, thanks, Clay." Audrey playfully punches Clay in the shoulder. "Well, to tell you the truth, Charlie purchased a book called The Glorious Birds of Central Park for me once. I would study it mostly when I was here with Charlie or V."

"And now you are an expert, bird woman."

Audrey smirks. "Well, maybe not an expert, but I know a fair bit." Audrey extends her arms over her head, stretching her abdominals. "Let's go over and feed them, Clay."

A look of concern appears on Clay's face. Audrey begins skipping back towards the picnic site. "I don't think we should feed them, Miss Audrey?"

"It's okay, Clay; people do it all the time."

Clay takes off after Audrey, anxiously yelling out. "Not the cake, please."

Audrey lets out a giggle, reaching into the hamper.

"Relax, Clay; I'm just giving them some bread."

Audrey takes hold of a bread roll. "Come, let's go over and say hi."

Clay follows Audrey as she saunters towards the Swans. "Be careful." Clay takes extensive steps to catch up to an excited Audrey. She pulls up several feet from the swans, tearing off a bite-sized piece of the bread with her fingers.

"Don't come any closer, Clay; you'll frighten them," Audrey whispers.

Clay holds his ground. "Ok."

Clay watches closely as Audrey moves carefully towards the swans, bending her knees slightly as she moves only within a few feet. She reaches out and presents the bread to the swans.

"Here you go, beautiful." She offers the bread in a soft voice. "Come and have some bread, baby."

The swans take notice of Audrey, crouched down with one knee now on the grass. One swan makes a kind of guttural warning call as Audrey inches forward. Clay looks on in anticipation.

"Be careful, Miss Audrey," he whispers.

The swan shows interest in the piece of bread, moving towards Audrey's open palm. "Come on, beautiful," she encourages them once more to take the bread. The swan cautiously inspects Audrey as she sways her palm back and forth. The swan creeps forward, its focus shifting on the piece of bread. "There you go," Audrey whispers. "Just...a little closer." The swan inches closer. Audrey extends her arm as far forward as she can. With a quick snap, the swan plucks the bread from Audrey's palm, guzzling it down without hesitation. Audrey turns to look at Clay.

"Did you see that!" she excitedly whispers. Clay becomes animated.

"Give him some more." Audrey turns her attention back to the swan. "Want some more, you beautiful bird?" Her voice is childlike.

The swan sizes Audrey up, displaying its eagerness as it notices the larger piece of bread in Audrey's other hand. It inches closer again, dismissing Audrey's presence for the plentiful meal. Audrey takes hold of the bread with both hands, still weakened from the surgery; she pries the bread apart with some effort, trying to extract another bite-sized piece. The movement unexpectedly throws Audrey off balance.

"Woe." Audrey voices, extending her arm to the ground to regain her balance. The swan becomes startled, but its focus remains on the food, sharply noticing the smaller piece in Audrey's fingertips. It lunges forward, snapping its bill at Audrey's hand.

"*Eeeh!*" Audrey shrieks, clumsily leaping back; the swan attempts to grasp the food, snapping its bill onto Audrey's sleeve. Audrey springs to her feet. "Oh my god, Clay, help, I'm being attacked," she says hysterically, laughing. The swan extends its wings, pursuing Audrey for the bread. Audrey heads off in the opposite direction.

"Run, Miss Audrey." A fretful Clay yells out.

Audrey runs across the park with the swan snapping at her heels, shrieking at Clay. "Clay!"

"Give him the food," Clay hollers out.

Audrey flings the piece of bread over her shoulder. The swan zeroes its focus on the flying object, retracting its wings as it slows to claim the food. Audrey quickly looks over her shoulder, relieved to see the swan has ceased its pursuit.

"Oh, my god," she pants, crouching in laughter. Clay quickly catches up to Audrey, unable to hide his smile.

"Are you alright, Miss Audrey?" Clay begins to giggle.

Audrey glances once more at the swan before turning her attention to Clay. "Far out, Clay, that bird's crazy."

Clay giggles uncontrollably. "That was so funny."

Audrey leans forward, slapping Clay on the chest.

"It's not funny, Clay; that swan could have killed me."

Clay becomes hysterical upon hearing Audrey's statement.

"That's it, Clay; I'm having all the chocolate cake," Audrey announces, racing towards the picnic setting.

"No, you won't."

Audrey looks around, squealing as Clay quickly catches up to her, picking her up off the ground. Audrey laughs hysterically as Clay effortlessly carries her under one arm, striding back towards the picnic area.

Chapter 28

It's a busy Sunday at the precinct, and Frank sits at his desk amongst the commotion, tapping furiously away at his keyboard. Miles is unbothered, leaning back into his chair, flicking through a fishing magazine.

"Hey, Frank, Captain Hamersley wants to see you in his office." Officer Rodriguez informs as he walks by Frank's desk. Frank retains his focus on the keyboard.

"I'll be there in a minute."

Frank slaps a few extra keys before rising to his feet. He picks up his coffee from the desk, taking two generous mouthfuls before tossing the disposable cup into the waste basket.

"Tell Hamersley hi from me, will you, Frank?"

Frank shakes his head at Miles' silliness. He heads across the crowded precinct, avoiding an array of traffic as he approaches his captain's office. The door is ajar, so Frank pokes his head inside.

"You wanted to see me, Cap?"

"Yeah, Frank. Come in, take a seat."

Captain Hamersley's office is sprawled with newspaper clippings, mug shots, piles of case files stacked around his desk, several commendation awards for excellence, including the Medal of Valour and even a photo of him with the former President of the United States, Barack Obama, whom he met at a fundraiser once. Frank closes the door and takes his seat opposite his captain.

"How's that assault case with the girl going, Frank?"

"No pleasantries, Cap? Just straight to the point." Frank jokes, adjusting his jacket for comfort.

"She's not ready to talk; the case has gone cold...for now." Frank shrugs his shoulders. "I might pay her another visit in a few weeks to see how she's doing."

Captain Hamersley nods his head.

"It happens, Frank, don't worry about it. As long as she's safe, leave well enough alone. Besides, guys like him will fuck up, sooner or later."

Frank nods. "Yeah, I know. Would have been nice to nail his ass to the wall for what he did, though."

"Next time, Frank." Captain Hamersley takes hold of a manila folder and tosses it in front of Frank.

"What's this?" Frank inquires.

"Intel, Frank. Remember that case you had a couple of years back, that Slovak scum piece of shit car thief who killed that woman whilst jacking her Tesla?"

Frank picks up the file, searching his thoughts to recall the case. "Yeah, Ladislav Varga, he skipped out on us. Rumour has it he's hiding somewhere in Florida."

"That's right! Good memory, Frank. So, now we got some intel that his then-girlfriend, who decided to join him on his interstate trip, is back in New York and living in Brooklyn."

"Dalenka Vargova." Frank reads the name on the file.

"That's her rap sheet. She's got a couple of misdemeanours," Hamersley states. Frank examines the file.

"So, Frank, I'm thinking that if she's here, then she probably had a falling out with Ladislav back in Florida. I thought maybe you and Miles might want to go to her residence in Brooklyn and lean on her a little since it was your case, to begin with. Maybe you can get her to give us Ladislav's location in Florida, so I can get Florida PD to pay him a surprise visit and bring him back here to face the standing charges of murder."

"She looks pretty clean. Nothing really to go on in the file."

Captain Hamersley gestures with his hands, offering an alternative solution.

"Maybe you can check her credentials, Frank. See if she's legal."

Frank agrees that it may be a possibility.

"If they parted on bad terms, it might be worthwhile to check her out."

Frank snaps the file closed. "Slovaks make nice food. Maybe Miles and I could have lunch there today."

Captain Hamersley smiles. "You, two, have a lovely time in Brooklyn, Frank."

Frank rises from his chair.

"Hey Frank, don't lean on her too hard. I want to find this guy, but what I don't want is another civil lawsuit on my desk."

"I'll tell Miles not to shoot her in the leg." Frank opens the door and salutes his captain. "See ya, Cap."

Frank walks directly back to his desk; he tosses the manila folder onto Miles's lap. "Read up; I'm going to take a leak."

"What's this, Frank?"

"You like Slovakian cuisine?"

"Slovakian? What, Frank?"

The Brooklyn Bridge, designed by John A. Roebling, was constructed in 1869 and completed in 1883. At the time, it was the longest suspension bridge in the world. The Brooklyn Bridge connects the boroughs of Manhattan and Brooklyn by spanning the East River. It was designated a National Historic Landmark in 1964 and a National Historic Civil Engineering Landmark in 1972.

Languetti leans forward, peering through the windscreen.

"I never get tired of looking at the Brooklyn Bridge. It's a wonderful achievement."

"Yeah, it's real nice, Frank. Hey, listen, let's go see this girl Dalenka first, and then we'll grab some lunch. Still too early for Goulash, Frank."

"You don't like Slovakian food?"

"It's alright. Head down Atlantic Avenue; it's quicker."

As Languetti manoeuvres through the Brooklyn traffic, Miles looks out the window, spotting the Barclays Centre, home of the Brooklyn Nets.

"Do you think the Nets will do well this season?"

Frank shakes his head with uncertainty. "Irving is injured, and Harden is on the way out. They need to find a new Point Guard."

"Harden is good for a couple more years. Turn right here, Frank."

Languetti turns the cruiser onto Rockaway Avenue.

"So, you think Dalenka Vargova knows where Ladislav is hiding out in Florida?" Miles poses the question.

"She knows. She was shacking up with him for the past two years. Question is, will she tell us?"

Miles raises his arms over his head, stretching his shoulder muscles. "Just up ahead, Frank. 229 Chester Street. Just pull up over there."

Languetti pulls the cruiser onto the curb. Miles grabs his coat from the back seat; both detectives hop out of the vehicle. The detectives cross the street, both men shifting their eyes about,

Brownsville having the most violent crimes per capita out of any neighbourhood in the city.

"Sun's bright today." Miles squints as he slides into his jacket. "Why the fuck would Dalenka choose this shithole of a neighbourhood to live in?" Miles loosens his tie, the warm weather adding to his discomfort.

"I don't know; why don't you ask her, Miles?"

Languetti pushes open a small gate. The frontage and driveway are enclosed by red brick pillars and black iron fencing, adding some security to the residents' possessions. Miles examines the property's façade. A single entrance door with two small windows on either side is surrounded by brick, and the side entrance to the right of the dwelling is secured by mesh fencing. Miles follows Languetti down the paved path that leads to the entrance stoop. Languetti takes hold of his badge, planting one foot on the steps as he leans forward, administering three decisive knocks on the front door. He looks away momentarily; the neighbourhood is barren, the sound of a shuffling lock bringing Languetti's attention back to the door. The door swings open. A beautiful Slovakian woman with dark golden-brown hair, wearing a floral mini dress, emerges.

"Áno?"

She smiles curiously at her visitor; Languetti raises his badge, presenting his credentials to the gorgeous woman.

"Bežať!"

The woman screams, turning to look behind her; Languetti shifts his eyes past the woman, a man lurking in the back, locking eyes with Languetti.

"Holy shit! Miles, it's Ladislav."

Languetti reaches for his weapon. Ladislav disappears quickly into the shadows.

"I'll go round the back, Frank."

Miles takes off to his right, scaling the mesh fence to access the rear of the house. Dalenka steps aside as Frank forcefully enters the house, his Beretta firmly in his hand, propped to the level of his eye.

"Prosím Ježiš."

Dalenka covers her mouth, clutching her dress as she backs up, pinning herself against the wall. Languetti cautiously navigates through the lounge; he hears a ruckus down the hall from one of the two bedrooms. He eases himself around the corner, leading with his gun, his eyes shifting frantically, wary of his prey. Languetti projects his voice down the hall.

"Ladislav, don't make this difficult, just come out of the room and give yourself up. We don't want anyone getting hurt."

Languetti listens for a response. Silence, the air is dead, the hallway dim, Languetti exposing himself as he ventures down, the nozzle of his Beretta pointing the way. The sound of glass breaking sounds out in the distance; Languetti is uncertain if Miles is the culprit, forcing his way inside via the rear of the house. Languetti inches further down the hallway, listening intently, pressing his shoulder against the wall as he guides himself further into the darkness. In the distance, a shadow emerges; Languetti is reluctant to speak. Still, he inches forward, two rooms on either side, one providing Ladislav with refuge. Languetti jolts, the shadow at the end of the hall taking form as Miles emerges; Miles raises his palm, signalling to his partner not to shoot him. Languetti exhales, motioning to Miles to cover the room to his right whilst he clears the room to his left. Miles acknowledges, shifting his position, his gun now firmly directed at the room to his left. Miles shifts his eyes onto Frank; his concern for his partners' safety is evident as Languetti takes a deep breath, relaxing his trigger finger, turning his full attention onto the door. He reaches out with his left hand, pressing the tips of his fingers against the door, readying himself for the confrontation. Miles shifts his eyes back onto the room to his left; the door is partway open, and some light from the window exposes the contents. Miles examines the partial view before shifting his eyes back to his partner. Miles watches intently as Languetti prepares to charge the room, a gleam catching his eye, light reflecting off Ladislav's watch face as he raises his gun towards Miles. The cracking sound of a bullet as it exits Ladislav's weapon is quickly followed by two more deafening shots fired in Miles' direction, sending the detective to the floor. Ladislav exits the room in a roar of rage.

"Prasa!"

Ladislav yells, now directing his fury towards Languetti. Languetti swings his Beretta to his right, the light coming from the room presenting Ladislav as he stands there with a nickel-plated Colt held firmly in his left hand. Ladislav raises the Colt towards Languetti; two consecutive bullets exit Languetti's Beretta and penetrate Ladislav's chest, the close range sending the bullets at peak force out of Ladislav's back, his heart absorbing both pieces of the hot lead. Ladislav falls back against the wall, his weapon leaving his hand as he slides down, his face void of life as he comes to rest on the floor. Languetti shifts his attention to Miles; Miles lies still on the ground, Languetti reluctant to move forward, the gun smoke clouding his view. An anxious moment passes before Languetti breathes a sigh of relief as he witnesses Miles lifting his head off the floor, using his elbow to prop himself upright, turning to see Ladislav's bloodied body only a few feet away.

"I thought he shot you?" Languetti is somewhat surprised. Miles focuses on Ladislav's expressionless face.

"Yeah, so did I, Frank."

Miles picks himself up off the floor. He examines his jacket, his left arm causing him some discomfort as he moves towards the light.

"You're bleeding." Languetti points out.

Miles pokes his finger through the fabric of his suit, one of the bullets penetrating Miles' jacket and grazing his bicep. "Shit! This was a new fucking suit." Miles holsters his piece in frustration.

A frightful scream draws the men's attention. Dalenka, at the other end of the hallway, is standing there, witnessing Ladislav's blood smeared across the wall, his body lying lifeless on the floor.

"Prosím bože, nie."

Dalenka falls to her knees in disbelief, wrapping her arms around herself, sobbing uncontrollably as she grieves her lover's death. Languetti bows his head with regret, holstering his weapon as he addresses Miles.

"Keep an eye on her while I go make the call."

Miles expels his anxiety as he leans against the wall, his thoughts on his improbable fortune, grateful as he watches his partner unassumingly make his way back to the front of the house.

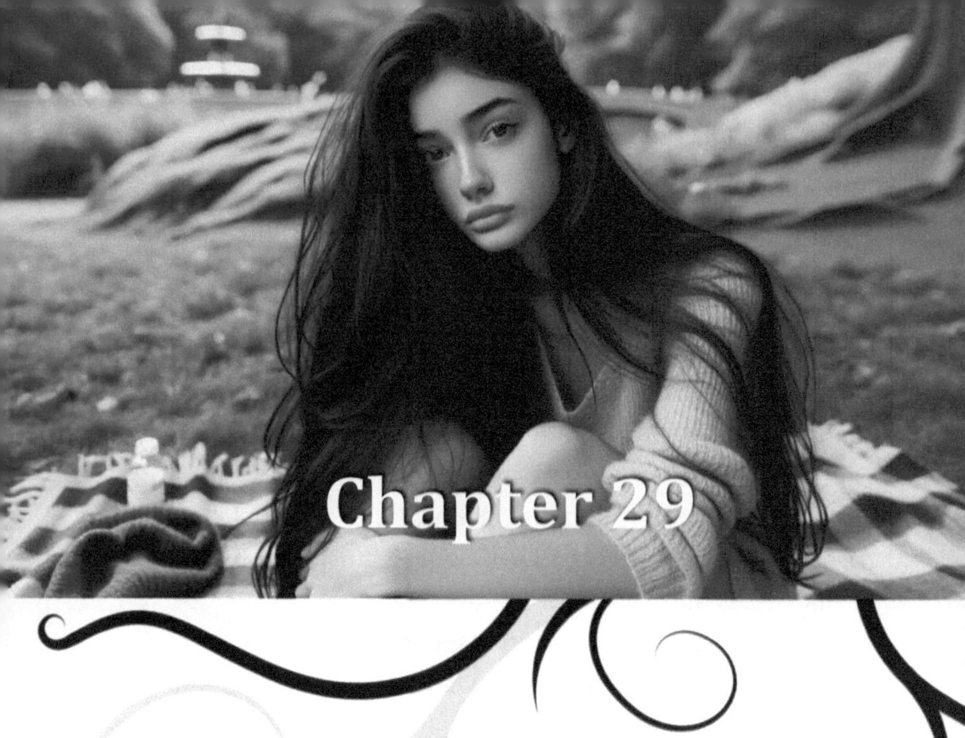

Chapter 29

Too few clouds have formed since the morning, and the sun is just overhead, blanketing Audrey and Clay with sunshine. Only scraps remain from the once neatly laid out banquet that Clay and Audrey shamelessly feasted on. Audrey is sprawled out, resting her head on the winter coat she has thoughtfully rolled to form a pillow.

"Oh my god, I can't believe we ate all that food, Clay," she moans, resting her hand on her stomach.

Clay sits upright; he, too, rubs his stomach, exhaling regrettably. "We sure ate a lot, Miss Audrey."

Clay notices Audrey's sunglasses resting on the hamper. He takes them into his possession, placing them on his face. The small frames outstretched over his cheeks, not quite reaching his ears. "Who do I look like, Miss Audrey?" he says smilingly.

Audrey looks over at Clay, raising her brow at the outstretched frames, too bloated to react. "You're going to break my Bre...uh Tiffany glasses, Clay," she says, unexpectedly burping. "Oops, excuse me!"

Clay chuckles at Audrey's emission.

"They don't fit your enormous melon."

Clay looks to the sky, swaying his head from side to side.

"You look like Ray Charles or is it Stevie Wonder?" Audrey is familiar with the impersonation.

Clay removes the sunglasses from his face, replacing them on top of the hamper. He looks up at the sky, squinting as he admires the beautiful weather.

"You like working for Charlie, don't you, Clay?"

Clay looks over at Audrey. "Charlie is a good boss."

Audrey turns onto her hip, placing her elbow onto the makeshift pillow as she confesses to Clay. "You both have been terrific friends to me. I don't think I can ever repay you for what you both have done for me these past couple of months."

Clay is humbled. "My mother always taught me to be nice to people. She said that some people are not nice, but I should always be nice, even if people are not nice to me."

Audrey thinks for a moment. "It's not easy to be nice to people who are not."

"No, Miss Audrey, it isn't easy. But my mother said that some people are just born like that, and sometimes people become less nice when terrible things happen to them."

Audrey rises off the pillow, sliding herself closer to Clay. She crosses her legs and faces him, looking him in the eyes. "I'm not sure if I agree, Clay. Terrible things can happen to anyone, like they did to me." Audrey pauses for a moment in thought. "And you."

Clay bows his head, feeling shameful for killing his father. Audrey reaches up, placing her hand underneath Clay's chin. Clay raises his head as Audrey removes her hand.

"You're one of the nicest people I have met, and you're that way because you choose to be."

Clay turns his head, looking out across the lake. "I did a terrible thing, Miss Audrey."

Audrey exhales with sympathy. "I know Clay."

Clay returns his attention to Audrey.

"Charlie told me," she admits in a soft voice. "But that's ok, Clay. You still chose to be a nice person, you didn't let that change who you are, and that's why I admire you."

Clay seems perplexed by Audrey's words. "It does not bother you that I committed murder?"

Audrey places her hand on Clay's knee, sharing a look of empathy. "No, it doesn't bother me, Clay. You were young, and you were protecting your mother. What bothers me is that you suffered in prison for almost twelve years. And I don't think that was fair."

Clay shrugs his shoulders, dismissing the severity of his punishment. "It was not that bad, Miss Audrey. At first, I was scared, but after some time, I got used to it."

As Audrey listens to Clay, she can't help but feel contempt for the justice system and why a judge decided that a sweet man like Clay, as she's come to know him, should lose twelve years of his life for protecting his mother.

"I made a friend in the library. His name was Caesar, and he was nice to me. I spent much of the time reading books, and he would teach me many things. We became good friends."

Audrey manages a smile.

"Is Caesar still in prison?"

"No. He passed on a short while back. He was old, and he got sick in prison."

"I'm sorry, Clay."

"He was a cheerful man. He was in prison for many years and liked being there."

Audrey huffs. "I've heard that before. I think it's called institutionalised. How could someone like being in prison, Clay? I'll never understand."

"He would often tell me that he liked that he always had somewhere to sleep and always had three meals a day. That was something that he couldn't always get on the outside."

Audrey leans back slightly. "I can't believe someone can feel like that, preferring prison to freedom."

Clay ponders for a moment. "I don't think he wanted to be in there. But he was in there for so long that I think he got used to it."

Audrey looks across the lake; the water is still. "I bet he would have liked to be here with you now."

Clay smiles at the thought. "Yes, I think Caesar would have liked that very much."

Audrey places her arms behind her, supporting herself as she leans back, looking up at the blue sky.

"Can I ask you something, Miss Audrey?"

Audrey tilts her head forward. "Sure, Clay, fire away."

"Do you regret not telling the policemen to arrest the man who hurt you?"

Audrey ponders for a moment. Her smile disappears. "I don't know, Clay." Audrey grabs her sunglasses. "Not really, no."

Clay fidgets with his shirt. "He shouldn't go unpunished for what he did to you," Clay uttered quietly, fearing he would upset Audrey with his revelation.

Audrey positions her glasses on top of her head.

"He won't, Clay," she says emphatically. Audrey's change in tone is audible.

"I didn't mean to..." Clay feels regret, wishing he hadn't voiced his thoughts.

"That's alright, Clay; I'm not upset with you. It's just that those fucken detectives made me feel like I was obligated to do something." Audrey's frustration is evident. "I hated feeling like that." Audrey sighs, placing her head in her hands, stroking her hair back with both hands, her glasses falling onto the blanket.

It was the first time Clay heard Audrey cuss; her emotions becoming heightened as she continued.

"Everybody is such a goddamn expert. The two detectives, Veronica! when she visited me in the hospital, even Charlie hinted at it the other day because he wanted me to feel safe when I return to work.

Clay clutches onto his shirt.

"No one has any idea what it was like, Clay; to be in a position where you're completely helpless; to have someone, someone with no fucken reason, break your hands and face."

Audrey snatches her glasses from the blanket; she takes a long, deep breath. Clay suddenly realises that her trauma is acute and is still very much with Audrey. It may never leave her, Clay wonders. Audrey takes a moment before looking directly at Clay. Clay sees her distress, sensing she has something more to say.

"Clay, there's something I haven't told you. Something not even Charlie knows."

Clay's assumptions are on point. He gives Audrey his full attention.

"William came to the hospital."

The revelation throws Clay back.

"He came that first week I was there, after Charlie left, after it got dark. He came up to me, real close and whispered in my ear." Audrey takes a breath. "He said if I talk, he would kill me."

Clay tries to process the information Audrey has told him. She waits patiently to see what Clay will say.

"Why didn't you say anything? If he threatened you like that, you should have said something to…"

Audrey looks away; an extended silence passes. Clay feels remorseful. He tries to make things right, offer her some comfort.

"Maybe he was only trying to scare you, Audrey. You know. Intimidate you so you don't have him arrested. In prison, inmates would say the same thing to other inmates all the time. They were acting tough. None of them really meant..."

"William killed his girlfriend," Audrey reveals, turning to look at Clay.

An eerie silence surrounds them both. Audrey looks across the lake as she recounts what Gloria had told her that day.

"Gloria told me, Amy, who had been dating William about five years ago, was found dead in her apartment by her mother. Her mother informed the police that William had been assaulting her and that she had bruises on her body in the past. Once, she had a black eye, her mother told the police, and her daughter was dismissive about her injuries, saying it was an accident, she was hit in the face with a tennis ball, Amy would say. Her mother knew she was lying and told her she needed to leave him. She remembers her daughter telling her two nights before she was found dead that she was going to break up with William and that she was sorry for lying to her mother. Her mother relayed all of this to the police, so they investigated. But they never charged him with murder. They never even arrested him. They stated that the presence of his fingerprints in her apartment meant nothing because they were dating and that the prior injuries had never been reported to the police. There was no documented history of violence. The lack of motive was also an issue. William saw to it that his lawyer friends twisted everything around, ensuring that he was never charged with her murder. They cited a string of break-ins and assaults in the neighbourhood as the likely cause of death."

Audrey looks directly at Clay. "He killed that girl and got away with it, and no one did anything. So that night, in the hospital, when he told me that he would kill me, I believed him, Clay."

Clay's eyes welled up, feeling Audrey's pain—guilt for misjudging the situation.

"I'm not strong like you, Clay." She forces a smile.

"I can't fight off..." Audrey shakes her head. "I'm tiny compared to most men."

"No one blames you, Audrey."

Audrey gives him a tired look. "I was afraid, Clay. I am still afraid to tell you the truth."

Clay moves alongside Audrey, placing his arm around her. "It's alright to be afraid; I get scared too. Especially of the dark."

Audrey laughingly clutches onto Clay. "You're such a goof."

"I won't let anything happen to you; I promise."

Audrey rests her head on Clay's chest, taking another deep breath, liberating herself from her ill feelings. "I might have to start paying you a protection fee, Clay."

Clay continues to cradle Audrey. "You can pay me with chocolate cake."

"I will," Audrey whispers as she closes her eyes, unexpectedly dozing off to sleep.

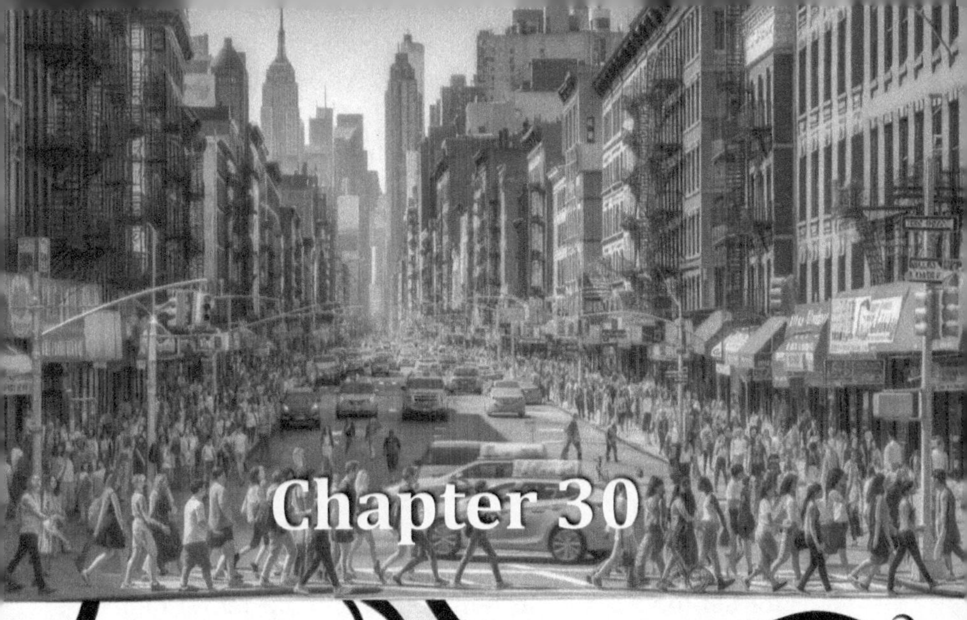

Chapter 30

Veronica places her hand on her head, feeling a headache coming on from the constant sounds of the hustle and bustle of the New York City traffic.

"Oh, God. Why does everyone have to always honk their bloody horns?"

It's just after noon on the following Wednesday, and Veronica, who's on foot, dodges the city's traffic as she heads for a Deli in the downtown city area near her place of work. A cab driver comes to a screeching halt, honking his horn at Veronica as she scurries in its path.

"All right, all right, I see ya," Veronica shrieks as she hurdles onto the sidewalk.

Wearing a taupe Gucci suit with matching stilettos and a piggy pink purse tucked under her arm, Veronica strides down the sidewalk, occasionally reaching up to lower her fashionable eyewear, peering at any handsome stranger who catches her eye. Veronica removes her sunglasses and nibbles the temple tip as she arrives at the street Deli. She begins to peruse the delectable options in the window, ultimately deciding on her choice of cuisine before approaching the Deli counter.

"What would you like, Miss?" A pleasant woman with a heavy Jewish accent inquires as Veronica steps forward.

"Hey, can I have roast beef with salad on a wholegrain roll and mustard, please?"

"Butter love?" The woman asks, holding the wholegrain roll in her hand.

"Yes, please, with salt and pepper, thanks."

"Sure, love."

The woman begins to assemble Veronica's order. As Veronica waits for her food, she turns her attention to the clutter of people filling the busy streets of the downtown area. She becomes somewhat amused as she spots a middle-aged man wearing a white suit jacket over a fluorescent pink T-shirt.

"Step out of the eighties, for crying out loud." Veronica huffs.

As she continues to manoeuvre her eyes from person to person, her attention is caught unexpectedly. Across the street, a man stands outside an office building, talking on his cell.

"That son of a bitch," Veronica whispers, now focusing with intent on the singular man.

"Here you go, love." The pleasant woman distracts Veronica as she thumps the sandwich on the counter.

"Anything to drink, love?"

"Um, yeah, an orange juice, please," Veronica replies in a distracted stutter, reaching into her purse for her wallet, her eyes partly on the man with the cell.

"That's six-fifty all up, love."

Veronica places the exact change on the counter, snatching her order in both hands before scooting off to the street crossing, still eyeing the man as she evades the chaos in her way.

"Come on, come on," Veronica mutters, squeezing her sandwich and beverage into her purse as she impatiently waits for the pedestrian signal to turn green. WALK: The sign illuminates. Veronica hurries inconspicuously across the street, still peering at the man with the cell. Skipping onto the sidewalk, Veronica slows to an amble as she approaches the man with his back turned. Veronica stops as she draws closer to him, tilting her head to the side, getting a glimpse of his profile before taking a few more steps. Now standing directly behind him, Veronica waits, listening to the man converse momentarily before distracting him from his conversation.

"So, it's business as usual?" Veronica remarks loudly and sternly, pulling the man out of his conversation.

The man turns his head, looking directly at Veronica, still holding the cell to his ear.

"I'll call you back, " the man says as he casually removes the phone from his ear and puts it in his coat pocket. "Well, I guess it was only a matter of time before we ran into each other, V."

William grins with a hint of contempt, sliding his hands into his trouser pockets. Veronica quickly feels infuriated by William's casual demeanour.

"I guess so, you sleazy prick," Veronica adds irately.

William lets out a laugh. "You were always the feisty one, V."

Veronica shakes her head. "I can't fucken believe you. You don't even give a shit for what you did to Audrey."

William acts coy, shrugging as he responds to the accusation. "I don't know what you're talking about; I haven't done anything."

Veronica clenches her jaw in frustration. "Deny it all you want, you fucken psycho. You're not going to get away with what you did."

William turns his head, acting aloof as Veronica's remarks begin to draw the attention of passers-by. Stung by Veronica's threat, William leans in closer to Veronica. "I already have, V." his voice is low and heavy. "And if you try to stir up any trouble, you will find out first-hand what your friend feels like right now."

Veronica squints her eyes at William. She is barely keeping her emotions under control. "I'm not afraid of you; you piss weak shit."

Annoyed by Veronica's taunts, William leans back, adjusting his coat and tie. He pretends to smile at a woman passing by, whose attention is taken by Veronica's high-pitched tone. "Lower your voice, V, I mean it."

Veronica lets out a loud yawp. "Fuck you, you cunt!"

William glares at Veronica; he tenses up. Noticing more onlookers, he puts on an embarrassed smile, lumbering towards the entrance of the building. A fired-up Veronica hollers one more insult towards William as he walks away.

"Asshole!"

William ignores her, scampering up the steps and through the revolving doors. Veronica holds her ground, her chest beating rapidly from a sudden adrenaline rush. She inhales, emitting a long breath to regain her composure, onlookers taking one last gawk before continuing their daily business. Veronica looks ahead, her attention drawn by the gleam of a black BMW, the vehicle turning into an adjacent driveway that leads to the underground car park of the building. Veronica grimaces as incoherent thoughts race through her mind, her attention slinging back to the revolving doors, peering through the transparent glass of the entranceway to catch one last glimpse of William as he enters the lobby elevator. A curious smile sweeps over Veronica's face as she hurries across the pedestrian walkway, turning cautiously down the drive that leads into the building's car park. She eyes the rear of the beamer as it pulls into the car park; the large roller shutter is now beginning to unravel. As it nears a close, she ducks underneath, the clacking sound of Veronica's heels echoing as she enters the void of the car park. One last squeak resonates through the carbon air as the roller shutter meets the pavement. Veronica watches closely as the black BMW parks a fair distance from her. She waits patiently behind a pylon; a man in a grey suit exits the vehicle and walks towards the lift, reaching back as he walks away, arming the car's alarm. Veronica looks over at the roller shutter, curious when the next car may arrive, turning her attention back to the elevator as it chimes. The doors separate; the grey-suited man enters before the doors close, capturing him inside. Veronica takes a calming breath, still flustered by her outburst at William on the sidewalk. She straightens her dress and walks down amongst the vehicles, looking both left and right, taking a moment to admire a classic red 1961 Ferrari 250 GTS California, just like the one in the movie, Ferris Bueller's Day Off.

"Sweet ride."

A smile forms as she remembers one rainy night, Audrey and she spent together curled up on the lounge with popcorn and chocolate, watching that very same movie.

"Save Ferris."

Veronica's smile almost turns to laughter, recollecting when they both jumped up on the lounge and sang, *Twist and Shout* along with the actor Matthew Broderick as his character Ferris joined the German American Appreciation Day Parade. Veronica's eyes sweep across the array of costly vehicles, her attention ultimately drawn to a single car parked on the far side of the lot, tucked against the wall, almost hidden in the shadows of the pylons. She walks towards the vehicle, the object becoming more apparent as she gets closer and closer. As she walks beyond the pylon, a silver C Class Mercedes is now in full view. Veronica gazes at the car momentarily, lowering her eyes to the vehicle's plate. The car's number plate, which reads WB-717, forces a smile on Veronica's face as she whispers the words. "Found-ya, you prick."

Veronica reaches into her purse, cautiously looking over her shoulder, ensuring she is alone as she scuffles through the items. The scuffle ceases. "Got it." She removes her hand, revealing a metal nail file, glimmering as it catches the light. Once again, Veronica looks over her shoulder; the dead silence of the car park is eerie, inducing paranoia. She takes a calming breath and glares at the flawless hood of the Mercedes C Class as it gleams from the fluorescents nearby. Her eyes again capture the initials on the number plate, causing an unexpected thought to reveal itself, two distinct words forming in her mind. An evil smile appears as she grasps the nail file tightly in her right hand. She takes two steps towards the car and leans forward, placing her left hand on the hood of the vehicle for support.

Suddenly, Veronica grabs her breath; the hairs at the back of her neck stand up as the thought of any pressure applied to the hood may set off an alarm. She hesitates for a moment. Still, there is silence; Veronica lets out a sigh of relief. She looks over her shoulder again, making one last sweep of the car park with her eyes. Reaching forward with her right hand, Veronica places the tip of the file on the hood. She begins to score deep and hard, the screeching sound of the metal resonating through the car park as she tears through the layers of paint. Random thoughts of Audrey and a cocky William fuel her determination. There is visible anger as she moves the file back and forth. Finally, she loosens her grip, completing the last of her vengeful strokes.

Placing her hand on her brow, she props herself upright, her heart pounding from adrenaline. Still holding the file firmly in her hand, Veronica looks down at the hood for a moment; she settles her breathing, looks over her shoulder, and scans the empty car park—nothing but silence. She returns the file to her purse, then uses her perspired hands to brush her hair back, emitting a contented sigh before promptly exiting the car park.

Chapter 31

Two hours have passed, and William exits a conference room on the 12th floor of the same building. He heads for the elevator, his thoughts returning to Veronica, reeling with resentment for her outburst in the street earlier that day. As the elevator doors open, William steps inside, slapping the button to take him down to the car park level of the building. He looks at his watch momentarily before loosening his tie, catching his reflection in the mirrored walls of the elevator. The lift comes to an easing halt on level five, the doors opening to reveal a young, attractive blonde-haired woman dressed in a smart business suit. She looks up at William and smiles before entering.

"What floor, Miss?" William quickly responds to her needs as the woman turns. His hand hovers over the panel of push buttons.

"Oh, I'm going to the car park as well." The woman replies, brushing her hair to reveal her ear to William. William sharply notices her opal earrings and compliments her.

"They look terrific." William gestures to the woman's earrings.

"Oh, thank you." The woman exposing her pearly whites. "They were a gift from my aunt," she adds, quickly feeling at ease with William's charm.

The elevator stops as it reaches the car park level; the doors open, and the stale air is evident to both. William extends his arm.

"After you."

The young woman again smiles as she exits the lift and is casual as she walks towards her vehicle. William notices her intent and makes a final attempt to seize the opportunity.

"Do you like the opera?" His voice echoes across the car park, the young woman turning, pretending she misheard.

"I'm sorry?"

"The opera. There is a show tomorrow night at the Metropolitan Opera House." William is confident as he approaches the woman.

"I've never been." She says, embarrassingly.

William smiles. "Well, I'd like to take you. Tomorrow night?"

The woman looks directly into William's eyes, admiring his confidence. "Sure, I'd love to go."

William extends his hand to the young woman. "My name is William."

"Jocelyn. People call me Jocey."

She slides her hand onto William's palm; William catches the aroma of her perfume as she leans in. "Pleasure to meet you, Jocelyn."

They converse momentarily, exchanging details before William walks her to her car. Jocelyn winds the window down, one last look at William.

"I'll see you tomorrow then."

William smiles. "Looking forward to it."

William takes a few steps back, giving her room as she manoeuvres the car towards the exit. Jocelyn looks up at her rear-view mirror to see William wave at her one final time. William holds his ground momentarily before casually walking towards his vehicle. He reaches into his pocket, presenting a grandiose smile as he retrieves his diamond-cut Mercedes-Benz key. He jingles the key ring in his hand, tilting his head and smiling as he visualises Jocelyn naked. William presents a beaming smile as he approaches the luxury car, looking ahead as he nears the vehicle's fender. His smile vanishes instantly; his face is dismayed at first as he begins to focus intently on the car's hood. His mood changes abruptly, and his thoughts turn to Veronica as he clenches the keys tightly in his hand. He looks over his shoulder at the empty car park, his emotions turning to rage as he again looks upon the hood of his Mercedes. Finally, he lets out a verbal roar, sounding the words. "You fucken- bitch!"

His voice echoes through the car park. He hunches over, placing both hands on the hood of the car, clenching his jaw as he tries to keep his composure. The once gleaming hood is now flawed with Veronica carving two distinct words: Veronica making clever use of William's initials as denoted on the car's number plate. William continues to fume, his blood simmering to a boil. He looks upon the hood of his precious car to see the words, scribed jagged and deep into the once flawless paintwork.

Chapter 32

Just after six that same evening, a weary Veronica enters her apartment, wrestling with two shopping bags chock-full of groceries. Using her rear to close the door behind her, she makes her way to the kitchen, groaning as she places the plentiful bags on the counter. Veronica enters the bedroom, removing her jacket before flinging it onto the bed on her way to the ensuite. She stands over the sink as she turns on the faucet, running her fingers underneath the water until she achieves the desired temperature. Cupping her hands, she fills them with water, leaning over as she splashes several scoops of the warm liquid on her face.

Feels so good, she thinks to herself. She takes hold of the smaller towel on a rack adjacent to the sink, wrapping her face and patting it several times until all the moisture is absorbed into the cotton fibres. She tosses the towel carelessly onto the vanity and proceeds back into the bedroom, reaching down and removing her stilettos, one at a time. She inserts her tired feet into her bunny slippers before casually walking back towards the kitchen. On her way, Veronica raises her hands over her head, grabbing her elbows as she stretches her torso.

"Time to get me some chow," she announces with an exaggerated yawn, reaching for the cordless phone that hangs on the wall above the kitchen counter. She pivots around to face the refrigerator, pausing to browse the multiple food menus scattered all over the freezer door, aptly secured with an assortment of colourful fridge magnets. She makes her selection. Yanking it from the door, she begins to dial the number to the restaurant as she walks over to the lounge area, falling carelessly into her luscious sofa.

"So hungry right now," she whispers, emitting another tired breath. Several rings pass before a male voice with a heavy Asian accent answers the phone.

"Foo Tong takeaway."

"Hey, Foo Tong, I'd like to place an order, please."

Veronica rubs her stomach, visualising the food of the cuisines she has previously ordered.

"Whut, you like, Miss?"

Veronica runs her index finger down the menu. "Can I please have the No. 12, basil stir fry with chicken?"

"Yes, one basil stir fry, chicken." The Asian man concurs.

"And two large spring rolls," Veronica adds.

"Two *spling rows*, yes…any *flied* rice?" The Asian man inquires.

"Just a small, steamed rice, please."

Veronica throws her head back and exhaustively waits for the man to confirm the order.

"Steamed rice for one, pick up or *derivery*?"

Veronica smirks as she responds in like. "*Derivery*, please."

Veronica gazes patiently at the ceiling as she listens to the faint sound of computer keys being punched through the receiver. Regular customers are located in the restaurant's database, which is retrieved by the caller's number.

"Okay, Apartment 87, 255 East side, yes?"

"Yep, that's correct, Foo." Veronica taps her bunny toes together.

"Ok, about a twenty-*fahv* minute."

"Sweet, see ya."

Veronica hangs up the phone and turns her attention to the grocery bags on the kitchen counter, sighing as she picks herself up from the sofa, dragging her tired limbs to unpack all the items she bought on her way home from work. As she's about to place the handset on the kitchen bench, she smirks in thought, deciding to call Audrey. Veronica presses speed dial three on the handset as she removes the items one at a time from the grocery bags, anticipating Audrey to answer.

"Hello?"

Audrey's voice sends a smile to Veronica's face.

"Hey, sexy, how are you?" Veronica responds in a deep, seductive tone, almost fooling Audrey.

"Hey, V." Audrey excitedly laughs. "What is new with you?"

Veronica fumbles inside the grocery bags as she responds. "Nothing much, same old crap. How are you doing?"

"I'm terrific. Started back at work this week."

"Oh, yeah, that's right. Wow, that's awesome." Veronica is delighted to see Audrey resume some normalcy in her life. "How are the hands?"

Audrey looks down at her hand, making a fist. "They still feel a little sore, but the doc says it's because the muscles haven't strengthened yet. He reckons it will take a few more weeks to regain my strength. All that pruning I do at work helps a lot."

Veronica opens the pantry and places selected items on the shelves as she listens. Audrey hears the obscure sounds in the background.

"What are you up to? I can hear strange noises."

Veronica laughs at the thought. "I'm putting my groceries away." Veronica groans as she stretches to reach the top shelf of the pantry with her free hand. Audrey's eyes widen as she hears the groan.

"Groceries, aye? Doesn't sound like it. Are you alone?"

Veronica smirks. "Yes, unfortunately, I'm all alone."

"Well, that's a first," Audrey remarks with tongue in cheek.

"Hey, what's that supposed to mean?"

They both laugh, conversing for several minutes about life, work, and sexual relationships or lack thereof; Audrey makes more fun of Veronica's adventurous love life. Audrey laughs out loud, Veronica reluctant to join her as she takes a jar of Italian sauce in her hand. Her thoughts shift as she looks at the label, which has an old lady with a wooden spoon standing over a pot. Veronica places both elbows onto the counter for support, contemplating her following words to Audrey as she examines the jar.

"Hey, guess what happened today?" Veronica tilts the jar in her hand back and forth.

"What?"

"I ran into somebody."

"What, with your car?!" Audrey is surprised, misinterpreting Veronica's vague statement. Veronica snickers.

"No…silly. On the street, in town, while I was getting lunch."

"Oh." Audrey huffs as she laughs. "Who?"

Veronica continues to study the jar in her hand; a moment of silence passes, and she is unsure if she should share her thoughts with Audrey. Audrey waits patiently for a response. "I ran into William." Veronica finally reveals.

Audrey remains silent, unsure of her response. The prolonged silence makes Veronica anxious.

"Hey, are you okay?"

Audrey dismisses Veronica's concern; she responds with a question. "What did he say to you?"

"Nothing." Veronica pulls herself from the counter and places the jar into the pantry. "I did most of the talking."

Audrey becomes uneasy; Veronica continues.

"I really let him have it. I called him all sorts of names right there in the middle of the city, in front of all these people walking by. It was fucken embarrassing, actually." Veronica chuckles.

Audrey smiles ever so slightly, picturing Veronica barking abusive taunts at William.

"You should have seen it, Audrey; I really gave it to him."

Audrey smiles at the thought. "He must have been really pissed."

Veronica's thoughts shift to William's Merc. "Not as pissed as he would have been returning to his car." Veronica carelessly reveals in a lowered voice. She leans against the counter, regretfully hoping Audrey misheard.

Audrey clearly heard Veronica's statement. "Wait, What! What did you mean by that, V?"

Veronica runs her fingers through her hair. "Oh...nothing." Veronica decides to retract the confession.

"V, what did you do?"

Veronica continues to backpedal. "Nothing, I'm just teasing, silly." Veronica diverts the conversation, remembering the Ferrari she encountered in the car park. "Hey, I have a great idea?" Veronica says excitedly.

"What?" Audrey is wary of Veronica's sudden change in subject.

"How about I come round Friday night, and we can have a movie night, just the two of us?"

"Yeah, I guess so." Audrey feels confused with Veronica's spontaneous suggestion, her thoughts partially on Veronica's previous statement.

"We can watch Ferris Bueller's Day Off."

"Ferris Bueller's Day Off?"

"Yeah, you remember when we watched it that night? Dancing like crazy bitches on your sofa?"

Audrey remains perplexed. She decides to shake off her incoherent thoughts and display her approval of Veronica's proposal. "Yeah… Sounds great!"

Veronica's intercom sounds. "Ah…yes! Foo Tong is here."

Veronica celebrates the arrival of her food with a fist pump.

"Who?"

"Foo Tong takeaway, I ordered Chinese before I called you."

"Oh…yum."

"Hold on a second, babe." Veronica makes her way over to the intercom. She leans across the counter, stretching herself to press down on the button. "Hello?" She groans.

"Foo Tong delivery." A male voice sounds.

"Cool, I'll buzz you in…just come straight up." Veronica presses the key button releasing the lock to the entrance door of the building. She raises the handset to her ear once again. "Hey, babe, my Chinese has arrived. So, I gotta go."

"What did you order?" Audrey inquires.

"Chinese food, silly."

Audrey rolls her eyes. "You're making me hungry," Audrey says, envious of the cuisine.

"Why don't you order something?" Veronica suggests. "There are heaps of takeaway joints near your place."

"I can't; I'm so broke…I've been eating baloney sandwiches for the past week."

"Oh…hun." Veronica begins to feel guilty, remembering how the ordeal cost Audrey most of her savings.

"We'll have a feast Friday night…on me, okay?"

"Can we have pizza?" Audrey requests.

"Anything you like, hun."

Audrey tries to take advantage of Veronica's sudden generosity. "What about lobster?"

"Lobster! Are you kidding me? I don't even eat lobster."

Veronica can hear the sound of Audrey's laughter; she pulls the handset from her ear, distracted by several definitive knocks on her front door.

"The guy's here, babe...I gotta go. I'll see you tomorrow night, okay?"

"Can't wait." Audrey was already wishing it were Friday.

"Luv ya, babe." Veronica places the handset on the counter, snatching her purse. "I'm coming," she yells, scurrying down the hallway, scuffling through her purse for money with her free hand as she reaches forward, pulling the door open. Her head is buried in her purse as she manages to locate a couple of twenties, finally looking up, yearning as she greets the deliveryman.

Her eyes widen in horror as she takes in a breath, unable to scream, her mouth swiftly covered by the force of William's palm. She reaches up, letting go of her purse as she attempts to struggle free. William shifts his weight forward, pinning her against the wall with brute force. William quickly reaches back, pushing the door shut with his free hand. Veronica latches onto his arm with both hands, trying in vain to free herself from his clutches. William throws his arm around her, twisting her round, pulling her towards him; her feet leaving the ground as he squeezes her back, tight against his chest. Veronica feels her anguish, her legs kicking freely through the air as William carries her down the hallway, entering the open area of the living room. She begins to feel intense pain in her jaw as William presses his hand firmly over her mouth, her nasal passages fighting to keep oxygen flowing in her lungs. William leans forward, Veronica's toes barely finding the carpet as he removes his arm from her torso. He reaches up, placing his palm on the back of her head; her eyes well up as he clenches his hand, taking hold of Veronica's hair. Without hesitation, William forces her head downwards, Veronica catching a glimpse of her reflection in the smoked glass as William brutally slams her head onto the tempered surface of the coffee table. The sharp sound of the glass fracturing sounds out; Veronica falls to the ground as William releases her from his grasp. Barely conscious, Veronica struggles to regain her composure. She places her hand on the side of her face, feeling the warmth of her blood that begins to spill down, her fingers sensing the gash amongst her sodden hair. William strides towards the balcony, sliding the door open with purpose, inhaling the cool air as it engulfs the room. He looks at Veronica, who has struggled to her knees; her hands shaking with fear and the blood flowing down her face. William casually walks towards her, a stone look on his face, as Veronica places her hands on the table, attempting valiantly to rise to her feet. William takes hold of her arm, seemingly helping her to her feet. She turns to face him, her heart racing as she reluctantly looks into William's eyes, his face expressionless as he stares back in silence. Suddenly, he jerks Veronica completely around, covering her mouth again, only now noticing the leather from his gloves pressing up against her skin. She again struggles to free herself fruitlessly as William picks her up and carries her towards the balcony. Veronica feels the cold air on her face as William steps onto the platform; her eyes widen in horror at the thought of what William may do next. She lets out a muffled scream, reaching out in vain to grasp onto the door. William walks towards the rail, lunging forward as he hoists Veronica into the air, releasing her body into the night sky. She lets out a frightful scream, the sound fading as her frantic torso passes each floor and, ultimately, she plummets to her death.

Chapter 33

Quiet tonight, Detective?" Flo places a cup of black coffee onto the table, sliding it towards Languetti. Frank inhales the aroma, savouring his beverage as he reaches across the table for the sugar.

"Yeah," he says, surprisingly, rattling the sugar packet in his hand, appreciating the rare moments of peace he seldom gets in his line of work.

Flo places a second cup of coffee on the table, reaching back to her serving tray for a piece of steaming hot Pecan pie; Miles makes noticeable, yummy noises as Flo places the plate on the table. "Here you go, hun," she winks at Miles as she leaves the men to dine.

"No pie tonight, Frank?"

Languetti stirs the sugar he added to his beverage. "I'm not hungry right now."

Miles looks suspiciously at Frank as he adds some cream to his beverage. He raises the cup to his lips. "Are you certain, Frank?" Miles takes a sip of his coffee.

Languetti nods his head with confidence. "One hundred per cent certain."

Miles glares at Languetti momentarily before leaning forward, sliding the plate over to his side of the table. Languetti looks up at Miles.

"What's this for?"

Miles leans back into his chair. "You earned it, Frank; I figure saving my life is worth at least one piece of Pecan pie."

Languetti takes a moment before responding. "The situation was what it was, Miles; we both did what we had to do. You don't owe me anything. We're partners; it comes with the territory." Languetti takes a sip of his coffee. "You would've done the same."

"Yeah, I know, but...I just wanted you to know I'm grateful for what you did."

Languetti acknowledges the gesture, collecting the fork off the plate. "Well, in that case." Languetti eyes the dessert. "Pie smells good." He slides the plate partway across the table. "Help me eat this, will ya? I'm trying to watch my weight."

Miles concedes with a smile. He leans forward and picks up his spoon, slicing off a piece from the nutty dessert and cradling it towards his mouth. "Hey Frank, I was thinking of going to Seneca Lake to do some fishing next weekend." Miles places the spoon into his mouth, wiping it clean as he removes it.

Languetti looks at Miles with a frowning smile. "I didn't know you knew how to fish. Did they teach you at Harvard?"

Miles dismisses Frank's humour with a ridiculous look. "I went to NYU, Frank. You wanna go with me or what? Get out of the city for a few days."

Languetti picks up his beverage, positioning it just below his bottom lip. "It's like a five-hour drive." Languetti points out as he slurps his coffee.

"Yeah, I know, so what. We can take turns driving. A quick vacation, get some R and R before the real cold weather hits."

Languetti uses the edge of his fork to slice off another helping of the Pecan pie. "Getting out of the city for a few days sounds like a good idea." Languetti places the pie into his mouth. He savours the taste, putting the fork on the table as the melody of his cell begins to sound. He reaches into his coat pocket, lifting the phone to his ear. "Languetti." Frank immediately recognises the voice on the other end.

"Hey Frank, it's Steph."

Frank instinctively looks at his watch, noting the time is six minutes past nine. "Hey, what's up?"

Miles looks on curiously, digging his spoon into the pie.

"Gremmer just handed me a report to type up, a homicide he was called to a couple of hours ago on the east side of town. The victim was a female in her late twenties."

Languetti listens intently as Stephanie continues.

"Report says she was identified as one, Veronica Park."

Languetti leans back. Instinctive thoughts rush through his mind.

"I remembered that name from the case you and Miles were on a few months back. A close friend of the victim? Anyway, I cross-checked the name to be sure. It's the same girl, Frank."

Miles' attention becomes more acute as concern sweeps over Languetti.

"Hey Frank, Gremmer said to give the case to you. He left the keys to the victim's apartment and the file with me."

"Don't leave; we're coming down." Languetti pulls the phone from his ear, promptly rising to his feet. "We gotta go."

With a mouth full of Pecan pie, Miles springs up on Frank's command. "Frank, where the hell are we going?"

"That dipshit lawyer, William, just made a big mess," Languetti yells over his shoulder as he continues out the door.

"Fuck me." Miles removes some money from his wallet and throws it onto the table, taking one last swig of coffee before darting to catch up to Languetti.

Languetti and Miles rush down to the Precinct, where they meet up with Stephanie, who hands Veronica's case file and the keys to her apartment to the detectives. Without hesitation, Languetti and Miles head to Veronica's apartment to investigate the crime scene, both considering if Veronica's death is linked to Audrey's assault in any way. As Languetti weaves through the traffic, Miles begins to recite Det. Gremmer's hand-written notes from his initial investigation earlier that evening.

"It says here she was found in the street," Miles reports, carefully dissecting Gremmer's notes. Languetti seeks clarification.

"He killed her in the street?"

Miles shakes his head.

"Nope, she fell from her balcony; eight floors, Frank."

"Was she shot...stabbed?" Languetti probes, turning sharply into a corner.

"The report says she died on impact. Gremmer wrote that she was likely pushed." Miles runs his finger across the report. "The report also states they found blood on the carpet, and the glass on the coffee table was cracked with traces of blood."

"So, he cracked her head onto the table and threw her over the balcony." Frank summates.

"We don't know that, Frank. We don't even know if anyone else was in her apartment. Maybe she just tripped?" Miles looks across at Languetti.

"Tripped. And fell over her balcony?" Frank glares.

"It's possible," Miles smirks.

"Someone was there, Miles. And you know who it was."

Miles studies the report. "No forced entry, Frank."

Languetti makes a sharp right. "That doesn't mean shit; he could have followed her home and forced her to let him upstairs."

"Why, Frank? Why not kill her downstairs?" Miles argues. "And if it was him, what's the motive?"

Languetti eases onto the brake as he rounds another corner. "I don't know. But something went down, I'm sure of it. That snake made his way into her apartment."

"I don't buy it. Why would she let this prick in her apartment, Frank? It could be just a freak coincidence that she was murdered. It may have nothing to do with the previous case."

"You don't believe that for one second, Miles. You know she was murdered, and you'd bet your badge it was that cunt, William."

In frustration, Languetti snatches the case file from Miles' hand and throws it on the dashboard. "Fuck what the file says. I'll do my own investigation."

Miles locks his fingers behind his head, pulling on his neck to ease his tension. "Fine, Frank, we'll investigate the crime scene ourselves."

As Languetti nears Veronica's building, he slows the cruiser, peering out through the windscreen at the police tape surrounding the pavement. A team of forensic officers are still at the scene collecting evidence as Languetti pulls up at the curb. Languetti hops out of the car; a cold mist surrounds the building; Miles takes the case file in his possession before joining Languetti on the sidewalk. Languetti takes a moment to look up at the high-rise before directing his attention towards the forensic officers.

"Hey, Frank?" One of the officers greets Languetti as he approaches. He questions Frank's presence. "Gremmer and his partner were here already. You know that, right?"

"It's our case now, fellas," Miles explains.

"What have you got?" Languetti places his hands on his hips.

"Oh, right." The befuddled forensic officer gestures to the ground. "The victim fell from the eighth floor. The point of impact was right here. Medic says it was most likely the main cause of death. We won't know for sure till the autopsy. You know how it goes. We're pretty much done here ourselves, just cleaning up the mess."

Languetti nods. "You finished upstairs?"

"Yeah, we're all done, Frank."

"I want that report on my desk a.s.a.p."

Languetti walks across the lawn towards the entrance; Miles takes one last look at the blood-soaked pavement before joining his partner.

Upstairs, Languetti approaches the door to the apartment. He pulls out a pair of latex gloves from the front pocket of his coat. Miles does the same as Frank sorts through the keychain. Locating the correct key, Languetti inserts it into the cylinder, easing the door open with his hand. He takes a small flashlight from his belt, checking the locking mechanism on the door jamb for any visible signs of damage before crouching down, avoiding the police tape as he enters the apartment. Miles also examines the entrance before crouching underneath the tape, following his partner inside. Languetti gradually moves down the dim-lit hallway, moving his eyes about, looking for any signs of a struggle. Languetti reaches the end of the passageway that leads to the apartment's main living area, stopping to take in an overall view of the room. His eyes focus on the bloodstains, the soiled carpet peppered with yellow markers by forensics that lead towards the far end of the room. Frank takes another step, shifting his vision to the glass of the coffee table, Miles joining him by his side, also peering at the cracked surface before shifting his eyes to the glass door that leads out onto the balcony. Languetti remains stoic, taking a moment to examine the crime scene, shifting his attention towards the kitchen, and taking note of the two bags of groceries on the kitchen counter. Miles watches Languetti walk towards the kitchen, sweeping his eyes over the area before turning to Miles.

"What items did Gremmer bag for forensics?"

Miles opens the file, taking a moment to locate the items Gremmer sequestered for prints or use as evidence in this crime. "Victim's purse." Miles rubs the back of his neck. "Some food items found on the kitchen counter and her cordless phone."

"That's it? Anything else?"

"That's everything, Frank. Just the general sweep for prints, blood, and fibres that forensics collected for analysis."

Languetti again considers the crime scene as he moves his eyes around the room; deep in thought of what might have led to Veronica's death. "Where was the purse found?"

"It was on the sofa." Miles makes his way towards the balcony. "We can check out the crime scene photos at the precinct, Frank."

Languetti takes several steps, positioning himself in the middle of the room. His eyes fall on the coffee table, tracing a bloodline of drops towards the balcony before addressing Miles.

"What do you think?"

Miles looks across at Languetti. "Assuming she didn't accidentally trip and crack her head onto the table, stagger out to the balcony for fresh air and then accidentally slip and fall over the rail to her death." Miles concedes. "Yeah, I'd say she was murdered, Frank." Miles walks to the centre of the room.

"It's a secure building, right? So, we have to assume she let her attacker inside. No forced entry. They argue, she's pushed, cracking her head onto the glass table. And then she is dragged out there and thrown over the rail."

Languetti is unable to come to terms with Veronica letting William into her apartment.

"Why would she let him inside?" He voices his thoughts.

"Maybe it wasn't him, Frank. Maybe it was some other guy she picked up. Could just be a coincidence."

Languetti shakes his head, trusting his gut instincts. "Nah, something's not right. I feel it. That prick was here."

Languetti heads off to investigate the other rooms in the apartment, instructing Miles to do the same. "Sweep the area again; I'm looking around inside the bedroom."

As Languetti moves into the bedroom, Miles carefully examines his surroundings, taking everything into consideration. He spots something wedged in one of the sofa cushions. On closer examination, Miles identifies it as a restaurant menu. Taking the pamphlet into his hand, he looks towards the refrigerator, the assortment of menus, and a noticeable void is visible. He yells out to Languetti.

"Hey, Frank!"

Languetti makes his way back into the room. "What have you got?"

Miles holds up the menu. "There was a menu for...Foo Tong's takeaway on the sofa. I'm thinking maybe she ordered out?"

Languetti looks at the kitchen counter. "Did they mention any takeaway in their report?"

Miles flips open the report. A moment passes before he shakes his head. "Nothing in the report about takeaway."

Languetti takes in the view around the room. He scratches his scalp. "That menu could have been there for weeks. Maybe it was from another night she ordered out. Hang onto it. We can check it out later, just to be sure."

Languetti and Miles spend several minutes going over the lounge area and balcony in the hope that Det. Gremmer and his team may have missed something vital. Standing in the middle of the lounge room, Languetti gazes at the blood on the carpet, finally removing his latex gloves, conceding there is nothing more he can do but wait for the results from forensics.

"We done, Frank?" An exhausted Miles wants to call it a night.

"We're done. We'll see what forensics comes up with tomorrow. Might give us something to work with."

Miles' thoughts turn to Audrey. "Hey Frank, we have to go see the girl."

Languetti nods regretfully, looking at his watch and noting the time. "It's late. We'll visit her tomorrow."

Languetti takes one last look around before heading for the door. Miles buries the latex gloves into his trouser pocket, the chilly air consuming his face as he stares at the balcony. He takes another moment, wondering how Audrey will take the news that her closest friend is dead. He wonders if William was the killer, and why. He rubs the back of his neck, filing his thoughts as he heads for the exit.

Chapter 34

The following morning, it's colder than expected despite the sun hovering bright over the horizon. A flaxen hue engulfs the stratus sky; Languetti stands over his kitchen sink, coffee in hand, and a myriad of thoughts occupy his mind. Having had little sleep, Languetti has risen early, eager to get to the forensics lab for the results of Veronica's autopsy. He takes one last sip of his coffee before placing the cup into the sink. He handles his coat and keys as he heads for the door. The bitter cold air pierces Languetti's skin as he steps out into the barren street, clutching his hands together as he walks to his car. The frosty eight-cylinder engine grumbles as he turns the key, the vehicle departing from the curb as Languetti pumps the gas—his first stop, to pick up his partner, who's waiting impatiently outside his home. 7:15 am sharp; Languetti instructed at the previous night's end. Miles shivers as he stands on the sidewalk, his thoughts on the case, trying to distance his conclusions until he reads the forensics report. He sighs in relief, spotting Languetti's cruiser rounding the corner. Languetti draws the car to the curb, Miles hopping inside quickly, slamming the door shut to keep out the cold. He greets Languetti with a weather report.

"It's cold outside, Frank."

"No shit."

Frank smiles as Miles fumbles with the heater controls on the cruiser's dashboard. Languetti eases his foot onto the gas pedal, the car pulling away; their destination is The Office of Chief Medical Examiner, where Languetti has arranged to meet up with forensics coroner Dr Evelyn Bridge.

Dr Bridge has been a forensic coroner for over nine years and has worked with Frank countless times. Languetti called Dr Bridge directly after he and Miles exited Veronica's apartment and asked if she could perform the autopsy the following morning as a personal favour to Languetti. Dr Bridge complied but demanded Frank take her to dinner in return. He agreed.

Miles is calm as he looks through the frosted glass of the cruiser, Languetti pulling across the street from The Office of Chief Medical Examiner; Miles suddenly remembers Frank's conversation with Dr Bridge the previous evening.

"So, have you decided where you're gonna take Dr Bridge for dinner?"

Languetti turns the engine off and reaches for the case file. "I don't know. Might take her to Noodle town, in Chinatown."

Miles looks across at his partner. "Noodle town, Frank?"

Languetti shrugs his shoulders. "Yeah, what's wrong with that? They make delicious Noodles."

Miles gives Frank a blank stare. "Frank, that's where we go to eat."

"Yeah, I know. So, what?" Languetti remains clueless.

"Frank. Why don't you take her somewhere nice? Like... The Golden Dragon."

Languetti pushes his head back. "The Golden Dragon. That's like a four-star restaurant."

Miles removes his seatbelt, preparing to disembark the vehicle.

"Frank! You dragged this woman out of bed at the crack of dawn, on possibly the coldest day in November's history, to carve up a dead body for you." Miles widens his eyes, emphasising his point. "I think that deserves four stars, Frank."

Languetti places his hand on the door handle. "Fine, I'll take her to dinner at The Golden Dragon, just to please you. Can we go inside the building now? I'm freezing my nuts off here."

"Yes, now we can go inside."

Miles is not eager to step out into the cold weather. Languetti hugs his shoulders as he exits the vehicle, pushing the door closed with his elbow. Miles adjusts his scarf as he leads Languetti across the street, eyeing the building's entrance. Both detectives are keen to get out of the cold and into the warmth of the lobby. They are greeted by a security guard just inside the door, both detectives exposing their badges as they march purposely towards the elevators. Inside the lift, Miles presses the button for the second floor.

"You think forensics will find anything?"

Languetti loosens his coat as he adjusts to the ambient temperature. "Who knows? If it was premeditated, then maybe he was careful not to leave evidence. He's a cock-sucking lawyer, remember?"

"Yeah, he's also an arrogant prick." Miles recalls their first encounter. "He knows how the law works." Miles reaches into his jacket and removes some peppermint gum.

Languetti checks his watch. "Yeah, but they always make one mistake, Miles."

"Let's hope so."

Languetti moves forward as the doors to the lift separate. He veers to his left, heading to Dr Bridge's lab, located at the end of the hall. Miles follows, placing a piece of gum into his mouth as he eyes the artwork on the wall.

In the forensics lab, Dr. Bridge sits at her cluttered desk, sifting through some file notes and taking small sips of brewed English breakfast tea from a royal-emblem mug cradled securely in her palm. She looks up from her desk, Languetti's frame blocking some of the light as he approaches the doorway. Dr. Bridge swivels her chair, leaning back, still cradling the tea in her hand.

"Oh look, my date is here." She grins, taking another sip of her tea. A wry smile appears on Frank's face as he greets Dr Bridge.

"Good morning, Evelyn."

Dr Bridge receives a warm sensation in her chest as she swallows another mouthful of tea. "Good morning, Frank."

Languetti walks towards Dr. Bridge, placing his hands into his coat pockets. Miles enters the room, raises his hand, and gestures to Dr. Bridge.

"Hey, Doc."

Dr Bridge acknowledges Miles with a wink before turning her attention to Languetti. "You're looking well, Frank. I haven't seen you much these past few months."

Languetti brushes his hair back. "There hasn't been too much going on lately. It's been a little quieter than usual."

Dr Bridge takes another sip of her tea. "Seems like the only time you call to see me of late is when someone dies."

Dr Bridge legally divorced a year ago and now lives with her only daughter, fourteen-year-old Sylvia. Frank, a lifelong bachelor, found himself attracted to Dr Bridge, and their professional relationship turned a corner when she sought comfort in Frank's arms after her marriage ended. At the time, rumours surfaced in the department that her marriage ended because something was going on between her and Frank. Because of this, Frank has been reluctant to pursue an intimate relationship with Dr Bridge, despite his feelings for her. Miles often encouraged Languetti to make his move, but Frank avoided the topic, fearing that those rumours would again surface. Dr Bridge was aware of how Frank felt, so she never forced it at the time. Last night, when Languetti called, she noted a hint of desperation in his voice and decided to seize this opportunity and entrap him into taking her to dinner. She was comforted when Languetti agreed, but wondered afterwards whether his decision was partly based on a desire to seek a personal relationship with her or solely to solve the murder case.

"I apologise. I should make more of an effort to call you. Not just when I need something."

Dr Bridge rises to her feet. "That's alright, Frank. You can make it up to me on our dinner date." Evelyn glares, reminding Frank of his obligation. Miles smiles, noticing Languetti's awkwardness. He decides to add to his partner's torment.

"He's taking you to The Golden Dragon, Evelyn."

Languetti purses his lips at Miles.

"Really!" Dr Bridge says impressively. "I've heard that's a fancy place to dine, Frank. This case you're on must be especially important to you."

Dr Bridge looks over at Miles, giving him another wink, enjoying themselves as they satirise Languetti.

Languetti lets out a small groan. "You both done?"

Languetti proceeds to the adjacent room, entering the sterile lab which houses Veronica's corpse. Miles walks over to Dr Bridge and places his arm around her as he leans in, whispering into her ear.

"You should wear something sexy on your date. Frank goes for that kinky stuff."

Evelyn snorts as Miles escorts her into the next room, both looking across as they enter the forensics lab, Languetti standing at the ready, just a few feet from Veronica's body. Miles slides his hand from Dr Bridge, patting her on the back before stepping to the side to join Frank. Dr Bridge approaches Veronica's body, the deceased resting on her back, covered from head to toe with a white cotton sheet. Evelyn places her tea onto a stainless-steel bench before taking a clipboard into her hand, which she utilised earlier that morning to make notes as she performed the autopsy. Dr Bridge observes Languetti, who is waiting patiently for her to speak. She raises her hand, curling her index finger.

"Come closer, Frank."

Languetti removes his hands from his pockets and walks over to Dr Bridge.

"Would you kindly hold this for a moment?" Dr Bridge hands the clipboard over to Languetti before leaning over the carcass, peeling the sheet back, and exposing Veronica's head and shoulders to Languetti.

"Thank you, Frank."

Dr Bridge takes the clipboard from Languetti's grasp. Frank reluctantly looks at Veronica, her face and shoulders battered and bruised from the impact of the fall.

"The report that I got from Det. Gremmer said that she fell, eight stories?" Dr Bridge pauses for validation.

"Yeah, that information is accurate."

Dr Bridge draws attention to Veronica's mouth. "See the bruising around her mouth, Frank?"

Languetti leans in to take a closer look.

"Consistent with a hand being pressed hard over her mouth. A lot of force, Frank. Most likely a strong male."

Languetti looks at Dr Bridge as she continues.

"Difficult to make out the exact size of the hand. The person who did this wore gloves. Not the latex kind; they were thick and smooth, probably leather, what most everyone wears during this time of the year."

Like a dipshit lawyer, Miles has his thoughts.

Dr Bridge continues on her train of thought. She points to Veronica's skull. "The trauma suffered on the left frontal lobe had fragments of glass. The report mentioned a coffee table with cracked glass and blood found in the victim's apartment?"

"That's accurate."

"The boys at the lab should confirm that the glass matches when they run some tests. I'll get the fragments over to them today." Dr Bridge stands erect before continuing. "The bruising and trauma are isolated from the rest of her body, Frank. The impact from the fall was on her right hip, and she came to rest on her back. The photos in the report confirm that. The cause of death was from massive haemorrhaging in the back of her skull caused by the impact of the fall. It was definitely the fall that killed her, Frank, but it appears that she got a bit of help over the railing."

Languetti nods his head, his thoughts solidified.

"I checked for signs of rape and scraped her fingernails. There was little residue to be found. I will send it to Alex in the lab for him to analyse. He should call you as soon as he's done."

Languetti places his hands into his trouser pockets, collating the detailed assessment.

"Not much else to work with here, Frank. Maybe forensics will find something you can use." Dr Bridge conveys her regret. Just the same, the evidence she provided validates that someone else was there, and it was indeed a homicide.

"Do you mind if I ask why Det. Gremmer passed this case on to you, Frank?"

Languetti exhales a breath. "The victim's friend was assaulted a couple of months back. There may be a connection."

Dr Bridge places her hand on Languetti's shoulder. "You look tired, Frank."

Languetti gazes directly into Dr Bridges' eyes. For a moment, he wonders how she would react if he placed his arms around her and held her tight against his chest. Miles notices the stark silence quickly becoming an awkward moment for him.

"Hey Frank, when you're done with your...whatever that is, I'll be outside waiting. We have other people to see, remember?"

A distracted Languetti is removed from his trance-like state. He fidgets as he collects his thoughts. "Yeah, he's right...We have to go." Languetti heads for the exit.

"Hey, Frank." Dr Bridge attracts Languetti's attention before he can walk out the door. "Tomorrow night? Say around 7:00 pm?"

"Sure. Tomorrow night sounds great. I'll come by your place and pick you up."

"Looking forward to it, Frank."

Dr Bridge smiles in admiration as she watches Frank leave the room. A vocal Miles projects his voice; it carries through to the room.

"Let's go, Don Juan."

Chapter 35

Languetti and Miles decide to stop at the local diner in midtown Manhattan to grab breakfast before visiting Audrey to inform her of the dire news. Beryl looks up from the counter as both detectives enter the restaurant, seating themselves at their usual booth by the window. She wipes her hands on her apron, taking pen and pad in her hand as she walks over to greet them.

"And how are you fine gentlemen doing this beautiful morning?"

Miles looks up at Beryl, still shivering, as he removes his gloves. "Beautiful morning? It's freezing outside, Beryl!"

Beryl looks out the window. "It is? Oh, I never feel the cold love." Beryl's hefty layers of fat surrounding her torso provide her with insulation. "What would you like, love?"

Although Miles makes a conscious effort always to eat healthy food, the smell of fried bacon in the morning often gets the better of him. "I'll have an Uncle Sam Breakfast, thanks, Beryl, with a large Orange Juice. Pulp Free if you would."

Beryl smiles. "I'll pass it through a sieve for ya."

An Uncle Sam's breakfast consists of three rashers of fried bacon, two fried eggs, a baked potato, and a fried tomato on buttered toast. Beryl scribbles the order down before turning to Languetti.

"I'll have the same." Languetti decides as he fights to remove his coat in the compact booth.

"Two Uncle Sams coming up."

Beryl makes her way over to the kitchen. Languetti looks out the window, his thoughts now on Audrey, imagining how she will react to the news of Veronica's death.

"Hey, Frank."

Languetti turns his attention to Miles.

"You should try to have a good time on your date with Evelyn."

Languetti arranges the items on the table as he listens to Miles.

"She's a nice woman. You should get to know her better."

"Know her better? What do you mean, get to know her better? Like how?" Languetti frowns.

"Relax, Frank; I'm not suggesting you have sex with her." Miles rubs his brow, avoiding the imagery. "I'm just saying that you two go well together, like ham and eggs. And on your date, you should ensure you are…a little less…your usual self."

"Ham and eggs. Who's the egg?"

"If you don't know who the egg is, then we're in real trouble, Frank."

"It's just dinner. It's no big deal. Just leave it alone."

Frank turns his attention to the passers-by through the diner window. Miles loosens his tie.

"Maybe you should make it a big deal, Frank?"

Frank continues to watch the street hustle.

"All I'm saying is that you should be with someone, and Dr Bridge looks to me as someone you should be with."

"Don't worry about me, Miles. I'll be just fine."

"Okay, Frank, just make sure you at least bring her flowers."

"Flowers. Why not a corsage?"

"Women appreciate flowers, Frank. It shows them that you're thoughtful."

Languetti leans back and flexes his chest with confidence.

"I know how to charm women; I don't need your help."

"Sure, Frank, I can see your charm has worked wonders for your love life," Miles mutters.

Frank straightens his posture, anticipating the arrival of his breakfast. "Last time I checked, you were single also!"

Languetti looks over Miles' shoulder as Beryl approaches, holding a tray with two steaming hot plates of food.

"Here you go, boys."

She places the food on the table, Languetti rubbing his hands together, almost salivating at the mouth like a hungry wolf.

"Enjoy."

Beryl departs, both men wasting no time as they reach for their cutlery.

"Oh, man, this is going to taste good." Miles leans forward, taking in the aroma of the cooked bacon.

Languetti reaches across the table, vigorously shaking the ketchup bottle and squeezing several dollops over his food, unashamedly digging in. Miles is mute, enjoying the moment, knowing in his mind that soon they will be with Audrey, painfully informing her of Veronica's death. Languetti follows suit, occasionally looking out the window between bites; now thinking about Dr Bridge smiling at him as she did earlier that morning, creating a feeling of warmth in his heart and quietly wishing he could wake up next to her and experience that feeling every morning of his life.

Chapter 36

It is just after ten the same morning, and Audrey is sitting on her lonesome behind the main counter of the florist, flicking aimlessly through a tabloid magazine. She looks up as the jingle of the wind chime sounds, attracting her attention. Entering the florist is Rose, struggling as she cradles a box of assorted fruit she purchased on her way to work.

"Oh my god, Rose!" Audrey jumps to her feet, racing across the room to assist. Rose fights to keep the door ajar as she backs up, using her knee to keep the box from falling. Audrey handles the door. "Are you right with that? You should let me give you a hand."

Rose groans as she heads straight for the counter, heaving the box onto the bench. "Oh *Jeesh*, that was heavier than I expected," Rose huffs, brushing her hair from her face.

Audrey places her hands on her hips. "You should have called me to help you."

"That's alright, love. You shouldn't be lifting heavy items just yet; your hands are still healing."

Audrey animates her hands for Rose to view. "My hands are fine, Rose, and you shouldn't be lifting anything that heavy with your bad back."

"Oh, Schmegegge." Rose flings her Yiddish at Audrey as she makes her way to the back of the store to wash her hands. A curious Audrey raises the lid off the box, exposing a range of luscious fruits. Her eyes focus on a small container of bright red strawberries. She looks over her shoulder as she reaches into the box, taking hold of the container of strawberries and placing them on the counter.

"Hey Rose, you mind if I have a strawberry?" Audrey projects her voice towards the back room.

"Have as many as you like, love," Rose yells.

A gleeful Audrey lifts the lid off the punnet of strawberries, removing the largest strawberry she could find and placing it under her nose. Rose walks out from the back and addresses Audrey in a stern voice.

"Audrey! Don't you eat that!"

Audrey turns and gives Rose a surprised look. "But you said I could have as many as I like?"

"You can. But not before you wash them first. Take them to the tearoom and wash them."

Audrey begrudgingly places the strawberry back and takes the container in her hand.

"Make sure you wash them thoroughly; you can't be sure what chemicals the farmers are using these days."

Audrey turns her head away from Rose as she rolls her eyes. "I promise to wash them super-duper well," she utters quietly.

As Audrey proceeds to the back, Rose sifts through the fruit for something to satisfy her taste buds. The wind chimes as Languetti and Miles cautiously enter the store; they look around the room, uncertain if this is the florist Audrey works at. Rose looks up to greet the two men as they approach the counter.

"How can I help you today, gentlemen?"

Languetti's response is interrupted as Audrey yells out from the back room.

"Rose, I think we're out of sugar." Audrey suddenly appears from the back. She stops, immediately spotting Languetti standing at the counter with Miles by his side. Languetti looks over at Audrey, nodding ever so slightly, a controlled look on his face.

"Audrey, we have customers," Rose announces.

"Detective." Audrey is surprised. Her tone is cautious.

Rose looks at the men, remembering that Audrey had spoken about her encounter with the two detectives and how she was interviewed about her ordeal.

"How are you, Audrey?" Frank asks.

Audrey forces a smile, her thoughts on his impromptu visit. "I'm well, Detective."

A moment of silence fills the room. Languetti hesitates for a moment. "I would like to speak privately if you have a few minutes."

Audrey senses the tension in Languetti's demeanour. "Sure, we can talk back here if you like."

Languetti proceeds behind the counter, Audrey leading him into the rear of the shop. Miles decides to hang back; he eyes the floral arrangements, not wanting to participate in this particular conversation. Rose senses something is amiss, but dismisses her thoughts as she watches the detective amble around the store.

"We have some lovely arrangements if you want to buy something for your wife or girlfriend, Detective." Rose cuts through the awkwardness.

In the back room, Languetti conceals his anxiety from Audrey, his mind circling with thoughts of how he will introduce the dreadful news to Audrey. He notices the small sofa to the left of the room.

"Audrey, why don't we sit down for a moment?"

Audrey acts on Languetti's instruction and gently eases herself onto the sofa cushion, awkwardly facing Languetti. Languetti begins to form a smile for just a brief moment before obscuring his mouth with his hand.

"Audrey. I need to talk to you about Veronica."

"My friend, V?" Curious thoughts quickly emerge. She refrains from interrupting the detective.

"Yes, that's right. Your friend Veronica. When was the last time you spoke with her?"

Audrey immediately recalls the previous night's telephone conversation.

"She called me last night. Around six."

Audrey's palms begin to perspire, anticipating unwelcome news forthcoming from the detective. Languetti probes for more information, fearing that Audrey may lose control of her emotions when she hears the news of Veronica's death.

"What did you talk about?"

Audrey thinks for a moment, her fingers jittery from nerves. "She asked me how I was, just girl talk. We only spoke for a short while." Audrey pauses momentarily, forcing a smile. "She is coming to my place tomorrow night to watch a movie."

Audrey quickly loses confidence in her last statement; she fidgets nervously, Languetti's eyes speaking volumes. Languetti dismisses Audrey's nervousness and continues to probe, his instincts telling him that Audrey has vital information that may lead him to Veronica's killer.

"What else did you two talk about?"

Audrey's thoughts go to William, remembering when Veronica told her she encountered him in the city that day.

"Did Veronica mention anyone else in your conversation?"

Audrey looks into Languetti's eyes, her emotions heightening at the thought that Veronica's encounter with William brought the detective here. She breaks her silence.

"She told me that she saw William in the city that day."

Languetti is unmoved. "She spoke to William?"

"Yes, V said she ran into him in the city...around lunchtime." Audrey hesitates for a moment, trying to untangle her chaotic thoughts. "She told me that she yelled at him in the street."

Tears begin to form; Audrey is concerned for her friend's safety and becomes impatient with Languetti's questions. "What's going on, Detective?"

Languetti places his hand on Audrey's shoulder. He takes a moment. Audrey is now fearing the worst and no longer wants to hear a response from the detective.

"Audrey...Veronica was killed last night."

Audrey freezes: her heart races as Languetti's words infiltrate her thoughts.

"I'm very sorry, Audrey."

Audrey is visibly shocked by the news; tears stream down her face, and she is unable to comprehend what the detective told her. Languetti remains eager to find out more about what Audrey may know.

"Audrey, I know this is difficult, but I need you to remain strong. I need to know what else Veronica told you when you spoke with her."

"Is she really dead?"

Audrey wipes the tears from her eyes, pleading for the detective to take it back. She wills herself to keep her composure. She takes a deep breath to calm herself down. She continues to recount her conversation with Veronica, and ultimately, she mentions the food Veronica ordered.

"Chinese food?" Languetti inquires.

Audrey begins to feel numb. The realisation that she will never see Veronica again hits her like a truck. Audrey sways, and her face is pale. Languetti take hold of her. Audrey struggles to keep herself upright. She holds her stomach, feeling nauseous. Languetti's words circle her thoughts. Languetti notices Audrey clutching at her abdomen and prepares himself, fearing that Audrey may puke. Audrey looks directly into the detective's eyes, her face now seething, and there is anger in her tone as she voices her thoughts.

"I want to press charges against him."

The sudden revelation throws Languetti. Rose enters the room. The distress in Audrey's voice inevitably drawing her attention.

"Audrey, what's the matter?"

Audrey rises to her feet, extending her arms to Rose for comfort. Rose quickly moves forward to meet her, cradling Audrey close to her chest as she lets out a high-pitched moan in anguish. Rose feels conflicted as she holds onto Audrey. Languetti is slow to his feet. Audrey's distress casts his decision to leave her alone to grieve. He addresses Rose.

"I'll come back another time to see her."

Rose presents a bewildered look. As Languetti proceeds to leave the room, Audrey raises her head from Rose's chest.

"She said something about William's car." Languetti snaps around to look at Audrey.

"What was that?"

"Veronica, she said something about him being upset when he sees his car. That's all she said."

Languetti stores the new information. "Thank you."

Languetti walks from the room, his stride increasing with purpose as he heads for the door. He looks at Miles, who's holding a single daffodil in his hand.

"Put the flower down, Miles; we're leaving."

Miles is fazed, following Frank out the door. "It's mine; I bought it!"

With a daffodil in hand, Miles jogs to catch up to his determined partner. As they approach the car, Languetti addresses Miles.

"Veronica ran into him yesterday."

"Who? William?"

Languetti nods. "She told him off in the street."

Miles absorbs the information. "And you think that's a motive?"

Miles places his hand on the handle of the car door. He waits for Frank to respond.

"No, I don't, but Audrey mentioned something about William's car."

"Veronica did something to William's car?"

"I think so." Languetti nods, instinctively confident. "Get Stephanie on the phone. I want to know where this prick works."

Miles pulls the door open and hops inside the cruiser, fighting to remove his cell from his coat pocket. He struggles, his coat bunched up and tangled as he wiggles around; cell in one hand, daffodil in the other. Languetti wastes no time firing up the engine.

"Hold on a second, Frank, I've got a better idea."

"What is it?"

"You said that Veronica maybe did something to his car, right? Well, it had to be something pretty bad for William to throw her off the balcony. I bet you anything that the car is at his place. There's no way he's had time to repair it, and if it is messed up in a bad way, he wouldn't have taken it with him to work today. I say we first go to his place and check to see if the car is there."

"If it is, maybe we'll find Veronica's prints on it." Frank is pumped. "Good detective work, young lad."

Miles finds his comfort, smelling his flower as he sits back. Languetti plants his foot hard. The cruisers' tyres screeching as Languetti peels away from the curb.

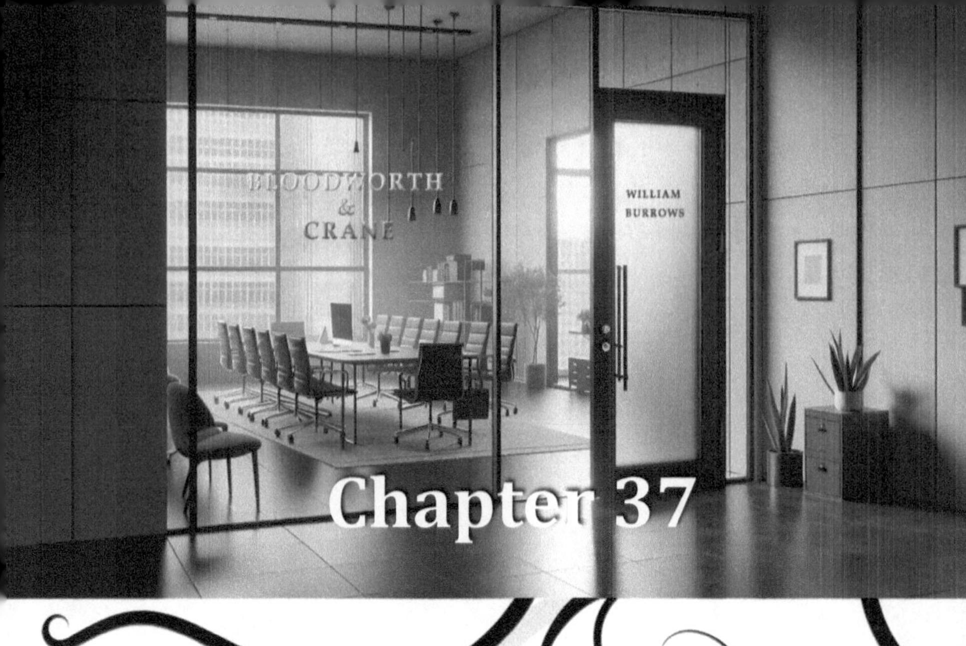

Chapter 37

The confident strut in Languetti's walk echoes as the heels of his leather shoes meet the black marble floor of the foyer. He walks directly up to the front desk, flashing his badge at a plump security guard who rises to his feet at Languetti's presence.

"Yes, officer." The plump security guard is coy, covering a half-eaten doughnut on his desk with his newspaper.

"Detective." Languetti corrects the security guard. "Can you tell me what floor William Burrows works on?"

"William...Burrows." The security guard reaches down and begins to search the digital register. Miles fiddles with his lapel, now garnished with the daffodil he purchased from Rose.

"He's on level six. Corporate Law. Would you like me to call him Detective?"

"No, don't call him. I'll go up." Languetti wastes no time as he heads for the elevator. The security guard looks at Miles.

"You can go right up...Detective?" The guard frowns. The yellow daffodil is obvious.

Languetti steps inside the elevator, quickly reaching for the button to take him to the sixth floor of the building. Miles leans against the elevator wall, exercising calm, the yang to Frank's anxiety. Languetti reaches around, checking his cuffs as he prepares for the encounter with William. The elevator doors open, directly adjacent, an expansive front desk made of dark cedar. Behind the desk sits a young woman with golden hair flowing over her shoulders, ready to greet the detectives with a smile as they walk towards her. Languetti directs his attention to the feature wall directly behind the receptionist. The firm's name in large black letters, Bloodworth and Crane, embossed with amber lighting. The young girl reveals her pearly whites to Languetti as he and Miles approach the desk.

"How can I help you today, sir?" Her tone is pleasing. Languetti displays his badge.

"I'm Detective Languetti. Please call William Burrows and ask him to come out here."

The young girl is startled by Languetti's demand, her eyes on the detective's badge as she clumsily reaches for the phone. She looks up at Languetti once more.

"Do you have an appointment?"

An occupational hazard ingrained in her from her many months as a desk clerk. Languetti glares at the girl as she nervously grins, dialling the office extension. She whispers into the receiver.

"Hi, there are two detectives here to see William." She sneaks a peek at Miles, noticing the flower on his lapel. "Yes." She replaces the handset and forces a grin as she addresses Languetti. "Someone will be right out, Detective."

With that response, Languetti steps away from the desk, eyeing the frosted glass door. His hand finds his cuffs as he waits for William to enter the foyer. Miles is ready. The frosted door swings open, revealing a short, balding man in a pin-stripe suit striding formally towards Languetti.

"Can I help you, Detective?" A hint of arrogance in his voice and a lawyer's stench.

"We'd like to see William Burrows." Languetti is now agitated at the presence of another person standing between him and his suspect. The dumpy lawyer is direct in his response.

"Mr. Burrows is not in the office at present. Can I ask what this pertains to?"

Languetti glances at Miles, the balding man's choice of words, aggravating him further. "No, you can't. Where the hell is he?"

The lawyer raises his chin; his physical displeasure at Languetti's directness is apparent. "He is out of the city on business. Unfortunately for you, Detective, I don't expect to see him back in the office for the remainder of today."

Languetti glares at the lawyer before looking at the receptionist; she has a ringside seat for the banter.

"If there is nothing else, Detective, I have other more pressing matters to attend to."

Miles weighs in. "No, we're done. You can go and press your matters."

The dumpy lawyer gawks at Miles, noticing the daffodil on the detective's lapel, before performing an about-face and walking back towards the frosted glass door. The young receptionist watches closely as the unsatisfied detectives head for the elevator—the receptionist peers across to see the lawyer exit the area, collating her thoughts on the interaction.

Downstairs in the lobby, the security guard raises his head from his newspaper, wiping his mouth of doughnut residue to see Languetti and Miles step out of the elevator and begrudgingly make their way towards the exit.

"Excuse me, Detective!" The guard's voice booms across the lobby. "Can you hold on a minute, please?"

The plump security guard waddles his way over to Languetti, pulling on his trousers as he approaches the detectives. Languetti stops, curiously annoyed at the guard's request.

"Detective, can you please wait here a moment? Someone from upstairs would like to speak to you."

Languetti looks at the guard before looking at Miles, wondering who that may be. All three men turn their attention to the elevator at the faint sound of the ping. As the doors open, the young receptionist enters the lobby, her stilettoes echoing as she hurries across the marble floor to meet the detectives. Feeling he's done his part, the security guard inches away, returning to his post. Languetti's interest increases as the girl draws closer. She peers over her shoulder as she completes her last few steps, catching her breath as she stands uneasily in front of the detectives.

"Detective. I have some information that may help you."

Languetti places his hands on his hips; he says nothing, allowing the girl to voice her thoughts freely.

"Look, William is a real jerk, so he probably deserves whatever he's got coming to him. If you want to find him, I know where he'll be later on tonight."

"Where?" Miles asks.

"He'll be at the Metropolitan Opera House."

"How do you know this?" Languetti inquires.

"I know because he sent me out to get his tickets. He was supposed to take me there tonight, but called this morning to cancel."

"If he cancelled, then why do you think he will be there tonight?" Miles is quick to point out.

The girl huffs at Miles. "Are you kidding me? The guy's a real sleaze. He said he had to take his cousin, who was in town, visiting for a few days. But I know that's bullshit. He's taking some other girl. I just know it."

Miles glances at his partner; Frank addresses the girl.

"What's your name?"

"Nicole, Nicky," she says, folding her arms in the process.

"What time is the show on tonight, Nicole?"

"The show starts at seven, but usually, people go earlier and hang out in the bar lounge for drinks. From like, six...six-thirty."

Languetti takes a moment to impart some sound advice before relieving Nicky. "Nicole, I want you to stay away from this man. He's dangerous."

The girl notes the seriousness in Languetti's eyes. "I will, Detective. Thanks."

Languetti rests his hand on Nicky's shoulder, expressing his appreciation for the information she provided. "Go on now, go back upstairs."

The girl graciously nods as she leaves. Languetti reaches for his cell, instinctively deciding to call forensics as he and Miles exit the building.

The Metropolitan Opera opened its doors for the first time on 23 October 1883 at 39th and Broadway. Wealthy New Yorkers, among them the Vanderbilts and Astors, financed the building, and it was no accident that special seating was provided for these patrons in 122 very visible boxes. After a fire gutted the interior of the building in the summer of 1892, the number of boxes was reduced to seventy, divided between two tiers. By 1940, to remove poor sight lines and increase seating, the Grand Tier boxes were removed, leaving only the parterre boxes. In the 1920s, John D. Rockefeller included a new home for the Metropolitan Opera in the plans for Rockefeller Center, but by the 1930s, the idea was shelved due to the Depression. In 1966, the Metropolitan Opera moved to its present location in the Lincoln Centre complex. The Metropolitan Opera House is located on the Upper West Side of town, at 65th Street and Columbus Avenue. Facing the opera house, the New York City Theatre is on the left, Avery Fisher Hall, the home of the NY Philharmonic on the right. The entrance consists of five high arches that span across the face of the building, which are made entirely of glass panes. At sundown, the sleek interior is bathed in golden lights, and while not the traditional architecture for an opera house, the graceful archways and the open glass entrance present the building with a strikingly elegant appearance.

Outside the main auditorium, groups of patrons are gathered together, the clamour of their voices filling the vastness of the lobby staircase. Drinks and canapés are served before the show, with black gowns, pearl necklaces, and diamond rings on display for all to praise. William brings the rim of the champagne glass to his lips, taking a small sip as he watches his date, Jocelyn, stuff a salmon canapé in its entirety into her mouth, endeavouring to remain graceful amongst the opulent crowd. She looks up at William, smiling at him with puffed cheeks, cautiously chewing her food and wondering what her appearance may look like to others.

Not very graceful, she thinks, placing her hand over her smiling mouth. William smiles back, commenting on her tenacious appetite.

"Don't stop at five."

Jocelyn keeps her hand over her mouth. Embarrassed by her gluttony, she gulps a mouthful of wine to clear her throat.

"I've hardly had anything to eat today," she explains. "Food here is so delicious."

William chuckles, taking note of her sleek form as she turns to admire the lavish surroundings of MET's lobby.

"This place is so nice." She peers over the railing; the marble staircase is draped in blood-red carpet flowing throughout. William takes another sip of his champagne.

"You come here a lot?" Jocelyn asks, pondering with her fingers resting on her lips, debating if she should snatch another delight from a passing waiter. A waiter moves by her, and she hesitates. Her window of opportunity closes.

"I've been here quite a few times."

William spots another waiter standing nearby; he signals for him to come over. The waiter is carrying a large tray covered in various hors d'oeuvres. Jocelyn's eyes widen as he approaches, her opportunity not squandered this time as she reaches for another canapé. This one is a flaky pastry filled with cream cheese, caviar, and the head of asparagus.

"Oh wow, this looks so yummy," she remarks, taking a generous bite. Her appetite amuses William. "Want to try some?" Jocelyn offers the half-eaten canapé to William.

William shows his palm to Jocelyn. "I'm good, thank you."

Jocelyn shrugs her shoulders, popping the remaining delicacy into her mouth. William's eyes wander around the room. Again, he raises the glass to his lips, sensing an eerie discomfort in the room. He takes a cautious sip of his beverage.

As William lowers the glass from his mouth, a shadow appears from his left shoulder, a hand quickly snatching the flute from William's grasp. Bewildered by the act, William turns to the figure at his side. Before he can voice his thoughts, a heavy hand takes a firm hold of William's forearm, forcing it away from his torso. William feels the blunt pain as Languetti smacks the cold steel cuffs down on his wrist.

"William Burrows, you are under arrest for the murder of Veronica Park."

William clenches his jaw with discontent as he glares directly at Miles, who stands guard, holding the champagne glass in one hand, his other resting on his firearm.

Jocelyn is startled. "What's going on?" She yelps nervously, watching in dismay as William is restrained. Miles extends his arm across the girl.

"Miss, can you please step back?"

Onlookers nearby flock together, asserting their attention to all the fuss. Languetti completes the cuffing, reading William his rights as he manoeuvres him towards the stairs. Miles attracts a waiter standing to his right, placing the champagne glass on the tray; he turns his attention to Jocelyn.

"Dates over; go home," he informs before clearing a path for his partner, leading Frank towards the exit as he forcefully guides William by his arm.

The room fills with muffled whispers as onlookers cover their mouths and inconspicuously point in William's direction. William tries to avoid eye contact as he passes the clusters, looking the other way at any hint of recognition, his frustration evident in his stride. A placid-faced Languetti diverts his attention to the crowds, noting the look on their faces. He returns his focus to a disgruntled William, relishing the moment and thinking that he could not have planned this any better.

Chapter 39

Back at the Precinct, Languetti directs William inside one of the interrogation rooms. A few steps behind follows Miles. The interrogation room is small and stuffy, with no windows and walls painted in a drab grey. On the far-right wall is a large two-way mirror adjoining a room with recording equipment. In the middle of the interrogation room is a rectangular table made from cheap laminated timber, supported by four partially rusted steel legs. Three dissimilar chairs surround the table, one facing the two-way mirror and the other two on the opposite side of the table. Suspended from the ceiling directly above the table is a light fixture, casting ambient light.

Languetti uses his leg to slide the chair from under the table, placing his hand on William's shoulder and forcing him down onto the chair. Miles closes the door behind him before making his way to the middle of the room to join his partner. Miles carries a manila folder containing the investigation file on Veronica's death. He places the folder on the table before taking a seat to the right of William. Languetti carefully pulls the last chair from beneath the table, directing a deliberate glance at the two-way mirror before taking his seat. He casually reaches across the table, sliding the manila folder towards him. He looks up at William as he opens the folder, removing the utmost photograph in the file. William unassumingly shifts his attention to the picture as Languetti places it on the table, sliding it towards him. Languetti stares at William, noting his indifferent reaction to the photograph before finally addressing him.

"Do you recognise this person?"

William shifts his weight forward, examining the photograph for a purposeful length, identifying Veronica's bloodied body lying in the street outside her apartment building. He looks across at Languetti as he leans back into his chair, considering his response.

"Hard to make out who it is, with all that blood, Detective."

William revels in mind games. Languetti reaches into the file, removing a second photograph and laying it directly over the first.

"Here's a better one; it's a close-up of her face."

William keeps his eyes on Languetti, refusing to look down at the photograph. Languetti is cautious not to let William's casual attitude affect his emotions.

"You can't possibly see leaning back into the chair as you are."

Languetti leans forward, taking the photograph into his hand and raising it only inches from William's face.

"Looks like Veronica," William says as he turns away.

Languetti nods, briefly looking over at Miles. "That's right. It's Veronica Park."

"She doesn't look well, Detective." William is brazen.

Languetti turns the photo around, looking at it momentarily before responding. "That's because she's dead, William."

Languetti reaches into the file, retrieving a third photograph from the crime scene. Again, he raises it only inches from William's face.

"This is a photograph of a coffee table in her apartment. Someone rammed her head into the glass." Languetti pauses momentarily. "And then they threw her off the balcony." Languetti places the photograph on the table.

"Eight storeys," Miles says.

William looks over at Miles. "That'll do it," he remarks, almost a hint of a smile.

Languetti swallows his resentment. "Where were you last night, say between six and seven?"

"I was home, Detective."

"Anyone with you?" Miles asks.

"Nope," William responds without hesitation, looking almost bored. Languetti keeps his eyes on William.

"Have you spoken with Veronica recently?"

William shakes his head slightly. "No, I haven't, Detective."

"Are you sure?" Miles asks.

William says nothing.

"Because we were informed you ran into her in the city around noon," Miles says.

Veronica must've told Audrey, William concludes. "Don't recall that, Detective. No law against it in any case," William confidently remarks as he adjusts his shoulders, feeling his arms cramping from the restraints.

"Do you own a car, William?"

"I own two, Detective." *But you already know this, so why ask?* William thinks to himself.

"Two!" Languetti nods his head impressively. "I have only one myself. Guess cops don't make as much money as lawyers do."

William remains unimpressed with Languetti's chatter, unwilling to lower his defenses.

"What cars do you own, William?" Languetti leans back in his chair.

"I thought you guys were detectives."

"We're not very good." Miles is quick to respond.

"Yeah, so how 'bout you help us out a little and answer the question." Languetti's patience wearing thin.

"I have a 2015 Mercedes-Benz C Class and a 2007 Chevrolet Corvette Z06."

Miles positions his hands behind his head, interlocking his fingers. "Impressive cars! One for work and one for play? Is that right, William?" Miles pauses for William to respond. William says nothing. "Bet you took the Vet out tonight, for your big date?"

"Ladies love the Vet, Detective. Gets them wet."

"Yeah, I bet it does." Miles unimpressively holds his stare.

Languetti draws attention to the case file, watchfully sifting through the numerous photographs. William is patient, reflecting on the questions he was asked about his cars. His thoughts go to Veronica, wondering if she had told anyone about the damage she caused to his car. His thoughts are realised when Languetti retrieves a photograph from the file, placing it in front of William. Languetti holds his silence, waiting to see if William will respond first. William's eyes briefly lock on the photograph, distracted by a strident knock at the door. William looks up as the door opens. A uniformed officer carrying a tray with three cups of coffee enters the room. He walks over to the table, placing the beverages before Miles.

"Thank you, officer."

Miles is quaint with a smile, reaching over to take a coffee in his hand. The burly young officer gives Miles a strange look before walking from the room, closing the door behind him as he exits. Languetti reaches over, taking a coffee in his hand; he slides the remaining beverage in front of William. William is amused by the gesture, knowing that Languetti is aware that William is in restraints. He looks over at Languetti; his smile is visible. *Same old tired mind games,* William thinks to himself. Languetti takes a sip of his coffee, and Miles does the same. Both detectives casually lean back into their respective chairs. Languetti takes another sip of his coffee, happy to allow William to ponder his thoughts.

"This your car, William?"

William says nothing; the image is telling.

Languetti takes another sip of his coffee. "I took this photo myself earlier today at your apartment building."

Williams unresponsive.

"The car was parked beneath the building's secure parking garage. We couldn't get in at first, but luckily for us, the caretaker was there at the time, and he was nice enough to let us in." Languetti looks over at Miles. "Really nice man. What was that nice man's name, Miles?"

"Fernando," Miles answers in a Hispanic tone. "Very accommodating little man."

Languetti nods his head in agreement. "Yes, he was very accommodating."

Languetti leans forward, taking a closer look at the photograph. "The hood is all scratched up; you can see that, right, William?" Languetti tapping his finger on the picture. "There was a plastic sheet taped over the hood when we first arrived, but we removed it to find it like this." Languetti continues to eye William.

"Any idea who did this to your car?"

"Vandals." William's response was prepared.

"Did you report it?" Miles asks.

"Nope."

"Why the hell not?" Languetti inquires. "This is a costly automobile."

Languetti looks over at his partner, Miles, agreeing with a pronounced hum. "I'd be pissed if someone did this to my car. I would want to catch the person and make them pay for something like this."

"Shit happens, Frank," William says carelessly. Languetti takes another sip of his coffee.

"When did this happen?" Miles inquires.

"Sometime yesterday."

"Around what time?" Languetti adds.

William shrugs his shoulders. "Midday? I wasn't there when it happened, Detective."

"Where was the car parked at the time?" Languetti inquires.

"Downtown."

"Where exactly?" Languetti continues to probe.

"It was parked at the Zenith building."

"I guess their car park security isn't too good?" Miles takes a sip of his coffee.

William tilts his head to the side, stretching his neck.

"So, you parked your car there, and when you returned to leave, you found it like this?"

"That's good detective work, Frank," William smirks.

"I can see why you covered it up. I wouldn't want to be driving around town with the words, Woman Beater, engraved onto the hood of my car." Languetti looks right at William. "Not something you can just buff out, is it?"

"Pretty nasty thing to do," Miles adds.

"I gotta say, William, in my opinion, I don't think this act of vandalism was random." Languetti raises the beverage to his lips. "Looks to me like this was very personal." Languetti takes a sip of his coffee. "Someone was pissed off at you, big time."

"Definitely some vengeful shit, right there," Miles says.

Languetti places his cup on the table.

"What's disappointing is that the car looked pretty clean when we arrived. Don't imagine we would find any prints on it now."

"Damn shame, we might have been able to identify the person who did this," Miles says as he sips his coffee.

William sits quietly, admiring his diligence in wiping down the car, ensuring no evidence of Veronica's handiwork remains.

"You know, William, it occurred to me that if Veronica did indeed do this to your car, as we suspect, I might add, there may be something in her purse to prove that fact," Frank reveals a smirk.

William conceals his thoughts, blinded by the oversight of not checking Veronica's purse while he was in her apartment.

"So, I called forensics and asked them to analyse anything sharp that was in Veronica's purse."

"Iridium-Silver, that is the colour of your car, right, William?" Miles asks.

Languetti reaches into his pocket, pulling out an evidence bag containing a metal object. He tosses it onto the table—William zeros in on the nail file like a hawk.

"We discovered this in her purse. You wanna guess what forensics found on it?"

William sits back. He contemplates the evidence, wondering if it's enough to prosecute. His presence outside her apartment is still not validated. He exercises patience, waiting to see what else the detectives have.

"So, according to this, William, we now have evidence that Veronica did indeed do this to your car. And that gives us motive. Pardon me, allow me to correct myself; I meant to say that gives you motive."

Miles smirks at William, who refuses to budge.

Languetti rises from his chair. He positions himself directly behind William. He reaches down into his left pocket and retrieves the keys to the handcuffs, freeing William from his restraints.

"Drink your coffee before it gets cold."

William rubs his wrists, peering over at Miles as he reaches for the beverage. Languetti ambles around the table.

"Have you been to Veronica's apartment recently?"

William takes an extended sip of his coffee.

"I told you, I haven't seen her lately, Detective."

"You didn't drive by her place at all… maybe say last night?"

William takes another mouthful of the coffee, vocal as he exhales a little steam.

"You like Chinese food, William?"

William leans back into his chair; he takes a moment before deciding to humour Languetti with a response. "Yeah, sure, I like Chinese food, Detective."

Languetti places his hands into his pockets. "There are a lot of Asian-type restaurants in New York nowadays; not so many when I was growing up." Languetti reminisces.

"Taking over the city," Miles adds. "Have to go to a ball game just to get a hot dog."

"Good food, though," Languetti continues, glaring at William. "There's one restaurant in midtown Manhattan that serves nice Chinese food: Foo Tong Takeaway. You know it, William?"

Languetti moves forward, placing his palms on the table as he peers at William. William refuses to be baited. He shifts his mood.

"You go there to eat, Frank?" William asks, concealing his impatience with the toiling questions.

Languetti raises his eyebrows, looking at Miles, pleasantly surprised by William's inquiry.

"Well, as a matter of fact, William, Miles, and I went there today for lunch."

William places his empty cup on the table. "And what did you have, Detective?"

Languetti indulges him with a response. "I had the seafood stir-fry noodles." Languetti glances at Miles.

"What did you have, Miles? I forget?"

"I had the chilli chicken with cashew nuts."

"You should go there sometime; you'd like it, I'm sure." Frank pauses momentarily. "The owner and his family, very nice people, have been in America for eighteen years. We had a chance to talk to the owner today, although he wasn't too happy."

William shifts his weight, impatience seeping into his skin.

"We asked him why he was upset, and he told us something that we found rather interesting." Languetti circles William. "He told us one of his sons was assaulted last night, whilst on a delivery. A delivery to the same building where Veronica lives."

The room fills with silence, a rush of thoughts entering William's head, wondering if there is any evidence he overlooked that may place him outside the building on the night of Veronica's death. Miles gets involved.

"Anything you want to share with us, William?"

It's a trap. William thinks to himself. They're just fishing— Miles peers at William.

"The kid told us someone came up from behind and knocked him out cold. Just as he was entering the building," Miles says as he shifts his weight forward. "He was dragged inside the building and left unconscious in the emergency stairwell."

"Conveniently out of sight." Languetti points out.

William tests Languetti's patience. "A lot of desperate, starving homeless people in the city, Detective."

William moves another pawn, irritating Languetti with his remark; Frank locks eyes with Miles momentarily before continuing.

"You know what's most interesting is that the food he had to deliver was ordered by Veronica," Languetti reveals.

William holds back a smirk. Veronica's decision to order takeaway last night aided him in her demise. William is careless; he pushes back to further irritate Languetti.

"So, you're looking for a killer holding a bag of Chinese food?"

Languetti grimaces, his frustrations beginning to surface as William's disrespect takes its toll.

"You think you're pretty funny?" Miles says.

William breathes a careless sigh. "So, what does any of this have to do with me, Detective?"

Frank looked briefly at Miles before shifting his attention to William. "We believe that the person who assaulted the delivery boy went upstairs and killed Veronica in her apartment."

William is confident there is no hard evidence. This charade was not fazing him.

"And we are pretty sure it was you, William." Frank glares at William. William glares back, resentful of the accusation.

"Is this a fact, Detective, or are you and your negro partner playing guessing games?"

"It's Detective Negro you dip-shit." Miles snaps back.

Frank leans forward, demanding William's attention.

"This is how we believe it went down, William. You encountered Veronica yesterday in the city, sometime around noon. You had an unpleasant verbal exchange. She was pissed at you, so she found where your car was parked and made the mess shown in this photo." Frank lifts the photo of the car off the table. "When you got back to your car to find it vandalized, you were pissed off, big time."

Miles interacts.

"So, you waited till it got dark and made your way to Veronica's apartment building, hiding in the shadows for the right opportunity to get inside," Miles adds, Languetti continues.

"Your window of opportunity opened up when you spotted the delivery. You waited until he was buzzed inside before you took him out."

William listens intently, exercising patience. Miles completes the scenario for William.

"You then made your way upstairs to Veronica's apartment, and when she opened the door, you stormed inside, threw her around just before tossing her over the balcony."

William smiles internally, *that's all their cards,* he thinks to himself. He calculates his response.

"That's quite the theory. Should I give up?" William mocks, raising his hands in the air. He leans back, pointing his finger at Languetti as he smirks.

"And... you have evidence to support this theory of yours, Detective? My fingerprints in Veronica's apartment? A witness, maybe?" Languetti and Miles eye each other momentarily.

They've got nothing. This is just a fishing expedition. There's no smoking gun. The nail file is too weak. William revels as his instincts were right. *I knew it. They arrested me out of spite. If they had any incriminating evidence, they would have produced it by now.* William recalls the arrest at the MET, the images of onlookers as he was cuffed. He becomes even more resentful than earlier. Now wanting to voice his dissent, knowing that the detectives have nothing on him. Nothing that can prove he killed Veronica. William leans in. Getting right up in Languetti's face.

"You've got nothing on me, Frank. Not one incriminating piece of evidence. What did you think? I would hear this theory of yours and roll over for you? Did you think you would frighten me into admitting to this crime? Do I look like some junky with depleted brain cells to you? Some lower-class, uneducated street punk, docile enough to fall for your old, tired mind games? This arrest was bullshit, Frank, and you know it. That's why I waived my rights to an attorney. So...with all due respect, fuck you and your theory, Frank."

Languetti manages to control his anger, staring intently at William. There's a sudden knock on the door. A grey-haired man sporting a suit complete with a vest and tie pokes his head in from behind the door. It's Captain Hamersley.

"Frank, can I have a word?"

Languetti holds his glare as he rises to his feet. William laughs, mocking Languetti once again.

"Yeah, fuck off outside, Frank," William utters resentfully.

The remark lights Languetti's fuse. Languetti extends his arm, collecting William flush on the side of the face, the unexpected blow knocks William off the chair and onto the floor.

"Frank!" Captain Hamersley yells out.

William props himself up, wiping his bloodied lip with his hand. William looks up at Languetti with a ridiculous smile.

"There you go, Frank. That's the spirit." William mocks once again. Captain Hamersley takes Languetti by the arm.

"Frank, outside now."

Languetti's frustration is prominent.

"Miles, help him back into his chair," Hamersley instructs.

Miles leans down, taking William by the arm, helping him to his feet. William eases himself back into his chair, his smile turning to a grimace as Languetti exits the room. Captain Hamersley leaves the room, closing the door behind him.

Just outside the room, Captain Hamersley approaches Languetti placing his hands on his hips.

"I don't like this, Frank." His voice is gruff, like an old dog. "What you did just then wasn't a smart move either. He decides to sue the department..."

"He's not gonna sue." Languetti cutting Captain Hamersley off. Captain Hamersley takes a deep breath, placing his hands into his pockets.

"What evidence did forensics dig up from the dead girl's apartment on this guy?"

Languetti is reluctant to answer, anticipating the outcome of the conversation he is about to have with his Captain.

"They came up with nothing."

Captain Hamersley takes another deep breath, exhaling from his nostrils. "What about the kid from the restaurant?"

Languetti shakes his head in frustration. "He got hit from behind, didn't see it coming."

"What about witnesses, Frank; solid evidence linking him to her death; anything?"

No response from Frank. Captain Hamersley gives Languetti a regretful look.

"Frank. you arrested this guy on your own accord. I haven't heard once piece of incriminating evidence in this interrogation. You didn't even run this by the D.A. because you knew as well as I do there's no way a judge would have issued an arrest warrant. But he's in there and now he knows that you got nothing on him. No concrete evidence that he was at the girl's apartment the night of the murder. It's all circumstantial and now you gotta clean this mess up before the mayor gets wind of it."

Frank swallows his pride.

"I'm sorry, Frank, but you have to let him go."

"I spoke to Audrey Mills this morning; she's willing to testify against him for the assault," Frank argues. Captain Hamersley pushes his shoulders back.

"I read the files, Frank. Ones got nothing to do with the other. The phone call about the car is hearsay and useless at best. I hate to admit it Frank, but this guy is right. He's no idiot, and he's not going to give himself up no matter how much you push."

Languetti's frustration is visible.

"Frank, you can't keep him here. He decides to call a lawyer, and we'll both be in deep shit. Let him go, Frank, now."

Languetti looks towards the interrogation room.

"You got an official statement from the girl he assaulted?"

"I'm bringing her in on Monday."

Captain Hamersley places his hand on Languetti's shoulder.

"Frank, get your statement from the girl and then we'll talk to the D.A. about laying the assault charges. Maybe they can find a way to tie the murder in with the assault."

Languetti looks at his Captain, conceding defeat.

"I know you want this guy, but all you've got is a scratched-up car with no witnesses, no forensic evidence and a suspect with no priors who knows his way around the law. It ain't happening with this guy, Frank. Let him go before things get out of hand."

Languetti slowly walks off, heading down the hall.

"Frank, where are you going?"

"Going to take a leak," Languetti mutters as he walks away.

Chapter 40

Inside the interrogation room, William checks his bloodied lip, wiping the edge of his mouth with the back of his palm. He shifts his eyes onto Miles, still bitter about his public arrest at the Metropolitan Opera House. Miles looks at William, sensing the resentful look.

"That this nation, under God, shall have a new birth of freedom." William quotes.

"What was that?"

William places both hands behind his head, slouching onto the chair. "So, Lincoln freed the slaves." William baits Miles.

"You a history buff as well as a murderer?"

William smirks, relishing the opportunity to take on Miles intellectually. "Big fucking joke. You niggers will never be free."

Miles adjusts his position slightly, absorbing the racial slur.

"What the hell are you ranting on about?"

"The chains around your wrists, you ignorant negro."

Miles raises both hands, exposing his wrists to William.

"Chains are still there, my black friend."

William runs his tongue below his swollen lip, still feeling the sting from the blow Languetti gave him.

"Look at you all dressed up in your pressed suit, flashing your badge like it means something to anyone. Bet you've even got yourself one of those fancy degrees. Strutting around, disillusioned to the real fact."

"And what fact is that, William?"

William leans forward, placing his hands on the table, eyeing Miles intently. "The fact that you're still a fucking slave." William glares. "Playing second fiddle to that white, has-been of a partner of yours; taking orders from him like a fucking dog. It doesn't matter how high you climb, there's always going to be a white man that you will take orders from. You are, and will always be, a slave. Detective negro."

Miles keeps his cool. Locking eyes with William as he rises to his feet. He walks away from the table, facing the mirror as he collects his thoughts.

"What's the matter nigger, *dids* I upset you?" William leans back in his chair, his arrogance on full display. Miles turns to face William, choosing his words carefully.

"You think you're a pretty clever guy, don't you, William? You're right; I do have one of those fancy degrees. Master's in criminal psychology at NYU."

"I'm real fucken impressed." William places his left foot on the table's edge, peering at Miles unimpressively.

"There's been something on my mind; maybe you can help me." Miles separates his coat, placing both hands into his trouser pockets. "Something I've been meaning to ask you."

"Yeah, what's that?"

"I was wondering why you beat up on Audrey?"

William is mute, unwilling to incriminate himself, knowing too well that the conversation is being recorded in the next room.

"The reason I ask is that in most assault cases, there is, more often than not, a genuine motive. For example, someone scratches up the paintwork on your $80,000 Mercedes, carving the words Woman Beater onto the hood. That would be a motive for the assault, or in your case, murder."

William exhales deliberately.

"In Audrey's case, though, there didn't seem to be a motive. And when there's no motive, it can only mean one thing." Miles moves forward, placing his hands on the back of his chair. "The person in question, that would be you, has a mental deficiency."

William clenches his jaw, resentful of the remark.

"I think you may find this information very helpful because there has been quite a lot of research done on unmotivated attacks. One study I read talked about one guy who would beat up on older women he dated; and the reason they found was directly related to his upbringing; specifically, his relationship with his mother."

Miles eyes William. William conceals his emotions. He looks away momentarily, his mother invading his thoughts.

"Your father left when you were very young, didn't he?"

William quickly looks back at Miles, the accuracy of the statement irritating him. Miles continues.

"Unmotivated physical abuse is commonly related to fear. Fear that the other person will leave them. You see, a person who fears abandonment will exercise harmful measures, often to control the other person, through intimidation, threats or acts of violence. They destroy the potential of the relationship with destructive behaviour. The reason they do this is to avoid pain. It's their way of dealing with the possibility of abandonment." Miles leans forward slightly. "How was your relationship with your mother, William?"

William glares at Miles; his blood begins to boil.

"What was she like with you? Did she make you feel like you were abandoned? Going to brunches with her female friends; having the help, tuck you in at night whilst she was out nights, fucking other men. Did she send you to boarding school when you were little to avoid raising you? How often did she cook you a meal and sit down with you while you ate?" Miles pauses momentarily. "After your father left, your mother abandoned you too, didn't she, William?"

William's chest starts to heave, his fury reaching its peak. His eyes shift about, unable to focus his thoughts. Miles continues to stare down at William.

"I'm curious, William. Do you still hug your mother when you visit her?"

Using his leg, William aggressively pushes the table over. He's quick to his feet. In one continuous motion, he extends his left arm towards Miles, his hand clenched with uncontrollable rage. Miles uses his hand to counter the aggression, taking a firm hold of William's wrist and pulling him off balance. Miles projects his leg, striking William below the knee, William's momentum carrying him towards the floor's surface. William's chest hits the floor, his left arm still restrained with Miles' firm grip, twisting it awkwardly behind William's back. Miles places his knee down onto William's neck, pinning him down. William groans as he tries to free himself, his anguish increasing as Miles suddenly jerks William's arm further up his spine.

"Get off me, you fucking prick." William roars with anger.

The door suddenly opens; Miles looks up to see Languetti casually enter, placing his hands on his hips.

"William. What are you doing on the floor?" Languetti's mocking tone announces his pleasure at the turn of events.

"Tell this nigger to let go of me." William barks.

"Now, William, we need to be respectful to the coloured folk also, in this here city," Languetti says in a southern accent.

Miles maintains his firm grip as Languetti shifts to the side, allowing two uniformed officers to enter the room for assistance. Captain Hamersley stands in the doorway.

"Let him up, Miles," Hamersley instructs.

The two officers gather around Miles as he releases his grip on William. Miles takes a few steps back, allowing the two officers to assist William to his feet, each taking their place on either side as a precaution.

"Get him out of here," Hamersley again instructs. William glares at Miles briefly before shifting his vision onto Frank.

"Enjoy the rest of your evening, William," Languetti smirks.

William continues to glare, running his tongue below his swollen lip, the impact to the floor adding to his pain. William exhales with bitterness; he's escorted towards the door. Hamersley moves to the side, making way for the men to exit the room. Hamersley looks at Languetti and then at Miles.

"Next time you guys bring him in here, he'd better have someone's blood on his hands." Hamersley holds his stare, making his point before heading off down the hall. Languetti turns to face Miles.

"I'm impressed. That whole abandonment thing you did there, fucking with his head, was a real masterpiece."

"You enjoyed that, eh!"

"Yeah, it was great to watch, especially the part where he lost his shit." Languetti becomes a little animated.

"Well, I aim to please, Frank."

"You know, every day, you're getting to be more and more like me," Languetti remarks as he exits the room. Miles shakes his head as he follows his partner out the door.

Chapter 41

The following morning, Audrey is curled up on her sofa chair, her feet tucked underneath her weary body, clasping a cup of warm tea as she looks aimlessly outside the living room window. Her eyes well up as she recalls Veronica's last words in her thoughts. *Luv ya, babe.* She reaches up to wipe away another tear from her swollen face. Taking a deep breath, Audrey leans forward and takes a sip of the fermented tea, feeling her chest warm up as it flows to her empty stomach. She places her hand on her face, brushing her hair back as she takes another deep breath, pleading for her pain to lessen. She barely hears the knock on the door, turning her head slowly, unsure if she heard anything. Again, there is a faint knock on the door; this time, she hears it clearly, looking across the room at the clock against the wall that reads half-past eight. She raises herself off the chair, removing her numbed legs from beneath her and placing her tired feet onto the cool floor. She makes her way slowly towards the door, still clasping the warm brew against her chest, her only solace at this time. As she approaches, she extends her weary arm unlatching the lock before easing the door open to reveal her visitor. She looks saddened at the man standing before her, letting out a crying sigh.

"Oh, Charlie," Audrey whimpers, clutching the tea tight to her chest with both hands, completely exhausted from the little sleep she could muster during the night. Charlie moves forward.

"Oh, Audrey," Charlie sighs as he places his arms firmly around Audrey, holding her tight as she lets out another muffled whimper. Charlie gently strokes her hair, pressing his cheek against her head, lending any comfort to ease her misery. Audrey tilts her head back and looks up into Charlie's sympathetic eyes.

"Why, Charlie?" She cries, looking to Charlie for an answer. Any justifiable response to help away the torment she is feeling. Charlie shakes his head in silence, unable to find the right words, no words that would justify what has happened to Audrey and the death of her closest friend, Veronica. He raises his palm to her temple, brushing her hair back.

"I'm so sorry, Audrey," Charlie says, his eyes welling up as he pulls her close again. They stand motionless in the doorway as Audrey grieves for her friend's loss.

Audrey eases herself back into the sofa, still cradling her tea in both hands. Charlie sits close beside her, placing his hand on her knee for comfort. Audrey looks down at her tea as she begins to tell Charlie about the time she last spoke to Veronica.

"She called me the other night." Audrey's voice is coarse. "She was coming over tonight. We were going to watch a movie together. Have ourselves a girls' night. Just the two of us." Audrey smiles at the thought, looking down at her tea again. "She was such a good friend to me." Audrey looks up at Charlie. "A good person, and she didn't deserve to die, Charlie."

Charlie rubs Audrey's knee. "No, she didn't, Audrey."

"I'm really going to miss her." Audrey wipes her cheeks. Charlie's compassion is evident as he places his hand on Audrey's shoulder.

"We're all going to miss her, Audrey."

Several minutes of silence elapse as Audrey and Charlie sift through their thoughts. Charlie adjusts slightly, making himself comfortable as he prepares to share his following thoughts with Audrey.

"Detective Languetti called me this morning." The statement draws Audrey's attention. "He asked me if I could bring you to the police station on Monday morning. He said you wanted to make an official statement about the night you were assaulted."

Audrey glances at Charlie, uncertain of what he thinks about her decision to suddenly come forward. Charlie offers Audrey a reassuring smile as he leans in.

"You're doing the right thing, Audrey."

Audrey looks down at her tea. "It's what Veronica wanted me to do. She made her point one day when visiting me in the hospital. I told her to butt out." Audrey looks up at Charlie, wiping away another tear. "She would probably be alive if I had listened to her, Charlie."

Charlie tilts his head. "It's not your fault, Audrey. None of what has happened is your fault. You mustn't blame yourself, Audrey. You were a good friend to Veronica, and I'm sure she is looking down on you right now thinking the same thing."

"He threatened to kill me," Audrey announces.

"Who, William?" Charlie is surprised by the revelation.

"He came to the hospital after you'd left, one night." Audrey looks at Charlie. "He's done it before, but you knew that, Rose told you, didn't she?" Charlie hesitates. "This is why you were so supportive of me when I chose not to talk to the police."

"I was worried he would come after you," Charlie pleads. "We almost lost you that night."

"It's alright, Charlie, I think we both made mistakes." Audrey manages a smile. She leans in closer to Charlie, placing her head on his shoulder for a brief moment. She dismisses her thoughts and addresses Charlie.

"Can I make you some tea, Charlie?"

"I could use some tea right now, but only if you let me help you make it."

Audrey manages another smile; she lifts her head from Charlie's shoulder. She places the cup onto the table, groaning as she rises off the sofa. Charlie keeps his arm wrapped around Audrey, and they amble towards the kitchen.

"Clay will be here a little later," Charlie announces.

"You spoke with him?" Audrey asks as she takes hold of the electric kettle and fills it with water from the faucet.

"He called me last night just after he left your place."

Audrey switches the kettle on and turns to face Charlie. "He was here when I came home yesterday. He stayed with me all afternoon and most of the evening. I must have fallen asleep right before he left."

"Clay told me what happened and how upset you were. He was also pretty upset at the news, but mostly concerned for you."

Audrey looks towards the window, feeling selfish for the attention she is getting, still bitter as she comes to terms with Veronica's sudden death. Charlie notices the dark lines formed beneath Audrey's eyes.

"Audrey, I want you to take it easy today. You should rest and make sure you eat something. It hasn't been that long since you were released from the hospital. I'm a little concerned myself, to tell you the truth." Charlie is fatherly with his advice. Audrey continues to gaze out the window, the sun peeking through the clouds.

"I'll be all right, Charlie. I promise I'll eat something." Audrey is dismissive. Charlie opens the cupboard above his head. He removes two teacups and places them on the counter.

"I have to go to work today," Audrey reveals.

"What for?" Charlie is perplexed. "Clay told me Rose gave you the day off to mourn."

"I left my purse behind and want to prune the batch of Roses we received. I never got a chance to do them yesterday."

"Can't that wait till Monday?"

Audrey shakes her head. "No. I have to do it today. Most of those Roses will be for deliveries over the weekend. Besides, I've taken too much time off from work lately."

"I'm sure Rose and Gloria will understand," Charlie argues.

Audrey approaches Charlie, placing her hands on his shoulders. "Charlie, I'll be fine. I need my purse, Charlie, and I could also use some fresh air."

Charlie is not pleased. "All right then, but don't stay too long. Just the hours you need to."

"Stop worrying, Charlie. I should be back by three."

Charlie pats Audrey gently on the head. "You know how upset Clay gets when you don't look after yourself."

Audrey smiles. "Sure, Charlie. I'll hurry back so as not to upset Clay."

The bell sounds on the kettle, signalling it's time to make some tea.

Chapter 42

Audrey walks steadily on the sidewalk, her head bowed and arms folded. Her earmuffs drown out the traffic noise as she heads for her destination. Up ahead, the florist where she works. Audrey suddenly stops as she approaches the entrance; her eyes examine the street traffic, paranoid thoughts lingering. She takes a deep breath before pushing the entrance door open with her palm. The chime sounds as she steps inside; the store counter is unmanned. Audrey removes her earmuffs and shifts her vision back and forth across the room. She becomes slightly anxious as she looks for any sign of human presence. She diverts her attention to the doorway that leads to the back. She takes another step. She hears a scuffle followed by the sound of the door to the rear entrance as it closes shut.

"Audrey!" John is startled as he appears through the doorway holding a water bucket full of Roses.

"Hey...John." Audrey breathes a sigh of relief, just pleased to see a familiar face. She walks towards John, removing her gloves and placing them on the counter with her handbag. John rests the bucket of Roses on the floor.

"I didn't know you were coming in today?" Rose informed John of the dire news earlier that morning. "How are you…feeling?"

"I'm fine, John." Audrey struggles to bring out her smile. John pauses, crossing his arms and nervously rubbing his elbows before addressing Audrey.

"I heard about…" He can't bring himself to complete the sentence. He looks at Audrey with sympathetic eyes. "I'm sorry about V, Audrey."

Audrey nods her head in appreciation. "Thanks, John," she folds her arms, deterring John from any physical comfort. She is mentally exhausted from all the human contact everyone has been giving her lately. She notices John's awkwardness and decides to change the subject.

"So…these some of the roses I have to prune?"

John glances at the bucket. "Yeah, that's some of them. There's more in the cooler out back. I'll go bring them in."

"Okay, great." Audrey is all business. John heads towards the back. "Where's Rose?" Audrey inquires, removing her coat. John stops at the door.

"She had to go out for a few hours. Said she'd be back about two."

"You hanging around?" Audrey does not want to be alone. John smiles at Audrey, anticipating the response she's hoping for.

"I'll stay here with you till she gets back."

Audrey's cheeks rose in appreciation for his thoughtfulness. "Thanks, John."

"No worries, Audrey." John gives her another smile before continuing to the back. Audrey looks around the room and takes a deep breath as she reaches for her gloves and pruning scissors beneath the workstation.

After one hundred and three minutes of pruning Roses, Audrey groans, wiping her sweaty brow with her sleeve. She looks over at John, kneeling by the store window, with a cloth and a cleaner in hand.

"Hey, are you hungry yet?" Audrey yells across the room. She removes her gloves and places them onto the workbench with the pruning scissors. John spins around on his backside to face Audrey.

"I'm starving."

"I could go for one of those falafel rolls around the corner." Audrey runs her tongue across as she smacks her lips.

"I heard that!" John springs to his feet.

"My purse!" Audrey remembers excitedly as she moves towards the main counter. She reaches into a drawer, retrieving her purse. She removes a twenty-dollar note, extending her arm to offer John the money.

"Can you also get me sparkling water?" She pleads, feeling that her body is completely dehydrated.

"Anything else?" John takes the money into his hand. Audrey puts on a naughty grin.

"Yeah, grab something sweet. Something with chocolate!"

John grins. "Sure thing, Audrey. I'll be back in ten."

John tosses the rag onto the counter before hurrying out of the store. Audrey brushes her hair back, again letting out an exhausted sigh as she heads for the kitchen to wash up. As she reaches for the faucet, she hears the entrance chime sound, curiously turning back around to see who it is. John comes leaping into the store with an embarrassed look on his face. He quickly makes his way behind the counter, grabbing his coat, which hangs by the door. He looks across at a smiling Audrey.

"It's freezing!" he shivers laughingly; Audrey shakes her head, amused by John as he scurries back out the door again.

"Crazy boy," Audrey mutters as she heads back into the kitchen. Audrey rolls her sleeves up as she reaches for the faucet; she again hears the entrance chime sound. She shakes out a giggle, rolling her eyes as she pivots on one foot, making her way back into the main area of the store.

"What did you forget this time?" she laughingly squawks. Her laughter quickly disappears as she enters the room. She looks across to see William standing there, unmoved by her presence. Audrey's limbs freeze up; her heart begins to race as she looks directly into William's wicked eyes. Muddled thoughts race through her mind, her body paralysed.

"Hello, Audrey." William's voice is heavy in tone, his face expressionless. Audrey's mouth dries up; she's unable to find her breath to respond or yell out her distress. She clenches her hands to suppress them from shaking; her eyes well up as William takes a few steps in her direction.

"Are we alone, Audrey?" he asks in a darkened voice. Audrey struggles to respond, raped with fear. She clutches onto the doorway, fearing she'll pass out as she struggles to breathe. William reaches the main counter. He leans forward, placing both forearms on the countertop to support himself. He eyes Audrey for several moments before once again addressing her.

"You don't look too good, Audrey." He shifts his eyes to her delicate legs before focusing on her petrified face. "Your eyes have darkened, and your face looks…unsightly pale." William ridicules, keeping the same bland expression on his face. "You really should look after yourself better."

Audrey reaches up, wiping the birth of a tear from her eye as she attempts to swallow what little saliva she has left in her mouth. She prises her lips apart, finding enough breath to address William.

"What do you want?" she whimpers. Her voice is trembling; her hands shake involuntarily. William smiles, relishing in Audrey's fear.

"I wanted to see you, Audrey."

Audrey keeps silent, still struggling with her composure.

"I thought we were friends?" William mocks. "Aren't we still friends, Audrey?"

Audrey says nothing. William lets out a small breath as he breaks a smile, easing himself up off the countertop; the smile diminishing from his face. William looks around the room, seemingly admiring the floral arrangements. Audrey shifts her focus towards the workstation, her sights falling on the pruning scissors. Her attention quickly turns back to William as he again begins to speak.

"I guess I should convey my condolences for the loss of your friend." William peering over his shoulder at Audrey, wanting to see her reaction. Audrey is mute; her thoughts are a blur as she struggles to breathe. Anxiety is getting the better of her. William reaches across, taking a single Rose from Audrey's workstation, resting it on his chin, and inhaling the sweet aroma.

"That which we call a rose by any other word would smell as sweet." he quotes softly, turning his head to look at Audrey once again. Audrey looks back over her shoulder; she considers darting for the store's rear entrance. William smiles as he steps towards her. Again, they lock eyes; William easing his head side to side to suggest that she shouldn't try to run. Audrey bows her head in resignation, knowing she has neither the speed nor the strength to escape from William. She stands there, feeling vulnerable, her heart rate increasing as William moves in her direction. Audrey fears what William may do as she watches him slither towards her. He navigates his way behind the main counter, holding the rose in front of Audrey's eyes as he moves in closer and closer, ceasing his stride only inches from her face. Audrey focuses on the rose before bravely raising her chin, looking directly into William's eyes. Several moments pass as William stares down at Audrey, his eyes revealing his lust for her. He directs the rose towards her, stroking the side of her face and down to her neck. William shifts his focus onto her breasts. He feathers the petals across her cleavage. Audrey stands there; her bare skin stimulated; she inhales the pungent aroma of William's aftershave as he leans forward, placing his hand on her shoulder, his cheek against her frontal lobe.

"Don't make me kill you, Audrey," he whispers in her ear. Audrey's lips separate as she takes a short breath; her eyes close as she exhales, and her mind drifts from reality as the warmth of William's lips touches her skin. William raises his hand from her shoulder, stroking her neck with his fingers and down to her breast. His hand caressing her gently. Audrey can hear the faint sound of William's chest beating heavily as he squeezes her breast tight in his hand. Unconsciously, Audrey raises her hand, placing it on William's broad shoulder.

"Oh god," she whispers, moistening her lips with her tongue, feeling sickened by her arousal.

Suddenly, the chime sounds as the front door swings open. John enters, holding a disposable bag and rubbing his limbs to shake off the cold. William backs off Audrey, both turning to see John standing in the doorway, John looking surprised at Audrey, her fear apparent. John glares at William.

"Leave her alone." John deepens his voice, exercising authority. William clenches his jaw, a wry smile appearing as he glares back at John. He is displeased with the command. He navigates from behind the counter and walks directly towards John. Audrey becomes fearful of what William may do. John takes in a deep breath, expanding his chest as William draws closer.

"Stay the hell away from her," he commands in a stern voice. William is unmoved as he stands a foot taller, hovering over him. His dissent for John is apparent.

"William, please don't hurt him!" Audrey pleads; John's thoughts confirm that this man hurt his friend Audrey. John clenches his fist, propelling his arm towards William's face. William is quick. He grabs John by the wrist, pulling him closer, taking hold of the smaller man by his clothing. John struggles to free himself from William's heavy grip, now feeling the pain soaring down his arm as William pressures John's wrist. William violently thrusts John sideways, throwing him across the room; John staggers as he tries to find his feet. His momentum ends as he collects several floral arrangements, falling awkwardly onto the floor.

"John!" Audrey yells, covering her mouth as she rushes to aid him.

"Leave him!" William growls: his voice filled with rage. Audrey ceases on William's command; she turns to face William. John struggles, raising his hand to nurse the side of his head; his blood is visible as he examines his fingers. He lays back, disorientated by the throw. Audrey glances at John again before reaching across the workstation and taking the pruning scissors into her hand. William moves towards Audrey, his breathing heavies as he stares at her. Audrey holds the pruning scissors out in front, her facial expression warning William not to come any closer.

"Do you think this is a fucken game?" William thunders away in anger. Audrey is startled by the penetrating sound of William's voice; clenching the pruning scissors tight, her hand begins to shake. She holds back her tears as she stands her ground in protest.

"Don't come any closer," she warns, her voice trembling with fear, knowing her efforts will be no match for William if he decides to attack her. William holds his ground, glaring into her eyes with conviction. A moment passes before he slowly shifts his weight towards the entrance, taking one last look at John as he thrusts the door open, stepping out onto the sidewalk. Audrey lets out a sigh of relief, loosening her grip on the pruning scissors. She hears John's voice as he struggles to get to his feet again.

"Oh god, John." Audrey rushes over to help, falling to her knees beside him. "You're bleeding," she says, regretfully taking hold of John by the arm. "Can you get up?"

"Yeah, I think so," John groans as Audrey helps him rise to his feet. "Are you alright, Audrey?"

Audrey nods her head slightly. "Yeah…no. Not really."

She places her arms around John, pulling herself close to his chest. They hold each other for a moment before Audrey puts her hand on his face, presenting John with a look of appreciation; the moment is tarnished with a hint of bitterness as she notices the blood smeared on the side of John's face.

"Well, that guys a real jerk." John makes light of the moment as he steps over the debris. Audrey forces a smile. She rushes over to lock the entrance to the store.

"Come on; let's go into the kitchen and fix up your head. You may need to use it one day."

John smiles. "That was kinda stupid of me."

Audrey places her hand on his shoulder as they make their way towards the back. "I thought it was pretty brave," Audrey admits.

John raises his chin. "Yeah! Maybe you…"

"The falafels!" she yells out, racing over to pick up the food John dropped. "Gosh, I hope they're okay."

"Audrey, I'm bleeding, and you're thinking about your stomach."

"Shut up, I'm blooming starving." Audrey takes John by the hand. "Come on, let's go fix you up so we can eat."

"You're so weird sometimes." John mumbles, nursing his head as Audrey pulls him across the room.

Chapter 43

Miles taps his index finger on his replica Rolex. "What time you got?"

Languetti looks at his watch as he sips his coffee. "Just after three."

Languetti falls back into his chair, perusing the articles in the Friday edition of the New York Times. Miles looks over his shoulder, glancing at the diners' wall clock; his eyes wander down to Flo as she prepares coffee for another customer. Miles looks back at Languetti, taking his beverage in his hand.

"Not long to go now. You must be getting pretty nervous." Miles takes a sip of his tea. Languetti looks up from his paper.

"Nervous? About what?" Languetti acts aloof.

"Your big date with Dr Bridge. You're picking her up tonight, remember?"

Languetti shrugs his shoulders. "I almost forgot about that; thanks for reminding me."

Miles purses his lips. "Yeah, right, Frank. Don't forget to buy her some flowers."

Languetti raises his palm at Miles. "We've been through this. Change the record already."

Miles swallows a mouthful of tea. "Did you make a reservation at The Golden Dragon?"

Languetti gives Miles two affirmative nods. Miles rests his beverage on the table; his thoughts divert to the murder case.

"What time is the girl coming in on Monday?"

Languetti turns the page on his paper. "Around ten."

"Someone else going with her?" Miles thinks of Audrey's safety.

"Charlie. I asked him if he could bring her in."

Miles looks at an adjacent booth, focusing on a little girl playing with her doll.

"Maybe we should go pick her up, just in case."

Languetti folds his newspaper, taking one last mouthful of coffee before responding to Miles. "I'd rather she made her own way to the precinct. I don't want her to get overanxious about the whole thing." Languetti places the empty vessel on the table before rising to his feet.

"Where are you going, Frank?"

"I have to do some stuff before I head home and rest for a while. You know, so I don't fall asleep at dinner tonight." Languetti looks across the room, gathering Flo's attention. She waves goodbye to Languetti from behind the counter.

"Take care, Frank."

"What stuff do you have to do, Frank?"

Languetti frowns at Miles, shrugging his shoulders. "You know...stuff."

Miles widens his eyes. "No, Frank, I don't know what stuff you mean." Miles seeks clarification. Languetti is reluctant to elaborate.

"I have to go and... pick up my dinner suit from the dry cleaners. Is that enough information for you, Detective?"

"You had your suit cleaned for tonight, Frank?" Miles grins as he takes a sip of his tea. Languetti looks irritably.

"Yeah, so what?"

Miles laughs softly. "Didn't you say the other day, 'It's just dinner. It's no big deal.'" Languetti adjusts his coat.

"It's not a big deal. It's just been quite a while since I've worn the dinner suit. I pulled it out last night to air it, and it smelt like fricken moth balls."

Miles leans back into his chair. He looks at Frank in admiration, like a proud parent.

"You want a ride home or what?" Languetti asks frustratingly.

Miles rises from his chair. "Yeah, I do." He turns and waves at Flo. "Catch you later, Flo." Miles follows Frank towards the exit. "Maybe we should stop by the drugstore and buy you some protection, just in case." Miles smiles and swings open the door for Frank to exit.

"Screw you," Languetti mutters under his breath.

"Not me, Frank, her!"

Chapter 44

"Clay, have you seen the big wrench?" Charlie groans as he picks himself up off the floor.

Clay turns his attention to Charlie. "Yes, boss. It's in the toolbox."

"Clay, I have the toolbox in front of me; I'm working out of it. It's not here." He responds in frustration.

"I don't have it." Clay pleads his innocence.

"Well, I don't have it, Clay. I don't even use the darn thing unless I really need to. It's too big for my hand." Charlie lets out a sigh. "Where the hell is that damn..." Charlie once again sifts through the toolbox.

"Boss," Clay takes a cautious step towards Charlie.

"What is it, Clay?"

"Didn't you use the big wrench yesterday when we fixed that leak in the water heater? In the storeroom out back."

Charlie looks up at Clay, quickly realising that Clay is right. He recalls needing it to tighten the large fastener on the water heater.

Clay wipes his palms on his overalls; Charlie's current mood causes him to feel somewhat anxious.

"Maybe I left it next to the water heater yesterday. I can go to the back and see if it's there."

Charlie resigns out of guilt. "Yes. Can you please go look for me?"

Clay stands there momentarily; he examines Charlie as he wipes the grease from his hands.

"You all right, boss?"

Charlie looks up at Clay, exhaling his grief as he responds. "Yes, Clay, I'm fine."

Clay casually makes his way towards the storeroom, ceasing his stride to turn and address Charlie once again. "I'm worried about her, too, boss."

Charlie gives Clay a sympathetic look. "I know Clay, me too."

Charlie looks to the entrance of The Parkway; he can hear the faint sound of the street traffic through the glass panes.

"You know it's almost five," he remarks. "Rose told me Audrey left the florist just before 3 pm. She should be back by now."

At that moment, the sound of ruckus and female laughter is heard. Both men focus on the entrance. Charlie tosses the greasy rag onto the counter. The door swings open; a giggling Audrey stumbles inside with her arm wrapped around John. Clay looks at Charlie; Charlie's eyes are entirely focused on Audrey as she looks across the room at Clay.

"Clay!" she yells, her voice echoing in the vast space. She peels herself away from John and clumsily skips towards him. Clay braces himself, his hands clenching his denim as Audrey quickly approaches. Her enthusiasm is frightening. She leaps off the ground, wrapping her thin arms around Clay's shoulders. She barely made it, her feet now dangling from side to side.

"*Hiya, Claye!*" she speaks in a high-pitched, squeaky voice. Clay presents Audrey with a nervous smile before glancing over at

Charlie, his facial expression telling, as he catches the stench of bourbon coming from Audrey's breath. He places his hands on Audrey's waist, supporting her as she slides down, her feet finding the ground.

"My big teddy bear," she squeals, wrapping her arms around Clay's stomach. Charlie looks at John, who is baby-stepping towards Audrey, his hands nervously placed in the rear pockets of his jeans, his eyes on Clay. Never having met Clay before today, John recalls several times when Audrey spoke about him, but can't remember Audrey ever mentioning how big Clay is. Astounded by his sheer size, John cautiously keeps his distance, uncertain of how Clay may react, given that John was with Audrey when she became intoxicated.

Charlie notices the fresh bandage on John's forehead and becomes curious. He shifts his focus to Audrey.

"It's five o'clock, Audrey. Rose told me you left the store at three." Audrey looks at Charlie; her smile diminishing as she notices how unimpressed Charlie is with her behaviour.

"Hi, Charlie," she whispers.

"Where have you been, Audrey?" Charlie inquires, peering at Audrey like a teenager who missed her curfew. Audrey releases her arms from Clay, miffed at the disciplinary attitude towards her whereabouts.

"John and I just stopped for a drink on the way home," she states emphatically. "Is there a problem, Charlie?"

She moves towards John, taking hold of his arm. John avoids eye contact with Clay, nervously tapping his toe on the marble floor as Clay looks down at him; John quietly wishes he were anywhere else right now. Silence fills the room; Charlie eases his glare, not wanting to condemn Audrey for her actions, remembering he had done the same on multiple occasions when his wife passed away. Charlie turns his attention to John.

"Were you also drinking, John?" John is only twenty years of age and still under the legal drinking age.

"No, sir, I mean, I had a Coke, is all. And some nuts."

"Some nuts," Audrey giggles.

Charlie assesses John momentarily. "Very well then, say goodnight to Audrey now and head on home," Charlie instructs. Audrey displays her resentment, looking at him unimpressively.

"I better get going, Audrey. It's getting dark outside." John resigns to the order, placing his arms around her, Audrey squeezing him tightly and close to her body.

"You're a good friend."

Clay watches closely as Audrey kisses John on the cheek; John feels embarrassed by the gesture; he blushes, looking down at his feet.

"I'll see you Tuesday, right?" John is chuffed.

"You *betcha*." Audrey is giddy, still feeling the effects of the alcohol; she points her finger at John, giving him a wink. John turns to look at Charlie one last time before slowly backing up towards the door, glancing at Clay as he swings open the door, bouncing out onto the footpath.

Charlie holds his ground; he's not done sharing his thoughts with Audrey. Charlie attempts to justify his militant behaviour. "You had us both worried, Audrey."

Audrey looks into Charlie's tired eyes; she decides not to burden him with the added knowledge of William's spiteful visit earlier that day. "I'm sorry, Charlie, but it's been a rough couple of days."

Charlie's mood returns to sympathy, and his love for Audrey is evident. Clay creeps closer to Audrey.

"You feeling alright now, Miss Audrey?" Audrey reaches out, touching Clay on the chest.

"Of course, I'm perfectly fine." Audrey staggers as she raises her finger in the air. "Just a little...tipsy is all." Clay places his hand on Audrey's shoulder.

"If you want, we can have lunch together tomorrow. Maybe order some pizza?" Clay is feeling hungry as it nears dinner time.

Audrey's smile is tiring. "Sounds like a good plan, Clay."

Charlie eyes the clock on the wall. "Clay, why don't you take off for the evening? We can finish this work up on Monday."

Clay acknowledges Charlie. Audrey extends both arms, falling face-first onto Clay's chest.

"You're my big...*muffles*." Audrey closes her eyes; she feels Clay's heart thumping through his chest, sending her off to doze. Clay jolts her awake from her peaceful slumber.

"I think I might have drifted off!" Audrey stretches her eyes, her voice announcing her surprise.

"You want me to carry you upstairs and tuck you in bed?" Clay teases.

"What!" Audrey shrieks. "OMG. Clay. I'm a lady, and I'm certain I can manage that all on my own." Audrey burps as she pulls her hair back, "Oops, excuse me."

Clay giggles as he heads home for the evening, exiting the lobby.

"Nighty night, Clay." Audrey waves.

Charlie moves closer to Audrey, securing her with his arm. "So, what's your poison, Audrey?"

Audrey blows a raspberry. "Bourbon."

"And how many bourbons did you have?" Charlie guides Audrey towards the stairs. Audrey holds up her left hand, extending four fingers.

"Really!" Charlie is impressed. "And you're still upright?"

"Yep." Audrey becomes animated. "I can hold my liquor, Charlie."

"Sure…you can, Audrey. I think it's time you went upstairs and slept it off, though."

Audrey pats Charlie on the shoulder. "Agree, good sir."

Audrey peels herself away from Charlie's arm. Charlie watches her, amused, as she walks drunkenly towards the stairs. Audrey stops, placing her hand on the railing. She turns to look at Charlie.

"Goodnight, Charlie Brown."

"Goodnight, Audrey." Charlie watches Audrey momentarily as she drags her weary legs up, one step at a time. He takes a deep breath, thankful for Audrey's safe return.

Chapter 45

After what seemed like a laborious task of reaching the top of the stairs, Audrey drags her weary body down the hallway, rubbing her shoulder against the wall for support, trying to remain upright as she approaches her door. Her vision is blurred, and the lights are dim, but she finds her focus as she begins to rustle through the many items in her bag, her fingers rejecting item after item until they find the elusive keys. Her hand was wavering as she inserted the key into the cylinder lock, releasing the door open; she again staggered inside, leaning back against the door and pushing it closed. Audrey makes her way down the narrow path, wiping her face with her hands, stretching her eyes as she lets out a regrettable sigh. She tosses her bag and keys onto the kitchen counter, gazing at the empty living room, her eyes shifting aimlessly, the alcohol disorienting her thoughts. She shifts her vision to the farthest end of the room, peering through the glass window to the building across the street. She smiles, admiring the deep golden hue omitted from the sun's evening rays as it blankets the brickwork. Audrey runs her fingers through her hair as she continues, taking small steps towards the bedroom, extending her hand to touch the wall, again lending support to her tired legs. As she enters the room, she again places her hand on her face, leaning against the doorframe, now beginning to regret her decision to stop for a quiet drink with John. Audrey pushes herself off the doorframe, walking towards the bed. Her hands struggle to take hold of the lapels as she removes her coat and drapes it on the end of the bed. She turns slowly, planting herself on the edge of the mattress, remaining upright momentarily, recomposing her thoughts as she reaches down, removing both her sneakers. She crosses her arms, peeling her sweater over her head, tossing it behind the bed. One by one, Audrey undoes the buttons on her blouse, pulling it back over her bony shoulders, exposing a lace bra made of delicate white satin. She rises to her feet, her fingers fiddling with the rugged denim as she unlatches the riveted buttons from their restraints. She slides the denim down to her ankles, feeling the dizziness in her head as she rises again. She pins the jeans to the ground using her toe, freeing one leg before doing the same with the other. Reaching behind with both hands, she unhinges her bra, the soft satin lace falling off her silky skin, exposing her ample breasts. She slides her hands over her stomach and down to her hips, placing her thumbs inside the lace of her panties, sliding them down her thighs, the soft satin material falling to the ground as she releases her hold.

Audrey stands there momentarily, her inhibitions fading as she looks across the room into the mirror, the redness of the surgical scars still visible. Her breathing slows, finding a solemn moment of peace, her thoughts far from her recent worries. She takes a calming breath and moves forward, reaching down to swoop a satin robe that rests on the floor. She pulls the robe close to her chest, brushing her hair back as she continues towards the door. She exits the room, making her way through the living area and to the bathroom of her apartment; the cold tiles beneath her penetrate the numbness in her feet. Audrey slides her hand across the wall, searching for the light switch, squinting her eyes in anticipation. The fluorescent light beams brightly onto her face. She closes the door behind her, placing the robe onto a rail hook before reaching across for the shower taps, the icy water quickly turning to steam as the temperature rises. Passing her fingers underneath the streams of water, Audrey waits for the ideal temperature before stepping into the cast iron tub, promptly pulling the curtain around and trapping the heat surrounding her.

"Oh God."

Audrey lets out a relieving sigh as the water heats her skin, holding her arms close to her chest as her body warms. She leans her head forward, completely submerging herself under the heavy pellets. Closing her eyes, Audrey raises her chin, exposing her face to the streams of water, indulging in the warm sensation as the ripples flow down her back. Several minutes pass as Audrey stands there, her thoughts drifting far from her troubles, random memories of her childhood seeping in, reminding her of happier times. Several more minutes pass before Audrey opens her eyes, taking the soap in her hands to lather her chest and arms. She returns the soap to its place, using the remaining lather in her palms to run her hands vigorously over her face and neck, raising her chin once more to allow the water to purify her pores. Audrey reaches forward, placing both hands on the shower taps; the water flow abruptly ends as she turns her hands; a few droplets of water manage to escape. As she slides the curtain back, a gush of cold air blankets her body, and goosebumps form on her skin as she steps from the tub. She reaches for a nearby towel, wrapping herself snugly, the thick cotton blend soaking up the water on her skin. She wedges the towel in her cleavage before reaching for a smaller towel aptly positioned. Audrey bows her head forward, wrapping the smaller towel around her hair before tossing her head back, securing her hair in the cocoon she has formed. Audrey takes hold of a hand towel hanging over the basin, pressing it against her face, trapping the air in her lungs as she holds her breath. She emits another relieving sigh as she lowers the towel, carelessly tossing it into the basin before lifting her robe off the hook.

The frigid air rushes in as she pulls the door open, her hand unconsciously reaching for the light switch as she exits the bathroom. Forgetting her slippers, Audrey leaves wet footprints behind as she ambles towards the bedroom, now in a trance state as she heads directly for the bed, pulling the quilt cover down and over itself. She places her hand between her breasts, loosening the knot she formed earlier, the damp towel falling at her feet. Audrey slides into her robe, her tired sole falling onto the mattress, her feet sliding beneath the covers. She pulls the quilt up to her chin, lying quietly on her back, her eyelids heavy from exhaustion. She looks across the room to the window; the last light of the day fades quickly; Audrey finally closes her eyes, falling into a deep and restful sleep.

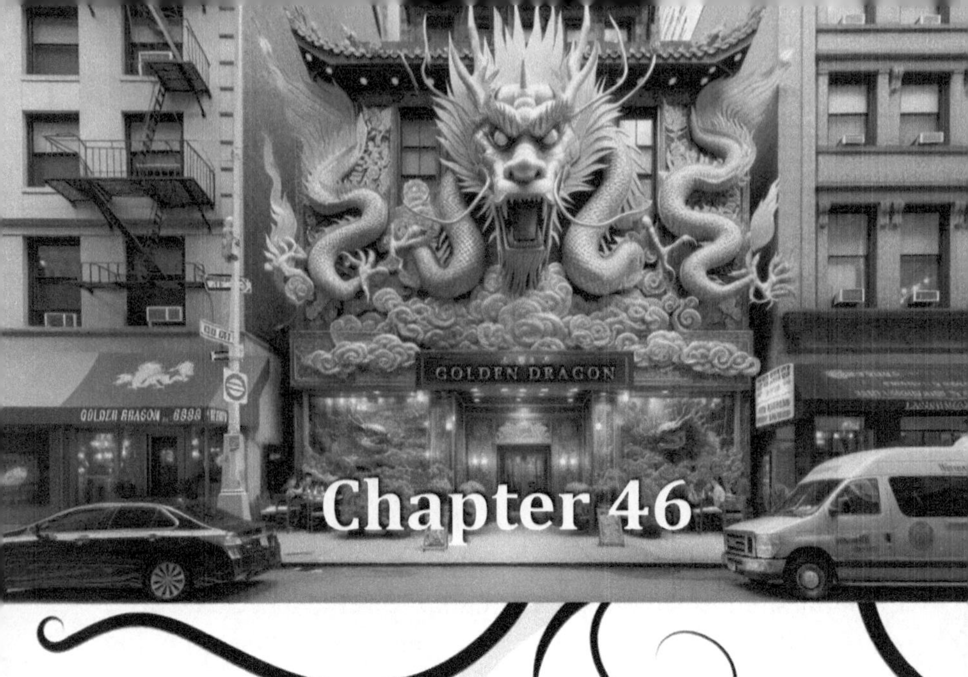

Chapter 46

Located on the east side of town, The Golden Dragon is in the heart of Chinatown and home to some of the city's finest Thai cuisine. It is just after seven, and ominous clouds hover over the city. They begin to emit light rain that quickly increases in density as the thunder announces the bleak forecast. Languetti feels the hard pellets of water on his back just moments before escorting Dr Evelyn Bridge inside the restaurant's waiting area, the fragrant smells immediately enticing the senses.

"Looks like your timing is perfect." Evelyn compliments Frank as she turns to look through the decorative glass windows of the lavish four-star restaurant, the rain now thumping away on the city's traffic. Frank's nerves are visible as he smiles at his beautiful date, running his palms over his shoulders to clear away the water beads on his newly pressed dinner suit. A man approaches, small in stature and of Eastern appearance wearing traditional chut Thai clothing.

"Good evening, Sir, Madam." The maître d' politely bows his head as he greets them both.

"Do you have a reservation tonight?"

Frank unconsciously bows his head. "Yes, we do. It's under Languetti...for two."

"One moment, please." The maître d' excuses himself before heading to a podium several feet inside the restaurant's foyer. Frank and Evelyn wait patiently as the maître d' rounds the podium, his eyes concentrating on the decorative register, which is traditional in its appearance and made from aged paper. Using his index finger as a pointer, he thoroughly moves his hand down the page, searching for Frank's reservation.

"Lane-gut-ti, yes?" The maître d' raises his head, mispronouncing as he looks at the couple for confirmation. Both Frank and Evelyn nod in unison. The maître d' props himself upright in delight.

"This way, please, sir, madam." The maître d's manners are impeccable, extending his hand towards the cluster of tables. Frank gently places his palm on Evelyn's lower back, directing her towards the seating area. The maître d' leads the couple, veering his way through the gatherings with precision. Frank's eyes scan the crowded room, an occupational hazard he can't seem to shake even when he's off duty. Frank draws his breath, taking in the appetising aroma of the Thai cuisine, just as they pass a couple being served their main courses. Evelyn looks impressively at the plates of food before turning to view Frank, her eyes giving him the seal of approval. Frank gives Evelyn a humble look, thoughtfully acknowledging his partner Miles for the wise suggestion.

"Here we are, sir, madam." The maître d' announces, sliding out a chair for Evelyn; Evelyn removes her coat, placing it on the maître d's arm, which is readily extended, before easing herself onto the plush chair. The maître d' quickly rushes over to assist Frank, who raises his palm, halting the man in his tracks.

"I can manage, thank you," Frank gestures as he seats himself facing Evelyn.

"A waiter will be here soon to serve you. So please have a lovely evening." The maître d' politely bows his head once more before heading in the opposite direction. Languetti watches the man as he leaves, promptly turning to address Evelyn.

"He took your coat!" Frank misses nothing. Evelyn finds the humour in Frank's observation, deciding to poke fun at him to help ease his tension.

"You going to arrest him, Frank?"

"Yeah, I might." Frank's wit is quicker since being partnered with Miles. They both smile as Frank reaches for the wine menu. Evelyn watches him closely, always finding humour in his diligence. Frank feels Evelyn's smiling eyes and looks up from the wine menu.

"What?" he says softly. Evelyn leans forward, placing her forearms on the table, her hands interlocked as she examines Frank.

"I'm looking at the wine selection." Frank feels justified. Evelyn widens her smile, her perfect teeth now on full display. Frank shakes his head slightly, returning his focus to the wine list. Evelyn peeks across the room to see a young couple a few tables down holding hands.

"Do you prefer red or white?"

Evelyn casually returns her attention to Frank. "I think white would be suitable for Thai cuisine. What do you think, Frank?"

Languetti bobs, thinking a big juicy steak probably won't be on the menu. "Would you like to look at the wine list? Maybe choose something you like?"

Evelyn gazes into Frank's eyes. "You can choose Frank. I trust you," Evelyn winks, sincerity in her voice. Languetti flips open the wine list again, holding an awkward gaze before shifting his attention to the menu.

"Nothing fruity, okay, Frank? Something dry." Evelyn adds, examining the table ornaments. She leans back into her chair and notices a very gay waiter, his smile beaming from across the room as he approaches the table.

"Good evening, my name is Manny, and I will be your waiter on this occasion."

Frank tilts the wine list, his face lamenting.

"And how is the lovely couple doing tonight?" The waiter is giddy as he addresses Frank. "You're looking very dashing tonight, sir." Evelyn chuckles, noticing the stark look on Frank's face. The waiter sways towards Evelyn. "Oh, I love that colour on you. It's so elegant." The waiter remarks, placing his palms together. Evelyn tilts her head to one side.

"Thank you, you're so kind."

The waiter observes the wine list in Frank's hand.

"Have you made your selection of wine, sir?"

"Yes, we'll have. A bottle of the No.7, please." Frank presents the menu to Manny, who scrolls his pen down the list, locating Frank's selection.

"The Wolffer Antonov. Oh, an excellent choice, sir."

"Is that a dry wine?" Evelyn inquires. The waiter scribbles down the wine selection.

"Oh yes, the Wolffer Antonov is a Sauvignon Blanc. Dry...unless, of course, you spill it on yourself." The waiter chuckles at his humorous anecdote, awarding it with a single clap. Evelyn glances over at Frank, who forces a smile for the waiter. The waiter removes two menus secured between his elbow and ribs, handing one to each.

"Here are your menus for tonight. As you will see, we have a wide selection, including three specials shown on the first page. I will return shortly with your wine selection, and if you are ready, I will take your food order!" The waiter presents them with a huge smile, performing a pirouette as he leaves. Frank looks over at Evelyn, who is quick to comment.

"Manny is adorable, isn't he, Frank?"

Frank produces a wry smile. "Yeah, he was very...upbeat."

Evelyn lets out a small laugh. "Upbeat? Is that your secret word for gay? Is it Frank?" Frank chooses to ignore Evelyn's question, pretending to be in deep thought as he studies the food menu. "He was right about one thing, Frank. You do look very dashing tonight."

Frank feels embarrassed, realising he has yet to compliment Evelyn tonight.

"You look very nice tonight as well. Your dress and hair..." Frank fumbles with his words, "you look perfect."

Evelyn smiles with appreciation. She leans forward; her tone is sincere.

"Thank you, Frank."

Languetti awkwardly returns a smile, diverting his attention to the menu items. Evelyn holds her gaze in admiration; inconspicuously, she breathes a sigh.

They both sit quietly for a few moments, perusing the menu items. The surrounding voices become one to emanate a soft hum that fills the room. The occasional clatter of cutlery is heard from those who have commenced dining on their selection. Seeping through the walls and ceiling, *Chopin's Piano Concerto No.2— Larghetto* dances romantically with the diffused lighting, offering a pleasant dining environment.

"I might go for the curry duck," Languetti announces with confidence.

"Which number is that Frank?"

"Err...number 17."

Evelyn runs her eyes down the page, stopping on menu item 17.

"Red Curry duck!" Evelyn looks up from the menu. "Sounds delicious, Frank."

"Yeah, I like eating duck. I've done some duck hunting in the past." Frank briefs over the menu one last time before closing it shut with confidence. He places it at the corner of the table before leaning back into his chair. Evelyn flicks over the page of her menu, Frank eyeing the surroundings as Evelyn, like the forensic doctor she is, scrutinises the many choices for the main course.

"I might try the...Spicy Seafood with Noodle." Evelyn ponders, raising her finger to her lips. Frank looks over his shoulder, sensing the waiter who is returning with their bottle of wine. Evelyn looks up from the menu as Manny greets her.

"Hello again. I'm back, and I have your wine selection." Evelyn greets Manny with a smile.

"Hi, Manny." Manny cradles the wine cooler in his arms.

"How are we doing with our food selections?" Manny places a basket of complimentary prawn crackers in the centre of the table.

"I think we're ready." Frank is confident. Evelyn eyes the prawn crackers as she places her menu on the table. Feeling peckish.

"Wonderful news." Manny says, as he places the chilled wine bottle on the table. "I'll prepare the wine for you first, and then..." Manny crouches down, putting the cooler on the floor at his feet. He springs upright once again. "I will take your order!"

Frank and Evelyn watch Manny as he unwraps the foil from the neck of the wine bottle, discarding the waste into a small pouch at the front of his apron. He quickly reaches into his back pocket, removing a fancy corkscrew. Placing the bottle against his hip, he drills the skewer into the cork with gusto. He places the bottle on the table and, using both hands, eases the levers towards the table. Again, he places the bottle against his hip, manoeuvring the cork side to side. It pops out like a party popper, a cloud of cool mist exiting the bottle. Cradling the bottle in one hand, Manny reaches forward, pouring a healthy amount of alcohol into Evelyn's wine glass.

"Thank you," Evelyn says politely. Frank waits patiently for his glass to be filled. Manny reaches over and pours Frank a similar portion before placing the bottle in the wine cooler.

"Let's put the wine over there, shall we? Out of your way." Manny reaches into his shirt pocket for his pad and pen. "Alright then, what will we have this evening for dinner?" He says smilingly, directing his attention to Evelyn.

"I'll have the Spicy Seafood Noodle." Evelyn reaches for her wine, wondering if she should spoil her dinner with a greasy prawn cracker.

"A stir fry, excellent choice." Manny scribbles down the order. "And for you, sir?" The waiter looks eagerly at Frank.

"I'm having the Red Curry duck with some vegetables," Frank announces, closely watching Manny as he again scribbles down the order.

"No. 17," Frank adds, solidifying his selection.

"Yes, No. 17, one of my favourites." Manny widens his eyes in an open display of delight. "So, our menu has a wonderful mixed entrée for starters. It has spring rolls, seafood cakes, lobster balls and satay chicken skewers. Great way to try a little of everything."

Frank looks over at Evelyn, who gestures her approval with her eyes.

"Yes, we will have that as well." Frank's appetite increases. He reaches for his wine.

"Wonderful, I wish I were dining with you two tonight." Manny giggles, his healthy sense of humour not going unappreciated. "If there is nothing else, I will prepare your meals for you." Manny shifts his head from left to right, anticipating confirmation.

"I think that's everything; we're good for now." Frank eyes Evelyn, who nods in unison.

"Wonderful. I will return shortly with your entrée. Until that time, please enjoy your wine with our complimentary prawn crackers." Manny once again performs his trademark 180-degree pirouette as he leaves the table.

"How's the wine?" Languetti asks, taking a small sample for his palette. Evelyn takes another sip.

"It's very nice, Frank. You chose well."

Frank takes a generous swig of wine, holding it in his mouth momentarily before swallowing, just the medicine he needs to calm his nerves. Evelyn leans in closer.

"How have things been with you, Frank? I've hardly seen you this past year."

Languetti places his wine on the table, his fingers caressing the neck of the glass as he considers his response. "I've been busy. Lots of cases. You know what this city is like."

A brief moment of silence passes, and Evelyn again probes Frank for conversation. "How's Shaun shaping up as a homicide detective?" Frank raises his glass off the table.

"He's good. Smart kid." Frank takes another sip of wine.

"Is he anything like you were when you started in homicide, Frank?"

"No, not really. He has a different approach. He's educated differently. It was different when I was his age. Streets were different. Criminals were dumber; they made more mistakes."

"Dumber?" Evelyn sniffs as she takes a mouthful of wine. She debates a prawn cracker as she listens to Frank elaborate.

"These days, they have more knowledge of stuff. Information is more readily available. Some criminals don't even leave their homes and yet, can steal thousands of dollars from people's accounts."

"You mean cyber-crimes?"

"Yeah. But the dirty crimes, like assault and murder... haven't changed. Still plenty of sickos out there. They keep me busy."

"And me too, Frank."

Frank leans back into his chair.

"Miles has a degree in criminal psychology. And these days, you need one to outwit some criminals out there." Frank taps the wine glass with his fingers. "We did it the hard way in my day."

Evelyn smiles. "They don't make them like you anymore, do they, Frank?"

Frank pushes his lips together as he looks at Evelyn, reminiscing about his early days on the force.

"He's lucky to have a partner like you, Frank."

Frank leans forward, feeling a little uneasy talking about the past.

"How are things going with you, your work?"

Evelyn takes a sip of her wine. "I don't hear any complaints from my patients, Frank."

Frank smiles ever so slightly. "And Sylvia?"

Evelyn succumbs to the prawn cracker.

"Sylvia is fourteen going on twenty-five." She holds off biting into the cracker. "She wants to go on a date with a boy who lives in our neighbourhood." Evelyn takes a tiny bite of the prawn cracker. "He's seventeen, Frank."

"Seventeen!" Frank looks surprised. "And what did you say to that?"

Evelyn points at Frank with the prawn cracker.

"I told her you would arrest him if he went anywhere near her. Needless to say, she hates me right now."

Frank leans back in his chair, acting like he has experience with the subject.

"She'll get over it...all part of the growing-up phase." Frank's extensive knowledge of child raising comes from a long history of television shows. Evelyn appreciates his input, nevertheless.

"She needs a father figure, Frank. Ever since the divorce, she has become increasingly demanding with her requests. I fear that pretty soon, she will stop asking me and do whatever the hell she wants."

"So, her father…"

"He went to live in California, Frank. Wants nothing to do with her."

Frank takes another sip of his wine, adjusting his comfort.

"I was thinking, maybe, if you think it's a good idea…we can take her somewhere one weekend. Like a hockey game or something."

Frank's offer completely throws Evelyn.

"Ah, yeah, sure, that would be…" Evelyn gasps. "Umm, wow, Frank. I never expected you…"

Frank smiles, chuffed that Evelyn has responded in kind to his suggestion. "Does she like hockey?"

Evelyn stares blankly into Frank's eyes. "I have no idea."

Frank chuckles, Evelyn joins him, taking a huge mouthful of wine to settle her anxiety. She places the glass on the table, cradling it with her hands.

"I don't know what to say, Frank. After the divorce…you became so distant."

Frank reaches out, placing his palm over Evelyn's hand. He hesitates momentarily, examining his thoughts before responding.

"I know I haven't been there for you much this past year. I wasn't sure of how you felt…and with me, my job. But I think now…maybe it's time we made some changes." Frank clears his throat. "I'd like it if we spent more time together." Frank looks into Evelyn's eyes, his openness welcomed by Evelyn.

"So would I, Frank, so would I."

Chapter 47

It's just after 7:30 pm. Charlie lets out a tired groan as he rises from his office chair.

"You're getting old, my dear fellow." He admits out loud, reaching down for his coat draped over the arm of the sofa. Charlie can feel his weary joints rub together as he slides his coat on, one arm at a time. He digs through his long trouser pockets for his keys, placing his hand on the doorknob, and taking one last look before turning off the light, gently easing the office door closed. The foyer of The Parkway has cooled since sunset, and Charlie can only imagine how cold it must be outside with all that heavy rain. He makes his way across the foyer, stopping one last time to peer up the spiralling stairwell; his thoughts are with Audrey. He lifts his weary feet off the cold tile and continues towards the exit. It's been an exhaustive day; he barely has the strength to push down on the lever, unlatching the door from its locking mechanism. Charlie pulls the heavy oak door towards him, the cold air biting his face like an angry asp. He reaches into his coat pocket, gathering his scarf and wrapping it tightly around his neck and face; the relentless rain still thumping away at the pavement. As he often does, Charlie turns one last time to look around the barren space before exiting the building. As he begins to pull the door to a close, a sudden dull pain stings Charlie on the back of the head; only a moment of consciousness now remains, just long enough for Charlie to see the marble tile draw closer as his body, void of life, comes to meet the cold hard floor—a sharp clanging sound as Charlie's keys leave his grasp and slide across the gleaming surface.

Chapter 48

Camille Saint-Saëns—The Swan, faintly surrounds the patrons as they dine. Frank sifts through the cacophony of sounds, easing his head to one side and projecting one ear towards the ceiling. Evelyn watches closely as Frank drifts, closing his eyes to aid him in isolating the music.

"What are you doing, Frank?" Frank takes a moment before responding.

"My mother played this piece for me when I was a child. It was one of her favourites."

Evelyn raises her chin, ignoring the clutter as she listens intently to the melody.

"She played?"

"Yes. My mother played the Cello." Frank's voice is soft, appearing distant as he pictures his mother and himself as a child, watching her play for him. "I haven't heard this in a long time."

Evelyn looks across at Frank, her eyes glazing over as she watches Frank reminisce. Frank looks across at Evelyn, a moment of silence surrounding them as they gaze at each other, neither one feeling the need to say a single word. Casually, they smile, turning their heads to see a familiar character approaching their table. This time, Manny is holding a large tray covered with an assortment of steaming Asian cuisine. He hovers over the couple, resting the platter on the table's edge.

"This tray is so heavy." Manny giggles like a Galah. "Oh my gosh. So, have we worked up an appetite yet?"

Evelyn takes her wine in her hand. "I certainly have."

Manny takes a moment to admire Evelyn, who looks radiant as she takes another sip of her wine. He looks suspiciously at Frank.

"Well, what has happened here since I last left you two alone?" Manny winks at Frank, adding a childish chuckle as he clears an area on the table. "Here is your assortment of entrées." Manny positions the large tray in the middle of the table. "Please take your time and enjoy every little bite. I will be back to check up on you in a while."

Frank leans forward, admiring the delicious array of cuisine.

"Looks pretty good, Manny."

"Thank you for the compliment. Would you like anything else before I leave you to dine?" Frank checks Evelyn. She gives Frank the thumbs up, eager to dig into the platter.

"I think we're good, Manny." Frank swipes his napkin from the table.

"Excellent! Enjoy." Manny bows, pirouetting once again as he leaves. Evelyn leans forward, inhaling intently, absorbing the aromatics of the eastern delicacies on display.

"The food smells terrific, Frank."

Frank agrees with delight, forgetting his manners as he takes a Spring Roll into his hand. Evelyn takes a moment, adjusting her chair as Frank dips the Spring Roll into the sweet chilli sauce. He twirls it to catch the dripping sauce, promptly biting down on the savoury pastry. Frank moans, feeling Evelyn's watchful eyes as he savours the moment. He looks innocently across the table.

"Hungry Frank?" Evelyn raises her eyebrows. Frank uses his tongue to push the food to the side of his mouth. Evelyn shakes her head as she raises her fork. "Slow down, Frank. There's more food to come, remember." Evelyn stabs a spring roll with her fork. Frank patiently waits for Evelyn to take her first bite before munching on his food.

"Tastes incredible." Evelyn's eyes are wide. She wipes her mouth, taking a mouthful of wine to wash it down. "How's that case you're working on, going?" Evelyn waves her hand across her face, the unexpected heat in her mouth causing her discomfort. "Woah! Hot spring rolls, aren't they?"

Frank wipes his mouth with his napkin, leaning back into his chair. "We're still working on it." Frank takes his wine glass in his hand.

"Did you find out who murdered that girl?"

Frank sips his wine, clearing his palate before returning the glass to the table. "We know who it is. But…we're currently having a lack of incriminating evidence problem." Frank feels mildly frustrated at the thought. He reaches for more food. Evelyn forks a lobster ball; her curiosity increases as her instincts for forensics take over.

"You said it was connected to another case of yours? An assault?"

Frank picks up a satay chicken skewer, dipping the end into the peanut sauce before placing it onto his plate. "There is a connection. Another case I was working on a few months back." Frank hesitates to bite the chicken, twirling the skewer in his hand. "A young girl was assaulted. She was hurt pretty bad and left for dead. Caretaker found her just in time." Evelyn anticipates that Frank has more to say, listening intently as she reaches for her wine. Frank rests the skewer on his plate, opting for another sip of his wine instead. "The murder victim was her best friend."

"And you suspect he also killed the girl, Veronica?"

Frank presents his frustration.

"We know this prick did it. Excuse my French." Frank tears off a piece of chicken from the skewer, chewing with purpose as he contemplates his ill thoughts on the subject matter. Evelyn places her wine glass on the table.

"Sorry, Frank; I didn't mean to upset you. Take it easy on the chicken. It's already been through a lot."

Frank smirks as he looks up from his plate.

"This case sucks right now." Frank lifts his wine off the table once again. "We'll get him." Frank is not as confident in his thoughts. "I'm meeting with the girl on Monday morning. She decided to press charges for the assault."

"Well, that's a start," Evelyn says.

"We're hoping the D.A. can somehow link the two crimes together. It's a stretch." Frank contemplates his theory, feeling agitated as he pictures a smug William in the interrogation room.

"That smug son of a bitch." Frank utters under his breath. He empties the glass of wine into his mouth. Evelyn reaches across the table, placing her hand on Frank's arm.

"Don't be so hard on yourself, Frank. You can't save every girl."

Frank calms his thoughts.

"Yeah, I know. But people like him..." Frank shakes the resentment off, drawing his attention to the platter.

"I think I'm gonna try one of these lobster balls. They look interesting."

Evelyn smiles, picking up her fork to join him. She stabs a lobster ball with her fork. Frank holds the golden, crusty ball of food on the end of his fork.

"You try it first, Frank."

Frank pops the succulent ball into his mouth. An explosion of flavours filling his mouth.

"Jesus! This food is the best I've had in a while, Evelyn. Miles was right on the money." Frank's mood solidifies, eagerly reaching for another treat.

"So...Shaun chose this place?" Evelyn grins as she places the food into her mouth.

Frank purses his lips.

"Miles suggested, but it was my decision." Frank stabs another treat with his fork. Evelyn chuckles with a mouthful of food, taking hold of the wine bottle to replenish her glass. They continue to dine, the exquisite cuisine delighting their senses. Frank leans back into his chair, glancing across the room and into the distance, his thoughts suddenly returning to Audrey as the relentless rain trickles down the unsheltered windows of the restaurant.

Chapter 49

A bright flash fills the room with light; Audrey's eyelids separate, waking her with the thunderous crack which quickly follows. She turns her head towards the window; her eyes struggle to focus. The room is draped in darkness. Another sudden flash of light causes Audrey to squint as it illuminates the walls for a brief second. Another thunderous crack soon follows; the sound is deafening. Audrey eases herself upright, her eyes sweeping the room, the rain pellets drawing her attention as they tap mercilessly onto the glass. The chilly air finds her skin as Audrey exposes her arms from beneath the covers. She runs her hands over her face, brushing her hair back as she exhales an exhaustive yawn. Tossing the quilt cover aside, Audrey plants her naked feet onto the floor, the contrast in temperature biting her toes as she makes her way to the dresser. Shivering, Audrey slides open the dresser's top drawer, taking hold of a thermal skivvy and underwear. She expels a chilled *bur*...as she disrobes, clenching her muscles tight as she quickly dresses with the thermal undergarments, re-wrapping herself with the satin robe, forming a tight bow around her waist to keep out the bitter cold.

Audrey manages her long, dark hair, taking careful steps out into the living area, the lightning again shimmering, filling the room with another blinding flash. She crosses her arms to keep herself warm as she inches towards the bathroom, her bunny slippers on her mind, recalling where she had left them earlier. Again, the heavens thunder away. Audrey suddenly stops, looking aimlessly across the room as the bright flash quickly fades, plunging her back into darkness. Disoriented from her nap, Audrey neglects the light switch, dismissing the thought as her eyes adjust to the dark. As she nears the bathroom, she notices the door is slightly ajar; a soft glow of light inside the room causes Audrey's heart rate to increase. She intensifies her stare, struggling to remember her movements from a few hours ago, resisting the thought telling her she had turned the bathroom light off before she went to bed.

Maybe I just thought I did, she thinks to herself, unconvinced that her thoughts are accurate, remembering her consumption of alcohol. She shifts her attention towards the front door, the distance too great to define any detail; just a black void is all she can see. Audrey turns her attention to the living area, the relentless lightning blinding her momentarily as she looks towards the windows, raising her hand to her face as she pushes her eyelids together to restore her sight. Audrey snatches her breath as a streaking sound breaks through the heavens, causing her to jitter as she again shifts her attention towards the light from the bathroom. She takes a deep breath, exhaling slowly to calm her nerves, raising her left leg off the floor, and stepping cautiously towards the bathroom; her palms are now moistened with sweat. Again, she glances down the long, narrow hallway, the front door presenting details as she draws closer. She breathes a small sigh of relief, feeling only slightly at ease to see the door is intact with no visible damage. Audrey creeps outside the bathroom, easing the door open to peer inside; she holds her breath as she notices that the light above the vanity cabinet is on.

The faucet is dripping rapidly, and the sound of the water reflecting off the porcelain bowl is drowned out by the heavy rain. Audrey raises her hand, placing her palm against the door to nudge it further. Like a frightened animal weary of a predator, she deliberately scans the room with her eyes, still disinclined to step inside. Leaning forward, Audrey looks at the bathroom mirror, checking its reflection that exposes the hidden area behind the door. Nothing; the room is empty. Audrey leans against the door frame, shaking her head as she closes her eyes for a moment. The paranoia is getting the better of her once again, she feels.

I was never like this, she thinks to herself. Audrey looks down, her bunny slippers bringing out her smile. Audrey steps inside the bathroom, gathering her slippers before twisting the tap to stop the dripping faucet. She looks at her reflection at length as she stands in front of the mirror, her face drained of colour, her eyes tired. She snuffs out the light with a flick of her wrist before exiting the room.

Coffee is what I need, she thinks, raising her weary head as she heads towards the kitchen. Audrey gravitates towards the floor lamp by the wall, just inside the living area. She looks ahead, sifting through the darkness as she fumbles for the lamp's switch. Audrey stops. Her limbs freeze as the lightning again fills the room with a white flash. The piano across the room claims Audrey's attention. Audrey's heart rate increases: the hairs on her neck rise as she catches sight of a human form that stands idle by the piano. Her heavy breath dries her mouth, making it difficult to swallow. Her eyes well up as she reluctantly toggles the lamp's switch, exposing her intruder. Audrey's worst fears are realised as she looks across to see William standing there, his arms sternly by his side. A thunderous crack ultimately follows, sending complete despair down Audrey's spine. Audrey's eyes display her horror, her lips separate as she attempts to scream, her only breath vanishing, preventing her from voicing her thoughts. William casually raises his finger to his face, motioning to Audrey to remain quiet. Audrey stands frozen, her limbs abandoning her when she needs them most. William moves towards her, stopping only inches from her face as he approaches; his fingers gently caressing Audrey's hair as he forces her head back, bathing her face with Aurelian light.

"That's much better." His voice is soft, his trademark smile non-existent. Audrey notes the seriousness in his demeanour as William extends his hand, loosening the neatly formed bow around Audrey's waist. He eases the fabric over her shoulders; the soft satin slides down her back as it falls to the floor. Her thoughts become grave as William brushes her hair back with both hands, his attention shifting to Audrey's physique, the thin thermal layer hugging her chest, exposing her shapely breasts. William's breathing heavies as he looks upon Audrey, his arousal evident as he leans forward to kiss Audrey. Audrey turns her head slightly, a single tear escaping as William's lips touch her cheek. William clenches his hand, trapping Audrey's hair in his palm.

"What the hell is the matter with you?" he voices, His frustration emerging. Audrey manages a whimpering plea.

"William, please don't."

William stares down at Audrey. His muscles become taut as his temperament shifts. He curls his arm, jerking Audrey by the hair towards him. Audrey grits her teeth from the pain, letting out a stifled cry as she reaches up to take hold of William's wrist. Using his other hand, William places his fingers over Audrey's mouth; two more tears flow down her face as she closes her eyes in anguish. He slides his thumb across her lips, caressing Audrey with his fingers, slithering his hand down past her neck and over her breast. Again, he uses his thumb, this time to fondle Audrey's protruding nipple, his bottom lip beginning to glisten as the saliva drips from his tongue. He continues to move his hand downward, Audrey taking in a quick breath as William's hand comes to rest on a small patch of skin exposed below Audrey's naval. He leans in closer, pressing his cheek against Audrey's temple as he pushes his hand firmly against her pelvis. She clenches her jaw as William brazenly extends his hand down beneath the waistband; his lips brimming with lust as the tip of his fingers converges with Audrey's soft pubescent hair.

With one continuous motion, Audrey shifts her weight back; her left arm extended as it travels swiftly through the air towards William, the stinging sound echoing in William's ear as her palm meets flush on the side of his face. William takes a step back. He is temporarily stunned by Audrey's objection as the thunder relentlessly shudders away at the windows once again. William quickly gathers his thoughts, clenching his fists in anger as he locks eyes with Audrey. His chest is now heaving with rage. Audrey holds her ground, raising her frail arms at William, her hands uncontrollably shaking as she reluctantly closes her palms.

"Don't touch me." Audrey's voice shivers as a single tear trickles down her pallid face. William chuckles, amused at Audrey standing there with her arms raised, ready to duke it out with him. Audrey holds her stance. Her body trembles as she glares into William's eyes; her thoughts confusing her as William unexpectedly relaxes his shoulders. She waits; her anxiety heightening as William stands there motionless, gazing into her eyes. William's face morphs, his eyes show compassion, and he bows his head unexpectedly. *Is this remorse?* Audrey wonders. Her breathing eases, and her arms begin to relax. She's distracted by the sudden change in William's mood.

Like a flash, William leaps forward with his right hand extended, taking hold of Audrey's wrist. He pulls her off balance, driving his clenched fist towards her, the might of the blow forces

Audrey's delicate frame into the unyielding wall. Audrey's knees buckle, her limp body collapsing onto the floor. Barely conscious, Audrey instinctively raises her hand to her face, the pulsating pain first unbearable, quickly turns to numbness. A thimble of blood seeps from the side of Audrey's mouth as she gasps for air. Without mercy, William leans forward, taking Audrey by the hair, pulling her up off the floor, rotating his shoulders, throwing her clear across the room. Audrey's left elbow shatters as it meets the dense oak floor. Neither hatred nor remorse are present in William's disposition as he walks towards Audrey. With his last step, he delivers a swift kick into her rib cage; Audrey curls up from the immense pain, her breath wheezing as she struggles to gather oxygen into her lungs.

Another blinding flash lights up the night sky as William stands over Audrey. His mood is calm as he watches her lie there, motionless. A moment passes before William carelessly looks up. His attention shifts to the beads of water trickling down the windowpanes. William brushes his hair back, releasing an anguished sigh as he enters the kitchen, using his elbow to toggle the light. He hovers over the sink, turning the cold water on, cupping his hand beneath the running faucet. He takes several gulps of the crisp fluid to quench his thirst before snatching the tea towel that hangs by his knees. He takes a long, deep breath as he wipes his hands dry, diligently wiping anything else he touched before neatly folding the towel and placing it back as he found it.

Audrey opens her eyes; her vision is blurred from the trauma. Disoriented, Audrey looks across the room, her eyes coming into focus on her grandmother's piano. The horrid memories quickly resurface as she senses the pain in her elbow, trying to raise herself off the floor, grimacing with tears as her first efforts fail. She takes several breaths; the agony is too familiar as she again attempts to rise, a blood-drenched molar falling from her mouth as she widens her jaw in anguish. Cradling her broken arm against her stomach, Audrey succeeds in her quest to rise, but only to her knees; her right arm, her only support, prevents her from collapsing onto the floor. She tries to regulate her breathing, the shooting pain in her ribs unbearable as her lungs fill with oxygen. Audrey gathers her thoughts, focusing on the coffee table and spotting the handset by the magazines only a few feet away. Using her arm, she begins to pull herself along the floor, the handset inching closer and closer as she labours her way towards her only salvation.

She ceases her movement at the sound of a single footstep, closing her lamented eyes as she realises that William is still in the apartment. Several more footsteps sound out as William moves towards her. Audrey bows her head, closing her eyes in despair as William rests on her path. Reluctantly, Audrey opens her eyes, confronted by the brown leather of William's boots. Her fighting breath still wheezes as she resists the urge to collapse onto the floor. William crouches down, Audrey closing her eyes again as he caresses her hair with his hand. He leans forward, whispering in her ear.

"All I wanted was the chance to love you."

William moves his hand through Audrey's hair, his voice deepening with hatred as he utters the following words.

"And you took that away from me."

William raises his toe off the floor, swivelling it on the ball of his boot and directly above Audrey's hand. He shifts his weight forward, two of Audrey's fingers giving way to the immense pressure, her agonising cries muffled as William swiftly places his hand over Audrey's mouth. Audrey extends her legs along the floor, kicking them back and forth as she struggles with the agony. Her plea for mercy is ignored. With his hand over her mouth, William rises to his feet, pulling Audrey up, pressing her back firmly against his chest. Audrey plants her feet onto the ground, the tears pouring from her eyes as she clutches both arms close to her body, every movement causing her immeasurable pain. William again leans in close.

"Don't you dare scream?"

He grits his threat through his teeth, slowly removing his hand from Audrey's mouth. A sacred moment of relief as Audrey takes in several breaths through her mouth, the pain in her side a constant reminder of her shattered ribs. Like a cat toying with a mouse, William stands behind Audrey, silently, his arms efficiently by his side. He watches cautiously as Audrey looks aimlessly ahead, her thoughts scattered and her mind too exhausted to gather them in. William expels a short breath in disbelief as Audrey moves away from him. Her feet stagger as she reaches the kitchen, leaning her shoulder against the wall to keep her weakened body from collapsing onto the floor. William remains curious, absorbed in Audrey's movements as she pushes herself off the wall, taking a groggy step onto the kitchen tile. William moves forward, shifting his eyes from item to item, targeting a chef's knife on the countertop.

She is going for the knife, William thinks to himself, admiring her resilience as Audrey struggles to keep herself upright. Another unsteady step towards the knife brings William's patience abruptly to an end. Taking several commanding steps towards Audrey, William raises his boot high into the air, the dull blow striking Audrey in her lower back, driving her forward into the kitchen cabinets. A painful gash opens as Audrey's forehead catches the edge of the marble counter, smearing her blood onto the cabinet doors as her body slides down onto the floor.

Chapter 50

Audrey cries out, closing her eyes tight as she fights to absorb the intense pain piercing her spine, her legs numbing from the impact. William looks on without remorse for his malice as Audrey gasps in agony, placing her trembling hand on her temple, stemming the flow of blood. Audrey pries herself off the floor, discounting her pain as she extends her fractured arm towards the cabinet door. William watches intensely as Audrey places her knuckles against the bottom edge of the cabinet door, forcing it partway open on her first attempt before gathering the strength to push the door aside with her arm. William crouches down, intrigued as he peers into the void; nothing but household cleaning products. William is cautious, taking note of the items inside: a can of bug spray, washing detergent, window cleaner and a few miscellaneous polishing solutions. Taking several determined breaths, Audrey reaches inside, brushing the items back towards William, her weakened arm only propelling them a few feet from where she lay. William observes the items as they scatter along the tile before him. Sorrow begins to seep in as he looks on; Audrey continues to resist the temptation to concede, searching valiantly for a weapon or anything that can be used to stave off William. The can of bug spray rolls in isolation along the tile, distracting William only for a moment before he again looks down at Audrey, her efforts in vain, her silent pleas for absolution ignored. She lunges one last time inside the cabinet, her shattered arm outstretched into the darkness, the relentless pain no longer bearable as Audrey finally ceases to move, coming to rest partway inside, her short breaths amplified by the void surrounding her. She lies there, still as a Rembrandt, her body torn and battered, her hands and face covered in her blood. Only a few breaths seemingly remain; her thoughts drift, and her troubles rapidly fade into darkness as her weary eyes finally come to a close.

Her new world begins with laughter, the sound of her own hands coming together as Veronica amuses everyone with her antics. By her side is Clay, with Charlie seated to her left, all joined in hysterics as Veronica circles the room on all fours, a game of charades. Audrey places her hand over her chest as she tries to catch her breath; even in her dreams, the task seems difficult. She leans to her right, resting her head against Clay's shoulder, her discomfort drawing Charlie's attention.

"Are you all right, Audrey?" Charlie displays concern. Audrey looks up at Charlie.

"Charlie, I can't breathe," she replies in a soft voice.

The sound of Clay's laughter fades into the background as Audrey closes her eyes. Charlie reaches out, gently placing his hand on Audrey's shoulder. "Audrey, can you hear me?"

Audrey remains still, her thoughts her only means of communication.

"Charlie," Audrey whispers. Moving her hand towards her shoulder. "I can feel your hand." Her lips sound out the words as she places her hand over Charlie's. She opens her eyes, turning her head to look at Charlie, her sight deceiving her, her eyes regaining their true focus. William, down on one knee, crouched over Audrey; his hand placed on her shoulder.

"You're still alive."

Audrey moves her hand away at the sound of William's voice, her thoughts rapidly simplifying as she looks up at William. A look of contempt in her eyes, no longer fearful of displaying her resentment towards him, Audrey's thoughts now turn to anger. William removes his hand. A slight smile is visible, his only response to the hatred in Audrey's eyes.

"You have something you want to say to me, Audrey?"

William taunts. Audrey remains silent at first, choosing not to feed William's hunger for torment. His smile baits her to respond, so Audrey gathers what little breath she has.

"You will always be alone," she replies. Her voice above a whisper, William's smile disappearing as Audrey's words circle his thoughts.

Rising to his feet, William clenches his fists in frustration as he paces back, Audrey's words igniting his fury. Audrey stares at him, the fear in her eyes non-existent, almost willing him to end her suffering. William moves decisively towards her, reaching down with both arms, pulling Audrey by her ankles, her torso falling to the tile as it clears the base of the cabinet. He places his hands on her shoulders, taking a firm hold as he pulls her up off the ground, drawing her closer, only inches from his face. He stares intently into her eyes.

"So, is this what you want?"

William's voice deepens with resentment. Audrey is immune to the pain as William squeezes tightly, applying pressure to her shoulders. Audrey says nothing, not a whimper, no longer willing to satisfy William by parading her pain, feeling the weight in her legs as William again loosens his grip. Seizing the opportunity to show her discontent, she directs her hand towards him, placing her bloodied fist onto his shirt, her knuckles striking William on the chin as she extends her arm towards the ceiling. The weakened blow was enough to penetrate William's pride. Audrey's reprisal catches William off guard, forcing him to unhand her as he takes a step back, a stagger in his footing as his feet brush against the items scattered across the floor. He wipes his hand over his chin before looking down at his chest; his shirt is now soiled with Audrey's blood. Audrey prepares herself; William's vengeance is inevitable as he looks up, glaring into her eyes with rage. He tears his shirt open, violently exposing his naked torso to Audrey, his taught muscles announcing his intentions, his wrath for Audrey. William lunges forward, taking hold of Audrey with both hands. Audrey pulls her arms close to her chest as her body is shifted back with brutal force. The motion suddenly halted as her back is thrust against the refrigerator door. William maintains his steely glare as he keeps her body pinned against the door; Audrey tastes the blood in her mouth as the impact causes her to bite down on her lip.

"Is that all you got?"

Audrey mocks, a wry smile appearing as she runs her tongue across her bottom lip. She moves her head slightly forward, staring intently into William's eyes, choosing to abandon her smile as she again voices her contempt.

"You piss weak shit."

William moves his head back. Audrey's words sting him once again. With frightful rage, William lets out an antiquated yawp as he rotates his shoulders, propelling Audrey several feet into the next room. The hurried momentum keeps Audrey off balance; her feet stumble beneath her, sending her face-first onto the dense floor. Her forearms again absorb the impact as her body comes to rest at the foot of the sofa. Without any uncertainty, William strides towards her, again using his hand to wipe his chin, the smear of Audrey's blood on his face providing constant irritation. Audrey remains still, her arms tucked underneath her body, her wheezing breath her only sign of life as William stands over her, gathering his rage for his final assault. He places his toe beneath Audrey's stomach, using the weight of his hip to roll her over onto her back; Audrey coughing numerous times to clear the seeping blood from her throat. She surrenders her left arm onto the floor as she looks aimlessly towards the ceiling. William takes note of the blood on Audrey's lips, a clear symptom that she has only minutes remaining. Deserting any remorse, William clenches his hands several times as he prepares to kneel next to Audrey, his thoughts simplified by his resolve to alleviate Audrey of her only sustenance.

William hesitates to act; he is unexpectedly drawn to Audrey's arm extended across the floor, his eyes fixated on her clenched hand, altering his focus in bemusement to identify something she is holding onto. William again shifts his vision to Audrey's face, her eyes no longer looking aimlessly towards the ceiling, her focus directed beyond William; the light suddenly dims over her torso.

Chapter 51

The rain has eased, and Frank is leaning back comfortably in his chair, one hand extended across the table. His thumb caresses the stem of his wine glass as he unexpectedly drifts into thought. Evelyn takes note, holding the last piece of strawberry cheesecake on her fork at bay, choosing to address Frank's abrupt silence.

"What are you thinking about, Detective?"

Evelyn pops the piece of cake into her mouth, sliding the fork out between her lips, wiping clean any evidence of the sweet, creamy batter. Still, her eyes are focused on Frank, who appears unmoved by Evelyn's question.

"Hello? Earth to Frank." Evelyn prompts Frank, relinquishing her fork to take hold of her wine. Frank casually looks across the table. "Did I wake you, Frank?" Evelyn whispers. Frank adjusts himself upright; his chair provides more comfort than expected.

"I apologise. I was just..." Frank pauses, still pondering his untimely thought.

"What is it, Frank?"

Evelyn is curious and gives her full attention. Frank hesitates, feeling somewhat uncomfortable offering her an explanation.

"I just felt something. Something..." Frank hesitates again, looking past Evelyn before resuming his train of thought. "I sometimes get these strange feelings...like something has happened. Call it a gut feeling. I don't know how else to explain it."

Evelyn pulls back a little. "What do you mean?"

Frank looks away momentarily, the awkwardness in his posture evident. "I've been a Detective for a long time now, and...every once in a while, I experience strange feelings when something significant happens. Specifically...like on a case that I might be working on at the time."

"So, you mean like the case you are working on now?"

"Maybe, I don't know." Frank brushes it off. "It's nothing. Sounds ridiculous, I know." Frank puts on a smile. "Probably indigestion," Frank states with a nervous chuckle. "All that Thai food we ate, maybe."

Evelyn presents Frank with a smile. "Premonitions, Frank?"

Frank grins. "I know how it sounds. I shouldn't have said anything. Sounds loopy when you say it out loud."

"Not at all, Frank...sometimes people, when they connect with someone, can often feel them when they are under duress. It means you care about them. Some people have that...gift." Evelyn winks, taking another sip of her wine.

Frank looks down at the half-eaten mud cake before him, embarrassed for sharing his impromptu gut feelings.

"You didn't finish your dessert, Frank?" Evelyn eyeing the neglected delicacy.

"I can't finish it." Frank takes his wine in his hand. "You're welcome to it if you like."

Evelyn's appetite is reignited at the thought, but she resists the temptation. "Oh, I really can't eat another bite." Her best performance is displayed as she waves her palm from side to side.

Frank is startled by a presence rounding his shoulder. Manny was in stealth mode as he approached the table; his high-pitched voice greeted them both.

"You two must be stuffed like turkeys for Christmas with all that food you ate." Manny giggles, delighted by his incorrigible sense of humour. "May I take your dessert plate?" Manny gently places two fingers on Evelyn's shoulder.

"Please," Evelyn says.

Manny reaches down to collect the plate before focusing on Frank's half-eaten dessert. "Are we dieting tonight, sir?" Manny continues to be playful.

"I have had enough food tonight, Manny." Frank pats his stomach.

"Very well, I will just have to finish it myself."

Evelyn stares intently at the cake as Manny handles it. "You should leave it; he may have a change of heart."

"Very well. Can I bring you anything else?"

Frank looks over at Evelyn. "I think we are all good."

Evelyn's smiling eyes causing Frank to blush.

"You two are so adorable." Manny giggles. "Just relax for a while, and I will return soon to present you with the bill."

"Thank you, Manny." Evelyn presents a delightful smile for his service.

"You are most welcome." Manny bows his head, performing his trademark pirouette again as he departs.

Evelyn is holding her wine as she leans forward and places both elbows on the table. She places one palm on her face, tilting her head slightly to one side as she suspiciously poses her question.

"So Frank, back to your place?" Gesturing the obvious with her eyes. Frank clenches his napkin, taking an anxious breath, as he searches for a verbal response. Evelyn lets out a purposeful snicker.

"Relax, Frank; I'm just toying with you."

Frank presents Evelyn with a timid grin. He becomes distracted; something sudden causes him to reach for his waistline. Evelyn immediately recognises the reflex, as she works in a profession where a pager is part of her everyday work attire.

"What is it, Frank?" Frank's eyes remain focused on the Pager's LED as he presses down on the retrieval button. The message is clear as it scrolls across the screen. 10-39 Parkway. Frank looks up at Evelyn, his expression telling.

"It wasn't indigestion, was it, Frank?"

Frank peers regretfully at Evelyn, shaking his head slightly. He leans forward, preparing to rise from his chair. "I will call you a cab."

Evelyn presents Frank with a smile. "Frank. Don't worry about the cab. I'll have Manny arrange it." She speaks politely, casually leaning back into her chair.

Frank rises to his feet, taking hold of his jacket in his left hand. His mind is already sifting through the possible variables of the message he received.

"I had a great time, Frank." Evelyn holds her smile. Frank looks down with mixed emotions before responding.

"Yeah, me too, Evelyn." Frank holds his ground momentarily, slightly turning his shoulders towards the exit.

"Frank."

Frank jerks back to face Evelyn. Evelyn extends her index finger, curling it towards her. "Come here, Frank."

Frank hesitates for a moment before taking a step towards Evelyn. Evelyn raises her chin as Frank leans down, Frank gently pressing his lips onto hers. The ambient music rises above the chatter as they both hold the kiss for what seems an eternity. Frank slowly pulls back, the music submerging as their lips finally separate.

"Thank you, Frank." Evelyn exhales with contentment. Frank manages a grateful smile.

"I have to go."

Frank suddenly turns and walks hurriedly towards the exit. Evelyn's thoughts are blissful as she takes her wine into her hand; delightfully, she reclines back into her chair. Suddenly, she pops up like a jack-in-the-box, the half-eaten mud cake on her mind as she looks over at Frank's empty chair. Without hesitation, she lunges forward, swiping the plate off the table and placing it in front of her.

"It's mine now."

Evelyn snatches her fork, slicing a generous chunk off and holding the sweet dessert before her mouth. She pauses for a moment, an odd realisation creeping up in the back of her mind as she eyes the delicacy.

"I just got stuck with the bill," she announces with a chuckle. She places the moist cake into her mouth and closes her eyes to savour the luscious, chocolaty delight.

Chapter 52

With the siren in full cry, Languetti plants his foot on the gas pedal. The roads are slick from the rain, the tyres squealing as Frank manoeuvres impatiently, tearing through the city's congested traffic. The sound of angry horns does nothing to deter Frank as he continuously examines the most accessible route to his destination. The tyres scream as the car veers violently left and right through the sodden streets, often coming dangerously close to colliding with the oncoming traffic. Languetti navigates the customised vehicle with the precision of a Formula One driver. The tyre's heated rubber hangs onto the bitumen one last time as the car makes its final aggressive turn; Languetti reaches towards the dash to kill the siren as the car approaches a cluster of emergency vehicles parked outside The Parkway. Languetti eases his foot onto the brakes, leaning slightly forward to peer through the foggy windscreen of his car as he pulls up to the curb. He places his hand on the ignition key, hesitating to kill the motor, allowing the wiper blades to make one more pass; the beams from flashing red lights distort Frank's view as fresh pellets of water quickly form on the pane of glass. Languetti cuts the vehicle's engine. He reaches across to retrieve his handgun from the glove compartment, which he had placed there earlier. Thoughtful not to wear his firearm during his dinner with Dr Bridge. He readies mentally before shoving the car door open, his eyes surveying the scene as he steps onto the street.

Languetti holds his ground momentarily, reaching behind to holster his weapon before heading towards the building's entrance. He takes note of the vehicles parked out front: three black and whites, an ambulance and Miles' Dodge sedan. Approaching the steps of the building, Languetti turns his head, purposely glancing at the two officers standing on the pavement. At the top of the stairs, a uniformed police officer stands on guard, thoughtfully making way as Frank approaches the door. Languetti enters the foyer, his eyes immediately falling onto Charlie, sitting on one of the lounge chairs near the base of the stairs; a poignant look of despair is visible, his eyes staring into nothingness. He's accompanied by a medic attending to a wound on the back of Charlie's head. Charlie looks up, noticing the detective standing there with his hands on his hips and a blank look on his face. Languetti is unwilling to foreshadow the crime scene. He holds his ground, and a sorrowful look appears as he locks eyes with Charlie. Charlie's grief is evident. Frank wipes his chin, placing his hand over his mouth, his eyes shifting towards the stairwell. He's reluctant to move forward, for what he may be confronted with as he reaches the top of the stairs. Languetti begins his stride, clutching his hands tightly as he advances each step, distancing his thoughts from Charlie as he draws closer to Audrey's apartment.

Languetti places his hand on the banister as he reaches the top of the stairs, gathering some oxygen as he prepares to venture down the long corridor that leads to Audrey's apartment. His right hand begins to fidget, his fingers nervously toying with the hem of his coat as he moves cautiously towards the entrance. The door is three-quarters ajar, the view shielded by a uniformed officer standing on guard. Frank stares intently as he approaches, parting his coat to reveal his credentials; the officer moving to the side as Frank furtively wipes his palms on the sides of his trousers, glancing at the officer before advancing. Languetti progresses down the hall, looking to the fore of the narrow passage, his eyes drawn to blood smears on the floor up ahead, tagged by forensics with a yellow marker. He continues, drawing closer to the crime scene, ceasing his stride as he enters the accessible area of the living room. He looks to his right to see his partner standing at the far end of the room, Mile's attention on the floor by his feet. Languetti looks to the floor, his view obscured by a forensic photographer hovering over what appears to be a lifeless body—a reluctant image of a deceased Audrey surfacing in Languetti's thoughts. Miles looks over his shoulder, raising his brow to acknowledge his partner. Languetti holds his ground, displaying his reluctance to join the two men. Languetti surveys the room, panning steadily from right to left, his attention once again drawn to the blood-stained floor by the sofa, the trail of blood leading his sights into the kitchen, his focus now on the assortment of household items scattered on the kitchen tile. An image Languetti has seen before recalling a case where a woman was looking for something harmful to spray in her attacker's eyes, maybe Audrey was looking to do the same; Languetti summates. Languetti shifts his eyes to the kitchen cabinets; more blood smeared over the cabinet doors, another sign of Audrey's desperation; Languetti exhales in frustration as he collates the barrage of images invading his thoughts.

"Hey, Frank." Miles calls out. "You better come take a look at this."

Languetti refocuses, turning his attention to Miles, his partner motioning for Languetti to join him as their eyes meet. Languetti begins to walk steadily towards his partner; Miles again turning his attention to the floor as Languetti draws closer, Languetti doing the same, the obscured view now becoming visible as the forensics photographer rises to his feet, making way for Languetti to move up alongside Miles.

"I've seen some weird shit, but this is…"

The forensic photographer shakes his head in dismay before taking another quick snap of the deceased's torso. Languetti draws his breath, concealing his staggered emotions as he comes to identify the body, the gruesome image immediately raising questions in his tangled thoughts, a look of disbelief surfacing as he gazes upon William's bludgeoned body, draped across the cold, hard floor. Languetti remains tacit as he inspects William's body from afar. His focus is drawn to the serrated marks on William's jugular, bewildered by the patterned bruising, likening the force to that of a primal beast suffocating its prey.

"You got what you deserved, you fucker."

Miles voices his thoughts. The forensics photographer peers across at Miles, feeling uneasy by the remorselessness of his remark. Languetti remains unfazed, examining the body, shifting his sights to William's right arm extending across the floor. His thoughts are puzzling as he focuses intently on William's hand, which is almost unrecognisable, the malleable flesh seemingly fused onto an iron poker that William has seized. Languetti looks across the room, eyeing the fireplace in Audrey's apartment; the cast iron utensils are overturned and sprawled across the floor. Languetti exhales in deliberation, raising his hand to his face and collating his thoughts as he tries to piece together the puzzle. He gazes intently at William's lifeless body; his mangled hand, his crushed jugular, and multiple blood stains consume his chest and arms. Languetti raises his head, his eyes shifting towards the sofa, recalling a memory from not too long ago when he visited Audrey. He ponders for a moment; then, suddenly, he turns to look at his partner. Miles nods as he locks eyes with Frank, his assumptions resolved, his telling stare reaffirming Frank's thoughts; ultimately, the detective concludes who was most likely responsible for William's demise. This was not the work of a delicate female like Audrey or an old, weary man like Charlie. Someone else was here, someone immense and physically powerful, someone who came to protect Audrey when she needed it most.

Chapter 53

William quickly turns, his eyes agape as he looks up above his eye line, indefinite thoughts congesting his mind as he comes to dread the presence standing before him. His sense of bewilderment becomes lost in a wave of emotions when Clay suddenly moves towards him, his hand now firmly wrapped around William's jugular, the oxygen rapidly diminishing from William's lungs as Clay squeezes his palm closed. William reaches out, impulsively grasping Clay's wrist with both hands; Clay extends his arm towards the ceiling, lifting William clear off the ground. William submits to panic, kicking his legs through the air in an attempt to free himself, his efforts futile, as Clay continues to hold on tight. Clay pulls William towards him, his other hand taking hold of William's groin; William grimaces in pain as he is lifted effortlessly above Clay's head. William persists to struggle; the strength of Clay's forearms restraining him, his efforts unmatched by the might of Clay's shoulders. Clay abruptly leans to his right, heaving his broad shoulders towards the far end of the room, the motion hurling William's body several feet into the air.

A flurry of sounds fills the room as William collides violently with the wall. The distinct sound of porcelain shattering onto the oak floor is heard as William's body brushes a floral vase that sits on the fireplace. A poker, long-handled broom and sweeping tray that lean against the fireplace are also disturbed as William's body comes to rest at the foot of the fireplace; the clanking sounds resonate to a fade as the iron utensils strike the floorboards. Clay turns his attention to Audrey, his eyes sweeping her battered torso as he eases himself down on one knee beside her. Audrey remains still, a warmth filling her soul as she looks up at Clay, smiling ever so slightly as Clay comes to look into her eyes.

"Hi, Clay," Audrey speaks in a soft breath, her sweet voice causing Clay's eyes to well up. Clay says nothing. His hand extended over her, reluctant to rest it on her torso, fearing he might cause her pain. He looks at Audrey's arm extended across the floor, her clenched fist causing Clay's cheeks to rise.

"You're a clever girl, Audrey."

Clay manages to speak, his voice uncontrollably shaking as tears stream down his face, fearing that those may be the last words he utters to her. Audrey turns her head slightly, her eyes glazing over as she looks up at the ceiling, her faint breath barely heard. Clay places his hand gently on her forehead, brushing her hair to the side. The sound of metal scraping against the floorboards draws Clay's attention towards the far end of the room, where William lies.

"Clay," Audrey speaks again. Clay quickly looks back into Audrey's eyes.

"Miss Audrey." Clay wiping the tears from his face.

"I will forgive you," she says softly, her eyes looking towards the ceiling. She no longer has the strength to move her head and look at Clay one last time. Clay, at first, seems puzzled by Audrey's words, unsure of her absolution. The sound of William's moan in the distance quickly resolves his thoughts.

William pulls his forearms close towards his chest, pushing himself off the floor and upright onto his knees, the iron poker held firmly in his right hand as he sways back and forth, disoriented from the impact. Scattered all over his chest and arms are multiple gashes that begin to ooze his blood, the several pieces of porcelain now embedded in his skin as William came to rest on the shattered vase. Looking aimlessly around the room, William squeezes his eyes shut several times to shake off the distorted view, a sharp pain above his brow evident as he reaches up to examine his wound, the open gash stinging him as his palm meets the exposed flesh. William looks around the room. This time, he can focus on his surroundings; a large black man crouched over Audrey, again, bewildering his thoughts. Drawing a deep breath into his lungs, William gathers his strength, digging the point of the iron poker into the floor as he lifts himself onto his feet. He stands there momentarily, staring at the unfamiliar figure crouched over Audrey, the expelled blood from his brow finding its way to the base of his jaw. Two droplets of blood, weighed down, escape to the floor.

A look of disbelief engulfs Clay as Audrey gradually closes her eyes. His trembling hand caresses her silky hair as she finally comes to rest in peace.

"I love you, Miss Audrey," Clay whispers as he removes his hand from her motionless body, pushing aside his tears as he closes his eyes, bowing his head in only a moment of grief.

In the distance, thunder sounds out, and a faint resonance causes Clay to open his eyes and look towards the window. William impatiently stabs the iron poker into the oak floor, repeating the motion several times, summoning his newfound enemy for one absolute battle. Clay expectedly rises to his feet, his rage surfacing through a wave of emotions as he slowly turns to face William. William stands there heaving, his chest pounding with resentment, the iron poker clenched firmly as he eyes Clay from across the room.

"Who the fuck are you?"

William's dissent is clear as crystal. Clay does not respond; the look of intent speaks volumes as he glares across the room into William's eyes. William's patience ends abruptly, hollering at the top of his voice, summoning Clay to approach him.

"Come on, you black fuck."

The room echoed with William's frustration. His angered yawp demanded satisfaction. Clay begins to move towards William, his arms remaining by his side as he draws closer with every step. William gradually raises the point of the poker on guard as Clay approaches, bringing Clay to a standstill only a few feet from William. William brazenly extends his arm towards Clay, digging the point of the iron poker into Clay's chest, exhaling in contempt as he takes in the full view of Clay's massive frame. Clay remains unresponsive, reluctant to act on his rage; his arms remain rigid as he waits for William to act on his hatred.

William swiftly pulls the poker away, raising it above and behind his head, before rapidly driving it towards Clay, expelling an enraged growl as he follows through with the motion. Clay reacts quickly, lunging forward and halting the action with his outsized hand, taking a decisive hold of William's clenched fist. William alarmingly pulls back, using his body's full weight as he tries to free his hand from the unyielding restraint. It's to no avail as he charges forward again, repeatedly striking Clay on the torso, the blows making little impact as Clay continues to hold his ground—an abrupt pain surfaces as Clay compresses his fingers down onto William's hand. William lets out a frightful cry as the bones in his hand eventually give way to the immense pressure. The fractured metacarpals push against and pierce the malleable flesh of his hand as Clay continues to apply pressure. Without any mercy, Clay directs his other hand towards William's throat,

William grimacing in further anguish as Clay's fingers bore into his skin, trapping the oxygen in his lungs as his hand clutches tight onto William's jugular. Clay begins to shake uncontrollably as he intensifies his hold, his eyes welling up as images of Audrey lying lifeless on the cold, hard floor invade his thoughts, igniting his rage further.

"I'm sorry mama."

Clay's voice trembles as tears run down his face. William lashes out, thrashing his legs towards Clay's shins, his efforts doing little to sway Clay from his intent, violently jerking William's forearm towards the ceiling to peter out his show of aggression. Pulps of William's blood begin to ooze between Clay's fingers, William feeling the full force of Clay's fury as he digs his thumb further into William's thyrohyoid gland. William's eyes roll back as his struggle ultimately ends, his left hand falling off Clay's shoulder, swaying as it descends towards the floor. Clay suspends the limp torso, gazing at length at the lifeless body, and finally releases his hold, allowing William to fall abruptly onto the floor. An eerie silence fills the room as Clay stands over the body. His staggered breath appends to the faint sound of the rain pellets tapping on the windowpanes like an audience applauding in the distance, saluting Clay for his accomplishment; for now, this wicked beast is dead.

Chapter 54

Languetti remains poised, preoccupied with a myriad of thoughts as he gazes out the window. The once darkened clouds, now white as snow, spread thin as if a small child had reached into the heavens and pulled them apart like cotton candy. The pellets of rain that linger on the windowpanes resemble diamonds, illuminated by the moonlight, and a kaleidoscope of red and blue lights is visible from the street traffic below.

"I've put the word out, Frank. We'll find him."

Miles' voice draws Languetti's attention away from the window. He looks across at Miles, both have come to the same conclusion: that Clay was most likely responsible for William's death.

"Must've been some crazy loon that did this to this poor bastard."

Languetti peers at the forensic photographer, who voiced his thoughts. "Where the hell is the rest of your team?" The dissent is evident in Frank's bark. He glares at length, startling the photographer, who quickly looks up at the detective.

"They're on their way, Detective."

Languetti gives the photographer a disappointing look. "I want every inch of this fucking room swept when they get here," Languetti growls, the forensic photographer nodding his head, acknowledging the detective's command.

"They will, Frank. I'll tell them."

Languetti maintains his steely glare, the photographer nervously looking at his equipment before looking across at Miles. Miles' placid look lending no comfort.

"And clean up that fucking mess." Languetti takes the edge off his tone, aware that his anger is misdirected, avoiding one last look at the unsightly carcass as he directs his sights elsewhere. Languetti moves towards the centre of the room, his eyes constantly jerking about, his focus again drawn to the blood-stained floor by the sofa.

"That's where the medics found her."

Languetti looks back over his shoulder at Miles. The remorse is noticeable in Miles' voice. Languetti maintains his silence; he exhales his grief, directing his attention back to the bloodied floor. Miles looks on as Languetti directs his focus to a small item by the foot of the sofa. He crouches down, narrowing his view on the inconspicuous object isolated on the wooden floor. Miles develops intrigue, Languetti's prolonged silence prompting him to inquire.

"What is it, Frank?"

Languetti focuses on the item, reaching up to his chest and retrieving a handkerchief from the inner pocket of his jacket. Miles watches closely as Languetti unfolds the handkerchief over his hand, reaching down to the floor and sequestering the item into the fabric. Languetti leans back, adjusting his balance as he raises his arm and exposes the item to the light above. His open palm exhibited a small rectangular object with distinctive markings. Miles squints, struggling to identify the object resting on the handkerchief.

"What the hell is that, Frank?"

Miles leans forward to get a better look. Languetti examines the object presented before him, flipping it over as he cradles it; a hint of recognition quickly drowns in confusion as Frank comes to identify the item in his hand.

"What the hell is this doing here?" Languetti wonders out loud, his eyes meandering around the room, looking for validation. He rises to his feet, taking another look at the item, questioning his thoughts as he turns it about in the handkerchief, ensuring he correctly identifies the component. Miles takes a step towards Frank, his view becoming more acute, watching intently as Languetti flips the item over once again, revealing markings on one side that read: 25A.

"Is that what I think it is, Frank?"

Miles prompts Languetti for a verbal response, seeking confirmation for his conclusion. Languetti remains unresponsive, and his interest is now elsewhere. Miles follows Languetti's line of sight, now directed towards the kitchen.

"Talk to me, Frank."

Frank is mystified as he approaches the entryway to the kitchen, his feet meeting the edge of the tile, his hands by his side, clutching onto the item as he scans the area with thoughtful eyes. Languetti narrows his attention to the kitchen cabinets below. One cabinet door swung open, the empty void once housing the items now scattered over the kitchen tile. Languetti proceeds into the kitchen, taking careful steps to avoid disturbing any of the items on the floor, the blood stains smeared on the tile a constant reminder of the torment Audrey suffered. Miles follows his partner, ceasing his stride at the entryway to the kitchen, looking on intently as Languetti again crouches down, this time focused acutely on the void of the open cabinet. Miles keeps his distance, choosing to remain patiently by the entryway. Languetti retrieves a small penlight, which he keeps holstered in the inner left pocket of his coat. Using his thumb and forefinger, Languetti twists the body of the penlight, the action igniting the penlight at one end. He places his right knee firmly onto the tile, leaning forward as he extends his arm into the void of the cabinet. The beam of light shone towards the rear corner, now illuminating the once-darkened void, revealing to Languetti its inner contents. A moment passes before Languetti retracts his arm from the void, looking away in thought. Again, he looks at the object in his palm as he slowly rises. Languetti looks across at Miles as he returns the penlight to its rightful place.

"Have you spoken to the old man yet?" Languetti inquires, inserting the small object into the outer pocket of his coat as he moves towards Miles.

"No, I came straight up here." Miles abruptly moves aside as Languetti strides past him. "You going downstairs to have a word with him?"

Languetti continues his stride. "Yes, I am."

Miles reaches for the back of his neck, squeezing his hand several times to relieve the tension that has begun to develop. "Care to share your thoughts at all, Frank?" Miles utters under his breath, looking around at the blood-smeared cabinets, deciding to make his way over and see what his partner discovered for himself.

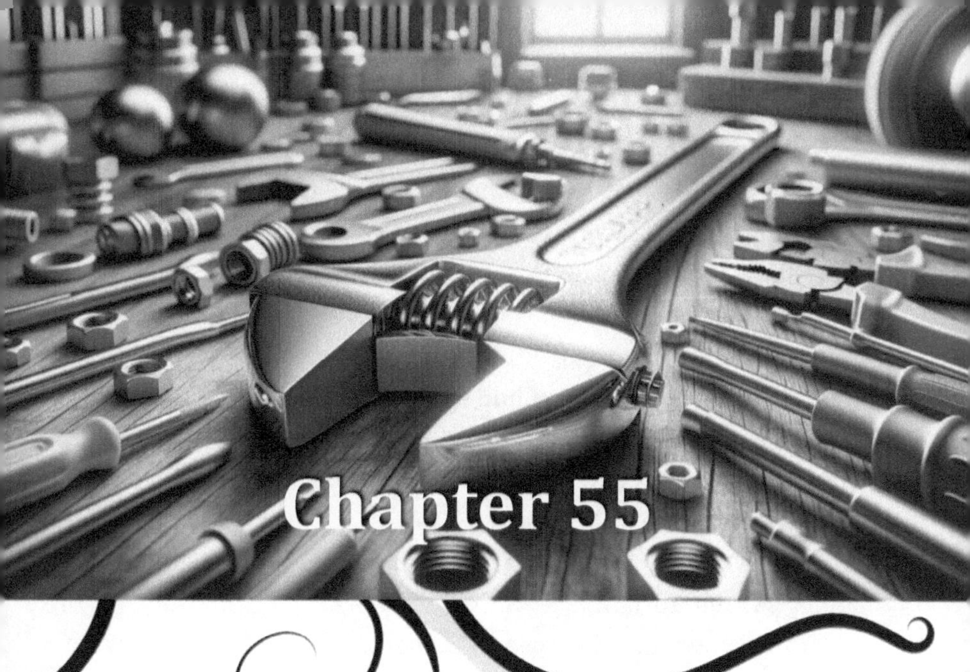

Chapter 55

As Languetti nears the base of the stairwell, he looks down at the lounge chair where Charlie had been seated earlier that evening. Languetti observes the foyer; Charlie is nowhere to be seen. The chair is now empty, and the female officer who had been attending to Charlie's wounds is crouched over an emergency medical kit.

"Where's the old man?"

The woman turns to see the detective standing over her shoulder. "He's in his office resting on the sofa, Detective," she explains, rising to her feet as Languetti steps into the foyer. "He's going to be alright, just a slight gash and bruising is all. Gave him some painkillers to help."

Languetti nods, eyeing the building's entrance. The forensics team enters the foyer, their respective kits in hand, as they head towards the stairs. They take note of Languetti as they approach. Languetti is tempted to voice his thoughts; instead, he glares at the men as he proceeds to make his way towards Charlie's office.

Inside the office, Charlie is spread across the sofa, a small table lamp by his side and two cushions aptly placed underneath his throbbing head: his eyes wide open, gazing at the flaking paint on the ceiling above.

"Hey, Charlie."

A soft voice calls out. Charlie looks across to see Languetti standing by the door, his silhouette partially lit by the light from the table lamp. Languetti tucks his shirt into the back of his trousers as he steps towards Charlie.

"Mind if I come in?"

"You may enter, Detective," Charlie groans as he attempts to adjust himself upright.

"Don't move, Charlie, please," Languetti pleads, motioning as he approaches.

"There's a chair somewhere in here." Charlie shifting his tired eyes about the room. Languetti takes hold of a rusty old chair; he places it by the sofa before sitting next to Charlie.

"How you feeling, Charlie?"

"My age and then some, Detective." Charlie's regretful eyes speak volumes.

"That cute medic out there assured me you're gonna be just fine." Languetti presents an awkward smile, provoking Charlie to do the same. "I think she's single. Maybe I can set you two up on a date."

Languetti's attempt at humour fails as Charlie places his hand onto his forehead, another pulse of head pain causing him anguish. Charlie closes his eyes briefly, thoughts of Audrey plaguing his mind, his mournful look returning.

"She couldn't tell me," Charlie opens his eyes, "the officer; she couldn't tell me how Audrey is doing, Detective."

Charlie looks across at the detective, appealing for answers. Languetti looks down at his hands, prolonging his response to Charlie.

"I can't be sure, Charlie. They took her away before I arrived." Languetti breathes, reluctant to speculate. "I'm sure they'll take good care of her." Languetti gives Charlie a mournful look. "Try not to think about it right now."

Charlie looks away, his eyes welling at the thought that he may never see Audrey alive again. He shakes his head, letting out a painful sigh.

"She didn't deserve any of this." His voice shivering with resentment. "It was him again, wasn't it?" Charlie draws his breath, endeavouring to control his emotions. Languetti gazes at Charlie. Charlie resolves his emotions. A moment of silence passes.

"I swear to the almighty, as long as I can draw a breath, I'm going to..." Languetti places his hand on Charlie's chest, disrupting his vengeful vow.

"William's dead, Charlie."

Languetti's sudden revelation causes Charlie to look up at Frank in astonishment. A moment of thought elapses before Charlie delivers a response.

"You mean Audrey...?" A bewildered Charlie poses the question. Languetti shakes his head, dismissing Charlie's thoughts. He leans back slightly, the rusty old chair proving to be a discomfort to Languetti's lower back.

"Charlie..." Languetti pauses in second thought, concealing his assumptions on Clay. "Charlie, can you tell me what happened earlier this evening? Were you here alone? Did you see Audrey at any time?"

Charlie closes his eyes; he massages his forehead with his palm, the two aspirin he was administered proving no match for his migraine. Charlie informs Languetti of the events that took place earlier that evening. Languetti evaluates his thoughts, the news that Clay had left the building proving to mystify his theory.

"You remained here, in your office?" Languetti inquires.

"I hung around here for a while; it was maybe half past seven or there-a-bouts when I decided to call it a night. So, I..." Charlie raises his hand to his head, closing his eyes to picture his movements. "I walked over to the front entrance and opened the door. It was raining, heavy rain, I remember." Charlie looks away in thought. "I don't really remember being hit."

"Do you remember who found you?" Languetti inquires.

Charlie shakes his head. "No one found me, Detective, I just came too. Found myself in here, tucked neatly behind the desk."

Languetti conceals his thoughts.

"I remember hearing sirens. So, I picked myself up off the floor and staggered out there to be greeted by your people."

Languetti leans back, reaching into his coat pocket.

"None of what I just told you really matters now." Charlie's thoughts again go to Audrey.

Languetti retrieves the folded handkerchief from his coat. Charlie notices and watches curiously as Languetti unfolds the fabric, revealing the item to Charlie. "I found this in Audrey's apartment."

Charlie leans forward, looking directly at the item. "It's a fuse." Charlie is puzzled.

"That's right. I think Audrey may have been holding this. I found in on the floor, near where she was found." Languetti states.

Charlie absorbs the information. He lies back, a hint of a smile appearing. Languetti holds the fuse in his open palm, waiting patiently for Charlie to respond. Charlie realizes what Audrey was trying to do. *But I was lying unconscious in this office.* Charlie places his hand over his eyes, concealing his grief. "I'm sorry, Audrey."

Languetti is puzzled by Charlie's words, he looks at the fuse and back at Charlie, who begins to lean forward, propping himself upright.

"Can you please help me up, Detective?"

Languetti slides his chair back as he rises to his feet, taking hold of Charlie by the arm and helping him up.

"Thank you, Detective." Charlie turns to face Languetti. "Come with me, Detective; I want to show you something."

Languetti escorts Charlie outside into the foyer area.

"Just over here." Charlie moves to the counter situated just outside the office. Charlie half-turns his attention to Languetti.

"Take a look behind here, Detective," Charlie says, pointing to the panel of lights beneath the counter. "Can you see these crystal lights?"

Languetti crouches down to get a closer view.

"Yeah."

"You see, Detective, all these lights are wired to the electrical mains in the storeroom out back, which is, of course, wired to every apartment in this building."

Languetti listens with intent.

"You see, I had this panel repaired a while ago."

Languetti examines the panel. "What do these lights do exactly?"

"Well, Detective, they are simply a way of indicating that a fuse has failed, in any of the apartments. This building is old, and it still has the original wiring from the time it was built. The designer had it wired that way; it was quite unique for its time."

Languetti looks up at Charle. "So, if a fuse fails..."

"Or if it is removed!" Charlie is quick to point out.

Languetti catches on quickly. "The panel would light up."

Charlie points to the lit crystal light, numbered 34—Audrey's apartment.

Languetti collates his thoughts. "And Audrey knew this?"

A regretful smile appears on Charlie's face. "Yes, Detective, she knew because I told her."

Languetti rises to his feet, taking another look at the fuse, and returning the item to his coat pocket. He looks across the foyer and to the stairwell leading up to Audrey's apartment, his thoughts drawing on the images he saw earlier. The kitchen area, the scattered items on the kitchen tile, and the blood stains on the cabinet doors. Languetti ultimately realised what Audrey was doing while fighting for a way to survive. Battered and bleeding, she dragged herself across the kitchen tile and to the kitchen cabinet, brushing the household items aside one at a time, not to deter William but to clear her path. Her desolate hope of survival was to get to the fuse beneath the cooktop, remembering the indicator lights on the panel in the foyer. Her only hope was that Charlie would see the light illuminated and come to her aid.

"It was Clay who killed William."

Charlie's words slice through Languetti's thoughts. He turns to look at Charlie, who has shifted ground and now stands near the end of the counter. His focus is now on a single item placed on the countertop. Charlie reaches out, gently stroking the prop once with his fingers.

"It was Clay who killed William, wasn't it, Detective?"

Charlie again voices his realisation, slowly turning his head, reluctant to receive any validation from the detective. Languetti looks at Charlie concisely before shifting his view to the left of Charlie; Charlie retracts his hand to reveal an oversized shifting wrench at the end of the countertop. Charlie stares out into the foyer, voicing his visualised thoughts to Languetti.

"I had asked Clay to get this for me earlier today. We argued briefly about its whereabouts. I had left the wrench somewhere in the storeroom out back. He meant to get it, but..." Charlie pauses, recalling that Audrey came stumbling in, intoxicated. "I sent Clay home before he had a chance to do so. But he remembered and came back for it."

Languetti takes a step towards Charlie.

"Clay noticed the light was on when he placed the wrench on the counter," Languetti concludes. Charlie nods, validating the detective's statement.

"We only repaired that fuse in Audrey's apartment a few months back; it would have been unusual for this fuse to have failed so soon after. I guess Clay realised the same when he saw the light was glowing."

Languetti places his hands on his hips, grieving for Audrey and wondering where Clay may have fled to.

"Clay is not a bad person, Detective. You need to understand, please."

Languetti places his hand on Charlie's shoulder. "You should be getting home now, Charlie. You need the rest." Languetti pats Charlie on the back. "Come. I'll have that cute officer take you home."

Charlie manages half a smile before addressing Languetti one last time. "Detective." Charlie ceases his stride, engaging the detective square in the eyes. "Clay has a lot of good in him; he doesn't deserve to be treated like a criminal. Please promise me you won't harm him."

Languetti presents Charlie with a confirming nod. "I'll look after him, Charlie. You have my word."

Chapter 56

With Charlie seated in the back, the police cruiser pulls away from the curb. Languetti stands with his hands in his trouser pockets, looking towards the night sky. The storm has since passed over, and the stars are now visible. Frank takes a moment, pondering his conversation with Charlie, before decisively turning back towards the entrance of the Parkway.

"Detective?" One of the officers standing on the sidewalk calls out. "It looks like they may have found your man."

"Frank!"

Languetti turns to see Miles at the top of the stairs, purposefully exiting the building.

"Central Park." Miles walks hurriedly down the stairs towards Languetti. "Just got the call, Frank. Two units are there right now."

Languetti strides over to the officer; he reaches out for the police radio. "Give me that."

The officer hands the police radio to Languetti.

"Who's on it?" Languetti demands, eager to address the caller.

"Car 22, sir, Officer Perez."

"Perez, this is Detective Languetti. You copy?"

"Go ahead, Detective."

"No one is to engage the suspect; I want you to hold till I get there."

"Copy that, Detective; we'll hold off till you get here, sir."

Languetti tosses the police radio at the officer. He moves quickly towards Miles' car. "You drive," Languetti instructs Miles as they make their way over to the Dodge sedan.

"What about your car, Frank?"

"I'll get it later."

With keys already in hand, Miles jumps inside the cruiser, looking over to his partner as he fires up the engine.

"Hit it." Languetti slams the door shut as Miles peels away from the curb.

"The call I got said he was spotted at the Bethesda Fountain, down by the lake." Miles leans forward, powering up the lights and siren before turning the car sharply into the next corner. "So, what did the old man have to say?" Miles inquires as he checks the street traffic in the rear-view mirror, swiftly changing lanes as he eases down on the accelerator.

"Nothing we didn't already assume." Languetti takes hold of the grab handle as the car veers from side to side.

"I really could use some fucking coffee, Frank." Miles lets out an exhaustive groan as he swerves through the traffic. "Exactly one hour ago, I was home, with my piece of shit, thirty-dollar Walmart heater maxed out on the highest setting, laying on the sofa with two minutes before tip-off. Nicks vs. Celtics on ESPN." Miles again turns the wheel, the tyres squealing as the car veers around another corner. "And you know what I had in my hand, Frank?" Miles examines Frank, who's hanging on tight as the car moves through the city traffic. "A steaming hot cup of Harris coffee." Miles quickly checks his mirrors before continuing with his grievances. "Every time I make plans on game night, some asshole goes and gets himself killed?" Miles honks the horn twice, clearing the way.

"Turn down here," Languetti points to West 68th Street.

"I got it," Miles grumbles as he turns the wheel, narrowly avoiding a merging vehicle. Languetti reaches to his waist and checks his firearm.

"How did your hot date go with Dr Bridge, Frank?" Miles again turns the wheel sharply, directing the car up 8th Avenue. Languetti feels reluctant to respond, knowing his partner will most likely mock him, given his grumpy mood.

"It was good. We had Chinese."

"Chinese? I thought you guys had dinner at The Golden Dragon?"

"We did."

"The Golden Dragon is a Thai restaurant, Frank."

Languetti shrugs his shoulders.

"What's the difference?"

Miles eases his foot off the accelerator.

"A whole fucking country, Frank." Miles directs the car onto Terrace Drive. He reaches forward, powering down the siren as the vehicle approaches the terrace, the heart of Central Park.

"Pull up here."

Languetti motions to the curb outside the terrace steps. Two police units already stationed outside are accompanied by two officers who quickly turn as Miles brings the car to a halt. Languetti exits the vehicle, looking directly at one of the officers as he approaches.

"Perez?"

One of the officers responds.

"He's at the bottom of the steps, Detective, just down by the lake."

Languetti moves quickly towards the steps that lead down to the terrace.

"Hey Frank, watch your step."

The rain, which has since ceased, is still proving hazardous on the smooth stone treads.

"Shit." Miles steps into a small pool of water. "Frank, slow down, will ya." Miles scurries, catching up to his eager partner. "Be careful going down here; these steps get slippery when it rains."

Languetti is cautious with his footing as he descends the stairs.

"Might break a hip at your age," Miles mutters, still pining for a cup of Harris coffee.

An open courtyard at the base of the steps houses the Bethesda fountain. Languetti looks around, easing his stride as he circles the fountain. He directs his sight towards the lake.

"Frank, eleven o'clock," Miles says, showing concern as he points out into the distance. Languetti refocuses; his vision hindered by the darkness surrounding the lake. He hears some commotion, elevated voices in the distance. As Languetti approaches, it becomes clear that both officers have their guns drawn, pointed directly at Clay. He hurries towards the lake.

Clay is standing, taught, shrouded in darkness, glaring at the officers as they approach him with caution.

"Get on the ground or we'll open fire," Officer Perez instructs.

Officer Schwartz begins to circle Clay. "On the ground now!" His adrenaline coursing through him as he flanks Clay.

Clay's eyes are filled with regret as he steps towards Officer Perez, willing him to shoot. *I'm not going back there.* Clay's thoughts are of prison and his now deceased friend, Audrey. His heart sunken with grief as he visualizes Audrey. All he wants is for the torment to end. Officer Perez cocks his gun as Clay takes another step towards him.

"It's your last warning, I will shoot!"

Officer Schwartz looks at his partner, unsure of himself, as he keeps his gun pointed at Clay, his finger resting on the trigger.

Perez begins to squeeze the trigger as Clay lifts his foot off the ground, deciding his fate.

"Perez! Holster your weapon." Languetti instructs as he approaches the trio.

Perez glances at Frank, hesitating as the detective moves towards him. Perez raises his firearm into the air as Languetti positions himself in front of Clay, blocking Perez's line of sight.

"Don't shoot." Miles shows his palms as he rounds Officer Schwartz. "Holster your weapon, Jimmy."

Both officers breathe a sigh of relief as the detective takes charge of the situation. Clay stays still while Languetti shifts his focus onto him.

"Clay...it's alright," Languetti says. "Just take it easy."

Clay stares at Languetti for a moment before turning towards the lake; he takes several solemn steps before sitting himself down on a protruding rock by the lake's edge.

"Don't take your eyes off him," Languetti instructs Miles.

Officer Perez approaches Languetti; his eyes fixated on Clay. Officer Schwartz raises his torch momentarily to identify the detective.

"Sir, it's Officer Perez; we spoke on the radio."

Languetti dismisses the introduction.

"Sir, he was just sitting on the grass, down by the lake."

Languetti's eyes lock onto Clay as he sits motionless.

"When we got the call on the radio, we were stationed up on 72nd, just grabbing a late snack. He fit the description, so we followed him. I stayed on foot; Jimmy drove the unit, but I told him to stay out of sight. He knew we were here, but he hadn't tried to run. Anyway, we decided to call it in instead." Perez looks across at Miles as he moves alongside Languetti. "He's a pretty big guy, Detective. Looks like a handful; that's why Jimmy called for backup."

Languetti looks directly at Perez.

"But then he stood up and began to walk towards us. We didn't know what to do, Detective. We told him to hold, but he kept on coming."

"Both of you can head off now." Languetti takes a moment to collect his thoughts. He commences his stride towards the lake. Perez is bemused at the request to leave.

"You don't want us to stay and help you take him in, Detective?"

Miles watches his partner closely, wary of the inherent danger.

"We'll take it from here, Perez." Miles' voice is soft. "Go back upstairs and finish your burrito."

Perez looks at Miles, who's focused intently on his partner. "Yes, sir."

Perez reluctantly accepts the order, turning and motioning to his partner as Miles takes a few steps towards the lake. Officer Jimmy Schwartz takes a glance at Miles as he walks by. Miles looks on as Languetti continues towards the lake. Miles holds his ground as he approaches a park bench. The thick air clears as Languetti nears the lake, the detective ceasing his stride approximately twenty feet from the water. His eyes adjust to the sparse light, his view clearer as he gazes down upon Clay. He takes another cautious step towards Clay, his bloodied hands placed aptly in his lap, his head slightly bowed, his solemn face now identifiable; Clay sits peacefully, looking across the lake into nothingness. Languetti holds his ground momentarily, unsure of his first words. He turns his head, looking across the lake's icy water, taking another strong breath as he decisively inserts his rapidly numbing fingers into his trouser pockets. Miles looks on at the ready, one hand hanging off his weapon, the other tucked away from the cold. Languetti resumes his focus on Clay, lifting his left leg off the dewy grass and commencing his walk, no longer wanting to prolong the inevitable. Clay remains still as Languetti nears; Languetti crouches and places one knee onto the damp surface. A quiet moment passes before Languetti decides to speak.

"Clay?"

Clay remains motionless, continuing to look across the lake's still water. Languetti reaches forward, placing his hand on Clay's shoulder. Clay turns his head slightly; his movement is subtle.

"Audrey and I came here just last week," Clay says, his voice trembling from the cold. Languetti listens acutely; a single tear runs down Clay's face as he recalls the day to the detective. "We ate so much food." Clay smiles, wiping another tear from his face. He visualises Audrey's smiling face. Recounting her antics on the lake and the time they spent confiding in one another. He looks across the icy lake. "It was the best day I've had since I was…" Clay holds off his revelation. Languetti remains patient. "Why do bad things happen to good people?" Clay gazes up at the detective.

Frank looks down at Clay's pleading eyes, Clay looking for an answer that will give him some comfort. "I don't know," Languetti admits.

Clay wipes another tear. "Audrey didn't deserve to die. She was my friend."

Languetti looks into Clay's mournful eyes, his grief consuming him. Clay bows his head slightly in thought.

"Sir? Am I going away again?"

Languetti remembers what Charlie had told him earlier and concludes that Clay has already served time. "I don't know, Clay." Languetti takes a moment. "But I promise I will do everything I can to keep you from going to prison for this."

Clay gazes across the lake, contemplating his future.

"Hey, Clay, it's pretty cold out here. Maybe we should go somewhere warmer and talk."

"Yes, Sir." Clay nods his head, conceding it's time to go.

Frank pats Clay on the shoulder. "Come, let's get something warm to drink. My partner was whining about his coffee the whole way here."

"Yes, Sir."

Languetti takes hold of Clay by the arm, both rising to their feet. Clay looks across the grass to see Miles standing by the park bench. Languetti places his hand onto Clay's back as they proceed towards the terrace, Miles looking on as his partner approaches, rubbing his hands together to stem the bitter air. Miles looks out onto the lake momentarily, reflecting on the night's events, before he, too, begins his tired stride, joining his partner as he escorts Clay towards the terrace steps, looking over his shoulder to catch one last glimpse of the Bethesda fountain in the moonlight.

Chapter 57

Raising the stick high above his head, the New York Ranger centre slams the face of his stick onto the puck, launching it along the scorched ice at a furious pace. The staggering Anaheim goaltender throws his body to the floor as the puck flashes past and into the back of the net, sending the New York crowd to its feet. Holding a large cup of Heineken in one hand and a half-eaten hot dog in the other, a heavily built patron donning his 1994 Rangers jersey leaps excitedly from his seat.

"You suck, Ducks." A piece of masticated sausage exits his mouth, bounces off his knee and lands by Sylvia's shoe. Sylvia looks to her right at the burly man seated beside her.

"Gross!" She presents him with a look of disgust. The burly man looks over at Sylvia and smiles.

"Sorry, miss, I didn't expect them to score so soon." The burly man raises his beer in the air. "Go you, Rangers!"

Sylvia squirms, jerking her head to her left, peering directly at Frank. "So, this is your idea of a good time?"

Frank smiles. "It's all part of the fun of Ice Hockey. You'll get used to it."

Sylvia looks past Frank, wide-eyed at her mother. "Mum!"

Evelyn mirrors her daughter's expression. "Why don't you ask Frank about the rules? If you understand how the game is played, you might enjoy it more."

Sylvia looks to the heavens. "Huh…not likely, mother." She raises her palm into the air, conveying her disinterest. Evelyn looks at Frank.

"You want her, Frank? She's all yours."

Frank smiles as the crowd again rises, for a striking penalty against Anaheim. Languetti leans in closer to Sylvia.

"See those two Rangers near the goal."

Sylvia rolls her eyes. "Ah…yeah. I'm not blind."

"These players try to stop the incoming play at their own blue line. They try to break up passes, block shots, cover the opposition forwards and clear the puck from in front of their own goal." Sylvia turns and gives Frank a confused look. Frank continues. "Offensively, they get the puck to their forwards, the wingers and centre, and follow the play into the attacking zone, positioning themselves just inside their opponent's blue line." Sylvia raises her hand, pointing to the ice.

"You mean like the guy at the other end who just scored?"

Frank nods profusely. "Yeah, he's the Rangers' centre."

The Anaheim defenseman hooks the Ranger winger, sending him to the ice. The crowd jeers as the referee again blows the whistle, awarding the Rangers a penalty.

"What just happened? Why is that guy going off the ice?" Sylvia inquires.

"The Ducks received a two-minute penalty for hooking."

Sylvia turns and looks at Frank. "Hooking?"

"It's a Hockey term."

Sylvia looks at her mother with a wry smile.

"You know, Mother and I came to Madison Square Garden last February."

"For Hockey?" Frank inquires. Sylvia looks at Frank.

"No, Billy Joel concert. Mum loves Billy Joel. She had a crush on him growing up. She has all his music, like on those big black plastic discs." Frank looks over at Evelyn, giving her a sweet smile. "He was great...Mum kept yelling out to him. It was kinda embarrassing, but it was ok because there were heaps of other old ladies there too, and they were embarrassing themselves also."

"Mature women, smart alec." Evelyn is quick to correct. A huge smile surfaces on Frank's face, withholding his urge to laugh out loud. Sylvia rolls her eyes as she continues her banter.

"Anyway, it was great because we hung around after the concert, and Mum got her precious Billy Joel—The Stranger shirt signed by Billy himself."

Frank gives Evelyn an impressive look. "Really, how'd you manage that?"

Evelyn leans in closer. "You remember Detective Rulky, who retired from that chronic neck problem a few years back?"

Frank nods. "Yeah, I remember him. He had that funny twitch when he turned his head."

"Well, he now does security for the Garden."

Frank leans back slightly, looking suspiciously at Evelyn. "I remember he had a little thing for you."

Evelyn smiles, tilting her head to one side. "Oh, Frank."

Sylvia jumps into the conversation. "And-still-does!" Sylvia emphatically points out to Frank. "You should have seen him slobbering all over Mum; it was *sooo*...gross."

Frank purses his lips, nodding his head. "That's a fascinating revelation, my dear."

"Yes, it is!" Sylvia continues. "Anyway, so Mum was like, so smooth." Sylvia becomes animated, waving her hands in front of her face. "She totally used it to her advantage. She had him wrapped around her little finger."

"I'm impressed." Frank bobbles his head casually. "You should be careful, Evelyn; he may want you to return the favour someday."

Sylvia places her hand on Frank's shoulder, confiding in him. "Don't worry, Frank, he's no threat to you." Sylvia begins to jerk her head to the side again and again. "He's still a twitcher, Frank," Sylvia says laughingly.

Evelyn reaches out towards Sylvia, giving her a gentle shove. "Oh, stop that. That is not a nice thing to do, Sylvia."

Frank can't help but laugh out loud. "That was a good likeness, I have to admit."

Evelyn raises her eyebrows at Languetti. "That's great, Frank, keep encouraging her."

Sylvia laughs out loud. "Oh, Mum, just chill." Frank looks at Evelyn, acting all teenage-like.

"Yeah, Mum, just chill."

The burly man rises from his chair at the sound of the referee's whistle. "That's horse shit." He suddenly remembers the young girl beside him and embarrassedly turns to Sylvia. "Sorry, hun." He plants himself in his seat. "The ref got us for high sticking."

Sylvia addresses the burly man. "Did the Ranger *high stick*?"

"Well...actually, yeah, he did." The burly man confesses.

Sylvia gives the man a sensible look. "Well... I guess it wasn't horse shit then, was it?"

The burly man laughs. "Well, I guess not." The burly man gives Sylvia a heavy nudge with his forearm. "Hey! You're alright, kid."

"Thaaanks." Sylvia places her hand on her shoulder; she turns to look at Frank, discreetly expressing her pain from the heavy nudge. "Got any ice on you, Frank?"

Frank smiles. "No, but how about we get some hot chocolate at halftime?"

Sylvia's eyes widen. "Ah, yes, please."

Evelyn can't help but smile as she looks on, savouring these moments, feeling truly blessed that Sylvia has taken an immediate liking to Frank. She leans forward, reaching down into her handbag, taking another peek over at Frank as he converses with Sylvia. Evelyn takes hold of an item neatly wrapped in brown paper. Frank takes notice, as a good detective would.

"What have you got there?" Frank inquires, with Sylvia curiously looking on. Evelyn smiles.

"I got you something, Frank." She extends her arm and presents the wrapped item to him. Frank smiles, reluctantly taking the gift from Evelyn's hand.

"For me?"

"Yes, Frank. This is a present for you."

Frank looks down at the item. "I...didn't get you anything. Didn't know I had to." He says foolishly.

Evelyn extends her smile. "That's alright, Frank, just open it."

Frank nods, looking curiously at the brown wrapping paper. "I wonder what it is," he asks, looking over at Sylvia, who quickly shrugs her shoulders at the notion. "Looks like you used a brown paper lunch bag." Frank points out as he examines what appears to be a solid rectangular item.

"Yes, Frank. I spared no expense on the wrapping paper." Evelyn jokes. Sylvia watches closely, acutely intrigued, as Frank tears away the paper to expose the item.

"A CD." Frank remarks. "*Classical Music Favourites,*" Frank reads the fancy script on the casing insert.

"Look on the back, Frank." Evelyn motioned with her hand for Frank to flip over the case. Frank turns the CD over; he focuses on the track listing, his eyes following the track names, ultimately reaching the eighth track title. Frank hesitates momentarily before announcing the selection in a soft voice.

"The Swan—Saint-Saëns." Frank looks over at Evelyn; his warmth and appreciation for the gift are evident.

"I asked Manny to find out the name of the CD, after you vanished into the night."

"This is…" Frank searches for a meaningful response but finds himself choked up by the gesture. He looks down at the CD once again before turning to face Evelyn. "I love it, thank you." His sincere voice cuts through the vocal crowd. Evelyn is chuffed at Frank's reaction; she smiles as she looks directly into Frank's eyes.

"You're welcome, Detective."

Sylvia is taken aback by their moment. "If you guys kiss, I'm seriously gonna puke."

Evelyn and Frank begin to chuckle at Sylvia's remark, but still, they maintain their gaze on each other, easing themselves towards one another, their lips gently pressing together. Sylvia lets out an awful shriek.

"Oh my god, I'm gonna puke." Sylvia places her hand over her mouth. The burly man notices and quickly reaches down, taking hold of an empty beer cup.

"Here you go, hun, puke in this."

An astonished Sylvia looks over at the burly man. She groans in horror, pressing both palms to the side of her face. "I'm in a nightmare."

Frank reaches over, placing his arm around Sylvia, cradling her towards him. Evelyn rests her head against Frank's shoulder as the crowd again goes up in a deafening roar. The New York Rangers scoring once again.

Chapter 58

It's Christmas morning in New York, and the streets are blanketed in four inches of white snow. The animals have burrowed into their nests to escape the bitter cold. The trees are barren of foliage, an exhibition of still life scattered throughout the city. Inside The Parkway, the warmth of the foyer is comforting, and Charlie is careful with his footing as he positions himself securely on a small wooden step ladder. He stands by the window just to the right of the entrance to the Parkway, taking a moment to peer through the frosted glass; two teenage girls on the sidewalk across the street. The sound of laughter as they chase one another with clumps of rounded snow, propelling it through the air with nothing but pure joy in their hearts. As he looks on, Charlie can't help wondering how this day could have been vastly different to what it has become. Charlie reaches up along the window's architrave, using his pin hammer to detach a length of red tinsel; repositioning it a few inches higher this time and pinning it down with his thumb. With the pin hammer firmly clutched in his right hand, Charlie prepares to secure the tinsel to the window. This time, to his meticulous satisfaction.

"Just a little higher, Charlie." Charlie immediately smiles at the sound of a familiar soft and sweet voice that fills the entire room. It's like a dream, but to Charlie's delight, this was not a dream but rather a Holy miracle. A day of celebration; to thank the heavens for this blessing and what may have been if not for the grace of God. Charlie turns to see Audrey standing behind him, gingerly on both feet.

"No crutches this morning." Charlie notices.

"I decided to go without today." Audrey's smile lighting up the room. Charlie secures the tinsel, just a little higher as Audrey suggested, careful as always as he steps down from the ladder. He turns to face Audrey; she stands there like a blessed angel, Charlie's heart filled with praise for this Christmas gift.

"Do you like what you see?" Charlie encourages Audrey to praise his efforts. Audrey explores the decorations, the glee in her eyes validating Charlie's good work. A few weeks have passed since Audrey last left the comfort of her apartment, and since that time, Charlie has completed his traditional Christmas decorations as he does every year.

"You've outdone yourself this year, Charlie." Audrey turned several times, admiring the ample decorations surrounding the room. "The foyer looks great, Charlie."

"Well, thank you, Audrey." Charlie places the pin hammer onto the counter as he walks towards Audrey. Audrey extends her arms out to greet Charlie as he approaches. Charlie does the same, carefully placing his arms around her and giving her a gentle hug. They embrace momentarily before Charlie releases his hold and looks down into Audrey's eyes.

"Merry Christmas, Audrey." Audrey smiles as she repays Charlie's well wishes.

"Merry Christmas to you, too, Charlie." Charlie smiles, gently placing his hand on the side of Audrey's face; her bruises have yet to heal.

"I see you are wearing the red sweater Gloria knitted for you," Charlie says.

"Yes, I really love it. Keeps me warm. She surprised me while I was in the hospital. It was my first Christmas present for the year."

"I can assure you, Audrey, it won't be your last."

Charlie and Audrey gaze at one another in peaceful harmony before a ruckus at the front entrance suddenly draws their attention. They both look curiously at the front entrance, observing closely. Beyond the patterned glass, just outside the door, a human figure clumsily mishandles the door's lever several times before finally releasing the latch. The cold air rushes in as the door swings open. A man wearing a long red coat stumbles through the doorway carrying a hefty utility sack over his left shoulder. Charlie and Audrey look on with intrigue as the man hurriedly does an about-face, pushing the door closed with his shoulder, confining the cold air to the exterior of the building. Seemingly out of breath, the man slowly turns to face his audience, brushing the snow from his coat as he does so. His face is completely concealed, wrapped in a plentiful scarf; only his eyes are visible through a narrow opening he has formed.

"And here I was, giving up all hope that Santa Claus really existed," Charlie remarks. Audrey expels a chuckle as she looks on in disbelief. The mysterious man reaches for the scarf to swiftly unravel it, pulling it up and over his head, revealing his grinning face to Charlie and Audrey.

"Ho-ho-ho...Merry Christmas." A cheerful Clay hollers out across the room. Audrey and Charlie both laugh as Clay's baritone voice fills the room. Charlie turns to Audrey.

"I think he just woke the entire building up, including the deceased." Audrey chuckles once again as she watches Clay toddle towards her. Clay can't contain his enthusiasm, yelling out again as he approaches.

"It's Christmas Day!" Clay says excitedly, his enthusiasm that of a young boy. Charlie smiles, a forgotten truth surfacing in his thoughts. This is Clay's first Christmas since he was released from prison. Charlie can't imagine how the last twelve years would have been for Clay at Christmas time. Not too impressive, Charlie thinks to himself. And the time before, his drunken, abusive father would have ruined every Christmas he had as a child. But still, that little boy inside him never died in all that time. He was only waiting, with the hope that one day he could experience the absolute joy of Christmas for the first time in his regrettable life.

Clay places the utility sack down on the floor.

"Merry Christmas, Miss Audrey." Audrey's eyes well up as she reaches out to Clay. Clay's face is beaming.

"Merry Christmas, Clay." Clay moves in closer, gently draping himself over Audrey. Audrey closes her eyes, latching onto Clay as tight as she can. Charlie looks on as they embrace, overwhelmed by the moment. Charlie's eyes also glisten, thankful that Clay returned that night and saved Audrey.

The detective kept his promise. He looked after Clay just as he told Charlie he would. He got Clay one of the top defense lawyers in New York, to represent him at the arraignment. It took the judge only seven minutes to dismiss the case, concluding that it was a matter of self-defence. Even the district attorney admitted afterwards that, given William's history, they would struggle to find even one juror to convict Clay of any wrongdoing. One of the most pleasing and unexpected moments to come out of all this was that the mayor himself issued Clay a certificate of bravery for saving Audrey's life.

Charlie exhales in delight, shaking his head with amazement at how these two souls found each other in their time of need.

Charlie bows his head momentarily, wanting to give thanks for this wonderful miracle.

"Hey Charlie, what are you doing?" Audrey inquires laughingly. "Are you praying?" Audrey mocks. Charlie looks up, giving Audrey a condescending smile. "Come on over here, silly." Audrey's laughter is like that of a muse as Charlie ambles closer; Audrey places her arm around Charlie's waist, pulling him towards her. Clay releases his hold on Audrey, reaching quickly to the floor. He turns to face Audrey and Charlie, displaying the utility, his face gleaming, unable to control his childlike giggle.

"I think Clay has bought presents for us, Audrey." Charlie presents curiosity in his voice.

"Maybe he really is Santa Claus, Charlie."

As Charlie watches Clay fumble around inside the utility sack, Audrey takes a moment, looking through the frosted windows, remembering her friend Veronica, and wishing she were here to celebrate Christmas together. Audrey removes her hand from Charlie's waist. She moves towards the window; Charlie watches her as she walks away.

"Audrey, everything okay?"

Audrey turns and smiles at Charlie. "Yeah, I'll be back in a minute, Charlie." Audrey continues towards the doors; she looks past the frosted glass at a man standing just outside The Parkway. She opens the door and steps outside, the door closing behind her. Audrey folds her arms to keep out the cold as she makes her way down the steps. He feet sink in the pillowy snow as she steps onto the sidewalk. She plods towards the man, who has since turned and heads towards his vehicle.

"Detective?" Audrey calls out.

Miles turns to face Audrey. "Hey, Audrey."

"Hey." Audrey smiles curiously at Miles. "What are you doing here this Christmas morning?"

Miles looks at Audrey, taking a moment before responding. "Just thought I'd come past and see how you were doing." Miles feels a little awkward. He attempts to justify his impromptu visit. "I was just on my way to Scarsdale. Christmas with the relatives."

Audrey tilts her head. "And you wanted to check up on me?"

Miles looks away, feeling somewhat embarrassed at the gesture. "Just wanted to make sure you are doing well, that's all."

Audrey appreciates the unexpected gesture. "I am. Thank you."

A moment of silence passes as they gaze at each other.

"So, how's Frank?" Audrey feels the cold numbing her face.

"Frank has a girlfriend now." Miles reveals.

Audrey raises her eyebrows. "Well, good for him." Audrey smiles laughingly.

Miles looks at the heavens, the mild snow brushing his face.

"So...anyway, you better get back inside before you freeze out here." Miles can't help but gaze at Audrey, his admiration apparent. Audrey compliments him with a sincere smile. "You take care, Audrey." A departing smile and wave from Miles as he turns to his vehicle.

"Hey, Detective?"

Miles looks over his shoulder, locking eyes with Audrey. Audrey hesitates for a brief moment as she gazes back at Miles.

"Merry Christmas, Shaun."

Miles presents Audrey with a grateful smile. "Merry Christmas, Audrey."

As Miles leaves, Audrey takes a moment to look up at the winter sky; the snow has begun to fall once again. Audrey bears the cold as she stands there, smiling at the wondrous sight.

"Audrey! You're going to freeze to death out there." Audrey turns to see Charlie standing at the door. "Get back in here."

"Alright, alright...I'm coming, Charlie. *Jeez.*" Audrey drags her feet through the snow, grumbling incoherently. "You're overprotective, Charlie," Audrey announces as she enters the lobby. Charlie shakes his head at Audrey; he turns to the sky to view the falling snow, taking a moment for himself before finally easing the door closed.

The End.

www.ingramcontent.com/pod-product-compliance
Lightning Source LLC
Chambersburg PA
CBHW030521190726
48283CB00006B/1719